Discover for yourself why readers can't get enough of the multiple award-winning publisher Ellora's Cave. Whether you prefer e-books or paperbacks, be sure to visit EC on the web at www.ellorascave.com for an erotic reading experience that will leave you breathless.

www.ellorascave.com

THE WARLORD'S GIFT
An Ellora's Cave Publication, July 2004

Ellora's Cave Publishing, Inc.
PO Box 787
Hudson, OH 44236-0787

ISBN #1-84360-954-1

ISBN MS Reader (LIT) ISBN # 1-84360-852-9
Other available formats (no ISBNs are assigned):
Adobe (PDF), Rocketbook (RB), Mobipocket (PRC) & HTML

Edited by *Kari Berton*.
Cover art by *Christine Clavel*

What the critics are saying:

The Warlord's Gift is an excellent story about one woman's journey to find happiness. The characters are easy to get into and you really feel as if you know them and can relate to them. The lead couple of Draven and Linea makes an awesome duo and are a perfect compliment to each other. Draven is strong and very commanding with a dominant attitude that will make you scream at times. Linea is strong willed and does not give in to Draven on any level. The sexual tension is very high and plays a part throughout the entire book, and when the couple comes together you better bring out the hoses. The Warlord's Gift is a wonderful story of paranormal activity and love found. It's easy to see why Veronica Chadwick is the great writer she is today.

--*Angel Brewer, Just Erotic Romance Reviews*

The Warlord's Gift is amazing fantasy story that will send you to a wonderful world of kings, queens, elves, and faeries. Ms Chadwick has created a sensual novel with lovable characters that will touch your heart. The Warlord's Gift is written with such emotional depth that as a reader you will feel the main and secondary characters happiness, their sorrow, their highs and lows. Linea and Draven are fantastic as hero and heroine. As I read this novel I cheered for them to overcome their plights. The love scenes were romantic, sensual, and passionate. I highly recommend this story for anyone looking for a once in a life time love affair. -*Susan HollyJust Erotic Romance Reviews*

The Warlords Gift is an exceptional lesson in stimulating sensual foreplay, this book captivated me. In my opinion this book is a necessary sensual read. -*Dianne Nogueras, eCataRomance Reviews*

THE WARLORD'S GIFT

Veronica Chadwick

This book is dedicated to:

Paul, my husband.
You are my safe haven, my champion,
My very own gift from God.
Thank you for always being on my side and never doubting me.
I'm so happy you're mine. I love you!

Lora Leigh. My sister, my best friend
Without your unconditional support, your unwavering love
and your promises to kick my butt when I got stubborn and
contrary
this story would have never been written.
I love you, sis! Thank you!

Prologue

The shove sent Linea sprawling across the cold uneven stone floor. She lay there like a broken doll for several moments, hoping he was done with her, praying he would leave.

"Your betrothed will come for you in a day or two. Clean yourself up, Linea. Try to do something about your appearance." His lips curled in disgust as his eyes traveled her naked bleeding body.

She pushed herself up on trembling arms, her empty stomach heaving. Standing, her body shook violently, the dark room tilted and she grasped hold of the short wardrobe to stay on her feet. She would endure; she had to. She could not let him see her crumble.

"Uncle." She raised her head, determined to meet his gaze. Gasping in pain, though her voice was level, she pleaded with him. "Don't give me to him. I won't try to leave again."

He moved too fast for her to react in defense. It would have done her no good anyway. Drawing his hand back and curling his fingers into a fist, he hit her face full force, the sick smack echoing off the walls. It seemed as though she fell in slow motion. Once on the floor she curled inward, trying to make herself smaller. He leaned down over her, his peppermint-scented breath hot and moist on her stinging cheek. She closed her eyes and focused on breathing slowly, deeply, to keep her dank world from spinning toward blackness.

"You dirty little twit," he spat. "Other than a breed bitch for a Kyrok you are of no value to me." He stood and paced slowly around her, disdainfully nudging her with the toe of his boot. "Nezzer Pandrum and I have reached a mutually satisfying bargain. One I cannot allow you to jeopardize. It seems he finds you comely. Only something uglier than you would."

He continued to pace, watching her. "I've tried, Linea. I've worked hard to save you but your sin is deeply rooted. It's in your blood and no matter what I did to purify you, no matter how I struggled to keep you clean before Iybae, still, your sin shows. Iybae, Omnipotent God, Lord of all, He requires much and you..." he stopped

7

pacing, completely caught up in the sound of his own pontificating, "regardless of my tireless attempts to purge your evil, have been…well…found wanting."

He leaned down close to her, his breathing labored. Her body tensed but she lay still, resisting her desire to move away from him. "I still see it in you. The filthy lust of the whores that shoved you from their heaving tainted bodies. I can feel it in you, just as I felt it in my sister," he said, then pressed his thick lips to her swelling cheek. She cringed, swallowing the bitter bile that rose in her throat, and opened her eyes.

With a grunt he stood, "I can't be around you for long, Linea. You beguile me with your iniquity. But know that I've tried. Your wickedness has held you captive here in this room."

From the corner of her eye she watched him survey the damp rock walls, blotchy with mold, crawling with insects. Clucking his tongue, he walked back to the rough wooden door. "You'll feel better soon, beloved niece. I hear Pandrum has voracious and unholy appetites when it comes to females of any species. A wanton woman such as you should tolerate his depraved affections nicely. You may even enjoy them. Mayhap it will tame the lust in you somewhat."

He shrugged. "Even so, all Kyrok males desire a human mate to improve their bloodlines. My willingness to part with you — according to the Pact, of course — makes you valuable, my dear. So you see it matters not what you promise. I won't give you a chance to escape again."

Linea heard the door slam then the scraping of metal against metal as Haig Orbane locked the door to her quarters and her hope. Finally, her screaming muscles relaxed into a dull ache and she swallowed the soft sobs that rose painfully from deep inside her. After a moment, she clutched at the bed frame and pulled herself up from the floor. Swaying a bit, she cautiously moved to the basin.

With a dirty rag she mopped at the blood that ran down her stomach. Without giving the wounds much attention she dressed in the only set of clothing she had now that the other had been ripped from her. Her struggle to keep the tears at bay was failing under the dizzying waves of pain and nausea. The pain grew in intensity, threatening to envelope her in complete darkness.

Sitting on the side of the makeshift bed she gently ran a hand under the mattress. Her fingers found the chain and pulled it free. The circle of gold twirled and gleamed in the dim candlelight as she held it up. Her mother's medallion always seemed to calm her somehow. Clasping it to her chest she sat back and leaned against the wall, closing her eyes against the hollowness she felt inside.

She thought to pray; to beg Iybae for mercy, forgiveness, restoration. Instead she paused on the brink of prayer, content to hover there on that plane in her mind where she could imagine God and her parents watching over her without apathy and censure. The unshed tears burned her eyes; the throbbing in her head grew worse and she inhaled deeply, letting go of the fantasy.

The possibility of ending it had crossed her mind but she knew she wouldn't kill herself, unsure if that made her brave or a coward. She should try to think of an escape with this fresh unknown fate advancing on her, but she was so tired and her head hurt so badly. She couldn't seem to focus. What, exactly, did mating entail? Pain, she assumed. More pain? Worse pain? She shuddered at the thought. What did Uncle mean by "unholy appetites"?

Moments later — or hours, she couldn't tell — Linea heard the key in the lock. She sat up straight, holding her breath, trying to control her pain and fear. *Dear Iybae, not again, please not again,* she pleaded with God, though she believed He couldn't tolerate her.

Angus cracked open the door and poked his head in. His small golden eyes narrowed as they adjusted to the dimly lit chamber.

"Miss Linea?" he whispered harshly.

"I'm here, Angus," she answered, trembling with relief.

He moved slowly into the room, setting a plate of crackers and cheese and a mug of water on the bed table. "Aw, Miss, are ye alright?"

The kindness in the young gnoll undid her. His overly large round eyes were bright with worry. She breathed in the dank air through her nose and held it till the burning behind her eyes eased and the lump in her throat melted. A nod was all she could give him.

"Now ye look here, Miss." He squatted in front of her. His bushy brows pulled together. His thin lips had an interesting sharp dip in the center when he smiled, like a wide V. Now they were nearly nonexistent as he pressed them together in an expression as serious as she'd ever seen Angus. "When I leave here, I'm going to forget to lock the door back…"

She mouthed the word "no," afraid that shaking her head would cause her to lose consciousness. She knew what her uncle would do to the youth if he helped her escape.

"No, Miss, now listen. I'm runnin' as well. I'm goin' across the sea to my homeland this night. He won't git his hands on me, I promise ye, Miss."

She searched his strange little golden face, trying to decide if she should chance it. If she ran and Angus was caught he would be killed...slowly, brutally. Angus had been the only light in her dark world, her only friend. He'd risked much for her already. Uncle Haig had bought him from kidnapping thieves when Linea was still very young.

She wondered how old he really was. Gnolls had a long lifespan but Angus always seemed to be young and so innocent. Too many times Angus had suffered punishment at the hands of her uncle because he'd given her extra cheese and bread after a "cleansing" or he'd been caught wasting time talking to her.

"I'd rather be dead than live here one more day, Miss," he murmured as if he read her mind. "Please, do this for me. You're like me own sis; I cannot leave knowing you're locked away. Miss Linea, ye cannot go with the Kyrok. That union, 'tis the one thing your stubbornness will not get you through."

Linea's brows furrowed and she opened her mouth to question him. Angus clasped her hand in his. His golden eyes widened to impossible size and glowed with desperation as he shook his head. "Listen, girl! You'll not live through it, I tell ye! I've heard things. Horrible things. You'll come with me. I'll take you with me and I'll keep ye safe."

"No, I'm weak right now. I'd slow you down." This time she stopped his protest. "I can't go with you, Angus." She lifted her medallion so he could see it. Angus sucked in his breath. "I'll go to Ingvar, I'll be safe there." He simply stared at the pendant, his mouth agape.

"What time is it?" she asked.

"'Tis nearly half night," he whispered. "I did not know that you had this... That you're..."

She frowned. There was so much she wanted to know about her parents, the medallion, Ingvar, and most of all, herself. She focused on her determination to know, to learn, to discover, and felt herself grow stronger. "Where is Uncle Haig?"

"He's retired for the evening in his chambers, Miss. I've been watching. He's been sound asleep for three hours. I heard him snoring real loud just moments ago. The rest of the servants are all in their chambers as well. And even if they weren't, they wouldn't see a thing. The guard at the back gate is passed out from too much mead and a bit of Rowena's special additive." He winked. "He won't be waking up till noon. Rowena assured me. I'll take ye to the gate."

"You go, Angus. Go now." Hope flared to life in her heart and she patted his hand still clutching hers. "I will leave soon. And, Angus, thank you."

"Promise me, Miss Linea. Promise me you'll leave here."

"Yes, Angus, I give you my word."

His thin lips curved into that pretty smile that looked as if someone drew it with flourish on his face. "I pray one day I'll look upon your lovely face again, Miss." With a wink he quietly slipped from the room, closing the door gently behind him.

Chapter One

Draven moved effortlessly, pushing though the dark branches and clinging vines in his path. Weary, hungry and annoyed he paid no heed to the two men who fought to keep up with his long strides. After tracking the thieving Gavril half the night, Draven and his men had lost him. The wicked elf had all but vaporized into the fog, cackling like an old woman gone mad. Damn this oppressive fog and damn that little imp, Draven thought. The elf's clever escape was only a temporary reprieve. When he caught the greedy toad he'd make him plead for mercy.

"Mason and I will gather some men when we arrive home." Armond spoke, breaking the tense silence. "We can have this issue dealt with before dawn. You have matters of more pressing need to attend to without having to hunt down these blasted elves."

"No." Draven's tone matched his dangerous mood.

"Use some common sense, Draven. You know Armond is right." Any other man would be a fool to argue; nevertheless, Mason knew his cousin better than anyone. Although he was neither as tall nor as big as Draven, he wasn't short. He was solidly built, heavily muscled and had been a challenging competitor.

"There's the meeting with the Endarian Overseer," Mason continued. "And you must prepare for your wedding at the end of the moon phase..." Draven cut him a sharp look. Mason smiled at Draven's grunt of disgust. "...or devise a way to avoid it."

Draven didn't break his stride. "All right, but not this night. The fog is growing too thick. Go at sunrise; the elf situation will hold till then. We all know where Gavril will hole up. Once you've found the elves and dealt with them, bring Gavril to me. The little demon will be sorry his mother and father ever met."

Draven stopped abruptly, sensing the presence before he heard it. Waves of fear, oily and acrid, came from beyond the darkness and assaulted his senses. Lifting a hand to stop the men and warn them to silence, he pivoted to his left and stood motionless. They heard the crackling underbrush, a thud and a muffled cry. Draven moved toward the sound and then stopped.

Through the cold gray mist that clung like damp gauze and the musty scent of moss and earth, he sensed a white-hot pain and panic. Knowing an injured beast could be more dangerous than a fit one, his muscles tensed, his hand gripping the hilt of his sword. Cautiously he moved through the dense vegetation that opened into a clearing. There, in a heap, lay a dark form crumpled across a fallen dead oak. A pale feminine hand reached out.

Perplexed at the unusual intensity of the emotions he received from her, his brows furrowed. Draven felt her nausea, the swelling pain in her leg and the tremendous ache that spread throughout her body. She lifted her head and looked up at him. Her face was shrouded in shadows but he couldn't look away. He felt her fear growing and knew the three of them were frightening her further.

He'd never sensed anyone or anything so sharply. The force of what was inside her threatened to overwhelm him. *Great Creator*, he thought in frustration, *why was he cursed with this affliction?* He had not the time to help every injured stray and weak little broken bird that fell across his path. He'd be better off to leave the girl here and let fate have her.

Even as the thought occurred to him he moved to her, knelt, and picked her up. She bit her lip; he'd felt the little twinge of pain. It amazed him that her senses were so overloaded she hadn't even noticed. In his arms, her body trembled with pain, panic, cold and a fear so dark Draven held his breath and bit back an oath.

He shared his warmth with her and she looked up at him, breathing heavily. Mesmerized by what he saw in her cobalt eyes, he held her gaze until her eyelids fluttered closed and her head rested limply against his shoulder. Pain enveloped him in hard unyielding pulses then faded away. It was good that she had passed out, Draven thought, his eyes narrowing as he absorbed her suffering.

Draven turned and started for home. Mason and Armond glanced at each other then reluctantly started after him.

Armond spoke first. "Let me take her to the temple, Draven. They will help her there. More than likely she lost her way in the fog."

"Yes," Mason agreed. "We can send someone to see that she is well cared for."

Draven pushed forward, ignoring them. Anger and an odd possessiveness rose in him.

Mason put his hand on Draven's shoulder. "Stop. Please, cousin, listen to us."

Draven stopped and glared at Mason.

"This is foolish," Mason continued, defying the unmistakable warning in Draven's eyes. "You can't attend to this woman now. You are king; you have too many demands on your time and attention at present." His voice softened. "Leave her to the wise men. They will treat her spirit as well as her body."

"Someone may be looking for her." Armond stepped forward. His green eyes full of concern, he held out his arms. "Delegate this problem, Draven. Give her to me. I will see that she gets the best care."

Draven's voice sounded more like a growl. "She is badly hurt, on my land, my subject. She is my problem. I will see to her care. Personally. You will stand down, Armond."

Armond held up his hands in a defensive gesture and backed away.

"For the love of Iybae, we only mean to help you see reason." Mason stepped closer and lowered his voice. "Block her, Draven. Shut it down."

Draven glanced sharply at Mason and moved on, doing his best to ignore him. He didn't think he could block her if he wanted to. Knowing that only added to his frustration and concern. No, he wouldn't let the girl out of his sight. She was decidedly more than she appeared. Where she had come from was unknown and he sensed a power within her he couldn't quite discern yet. He frowned at the thought. She was a threat to him and his people...a potentially fatal one.

Mason sighed and waved his arm, following behind. "You aren't using rational thought..."

"Mason! Do you think I need coddling?" Draven shouted. "If you mean to be so damned helpful, go and clear the brush before me."

They trudged along in tense silence until they came to the clearing where their horses were still tied to the trees where they left them. Draven gave Mason a hard stare and handed him the girl while he mounted his horse and settled into the saddle. Silently he leaned down and took her from Mason, positioning her sideways in the saddle, keeping one arm around her to hold her in place as he held the reins with the other.

The last of their journey home they rode at a smooth canter, the girl resting limply against Draven's chest. She didn't turn to him or cuddle closer, instinctively seeking security as he had expected. She simply lay in his arms limply, her head bouncing softly against his shoulder. He held her frail body close to his. There was so little warmth in her and she seemed so weak.

She needed help but he was not unaware of the danger she presented. He felt something surrounding her, and from beyond her; something corrupt, something adverse. His frown deepened and his arm stiffened around her. She moaned but he didn't loosen his grip. Silently he offered prayer to Iybae for guidance and wisdom.

Chapter Two

When they were only yards from the gates of the keep, Armond galloped ahead to announce their arrival. He and Joeff, Draven's manservant, met them at the top of the great stone steps. Two boys stood ready to take their horses to the stables.

Draven reluctantly handed the girl down to Armond and dismounted with ease. His horse, Mandrake, turned his head, gently nuzzled the girl and snorted softly. Draven took her from Armond, meeting his gaze, and settled her limp body into his arms. Taking note of the curious eyes subtly stealing glances at him and his strange burden, Draven swiftly ascended the many steps leading into the great doors.

"Have Netta meet me at the baths," he said sternly without slowing.

Always somber, Joeff merely nodded and turned, spearing several nosy servants with looks of reproof.

Draven walked into the great hall and turned to the right. A young boy, a servant's son, ran ahead of him to the door tucked in the nook to the right of the wide staircase and pulled it open. He stood holding the iron door handle, his thin arms shaking from the weight of the door, his face tilted upward proudly, bright eyes following the mighty warlord. Draven tilted his head, met the boy's gaze and mumbled a thank you, quickly brushing past him on his way through the door and turning down the narrow passageway.

He descended into the baths, his boots nearly silent on the granite steps. The dimly lit hallway opened up into a large room completely tiled in slate rock. Two long, wide, padded benches were placed parallel to each other in the middle of the room. Along the back wall sat a large table and a copper basin. Draven laid her down on a padded bench, then stood. He crossed the room, opened the valve and filled the basin with warm spring water. He went back to her and knelt down on one knee, pushing the hood of her cloak back from her face.

Thick, dark, copper-tipped eyelashes lay against the dull blue smudges under her eyes. She was too thin. Her creamy pale skin was taut over high cheekbones, a strong jaw line and a soft gentle chin. Her nose was unremarkable and straight but not sharp, neither puggish nor beaklike. Her mouth was wide, her pink lips soft and full.

He clenched his teeth, clearly discerning the shape of knuckles in red and blue along her swollen left jaw. The bruise was beginning to spread up her cheek. Draven had no patience for men who took their aggression out on women. Perhaps that was the sinister feeling surrounding her. Perhaps she was running from an ill-tempered ass of a husband. He truly hoped that was it. An ass was easily dealt with.

It wasn't long before he heard the pitter-pat of Netta's slippers on the slate. He had begun unbuttoning her bulky, black cloak. It was obviously made for a man and it completely engulfed her. He looked up as Netta entered the room, thankful for her presence. The many cycles she had seen had made her patient and wise rather than bitter. She was a short, plump woman with warm brown eyes and a rosy round face. Her small bow-shaped lips seemed always curved into a sweet smile.

"Joeff told me about the girl. He's sending for the healer. I thought you might need these," she said, holding up a cake of soap and a clean sleeping gown. Focused on what he was sensing and trying to discern the significance thereof, Draven didn't answer but continued to disrobe the girl. Netta always understood his single-mindedness when it came to his gift and he was thankful for that. She silently set the things down on the table and came to help him.

Draven looked up as he finished unbuttoning the last button. "I'll lift her up and you remove her clothing."

Netta nodded and smiled at him, trying to hide her own concern. Whether that concern was for him or the girl he wasn't sure.

He sat on the edge of the bench and reached inside the girl's cloak. His hands moved up her sides, frowning as his fingers skimmed over her prominent ribs. He held her just under her arms then gently lifted. He rested her upper body against him with her head lying against his shoulder. While Netta carefully removed the cloak, Draven unwrapped the scarf that wound around her head. Loosed from its binding, her tousled dark hair tumbled down her back.

Netta looked up at him, her brows raised. "Ah, how lovely. We women should all be so blessed."

Draven knew she was trying to relieve the tension, but he ignored her and gathered the thick mane to the side to fall over the girl's shoulder so that Netta could deal with the buttons at her back. His fingers brushed against the chain around her neck and he lifted the gold pendent that hung between her breasts. It was small and round, engraved with perhaps a coat of arms.

Frowning, he unhooked it and rubbed a thumb across the pendent. It wasn't a coat of arms but a small orb with tiny lines fanning from it resembling light. Words he could not translate curved along the outer edge. The language was familiar but he couldn't remember when or where he'd seen it. He would make a point to find out, he thought, setting the pendant aside and shifting his focus back to helping the girl. Netta had finished with the buttons; he pulled the dress down and freed the girl's arms.

"Oh." Netta paused then whispered, "Lift her arms, Draven, so I can get her chemise over her head."

Without moving he watched Netta's smile melt into a frown, her brows knit together in concern. He felt sudden sharp alarm shake Netta to the core and then soften into sorrow and compassion. Narrowing his eyes he put his left arm around the girl's waist and with his right he took the knife from his belt. "Just cut it off," he said, holding it out to her.

She looked into his eyes and he nodded sharply as she hesitantly grasped the knife. He could feel the girl's breath on his chest; he could feel her heart beat in a slow steady rhythm. His right hand held her head against his shoulder as he watched Netta gather the thin material and carefully cut the chemise from her back.

He heard Netta gasp but he couldn't look away. He swallowed the roar that threatened to erupt from him. Bruises stained her back, shoulders and arms with ugly splotches of blue, purple, red and greenish-yellow. He skimmed his fingertips over the velvet skin, gently probing for broken bones. Then he traced the slick white lines that crisscrossed and overlapped. There were so many, different lengths, different widths. Anger seared his stomach. No animal should be treated this savagely, let alone a woman, not for any reason.

An intense desire welled inside him to protect her and save her from whoever had caused this pain. The powerful surge of intuition warred with his wisdom that this girl was not what she appeared to be. He couldn't ignore the veil of danger he sensed hovering around her and until he unraveled the mystery of who she was and where she came from and why, he'd consider her a very real threat and, God help him, he'd treat her as such.

He lifted her away from him and began tugging the ruined chemise from her arms. It was then he noticed the rusty brown stains that caused the garment to adhere to her breasts. He looked up, meeting Netta's tear-filled gaze.

"Get me some water," he growled through clenched teeth as he laid the girl back down on the bench and knelt beside her.

Netta went to the basin filled with warm water, dropped in the clean sponge and carried them back to the bench. Draven trembled with fury as he took the sponge from her and pressed it against the girl's body, saturating the thin material. Carefully he lifted the chemise away. Fresh blood wept from the wounds. He hissed through his teeth and thanked the Great One that she slept.

She was young, likely no more than twenty cycles. Her injured breasts were very full, round and firm; their peaks were still pink, telling him she had yet to bear children. The wounds weren't terribly deep, save for the slice that cut into her right nipple, but they were so many.

His fingers glanced over the white scars and the raised red welts across her breasts and stomach. Several angry slashes broke the skin. The person who had beaten her, likely with a whip, had concentrated on her breasts. It had been incredibly painful for her and would be again, but he could take away the worst of it.

"She should be bathed, Draven. She's filthy and all these cuts are in danger of becoming infected." Not one to hide her emotions well, Netta spoke sharply, her voice cracking with emotion. "The minerals will help in healing as well. I'll go fill the bath."

He glanced at Netta then stood. "No, I'll take her into the pool. It will be easier that way and the healing properties of the spring water are more potent there."

He pushed the girl's skirts up and ran his hand lightly down her leg. He didn't think the bone was broken but her ankle had turned an ugly purplish-blue and was swelling. Mindful of the injury, he pulled off her worn slippers. Her feet were battered from her long run. The soles and high arches were bruised and blisters had been rubbed raw, leaving bloody wounds on her heels and toes.

Taking the knife from Netta's hands, he lifted the haggard dress bunched at the girl's waist and with a twist of his wrist, easily cut through the inferior material. The girl shuddered, her stomach quivering against Draven's knuckles. He opened his hand and rested it there, absorbing more of her pain and queasiness. He closed his eyes against the sensations as they mingled with his own rage.

When he opened his eyes he saw that the welts continued lower on her stomach and the new wounds crossed old scars farther down and around her hips. He fisted the ruined material of her dress in each hand and ripped the remaining cloth away with a few tugs. Kneeling again he lifted her head and brushed the long, warm brown hair from under her to cascade into the basin.

Without turning he held out his hand. "Soap." His voice was low and vibrated with fury.

Netta's soft pudgy hand touched his forearm and he breathed deeply. "Draven, stop. Let me," she said softly, her voice wavering with emotion.

He turned his head and stared at Netta for a moment before he stood and walked away to find the healer.

Joeff met him at the top of the stairs; his eyes widened and he took two steps back. "Lord Amaranth, the healer is here. He waits for you in the hall."

Draven said nothing but walked through the passageway and into the hall, sorting through his conflicting emotions as he went. In order to handle this situation correctly he would need to focus on discovering who she was while protecting her. There was no place for attraction here, he lectured himself, and certainly no place for possessiveness.

Brussoe Kendrick was an imposing figure of a man. He stood nearly eye-to-eye with Draven and, though most of his bulk had gone soft over the years, thickening his middle substantially, he was once as strong as the warlord. His silver-gray hair waved back from his face and was cut close. His smiling mouth was hidden under a bushy gray mustache. Waiting patiently in the hall he shuffled his feet, both hands folded over the handle of a worn leather satchel. Brussoe had known Draven from the time he was a boy and was well respected by the people of Lanthor as well as their king.

"Greetings, my lord…" The look on Draven's face caused Brussoe's smile to falter. His shaggy gray brows collided over sharp brown eyes.

Draven met his gaze. "Follow me." His statement left no room for discussion. He turned and retraced his steps.

Netta had just finished braiding the girl's damp hair. She glanced up at Draven. "She's ready for the pool. Should I have a bench carried into the water?"

"No," he said as he sat and pulled his boots off.

"Draven." Netta took a deep breath when he raised his head and scowled at her. "Take care with her head," Netta told him, pointing to an area above her own temple. "She has a nasty lump."

He simply stared, struggling to rein in the violence welling up in him. Dealing with the man who did this would take formidable control; at this moment, he wasn't sure he had it. What he had was a desire to tear her attacker apart, shed his blood, make him scream in agony the way he was sure this girl had screamed.

He stood and pulled his shirt over his head. Flinging it aside he quickly unlaced his leather pants, discarding them with the rest of his clothing. Brussoe cleared his throat. Netta averted her eyes and backed up, mainly because she wasn't far above eye level with his hips. She handed Draven a soft cloth and the cake of soap.

He lifted the girl into his arms, walked through the archway and stepped down into the pool fed by hot springs. The girl's lips parted and a low moan escaped between them. Her hand pushed at the center of his chest, fighting even in her sleep. He held her body close to his, absorbing her pain, and watched her face as she began to relax. His body responded to her immediately, though he tried to focus on his task at hand.

He knelt on one knee, positioning her to sit and lean against him. Her lower body was submerged in the mineral-rich, hot spring water. He slung the cloth over his shoulder, cupped his hand and poured the water over her chest and down her back as sweat beaded across his forehead and dampened his hair. With the slippery cake of soap, he rubbed lather over her shoulders and down her arms.

She was thin but he had been wrong; she was no weakling. The muscles in her arms were long and well-defined, as were those in her legs. Her hands were scraped, blistered and callused. Her head rolled back as her body slowly absorbed the warmth surrounding her. The sudden desire to kiss her hummed through him.

He wanted to taste the warm skin that pulsed at the base of her throat as her heart slowly pumped life through her. Trying to distract himself, he soaped the cloth and began washing her forehead, her cheeks. He wiped the dried blood from her bottom lip and breathed deeply, moving the cloth down to her neck, over her shoulders, between her breasts.

Yanking himself back to reality, he examined her wounds. Her nipple was swollen and red, the torn flesh ragged. He carefully cleaned the dirt from it and clenched his teeth as it oozed fresh blood.

"Uh, Lord Amaranth." Brussoe cleared his throat again. "We should see after that ankle soon. Soaking too long in the heat will do more damage than good."

Draven nodded. He finished washing her and rose from the water, heedless of his heavy erection. Unabashedly he carried her to the bench and gently laid her down. "Netta, when she has been tended to, have her put in the room next to mine." He kept his gaze on the girl. "Have someone find her some decent clothes. Call for me as soon as she awakens."

Draven pulled on his leather pants, leaving them untied. He bent to pick up his shirt and noticed the pendant he'd taken from around the girl's neck. He picked it up and clasped it in his hand. "Brussoe, do your best to repair her nipple. She's young, I want her to have no trouble nursing her babies someday and it's important that she be able to receive pleasure as well." Grabbing his boots, he left Brussoe and Netta to their ministrations.

Mason was standing in the hall between Draven's two hulking wolfdogs, Rolf and Aletha. Draven softly clicked his tongue and the dogs fell into step behind him, their big heads lowered.

"Is the girl alright?" Mason stopped him as Draven turned to mount the stairs.

"She will be," he answered harshly.

Mason frowned. "You're still angry with me."

"No, Mason, not with you."

"Armond?" He stopped him again.

"In the name of Iybae, Mason!" Draven hissed through his teeth, slamming his fist against the banister.

Mason lifted a brow at the soft crack of the impact. "Shall I send word to the villages that the injured woman is here?"

Draven thought for a moment. "Not just yet. Tell Armond as well. Keep your mouths closed for the moment. I'm to meet with Haig Orbane tomorrow morning. We will discuss it further after I'm finished with him and the elves are dealt with." Draven took two stairs at a time, leaving a puzzled Mason standing there with his hands on his hips.

Chapter Three

Looking into deep blue pools, Draven's hands glided over her soft skin. Desire was there in her eyes, her body warm and trembling with need. She arched against him; her moan seemed to echo around him, through him. Her lips lightly caressed his shoulder, his chest. Her tongue teased his nipple, drawing a groan from his very soul.

Her hair was like silk, softly waving around his fingers as he brushed it back from her face. Pressing a kiss to her temple his hand moved over her small shoulder and over the slope of her breast. Her erect nipple grazed his palm as he cupped the full, swollen globe. "So soft, so hot," he murmured into her hair.

Wide eyes looked up at him, hope mingling with desire. Lowering his head he tasted her plump parted lips and she curled into him, purring like a kitten searching for warmth. He stroked a hand down her back, pulling her closer to him. Her body, so frail and soft, seemed to merge with his.

He groaned as he rolled her onto her back, settling between her thighs. Breathtakingly lovely, she opened to him. Her cheeks flushed a deep rose, her lips swollen from his kisses; her round breasts rose and fell with every breath that shuddered from her.

While his chest tightened with emotions he didn't wish to interpret, his body urged him to take her, flooding him with waves of sensation. His shaft pulsed with every heartbeat, yearning to plunge deep inside her, feel her channel convulsing around him. He braced his weight on his forearms, feeling the slick heat of her as his hips settled between her thighs.

His mouth closed over her nipple and her hands grasped his head as she cried out. Sucking and licking the hardened flesh sent ripples of her pleasure radiating through him. His cock flexed with need. Reaching between them, his fingers found her plump silky folds, sodden with her juices. He opened her, sliding his fingers over the taut little bud and then lower to the tight opening of her sheath.

Moving up her body he positioned the head of his cock just inside her snug entrance. He clenched his teeth as he looked down at her, watching the emotion swirl within the blue depths of her eyes as it swirled within him, weaving with his own.

"Please," she panted, her blue eyes stormy. "Love me."

* * * * *

Light…soft dusky light glowed around her, and warmth. Linea felt cocooned in heat and light and warm, soft colors. She parted her lips on a sigh as the heat filled her. Pleasure…oh it felt so good; the pleasure cascaded over her.

She felt her breasts swell and heat, their peaks cresting, aching, but not with pain. The air around her seemed humid, hot and spicy. Her body reacted to an unseen touch and she couldn't resist the desire to arch against it. Wanting more, she wanted it to never end; the warmth, the security and…
"Oh yes," she groaned…the way she felt.

The sensations ebbed and flowed and she seemed to float on emotion. She felt safe, she felt treasured – no, something wasn't right. Was she dead? Though she tried to contain it, a strangled cry escaped her throat as the pleasure grew intense.

Hovering there in some otherworldly space, she opened her eyes. Slowly turning, gasping for breath, her body was subjected to waves of sensation and emotion. Wisps of color whirled around her and converged into silver eyes shining outward from a beautiful masculine face.

"Breathe me in," he moaned seductively.

* * * * *

Wondering for a moment if she was still asleep, still dreaming, Linea lay still, trying to regulate her breathing. She thought she was awake but she still felt as though she was floating, enveloped in warmth. So warm and restful, her limbs felt liquid, her mind clear. A hint of the intense pleasure from the dream rippled through her.

It was easier to breathe at least, she thought as she inhaled deeply. There was no pain, for the first time in a long time, no pain. The scent of herbs and baking bread made her mouth water. No, it couldn't be real, and she wasn't ready to face reality yet so she laid there, her eyes closed, and tried to recapture her dream.

But somewhere far off she heard a lovely sound, a song, someone humming. She was dead — she must be — and Iybae, the great Creator, in His infinite mercy had looked past her sin and had granted her a place in His paradise. It was quite possible that she had expired. After all, she had hit her head when she tripped over that fallen oak.

No, it felt too real, she thought as she stirred apprehensively, her hand brushing over the soft surface she lay upon. It was very real. She wasn't dreaming and she wasn't dead. She opened her eyes slowly and lay still, allowing her surroundings to come into focus. She wasn't dead, but she thought maybe she was in paradise. The bed she lay in was so wide and cloud-soft, canopied and shrouded in yards of sheer ivory material. Beyond the haze of the shimmering folds the room was warm and welcoming.

Several flickering candles sent shadows dancing. She could see the outline of a large wardrobe against a far wall. There was a fireplace to the left of her; she could hear the snapping of a fire and smell the wood smoke. Facing the fireplace was what appeared to be a darkly colored, oversized chair. Everything seemed to spread out and tower. She blinked, wondering for a moment if she'd shrunk.

She felt shaky and unsure. Her hair had been braided and she'd been dressed in a sleeping gown. It was too big for her but it was soft and billowy against her sore body. She couldn't remember when she felt so clean, and the two nights she'd spent running from her uncle had left her covered in grime and sweat. Lifting a hand to her throat, she found her medallion was gone.

Someone had taken her medallion and stripped her of her clothes. Someone had stripped her...a tremor of fear spread through her. They knew. Now they would send out word about her. He would come for her. Sitting up, she pulled herself back against the padded headboard. Her injured ribs screamed in protest, momentarily taking her breath away and then fading to a dull ache.

The humming stopped and she looked up to see someone moving to a doorway. There was whispering, followed by retreating footsteps. Pain budded in her temple and slowly began to bloom. She pushed the thick quilt to the side to see her foot had been wrapped tightly. The bandage covered her ankle and calf halfway to her knee.

She wiggled her toes and flexed her ankle, sucking in air through her teeth at the sharp stab of pain that radiated up her leg. At least it wasn't broken, as she'd first thought. Her breasts began to sting, but the incredible throbbing pain had subsided. Pulling her gown away from her chest she stared in horror at the bandages that covered her breasts.

Pain or no pain, she couldn't lie there and wait to be taken back. She concentrated on keeping her breathing shallow and her ankle still. Getting her feet on the ground was the ultimate goal, if she could just swing her legs around to the edge. She leaned over to judge the distance to the floor and bit her bottom lip.

She would have to sit on the edge and slide down. Attempting to reposition herself, she pushed up on her hands. The curtain at the end of the bed parted abruptly. Linea yelped and looked up into the same piercing gray eyes that had captivated her the night before...and in her dream.

"Where am I?" She had meant to sound much more forceful, but instead her voice sounded far away, breathy, small. She nearly grimaced.

His intense eyes moved to her mouth and trailed down her body. Something in them made her feel naked and she pulled the quilt back up to her neck. Fear gripped her and she tensed, causing her body to ache. It frustrated her that she felt her cheeks grow pink with heat. She so wanted to be strong, to shake off the terrible vulnerability that hung over her like a shroud.

He was a dark mountain of a man, dressed in a shirt the color of brandy wine that pulled tightly across massive shoulders. The long sleeves were pushed up to just below his elbows, exposing thickly muscled forearms sprinkled with black hair. The shirt had no buttons or collar but had an open V with untied laces. His black pants clung to narrow hips and thick, powerful thighs. Black brows pulled together above his stormy eyes. The goatee that framed his well-defined, unsmiling mouth was trimmed short and dark. Thick black hair parted in the middle and hung in waves to his wide shoulders.

"You're a guest in my home, at the moment." His voice was a deep bass and commanded obedience. His gaze moved over her body once more, leaving her feeling flushed and nervous. "The pain is back."

It was not a question. She looked down at her bound chest, when she looked up again he wasn't there. She jumped then recoiled when the bed sagged beside her under his weight. His hand came toward her and she shut her eyes, braced for the impact. Warmth spread through her as he softly touched her cheek and turned her face to him. His hand was so hot and calloused but achingly gentle. The muscle in his jaw tightened and he frowned; his eyes darkened as his thumb glided across her bottom lip.

* * * * *

Draven felt her flinch, both physically and mentally. He clamped down on the rush of anger, reminding himself of what she'd been through. The pain she'd endured was abhorrent. It amazed him that she had been able to walk, and yet she ran.

"You bit your lip," he murmured. "This balm will help."

He felt her reaction to his touch, an unexpected mixture of emotions radiating throughout her body, and was taken aback. Taking a deep breath he pushed away memories of the dream he'd had the night before and tilted her face away, studying the discoloration along her cheekbone and jaw. It was a bit bluer now but the swelling had gone down some and her skin had pinkened a bit.

Tenderly, Draven held her head still and smoothed his free hand over her silky hair. He felt the knot above her temple and paused there, absorbing the pain. He watched her eyes flutter closed and felt her intake of breath. Slowly leaning across her, he placed his left hand on the bed beside her right hip.

Never taking his eyes off her face he braced himself as his right hand moved slowly down her throat. She gasped and her eyes opened wide. He stared into them, feeling her mind and body brace to fight as fear surged through her. It occurred to him that she might wonder if he'd strangle her and the idea did not settle well with him.

Holding her gaze, the slow shake of his head was barely perceptible. Her pulse, pounding against his hand, slowed a bit. His gaze moved to her lips and his hand brushed against her hip as he leaned toward her. Touching her made him want to feel more of her, kiss away the fear, to melt her into him.

He raised his gaze and looked into her eyes as his hand moved to her chest, just above the bandages that wrapped her breasts. He absorbed the pain there, watching her eyes darken. Feeling the heat of her tightening arousal mingling with confusion, he endeavored to control his own body's response.

He prided himself on being a man who knew his limits and had the good sense to exercise self-restraint. He held her gaze as he withdrew his hand, frowning as she trembled, swallowed hard and looked away.

"Don't," he said hoarsely as heat surged through him. "Don't lick your lip, you'll lick the balm off."

It was a logical reason, more logical than the truth. The sight of her small pink tongue darting across her bottom lip enticed him to taste her. Damn it all to hell, he thought, where had this wild lust come from? He'd have to control it, there was too much at stake. He was to be married soon, he reminded himself, not to mention that for his thirty-five cycles this girl was much too young.

Netta, his salvation, came into the room bearing a tray of food for the girl.

"Where are you from?" he asked, a bit more harshly than he had intended.

She looked from Netta's tray back to him. Fear again, and anger.

"Be at peace, girl," he said with frustration. "Who hurt you?"

She looked past him, pressing her lips together.

"I've brought you food," Netta interrupted. "You must be ravenous. You're wasting away."

"At least tell me your name." He sighed, glancing pointedly at Netta.

Her blue eyes narrowed as she looked from the woman to the warlord. "Joan."

He held her gaze, knowing she lied. "Joan?" He gritted his teeth against his burgeoning anger. He'd let her keep her lie, for now. "How old are you?"

Relieved that he seemed to believe her she relaxed a little. "I've seen twenty-five cycles."

He narrowed his eyes dubiously. "You look no more than nineteen, twenty possibly."

She frowned. "I am twenty-five. But believe what you wish," she snapped and looked away again. With a sigh she turned back to them. "You've been more than kind. I regret that I have nothing to give you in return for your kindness. If you will return my things to me, I will relieve you of the burden of my presence."

"But that's not possible, dear," Netta said as Draven took the tray from her and placed it on the girl's lap. "Your clothes were, well...they were, destroyed."

"What?" she rasped. Her wide blue eyes darted between the two.

Draven felt her panic rise and he poured the hot tea and added honey. "Joan," he sneered. Raising his gaze to meet hers without lifting his head he handed her the cup. She was a terrible liar. At least that said something for her. But she deemed it necessary to lie about her identity, and that did not bode well for her. "Netta will find some clothing for you."

She needed to eat, she was too thin, he thought as he broke open the bread and smeared on fresh butter. "At this point you are in no shape to leave."

It wouldn't matter if she was, but there was no reason to tell her that. Searching her face, he laid the bread beside the bowl of steaming broth. A strong vein of resolve had her chin lifting in defiance, but Draven felt the fear, the anger, and the sultry wisps of desire swirling around it. "Now, you will eat," he grumbled at her.

She shuddered at his demand and pressed her lips together tightly. In his frustration he wanted to intimidate her, demand the truth. It was that bitter fear swirling inside her that held him back, looking into those incredibly sad blue eyes. With a deep breath he stood. "No one will have an opportunity to hurt you while you're here." He placed his hand over hers, still fisted in the quilt at her neck. "You have my word."

* * * * *

Frowning, she watched him leave. The old woman walked around the bed, pulling back the curtains. The room, decorated in rich warm colors, opened up for Linea and she breathed easier.

"I'm Netta, dear. Is there anything I can fetch for you?" The woman's smile was so warm, her words soft and comforting.

"What time of day is it?" Linea's question was almost a whisper.

"It's almost noon." Netta smiled over her shoulder at Linea as she moved to open the window drapes.

Linea gasped. "I've slept too long."

"Nonsense!" Netta grinned and sat down on the side of the bed. The mop of gray curls pinned on top of her head wobbled. "You've slept because you've needed sleep."

She looked at the cherubic woman sitting with her hands folded over her round belly, watching her expectantly.

"Who is he?" Linea asked, nodding in the direction of the door.

Netta chuckled, dramatically waving her arms. "He's Lord Amaranth. Master of this keep and King of Lanthor."

Netta's eyes sparkled with humor but Linea forgot to breathe. What kind of cruel fate was this? She was being held in the keep of The Butcher King. Lord Amaranth was his son, her family's adversary. There had been rumors, horrible tales of what happened to those who crossed Amaranth. They said the son, though he struggled to rein in his temper, was possibly more volatile than the father. An icy shiver slithered down Linea's spine. Iybae must be livid with her.

"Goodness, you've gone completely pale. Don't let his reputation frighten you, dear." Netta patted Linea's hand and laughed as she looked over her shoulder after him. "He's really a good boy."

Linea lifted her brows and swallowed the knot of anxiety that clogged her throat. "Boy?"

"Ah well, Lord Amaranth will always be a boy in my heart." Her warm brown eyes sparkled with pride.

Linea's eyes widened and she coughed. "You bore him?"

Netta's laugh sounded like bells. "Oh dear, no! I doubt I would have lived through such a bearing! Lord Amaranth was born weighing thirteen pounds."

Linea blinked and stared at Netta wondering what kind of woman it would take to endure giving birth to such a babe.

"I was his mother's maidservant. She was a tall, strong, hearty woman." Netta glanced at her. "Much like you." Netta went on before Linea could comment, "I cared for Lord Amaranth and brought him up after she was killed." Her smile faded. "I miss her still; we were very close. She would be so proud of her son."

Sighing heavily she stood and patted Linea's knee. "I have freshly pressed, clean clothing for you, maybe a bit short, perhaps a bit large. You're too thin. Finish eating and then, if you're up to it, I'll help you dress."

"Yes, thank you." Linea tried hard to picture the king as a boy but just couldn't imagine him as anything but the oversized warlord he appeared to be.

"You are welcome here, dear." Netta's eyes sparkled and her smile was so warm, Linea could barely resist the urge to hug her. Humming sweetly, Netta turned and padded out of the room, leaving Linea staring after her.

Chapter Four

It disturbed her to realize just how starved she was for a simple smile, some small, kind affection, a gentle touch. Not since her mother and father died had she been touched in a way that even resembled care. That would explain her peculiar reaction to the king and his generosity. She didn't deserve it; she hated that she allowed herself to accept it.

Never having been served or cared for, she felt shamefully lazy, wicked in her indulgence. The bed sheets felt wonderful against her skin. She couldn't remember ever having felt so warm, so clean. Even in the hot seasons she had felt cold all the way to her bones.

Overwhelmed by her conflicting thoughts and emotions, Linea nervously nibbled the buttered bread; it seemed to melt in her mouth. She dipped it in the herbed broth and began munching greedily. In her mind flashed the image of Lord Amaranth's long fingers as he buttered her bread. An unfamiliar ripple of liquid heat infused her and her mouth went dry. Linea squeezed her eyes shut and shook her head but the image wouldn't dissolve.

She laid the bread aside and gulped warm, sweetened tea. Her body was tormented with sensations foreign to her. Her breasts pressed against the bandages with every breath. Their tips felt tight and they stung. The pain and pleasure together sent tingling waves pulsing along her nerve endings, making her want more. What kind of power was this? What had he done to her?

She had heard of the king, Lord Amaranth. She had heard her uncle's servants whisper horrid tales of his conquests, testimonials and stories of the carnage and bloodshed left in his wake, and they had only paled in comparison to those of his father's before him. He was known for his brutal violence and apathy. She knew what those hands were capable of and she knew he despised her family; she'd overheard her uncle say so, many times. If he knew who she really was, he wouldn't be kind; he'd kill her.

Lord Amaranth was such a large man. With those strong, callused, bare hands, he could kill her so easily. And yet he had been so gentle.

His finger gliding over her lip had been so hot it still tingled. The aching in her nipples increased and she cupped her breasts gently, feeling the hard knots push painfully against the bandages, against her palms. Gently she rubbed at them to relieve the tension there.

Waves of pleasure danced through her body, bathing her in heat. She gasped as the most intoxicating feeling overshadowed the slight stinging she felt. Every slight rub sent bursts of sensation radiating through her; her pain seemed to fade in the veil of this strange desire. She moved her fingers over her nipples, testing. They were round and hard, hardening even more with her touch, straining against their bindings. She liked the feel of them against her fingers, the sharp pain and pleasure that spiraled through her, spearing lower.

She slid down in the bed and laid back, a shuddered breath escaping her lips. In awe of what she was feeling, she let her hands explore. With each stroke the desire for more grew, heating her body further. Her eyes drifted closed as she warred with her emotions. She should stop, she knew she should stop, but she liked the new feeling. There was tension, she felt something building, but it wasn't like being afraid.

With one hand she clutched a pillow and pressed it to her lower abdomen. She continued to gently massage each wounded breast lightly, lavishing in the rain of warm sensation. She squeezed her legs together as the pressure built at the core of her and a tightening began between her thighs, pulling, urging her toward something... something she couldn't name.

* * * * *

"That's it, Nathaniel! This time without the dramatics." Draven stood in front of the young warrior, legs apart, knees slightly bent, thighs braced. "Conserve your energy. Lunge with sure, determined strokes. The power will be there." He shifted from one foot to the other as he held his sword in both hands, ready for the next attack. "It's not with force that the stream carves the stone but with unyielding consistency. Now, when you're ready..."

Nathaniel grinned. "Yes, ready, my lord." And with a war cry, he lunged forward. Draven easily blocked him with a sharp clang of metal against metal, a sound Draven both loved and hated reverberating off the surrounding mountains. It was a perfect day for exercises. All of Lanthor was bathed in warmth and light. Draven loved his kingdom with its lush forests, rocky mountain peaks and the blue-green rolling hills. The fact that they had little flatland was fine with him.

In the valleys lay lovely little villages. Race or species didn't matter. Everyone lived together in peace, for the most part. And, he was proud to say, he had their respect; therefore, they tended to obey the edicts. The elves were the exception. Thieving, mischievous scoundrels they were. The mere thought of Gavril and his horde of miscreants put him in a bad temper, so he pushed them from his thoughts.

He loved training; he was especially fond of Nathaniel. The youth had fire and a drive to succeed, but he was fair and considerate. Nathaniel was learning fast and he had the strength of mind and body to become a fine warrior. However, he was still a boy and liked to show off as if on stage. Like most eager young men, he lacked self-discipline.

The corner of Draven's mouth lifted as Nathaniel charged at him again. He locked Nathaniel's feet and sent him to the ground just as erotic sensations gripped Draven. His grin faded into a frown, his brows knit together in confusion as sensual waves crashed over him. He froze, tensing for a fight as he fought to understand what was happening.

"My lord. Are you well?"

"What?" Draven said a bit sharply, his increased breathing having nothing to do with swordplay. He looked down at Nathaniel, who lay below him. Nathaniel had dropped his sword and held both hands open, palms up, the tip of Draven's sword hovering a hairbreadth from Nathaniel's Adam's apple.

"Damn." Draven narrowed his eyes as he sheathed his sword and stepped away. As he focused he located the source of the sexual onslaught. It came from the woman. His eyes narrowed as he absorbed the pleasure of her timid caresses, her growing desire. He felt his cock swell and pulse with each wave of sweet torment. His hands...he wanted his hands on her tender breasts. He wanted to devour them with his touch, with his tongue. He wanted to give in to what she was doing, close his eyes and focus on it, intensify it or better still, go to her, increase her pleasure and his own.

"Did I do something wrong, my lord?" Nathaniel asked warily.

He had to snap out of this. What was he thinking? "No! No, Nathaniel. Excellent work. Go now, that's enough for today." He looked around to see Armond with his head cocked to the side, his brows furrowed, those green eyes assessing him.

Mason leaned against a post, his arms crossed and his eyes bright with humor, a smile teasing the corner of his mouth. Even without the gift his cousin could always read him. Mason, a clever mocker, loved that he knew Draven better than anyone and used his knowledge whenever he could to plague him unmercifully. Usually Draven found the humor in Mason's jests but this time he was too torn between fighting his predicament and giving in to it.

"Wonderful," Draven grumbled under his breath and stumbled as strong sensual sensations speared through him, gripping his body with lust.

"Lord Amaranth. Are you well? You're turning red." Nathaniel laid a concerned hand on Draven's shoulder.

"I'm fine, Nathaniel. You have work to do at home, don't you?" Draven sniped. He was immediately sorry for snapping at the boy but he couldn't think rationally at the moment.

"Yes, my lord." Nathaniel shrugged as he turned and walked away.

Draven made his way across the yard to where Armond and Mason stood. Fear — the woman's fear — began to cloud and weaken the pulsing desire. Hopefully she'd stopped her self-exploration. He had too much to do and he didn't think ravaging her was an option in her present condition.

Armond lifted a brow but said nothing.

Mason smirked. "Are you getting too old to train the young bucks, cousin?"

Draven glared at Mason. "You're only one cycle younger than me, Mason."

"Yes, but I'm crafted so much better," Mason said as he flexed his muscles.

Armond made a sound of disgust and rolled his eyes. "I'm going to see about the horses. I have some leather work to do." They watched Armond saunter to the stables, shaking his head.

Mason crossed his ankles and leaned back against the fence "So, you're hot from training or you're hot and turned on? It's not that hot today. Please, Draven, tell me you don't have a thing for the boy."

Draven gave him a menacing scowl. "The way your mind works unnerves me, cousin."

Mason chuckled, then his eyes widened as an idea struck him. "You picked up something from the girl!"

"Shut up, Mason," Draven said through his teeth. He needed to get away from him. He was hot; sweat beaded at his temple. His cock strained uncomfortably against the binding leather of his pants.

"You did!" Mason grinned, moved closer and elbowed Draven. "Fluffin' her duff, was she?"

Draven stared at Mason for a moment. "Mason, there are times when you can be absolutely repugnant." He glowered at him then started to walk away before turning back and facing Mason nose to nose. "If you say anything about this to anyone at anytime, I won't hesitate cutting your cursed tongue out of your over inflated head."

Mason straightened, giving Draven a pained look. "I'm wounded, cousin. Wounded, I tell you! How could you think I would malign your reputation in that manner?" He swiped at an imaginary tear. "Why, if it got out that you were more than a bloodthirsty warlord..." Mason's eyes widened. "Well...Iybae only knows what would come of such a revelation!"

Draven shook his head, annoyed that a smile tugged at the corner of his mouth. Mason could make the dead laugh, which made it nearly impossible for Draven to stay mad at him. "Exactly," he grunted.

"Besides, if the women knew the king was so hot-blooded, they might be more inclined toward you. Now just where do you think that would leave me?" Mason asked, grinning.

Draven snorted. As if Mason would ever want for female attention. "You have nothing to fear. Whether they find out or not, I'll be married soon," he said, leaning against the fence beside Mason and watching the horses romp in the pasture.

Mason turned serious. "Draven, you have to find a way out of this."

Draven cut him a warning glance. "I need a wife." Now more than ever, it seemed. His body was raging with need. Although he had the sinking feeling that taking the straitlaced widow would do little to assuage his lust.

"You don't need Cynthia Randall Madison," Mason said.

"Cynthia Madison is a lady. She's well-bred and respectable. She'll be a beloved queen," Draven said dryly.

Mason shifted to look at Draven. "That's incredible, Draven. You're starting to believe that, aren't you?" Draven was surprised by the anger he felt budding inside Mason and shot him a bemused look. Mason almost never got angry. "Look, Miss Cynthia is spoiled and annoying. Draven, she's a cold, unpleasant little brat."

Draven's mouth hung open at Mason's indignation. "Mason, how do you know Miss Cynthia?"

"I don't...not personally," Mason said, frowning. "But I've heard things. Gossip, women just love to gossip, you know."

Draven smiled now and pushed away from the fence, shaking his head. "Is that what you've resorted to, cousin, gossiping with the ladies? And all this time you had me believing you were a hot-blooded stallion. A lover so intense, so powerful, that you could render a woman speechless with your sexual arts and leave them gasping and weeping with joy in your wake. Mason, you are a fraud, you are but a gossiping ninny."

"The hell I am!" he said with wide eyes. "A woman must be wooed. They like a man that will listen to them. He tilted his head and narrowed his eyes at Draven. "Perhaps you have been too long without a woman to know these things."

Draven chuckled. Oh, this was magnificent. Absolutely wonderful. It was just what Draven needed to cheer him up. He loved it that he finally got the chance to fluster Mason. "Sad, Mason, truly sad." Draven turned, waving, and headed toward the keep.

"All right, go ahead. Laugh," Mason said after him. "But don't come crying to me when the cold snipe freezes your dick off."

Draven tilted his head back and laughed.

Chapter Five

Draven stood at the expansive window and watched Armond drag Gavril by his collar across the field below. Only the crackle and hiss of the fireplace broke the silence. Lifting his mug, he swallowed what was left of his coffee and absently ran a hand down the claret-colored, velvet drapes. A grunt of satisfaction rumbled in his chest. Rolf raised his head expectantly then lowered it again, keeping his eyes on his master.

Draven's war room was created and decorated to intimidate. The far wall was lined with books in a wide range of subjects, most of which he'd read, some more than once. On another wall hung the Amaranth crest. Flames reflected from the fireplace flickered over the hammered silver image of a wolf; its eyes of smoky topaz glittered, its long fangs bared. Various swords, knives, bows and spiked weapons were mounted along either side of the crest. Maps from before the Great War to the present were hung around the room. The desk was dark mahogany wood; carved by his mother, it had been a gift to his father.

From the painting above the fireplace, Draven's infamous father, Rayne, scowled down at him. His nose flared slightly beneath ever watchful, obsidian eyes. Draven mirrored Rayne's dark brooding features in all aspects except the turbulent gray eyes he'd inherited from his mother. Rayne's well-defined mouth was set in determination; his strong jaw clenched in preparation for battle. This room was known across the land to be an unnerving, if not frightening, place to be, and yet it was the one room in the keep Draven found the most serene.

The Endarian holy men seated across the thick wooden desk exchanged a puzzled look but said nothing. They held themselves rigid, occasionally hazarding a glance toward the wolfdogs that lay deceptively peaceful near the hearth. Without lifting her head, Aletha looked up at them, bared her teeth and growled softly in warning.

Draven turned and glared at the men. Setting his empty mug on the desk with a clunk, he slumped down in the tall leather chair with one arm slung over the back and studied them. They sat up straighter in their respective chairs, avoiding his gaze.

Both men wore black cloaks with the Endarian crest embroidered over their hearts. The man to Draven's left sat with his bony hands clasped together in his lap. His ferret-like features matched his restless and wily personality. The man seated to Draven's right was larger in all aspects but had an innocent, almost feminine face and a friendlier demeanor than his companion.

Draven continued to stare as he opened the block just a bit. He felt the small vein of fear weaving through their nervousness. A good and healthy reaction, he thought to himself. He waited just a moment more, enjoying their disconcertedness, before he blocked them again. Draven sat forward. He rested his muscular forearms on the desk and leaned in, frowning darkly.

"Why did Orbane not come and face me himself?" Draven questioned, though he knew why. The overseer of Endaria was a contemptible coward. His love and respect for Orbane's mother and stepfather had caused Rayne to suffer Orbane's lack of character with a tight lip. He had expected Draven to do the same but Haig Orbane was consistently making it impossible to honor his father's wishes.

"Sir Orbane sends his apology. He had fully intended to keep his appointment with you, my lord; however, this morning presented him with a matter more pressing." The thinner of the two spoke quietly.

Without moving his head, Draven cut his gaze to the other man, who nodded quickly and averted his eyes. Draven resisted the urge to snarl at the man's obvious weakness and shifted his gaze back to the skinny man. "What matter could have been more pressing?"

"With respect, Lord Amaranth." He bowed his head and cleared his throat. "I may not divulge our overseer's business."

Draven's eyes narrowed. "Your overseer's business is my business."

The man's thin lips pressed together. "Yes, my lord, I apologize; however..."

Draven stood, halting him with a piercing glance. The wolfdogs lifted their heads. Rolf bared his teeth, sensing the fear rise in the men. "Haig Orbane is a spoiled, angry boy who is raping the land and my people. I have suffered the impotent coward and his pathetic underlings far too long," Draven stated, his voice deceptively low and smooth.

The man frowned, his brows lowering. "Lord Amaranth, I beg your pardon. Sir Orbane is overseeing Endaria with the strong hand required to be a great leader—"

"I am not as blind to Orbane's dealing as he hopes I am, nor am I the idiot he says I am. I have warned him about his mistreatment of my people and he refuses to comply. He is subject to me whether he likes it or not and I'm done with being lenient with him."

The man shook his head and rushed to defend the oppressive overseer. "My king, you are misinformed. Sir Orbane—"

"Enough!" Draven snapped.

The men started at Draven's sharp retort. They recoiled as if expecting an assault as Draven stepped around the desk. He heard their collective sighs of relief as he walked past them, crossed the room and opened the door.

Draven walked toward two warriors who stood watching by the fireplace. They had seen the look in his eyes and had met him halfway across the great hall. They stood straight, their bulky bodies stiff, heads tilted, not wishing to miss one word of the orders from the Warlord King.

To ask him to repeat his words would be not only useless but also humiliating, and would disintegrate any hopes of advancement. They nodded, grim-faced, and Draven met both gazes.

Laying a heavy hand briefly on their shoulders he turned and strode back to the war room to glower at Orbane's men. "These men will escort you to Endaria and bring Orbane back to me."

Both men stood. The skinny man's eyes widened. "But, Lord Amaranth...my king—" he began.

"Get out," Draven growled through his teeth.

The man's mouth snapped shut and they said nothing as they walked quickly past him. Draven watched as the warriors flanked them and escorted them from the keep.

"Well, aren't you a fierce one." The gravelly voice chuckled.

Draven glanced down at Gavril. "Yes," he said without expression.

"You don't frighten me, Amaranth, you human scum," Gavril grumbled, stamping his foot. His gnarled face turned red as he grappled against the ropes that bound his stumpy arms. "You can't terrorize me. You're just a muscle-bound oaf; you can't do anything to me. King or no king, you have no authority over a noble elf. Ha! You're donkey dung!"

Draven watched the elf fruitlessly fight his bindings with a humorless smirk. "Gavril, you are truly simple. Save your energy." He motioned for Mason and Armond to follow him. "You're going to need it soon."

Draven turned, shaking his head, and walked back to sit in his chair. He would love nothing more than to banish Gavril from Lanthor. The grizzly little elf was tiring to deal with. More than anything he wished the faeries would return. Maybe they could do something about Gavril's ornery and troublesome ways. They could most assuredly deal with him more effectively than he could. All he could do was dole out discipline, and he'd lost all thought of being compassionate about it.

Armond shut the heavy door behind him. He and Mason were still grinning as they sat in the chairs the Endarian men vacated. "You have to allow us to watch you torture the little ass. He's been a cursed imp to deal with," Mason said.

Draven nodded. "So I take it the elves have been dealt with?"

"Yes." Armond sat back in the thickly cushioned chair and propped an ankle on his knee. "It took a while but we rounded them up and marched them through the town. We have them locked up in the hold under the Temple. The villagers are thrilled."

Mason grinned. "Especially the girls." He waggled his eyebrows at Armond. "One such girl rewarded Armond with the privilege of a kiss."

Armond frowned, his ears slowly reddening, his expression serious as always. "She was merely expressing her appreciation."

Draven barely suppressed a smile as he watched his childhood friend squirm. Armond wasn't considered particularly handsome but he had a most interesting face. His large, round green eyes avoided Draven's gaze. A long sharp nose was the focal point of his clean-shaven oval face. His lips were just a bit above thin. A small scar curved along his right jaw. He kept his light brown hair pulled back and tied with a leather cord. Something about Armond was very much appealing to the opposite sex. Some were truly smitten, but Armond was usually oblivious to their interest or maybe too stubborn and timid to do anything about it.

Mason patted Armond on the shoulder. "You're aging, old boy. You'd better make a move before you grow too old to know what to do with a woman."

Armond scowled at Mason then turned to Draven. "What are you planning to do with the elves? We can't just keep them locked up."

He absolutely could just keep them locked up. However, that would mean he'd have to feed them. When and if he let them out, they'd more than likely go back to causing havoc.

"Put them to work in the fields," Draven decided. "They will work there until they make compensation for the damage they did to the village and replace the things stolen from the villagers. Have a few elves work on the broken gates and stables. Let the villagers supervise, and need I tell you they must be guarded?"

Mason frowned, shaking his head. "That's it?"

Draven lifted a brow. "You have a better idea?"

"Yes." Mason stared at him incredulously. "Pain…lots of pain."

Draven smirked. "Ah, but it is extremely painful for an elf to be forced to work."

Mason looked disappointed. "Whatever you say, cousin. What about Gavril?"

"As leader of the destructive horde, Gavril will need a bit more discipline." Draven watched Mason's expression lighten and shook his head. "What would you have me do, Mason, tie him up and torture him?"

Mason nodded slowly. "Not a bad plan…not bad at all."

Draven's brows rose. "You need to go on a hunt. Your bloodlust is becoming bothersome."

Mason shrugged. "But you do intend to beat him. Tell me you'll beat him, Draven…"

Joeff interrupted, knocking twice and slowly opening the door. "I brought coffee." He walked across the room and set the tray on the desk between the men. Looking up he met Draven's gaze. "We will have pastries soon, my lord. Shall I bring them?"

Draven opened his mouth to decline when Mason and Armond said, "Yes!" in unison.

Joeff bowed with a smile and left the room. Draven poured the fragrant hot coffee into his mug. "As to Orbane…" He paused, taking a sip. "He failed to answer me about the problems with the people of Endaria. He insisted there were more pressing matters."

"You let this go too long, Draven. You are weakening in your old age," Mason snapped.

"Be cautious, Mason," Draven grumbled.

"I apologize." Mason sighed. "But Orbane should have been dealt with long ago. You have warned him about his savagery toward the people and about his bleeding the land dry for his own gain. Every moon phase he takes more and more from those subject to him. They are turning to you now, as their king. Draven, the bloated ass has had enough time!"

"Mason, don't mistake my calmness for patience." He glared at Mason for a long, silent moment. "I don't take lightly the oath I pledged to my father. I will not dishonor him but, rest assured, I will not stand by mildly while Orbane ravages this country or its people. I have sent my men for him. He will come with them, one way or the other."

Armond spoke quietly. "Draven, there's been talk that there is a faction of dissenters against the throne."

Draven met Armond's ever perceptive and wise gaze. He knew about the faction. He'd been covertly looking into the situation on his own for a while now. Still, he hadn't been able to pinpoint who the principal player was or what motivated him. It had become clear that Orbane was involved.

The whole dilemma was particularly uncomfortable for Draven. He knew the legacy that followed him, knew many of the stories bantered about were greatly exaggerated. Yet he'd gone out of his way to prove he was neither unfair nor unnecessarily brutal, ruling with a firm but kind hand.

He was certain an emissary had ensconced himself in the keep, spying on him and his men, and because of that he kept his investigation secret. He hadn't made Mason or Armond privy to what he was doing because he knew they wouldn't rest until they found the rat, and at present he needed everything to remain as routine as possible.

"Yes, I'm aware of it," Draven answered solemnly. "I'm looking into it."

"What are you doing about it?" Mason grunted sarcastically.

Draven smiled at Mason. "I'm being patient. I'm becoming adept at it in my dealings with you."

Mason snorted and rolled his eyes.

"Rest assured, my eyes are wide open and when the time is right I'll do what needs to be done. Until then, trust me," Draven said, eyeing Mason. Armond merely nodded. Mason's mouth tilted at the corner sheepishly.

Draven's smile melted as his gaze shifted to the closed door behind the men. She was near. It stunned him that he could sense her, even through the block he'd constructed. He stood as he felt her life force wrap around him, pulling him to her. He tensed as he recalled her earlier activities, his body immediately responding to the memory of her heat.

The woman was a complexity of emotions that threatened to overwhelm him. He struggled to separate them, sort them out. One sensation grew more intense than the others as they spiraled though him; it was surprise. She was astonished, bewildered.

Chapter Six

Draven moved around the desk and swiftly strode across the room. He flung open the door and there she stood, looking like a lovely goddess. Her gown of blue was a bit too large, a bit too short. The neckline rode just above the swell of her breasts and revealed much of her shoulders; long wide sleeves nearly covered her hands. The silky material draped sensually over her full breasts and hips and outlined her thighs as she moved. Her brows knitted together. One hand fanned nervously over her stomach, the other arm braced around Netta's shoulders.

She was tall and strong, well built, if just a bit thin. Her thick, walnut-colored hair had been brushed out and shimmered with strands of dark copper and burnished gold. It had been pinned back, but a few loose tendrils curled around her heart-shaped face. Her pink lips were parted, her top lip was softly curved, and the bottom lip was full with a tiny dip in the center.

Draven's arousal intensified, thickened, pressed tightly against the confines of his snug pants. He was intrigued by the intelligence, sadness and mystery her wide, deep blue eyes held. What intrigued him more was why those enchanting eyes were so full of compassion as she stared down at Gavril while he knelt at her feet, pledging to her his fealty.

Draven stood, watching warily, his eyes narrowing as Gavril took her hand in his small bound hands and kissed it. Draven felt faint waves of adoration and respect wrapped in strong bands of joy spiral through him, and knew the emotions came from someone other than the woman. It didn't take long for him to realize it was Gavril he sensed.

Briefly he wondered if he'd lost his mind. Elves couldn't be sensed. As quickly as the feelings came, they evaporated. Gavril's head jerked around. His bright eyes widened as they met Draven's hard gaze.

"Aw, three hells!" Gavril whined. "Not him." He looked back at the woman. "Please, my lady, tell me it's not him."

Draven cocked a brow and stared down at the elf.

"I...I..." she stammered. He felt her confusion spread like a thick fog within her, softly unfolding. She frowned deeply, shaking her head, and looked up at Draven for understanding. "Why do you have him bound so?"

Annoyed, Draven stared at her. "Why do you care?"

She winced at his unyielding gaze and harsh tone, but held her ground. "H...he's small and defenseless." She lifted her face and met his gaze. Draven knew she fought to control the tremors that danced up and down her spine. "Why do you want to hurt him?"

Draven tilted his head to the side, dark brows knit together as his own confusion dissolved into irritation. "This is none of your concern...Joan." The last he said sarcastically, making his point that he knew she lied.

Joan, as she insisted on calling herself, shifted and Draven felt the sharp pain that traveled up her leg. He watched her face with narrowed eyes and wondered how she kept her expression blank. She had merely blinked in response to the ache that now throbbed there. He looked at Netta. "Why in hell is she out of bed?"

Netta scowled. The girl patted the older woman's shoulder, took a deep breath and ignored Netta's urging to move on. She thrust her breasts out as she breathed in deeply. Draven groaned inwardly, his gaze settling on those luscious breasts.

She stiffened her back as she raised her chin. "My king, Lord Amaranth, I appreciate all you've done to care for me and the gift of your hospitality; however, I will not be bullied."

Draven felt her rage override her healthy fear and her pain. Her body trembled visibly and he felt hot fury crawling up his neck. He opened his mouth to speak when she raised a small, shaky hand to stop him. Her long elegant fingers were marred with blisters nearly healed now and tipped with ragged nails. Clenching his teeth he stared at the palm that should have been soft and rosy but was red, lightly calloused and scraped raw.

"I won't let you hurt this elf." She laid her hand on the grungy elf's head as though the devil spawn were a child.

Draven's eyes narrowed at the audacity of the woman. "I am master of this keep, woman, and while you are here I am master of you; therefore, you *will* do as I say and you will not question me. As I've said, what I do with this elf is no concern of yours. You'd do well to hold your tongue." The last he hissed through his teeth.

Her eyes lifted stubbornly. She met Draven's furious gaze and he felt her flinch. As well she should be afraid, he thought, yet she persistently continued to plead her case. He couldn't help but respect her for her dogged determination.

"Yes, my lord, I will do my best to do as you say but I can't hold my tongue. This elf is of importance to me." She looked down into Gavril's adoring gaze. "I cannot see how he could be of any consequence to you." She looked back at Draven. "Surely he's too small to cause any harm. Please, Lord Amaranth, you must release him to me."

Draven felt the men standing behind him. He knew that his decision affected more than just an odd woman and a disgusting elf. Furthermore, he didn't appreciate being backed into a corner. The situation would be different if this were just a woman and an elf; however, that was apparently not the case.

No elf ever bowed to anyone, for any reason. Gavril, elder, leader of this thieving band of elves, had not only bowed but went further still, pledging his life, his service to this woman. More proof that she was more than she appeared.

Draven fought to rein in his impatience. He was taken aback by the combination of raw fear and courage he saw in her bright liquid eyes. He felt the spiky pain she seemed to ignore somehow, and the frustration that pushed her on. He warred with the anger that swirled in his gut and the desire to pick her up, carry her back to bed and replace her pain with pleasure. He looked down at Gavril. The elf stood transfixed, gazing reverently up at the woman.

For a moment Draven wondered if he'd somehow been sucked into a parallel universe, some other dimension, like those from the stories his grandmother had told him about. Most of the villagers had lost a night's sleep and a day's work herding livestock after a horde, led by this "sweet little elf," opened all the stable stall doors and corral gates one evening. They had stolen and destroyed what amounted to several months of backbreaking work for the fun of causing mischief. For that, they would indeed pay.

"No." His tone left no room for further debate. "Netta, take her to the garden or back to the bed. Anywhere. Just get her away from me!"

Netta scowled at Draven again and pursed her lips. "Come, dear. No, don't argue anymore," she whispered as she steered the girl toward the garden entrance.

Gavril looked up at Draven, his violet eyes swimming. "You are a heartless bastard," he cried as he waddled over and stomped Draven's foot as hard as he could.

A growl rumbled in Draven's chest at the elf's ineffective assault. He reached down and lifted Gavril by his shirtfront to look him in the eye. "Lest you forget, Gavril, I am not a gullible little girl that you can manipulate. You and I both know what you are. And you better damn well remember who I am."

"Have you a death wish?" Netta asked as *Joan* pulled away from her and quickly limped back to where Draven stood.

"Put him down." Her voice shook with indignation.

Surprised at her impudence, Draven dropped Gavril on his bottom and with his boot scooted him toward the warrior that had come forward. He took two steps forward to tower over her. She never looked away in spite of the fear he felt keening inside her. He watched her chest rise and fall with fury and felt the growing pain that pulsed throughout her body.

"You are being a tyrant," she breathed; her voice was low and husky with emotion. "It's easy for someone of your size to harass and abuse someone smaller, weaker than you."

Draven clenched his teeth against the fury in himself and the pain and resolve he felt throbbing inside her. The fear had been pushed away but it was still there. "You are fighting a battle you do not understand," he said, restrained violence evident in his voice.

"No, you don't understand. I have to be with him. He needs me and I will not leave him."

Draven's frown deepened. She gasped as he took her by the shoulders. "Do not challenge me, lady!" he growled as he absorbed her pain, his eyes narrowing at the intensity. How in the name of Iybae did she stand it without showing it in her expression? Ah, but he could see it in those ocean-deep cerulean eyes of hers, feel it in his own body.

Draven took a step closer and started to speak, when he heard a plaintive whimper. Keeping his big scraggly head down, Rolf eyed his master warily as he moved his big body between them, effectively protecting the lady. Aletha lumbered up beside the woman and gazed up at her much like Gavril had. Rolf gently nudged Draven, his eyes pleading for mercy. Draven scowled down at them with disappointment at their lack of loyalty, but only Rolf had the good sense to divert his eyes.

He let her go suddenly and she swayed on her feet. He reached out to steady her and she took a step back. Lifting his brow he took a deep breath and struggled to speak softly. "This elf is guilty of criminal acts against my people, and he will be punished."

He would not stand here in his home and quarrel with this woman...this enigma of a girl. What he truly wanted was to throw her over his shoulder and carry her to bed where he could tame her and that damned defiant tongue of hers. He swallowed a groan as the vision of her caught up in the pleasure he gave her, moaning and writhing beneath him, played out in his mind.

The girl blinked at Draven, as though she were momentarily thrown off balance. "Then, I...I will go with him."

Rage and frustration clawed at him. "Fine! Take them to the hold."

"No, wait, my lord, please," Gavril pleaded.

Draven turned away as the warriors snatched up Gavril, took the girl by the arm and began to lead them away. Aletha growled and followed after them. Rolf grumbled low in his chest and circled Draven's legs.

Netta hurriedly moved to Draven and grabbed his sleeve. "You can't do this," she whispered harshly. "You've seen her wounds; you can't send her there. She still needs care."

"It's her choice!" he bellowed. What kind of spell had she put on everyone that they had all turned to her? Even his wolfdogs appeared to have disregarded their loyalties.

"Draven, please..." Netta nearly sobbed.

She was right. She had not had the chance to heal, and though he was humane to those he held prisoner, the hold was not clean enough. With so many open wounds she could develop a fever. He closed his eyes and sighed. "Wait!"

The men stopped and turned, a bit wary but awaiting orders.

"Take her to her room and lock her in." Without looking at the girl, he turned his cold gaze on Gavril with unbidden disgust. "Take him outside and wash him down like the dog he is. When he's reasonably clean, take him to the room at the far end of the hall and lock him in as well."

He watched as his men dragged the small man, screaming and fighting, from the great hall. He looked up to see the girl being escorted up to her room, his two faithless wolfdogs following behind. He wondered if she would glance back. He could sense her anxiety pulsing strongly just beneath her densely woven anger and determination.

Chapter Seven

The king's warrior never spoke, but shook his head at Linea. She caught a hint of a smile before he closed the door softly and locked her in. Limping to the bed, she sat looking down at her hands clasped in her lap, frustrated with the impotent anger still swirling in her stomach. Poor little elf, she thought. What kind of man could be so hateful? At least he gave little Gavril a room, and not too far away.

Perhaps she could talk Netta into letting her visit with him occasionally. She could offer to work. It was only right that she pay in some way for her room and board as well as the care she had received. Now that the elf would need food and shelter as well, she would see to it that she and Gavril did not take advantage of the king's generosity. Her brows furrowed, remembering Gavril's solemn little face. *"My life for you, my lady,"* he'd said reverently. *"For you, as it was for those who sired you and as it will be for your generations to come."*

Those who sired her were gone. She had faded memories of her parents, but no matter how hard she tried she couldn't recall their faces or anything of her life with them. That fact made her feel hollow inside, even though she remembered that they had loved her fiercely. There was a distant smoky memory of happiness and affection.

That love had died with them. The memory of it had been clouded by the agonizing pain in her body and her spirit. She wondered if perhaps their love was only a wishful dream; it had been at times easier to believe that it was. With all that was in her she had to believe that it was not. The memory of their love meant that love existed; that was all that had kept her sane.

She couldn't see how there could ever be a "generation to come." Even if her uncle never found her and she managed to live through her defiance of the king, she was an unacceptable bride. She had no real family, no legacy. She had nothing to offer a man; even her body had been ruined and was undesirable. To keep her pure, Uncle had said. She was barely fit to mate with a Kyrok. She shuddered remembering the one time she'd glimpsed Sir Pandrum.

He was as tall as Lord Amaranth but bulkier and hairier. His hands were huge and clawed. She wasn't sure what it meant to be mated but she had a good idea, and the thought of what it could mean filled her with horror. Hopelessness weighed on her but she shoved it aside and shifted her thoughts back to the elf.

There was a bond of some sort there and she had to make Lord Amaranth understand, but how, when she didn't quite understand it herself? The corner of her mouth tilted. Standing up to the king had been exhilarating, and he hadn't beaten her for her impudence...not yet, anyway.

It was a foolish, stupid thing to do, but she'd been imprisoned and beaten for too long. It had taken twenty-five cycles for her to decide to fight, and fight she would. The king could kill her, or worse, he could send her back to her uncle, but not without a fight. If somehow he succeeded, she thought with a shrug, Uncle Orbane would end up killing her because she refused to bow to him or anyone else ever again. She'd rather die fighting than to submit to his torture any longer.

It was disconcerting to her that the king had been kind to her so far. He had seen that her wounds had been treated, that she'd been fed and cared for. She didn't believe him to be cruel as so many did. She seemed to understand him, although she couldn't fathom how.

Earlier, when he grabbed her, it was as though he absorbed the pain that had been building in her ribs and leg...she felt them drawing away and they faded. Now she was achy but the sharp throbbing pain was gone. She raised her hand and touched the knot on the side of her head and frowned. Perhaps her thoughts were jumbled because of it. And the wolfdogs, she could have sworn she understood them, their intent to shield her, to comfort her, their love for their master. She must be imagining things. "Great Creator Iybae, what is to become of me now?"

* * * * *

Lord Haig Orbane watched the giant beast pace the floor and wondered briefly if he'd wear a hole in his lovely expensive rug. Pandrum was half Kyrok, half-human. The Kyroks were a savage species admired for their size and might. They had found that mating with humans produced even stronger and more agile beings. They were usually lacking in the area of intellect. Human blood didn't seem to improve on that trait. Pandrum was no exception. "I have men looking for her, Pandrum."

"What makes you think I still want her, Orbane?" Nezzer Pandrum stopped and looked at Orbane with disgust. "She's obviously disobedient and unruly."

"Let's not play this game, Pandrum. We both know that you want Linea. You need her — we all need her and when she's found she will be dealt with." Orbane crossed his long, skinny, velvet-clad legs as he stuffed cherry-flavored tobacco into the bulb of a hand-carved pipe. "She won't think of leaving again when I'm done with her."

A tremor of satisfaction hummed through him at the thought of punishing her one last time. The power of the Great Creator, Orbane told himself, confirming his righteousness. Linea was such a heady combination of sweetness and purity when she was a child. He had watched the perfect little girl grow up too quickly.

In spite of all his efforts, the Evil One, Asmodeus, had corrupted her in order to steal his soul. Orbane saw it happening and though he'd tried, could not save her. He went to his room and defiled himself because of her. Asmodeus used her to taunt him, making him want her, and all the while she knew. He knew she knew. Now she wore proof that he had tried.

Her beauty was forever marred. Her lush body branded. She would forevermore wear the proof that she was cursed, a whore who could not be purified. Still, he hated having to give her up now, though it was for the best. She was gifted and so strong. She herself was a gift, meant to be used, and used she would be.

Oh, how he would so miss watching her fight against the pain, refusing to cry. He would then pray and go to bed with the hope that this time, the purification had sanctified her that she might be useful to Iybae. Yet the next time he saw her bent over the basin scrubbing the laundry or on her hands and knees polishing the kitchen floor, hellfire would flame to life within him again.

He would forever want her; it was her fault and her sin and she would forever bear the iniquity of his lust. Now was the time. They had the power now and she had the gift to channel it. And when it was done, Pandrum would take her and he would let him. He sighed and lit his pipe, taking long puffs. As much as he hated to let her go, Linea's union with this Kyrok was of great value to him in so many ways. For now it was best to let Pandrum think he led the Council. When he became king, he would need to be rid of all stumbling blocks, including Pandrum and the evil Council.

"Yes." Finally, Nezzer Pandrum folded his substantial frame into the chair across from Orbane. His sweaty forehead wrinkled in thought as he scratched his grungy beard. "It occurs to me that her untamed spirit may be more of an asset. I will enjoy breaking her." He looked Orbane over. "In any case, I have doubts as to your ability to control a dog pup. I'll deal with the shrew myself."

Orbane frowned and cleared his throat. "Yes, well, when we find her and I turn her over to you, our contract will be binding?"

"Yes, Orbane, you pig." Pandrum grinned, unashamed of his rotten, jagged teeth. "I'll help you defeat the great and mighty King Draven Amaranth." The warrior's smile faded. "But if I find that you've already rutted with the little bitch, I'll kill her and then I'll kill you, after I've cut off your stones and fed them to you."

Orbane blew smoke from between his lips. He laid a hand on his burning stomach as the acid began to churn. "She is still a maiden, Pandrum. I'm her uncle. I have not touched her and she hasn't been out of my care since she was five cycles old."

Pandrum gave him a sideways glance. "She's out of your care now. And how do I know you never had her?"

"She is my niece, for God's sake!" he snarled. "You have my word she is an innocent. She's never even seen a man's member."

"You mean you didn't wag your stubby sausage at her while you were beating her, Orbane?"

Orbane felt the acid rise in his throat and his face grew hot with fury. "I only punished her when she needed purification."

"And she needed purifying often, didn't she, Orbane?" Pandrum chuckled. "Little Linea was a bad girl, wasn't she? Little bitch made Uncle sweat, did she?" He was sneering now. "Besides, isn't she only your half-sister's daughter?"

Filthy Kyrok. "Yes, Pandrum." Orbane sighed impatiently and hoped the heat crawling up his neck wasn't obvious. "But I haven't defiled her."

Pandrum stared at him with narrowed eyes for a while. "If what you say is true—and I doubt it is—then she will prove as tasty as I've imagined. It will be my pleasure to help you deal with Amaranth. I'll even consent to hold the great king still while you slit his pretty throat."

"Oh no, I have plans for Amaranth...long, drawn-out, excruciating plans." Orbane's mind gave way to his lifelong fantasy and he nearly whimpered with anticipation. With the pure bulk muscle of this stupid Kyrok army behind him, he would have the revenge he'd ached for. The reward of seeing Draven Amaranth torn and broken would be well worth sacrificing the sweet Linea. With her properly wed to Nezzer Pandrum, there was nothing to keep him from ascending the throne. His throne!

Pandrum stood, stretched and yawned, his foul breath tainting the cherry-scented air. Orbane scowled at him without getting up. He laid his crossed wrists on his knee, waiting impatiently for the Kyrok to take his leave.

"My men and I will be doing some searching on our own. I'll let you know if we unearth anything interesting." Pandrum turned and lumbered to the door. He stopped, his hand on the knob. "If I find her first, I will have me a taste. Make sure she's mine, ruin her for any other." He threw his head back with a high-pitched lusty laugh that hurt Orbane's ears.

"You'll do no such thing. You'll bring her to me so that I may have you wed properly. Rightly in the eyes of Iybae." Orbane was trembling with fury. He grasped the bowl of his pipe tightly, his knuckles turning white.

Pandrum grinned, watching him, then turned the knob and left, his laughter screeching through the small keep.

Chapter Eight

Warriors of Lanthor, large hulking men, sat and stood warily around the great hall. Watching their king pace back and forth in front of the vast stone fireplace, they occasionally exchanged glances of confusion and dread. No one played the lute or sang. No one smiled. They all felt the tension radiating from their noble leader. The muscle in Draven's jaw pulsed with agitation. His fists were clenched at his sides.

A demure servant girl quietly entered the hall bearing a tray filled with cheese, bread and fruit. Quickly, without lifting her face, she set the food on a table then curtseyed stiffly and left the room. No one spoke; there were no flirtations, bawdy jokes or sly winks. Finally Draven came to a halt, turned and faced them.

His expression kept them silent. Though Lord Amaranth was, for the most part, jovial, this was one of those times when there was no room for frivolity. His voice rumbled with barely controlled anger as he gave them their orders plainly and to the point. Because they knew their king never asked anything of them that he wouldn't expect of himself, the thought never crossed their minds to defy him or deny him anything he asked.

"Haig Orbane, the overseer of Endaria, will be arriving soon." Draven noted the deepening frowns. Carefully he opened the block to sense those around him as his gaze traveled the room, searching faces, though the strong emotions washing over him revealed nothing. He knew there was a traitor somewhere. He prayed it was not one of these men, these warriors, betraying him.

He shook off the uneasy feeling and closed the block before continuing. "While he is in Amaranth Keep, he will be guarded, as will anyone he chooses to bring with him. I do not want him or his people left alone, for any reason. He is not to have contact with any of you, the elf, or the girl."

Draven turned to Joeff, who met his gaze. "The servants are to be apprised that they are not to converse with Orbane or those with him other than polite pleasantries. They will take their orders from me."

"Yes, my lord," Joeff answered.

Draven selected three men to leave for Hessum, taking with them a rather stern request for a meeting with the Kyrok overseer, Lord Graeme Sierra, and his war councilor, Nezzer Pandrum. As he walked deliberately toward the stairs he directed those who remained, "You'll go now and ready yourselves. Patrol the forests. Armond, select those you see fit to go into the villages."

Armond gave him a curt nod.

Draven motioned for two men to follow him and mounted the wide staircase two steps at a time. The balcony consisted of three corridors. Carved marble archways opened them up to a view of the great hall below. Doors leading to various rooms lined the parallel walls.

The woman had been confined to the room opposite the stairs. He had Gavril taken to the room at the far end of the eastern corridor. Draven's quarters were at the east end of the central corridor and, therefore, he was effectively between them. He didn't want to be far from either in the event they attempted anything malevolent.

Rolf's big body lay across the front of her door. Aletha sat like a sentinel, her big whiskey-colored eyes sharply assessing them. Draven eyed her with disappointment, then with a grunt turned to the men. "Gavril will be brought in from his work in the stables soon. Never leave his nor the woman, Joan's, door unguarded." The name on his tongue made him want to spit. "Ever."

The two men nodded and Draven watched Gavril's guard walk down the hall, turn left at his own door and continue to the small door at the end to wait. Turning to the other man he said tightly, "No one goes in this room without my prior knowledge or permission. Is that clear?"

"Yes, my lord," the warrior replied, meeting Draven's gaze.

Draven nodded. "Rolf," he snapped. The wolfdog's head lifted immediately and met his master's gaze. "Move." Rolf grumbled but lumbered away from the door and plopped down on the other side of Aletha. With a snarl of his own, Draven unlocked the door, threw it open and stepped in. The sound of the slamming door echoed through the hall and reverberated off the walls.

* * * * *

The sound made Linea jump. She looked up to find Lord Amaranth standing before her, his fisted hands on his hips, his mouth pressed into a straight line. His dark brows furrowed over narrowed eyes that were sharp, hard and cold like the metal of a sword. For a moment she wondered if he would breathe fire.

"Who the hell are you?" His voice was so quiet she almost didn't hear him.

She opened her mouth to speak and he lifted his hand. "Don't tell me you are Joan. The very sound of that name sours my stomach."

Linea lifted her brows at the intended insult, but remained silent.

His reaction was lightning fast as he moved to her. Taking her by the shoulders, he lifted her to her feet and shook her gently. "Answer me!"

Her heart pounded in her chest as she struggled with the growing flood of fear and fury. Every muscle tensed, ready for the blows that she expected were next. She hated that she couldn't control the tremors that wracked her body. She swallowed and forced herself to look up. The muscle in his jaw jumped; his nostrils flared slightly.

She finally met his gaze. A storm brewed there, threatening to rage out of control, but she refused to look away. It struck her in that moment that he was frighteningly beautiful. His eyes widened slightly. Her body heated; she felt the warmth crawl up her chest, her neck. That strange pulling began low in her belly. She looked at his mouth again and had the ridiculous urge to run her finger across his bottom lip. Frowning at the insanity of her thoughts, she shook her head in hopes of clearing her mind. She met his gaze again and shuddered at what she saw there. His eyes had darkened, dilated; they looked hungry.

She took a steadying breath and opened her mouth to speak. His head lowered till she could feel his breath on her lips. Her body tensed; the smell of leather, spice, and something darker intoxicated her. She suddenly felt spellbound. She wanted to run fast and hard. She wanted to lean into him, to taste his mouth.

Lord Amaranth's hands were achingly hot on her shoulders, even through the material of her makeshift dress, and she wanted the feel of them on her skin. As if he knew her mind his hands loosened their grip on her shoulders, gentling their touch. His thumb rubbed over the maddening pulse that throbbed at the base of her neck. Her breath quickened and she trembled, afraid of this new awareness developing in her, afraid of what the king would do to her, of what she wanted him to do.

"Tell me your name." She could barely hear his hoarse whisper for the sound of the blood pounding through her veins. She felt his words flutter on her lips. *Linea. I'm Linea Wyndham.* It was on the tip of her tongue. She so wanted to be truthful with him, but even more, she wanted to live. She had to live.

"My name is Joan," she whispered.

He searched her face for a second before he let her go and stepped back. His hands fisted at his sides. "Damn you, woman!" he shouted.

She shut her eyes, waiting for him to strike her. She wavered then sat back on the bed and swallowed hard. Her mind was completely befuddled, her body aching with need and pain. She opened her eyes, blinking. He hadn't hit her, but she was sure he was going to. She felt the heaviness in her breasts, the extraordinary mixture of pain and pleasure that radiated from her contracting nipples and the exquisite tightening lower in her abdomen, deeper inside her. The new sensations had Linea feeling afraid, frantic and a bit hysterical.

Lord Amaranth walked away from her, running his hands through his thick hair. She could swear she heard him growl like a wolf stalking his prey, could hear it rumbling in his chest, feel it seep into her, reverberating through her body. Bracing herself against the sharp waves of sensation that washed over her, she wrapped her arms around her stomach and bit her lip.

She wondered at the power he seemed to have over her. Feeling weak, drugged, she sat swaying, slowly becoming more aware of the anger, a fierce frustration growing inside her. It seemed tangled with a hot desire to strip off her clothes and run her hands gently over her tender breasts, to taste her nipples as they hardened against... No, she squeezed her eyes shut and shook her head. What an odd image, she thought.

No, it was his naked skin she wanted to touch, see if it tasted dark and spicy like he smelled. She wanted to touch the hard planes of his chest, his stomach and lower... No... Yes. She groaned, covering her face with her hands. She was losing her mind.

With a roar, Lord Amaranth whirled around and stomped back to her. Anger and irritation mounted rapidly in her. She felt animal lust and aggression, although she didn't understand why. He advanced on her like she was his prey, braced his arms on either side of her and loomed close to her face. This time she was sure he was growling, baring his teeth. She couldn't seem to help the sudden intense emotions—emotions that didn't belong to her but seemed all of a sudden a part of her, driving her. She clenched her teeth, her breaths coming in pants. "My lord…" she breathed.

"I'm not a simpleton! I know you are *not* Joan!"

Linea refused to back away, refused to show any fear, though it gripped her. She knew she shouldn't defy the king. She knew her life was at stake, but she couldn't control the torrent of emotion surging through her.

"Back away from me now." Her low sultry voice surprised even her.

Lord Amaranth's eyes narrowed but he didn't move. "You are a sorceress." He leaned closer. "Who sent you here to torment me?"

She held his gaze and blinked.

"Well?" He stood and bellowed.

"Me? Torment you?" She was beyond indignant. She felt hot with anger and itched to touch him. It infuriated her. She stood then, forcing him to back away, glaring at him, growling at him. "I didn't come to you, Lord Amaranth. You brought me here against my will. I asked you for nothing!"

"Did you expect me to leave you out there broken and bleeding for the beasts of the forest to devour—or worse…a Kyrok? Are you daft?"

She paled, remembering her betrothal, but recovered quickly, lifting her chin. "Ha! One beast is no different than another!"

"You silly fool." His chuckle lacked humor. "You are truly naïve. A beast I may be, my sweet one," his gaze traveled over her body, "and devour you, I may. Have no doubt, there is a great difference."

Her eyes widened. She thought she understood exactly what he meant and what disturbed her most was that she wholeheartedly believed him. She shook her head again, choosing to ignore his declaration. "You have but to free me and the elf and we will trouble you no more."

His mouth tilted at one corner and he took a step toward her. "Not till I know who you are, the nature of your connection to Gavril, and from whom you are running."

"Just who do you think you are?" she asked boldly. Taking a step toward him, she poked him with the index finger of her right hand. His chest was as hard as she imagined. Her palm itched to explore it and she momentarily wondered if it was bare and smooth or if there was hair.

He looked down at her offending finger and then without raising his head he lifted his gaze to hers and gripped her hand tightly. "I am your king."

"Such an honorable king," she spat. "Ha! You are a bully who likes to pick on those smaller than yourself!" she snarled at him and struggled to free her hand from his grip.

His expression darkened as his other hand curled around her neck and lifted slightly until she stood on her tiptoes. He yanked her close until the tip of his nose touched hers. He was seething, as was she, their breath pumping in and out of their lungs. She felt hot fury surging through her and raw hunger and her own fear.

"Do not challenge me," he warned her. "You don't have what it takes to take me on. I will break you." He released her, scowling down at her as she fell back onto the bed then bounced back up. Her hand went to her neck and she scowled back, narrowing her eyes, her gaze never wavering from his. "Little fool."

She clenched her teeth against the rush of emotions she didn't understand, trying to think.

"You will remain in this room until you give me answers," Draven told her. "Truthful answers. You'll have no freedom until I get them. You will have no contact with the imp down the hall until I have them."

Linea stood speechless as he walked from the room and quietly shut the door behind him, locking her in. It wasn't until she heard Lord Amaranth's retreating footfalls and the thunk of the guard's big body as he leaned against the door that she gave in. Her body shook violently in frustration. She punched a pillow then threw it against the wall.

She wanted to throw more things, kick and scream, but she was afraid it would hurt too much. She sat on the bed and lay back, breathing heavily.

"That damn, arrogant, self-important, ass!" Oh, it felt good to say that. This rage pumping through her felt so liberating. It broke loose inside. She wished she had said it to his face.

She rose from the bed and pulled herself back against the headboard. Absently she rubbed her ribs and frowned. Her head was beginning to throb, making it harder for her to think clearly. She felt bothered and irritated, but strong and powerful. She felt alive like she had never felt before. At the same time, to finally escape one tormenter only to find herself in the clutches of another was infuriating. This captor, however, was perhaps more tolerable than her previous one. He wasn't going to hurt her, not really...at least not until he found out her true identity.

Chapter Nine

Draven took his walk to the stables slowly. The cool breeze did nothing to bank the fire that still burned from his altercation with the girl earlier. The pleasant scent of evening dew and fresh hay filled the air, but his mind was on her and it was her scent he thought of. It was rich and sweet like warm honey. Knowing she would taste just as delicious had him swallowing a groan. The woman was making him crazy. She kept him frustrated in every way possible. He needed answers quickly, before he threw her on the bed and devoured her, driving them both insane with erotic pleasure.

Grouchy elf curses reached his ears while he was still a distance away. Draven wasn't above physical discipline when warranted, but elves were notoriously lazy and Gavril would have most likely preferred a beating to the full day of hard labor he'd suffered.

Draven found Gavril oiling saddles. Smiling, Draven clasped hands with the guard that watched over the elf and indicated with a nod that the man was relieved to go home. Draven took the lantern the guard offered him and hung it on a peg. Leaning against a post he crossed his arms and listened to the old grumpy elf mumble about injustice and foul-smelling humans.

"Gavril, is there no hope for you?" Draven asked quietly.

Gavril's head jerked up, his face pinched in anger. "You hateful hell beast! I'm severely fatigued. You have worked me till I'm done in! I have no more energy left and I smell like horse sweat! Have you no heart? Have you no feelings?"

"No, not really."

"No, I know you don't." Gavril squinted up at him. "You don't need your own, you can feed on the emotions of others."

Draven's brow lifted, glaring down at him. Did he know? How? How did he know? "Explain."

"Idiot!" Gavril spat.

Draven's eyes narrowed.

Gavril's rage turned into a whimper. "You...made...me...shovel...horseshit! Do you know that?"

Draven would have grinned were he not so shocked by the tears that left dirty tracks on the elf's pockmarked cheeks. "Yes, I know. But be at peace; you won't be shoveling horseshit tomorrow."

Gavril looked up hopefully. Draven held up a hand to stay his thanksgiving. "The sheep stalls will need tending tomorrow."

"Oh, precious Iybae, Creator of life!" Gavril said as he fell to his knees, raising his arms to the sky. "Save me from this affliction, this evil one who delights in my suffering!"

Draven chuckled and rolled his eyes. "Save the theatrics, Gavril. Iybae knows how troublesome you are and He's on my side." He sighed and pushed away from the pole. Bending, he lifted the saddle and hung it back where it belonged. "Now, if you're finished I'll escort you back to your room for the night."

"No!" Gavril scowled defiantly, his hands on his hips.

Exasperated, Draven turned and grasped Gavril's torn collar. "Would you rather snuggle up with one of the horses?" Gavril laid a fat little hand on Draven's. His violet gaze met the hard gray gaze of a man who was nearly out of patience.

"Please, Lord Amaranth." He spoke softly. "Let me talk with her." He paused. "I must speak with her. There are things she must know."

"What things?" Draven frowned.

"Please, I'm not pranking this time. I swear," Gavril pleaded.

Draven saw sincerity in the elf's eyes and it troubled him. "Tell me. I'll pass on your message."

"You don't understand. I have to help her." Gavril sighed. "All right, fine. I'll let you sense me, then you'll know."

Draven tilted his head. "Sense you?" His brows knitted together in uncertainty as Gavril's frustration, desperation, flooded through him. He felt Gavril's need to serve the woman and knew it was beyond the elf's control. He jerked Gavril to eye level. "How do you know about me? Who is she, Gavril?"

"Lord Amaranth, let me explain..." Gavril gasped.

"I'm not stopping you." Draven glared down at him.

Gavril squeezed his eyes shut. "I am honor bound to watch over her."

"You were doing a pathetic job."

The elf grimaced. "I couldn't find her."

"You know who she is. Tell me." Draven gave him a little shake and Gavril yelped.

"Argh, you're so thick-headed! I can't tell you now," he snapped. "In time you will know."

"Now!" he bellowed, shaking the elf harder.

"You're leery of her. There's no need to be. She's not out to cause you or your kingdom any harm. Stupid human, you have but to look into her eyes to know that."

Frustration mounted in Draven's chest. His heart pounded with it.

"Lord Amaranth," Gavril squeaked. "I...can't...breathe."

"Eyes can deceive. I want facts, you runt! Is she a spy?" Draven growled through clenched teeth, reluctantly letting Gavril go.

"A spy." Gavril stared at him for a second then rolled his eyes and shook his head. "Hell, no. Even I thought you had more brains." He crossed his stubby arms over his barrel chest and narrowed his eyes. "Is the big bad kingy wingy afraid of the widdle girl?"

Draven's smile lacked humor. "How did you know about me?" he asked again.

Gavril dropped his head, shaking it like a frustrated parent. "You underestimate elf abilities, my lord. You humans think your height and bulk is so very important. Our gifts are many. 'Knowing about you' is one such gift.

Again Draven narrowed his eyes. "What exactly do you know about me?"

"Well, obviously more than you know," Gavril said smugly.

Frustrated, Draven snarled, "I'm sick of your games, elf. You underestimate my height and bulk." Draven grabbed him by the waistband of his britches and headed for the keep in long strides. "Time for bed, insect. You have a long day tomorrow."

Gavril kicked and groused the whole way back to the keep. Unfortunately Draven was beginning to believe the irritating little elf, and he needed some answers. He focused on Gavril again but came up against a wall.

"I told you, simpleton, you can't scan me without my permission or without...her." Gavril sneered.

Draven dumped a very pissed-off Gavril in his room and locked him in soundly. The vexatious elf. Draven paused to listen, meeting the gaze of the warrior guarding the door. There was no sound coming from the girl's room but Draven was certain he felt her pulsing inside him. Her emotions had swum through him, he was used to that. What took him aback was that he felt her receive from him. Was it possible that she had the same gift he was cursed with?

His spirit knew this woman, was drawn to her. His body ached, heat pooled in his groin, his member became hard, demanding to know her better. His heart wanted to protect her, erase her pain, both in body and soul. His mind, however, reminded him of her age and her questionable identity, not to mention her sanity after her protest over that idiot elf.

She hadn't backed down or given in to her fear. On the contrary, this woman's fear seemed to strengthen her courage. Her battle was one of passion. One that, now that he thought about it, she had won. Her passion had been extraordinary in every way, and every cell in his body seemed to respond to her. He breathed deeply, reminding himself that he couldn't let this situation drag on and he couldn't allow himself to indulge. His frown deepened. She was too young and he was too old to be led by his cock.

Chapter Ten

"Find Mason and Armond," Draven said sternly as he passed Joeff on his way to the war room. He meant to slam the door but Joeff stopped him.

"Pardon me, my lord, I was just coming to inform you that guests have arrived for the noon meal," Joeff said cautiously.

Draven turned slightly, still gripping the open door, and scowled. "I have no time for guests today."

Sympathy was plain in Joeff's expression. "I'm sorry, Lord Amaranth, it is your betrothed, Mistress Cynthia, and her attendant."

"Aw, f-f..." he started, banging his forehead lightly against the door's edge. His betrothed. He kept forgetting his betrothed. She would soon be his wife, his lover. He'd do well to keep her foremost in his mind at present, he admonished himself.

Yet another reason he had to find out who this Joan woman was and be rid of her. He tried to remember if they were supposed to meet today but couldn't recall any such arrangement. They weren't supposed to meet again until a week before the wedding. "Is her father with them?"

"Only she, my lord, and her attendant. Shall I send them away?"

"No," he said in disgust. "Invite them to make themselves comfortable in the sitting room. Keep them entertained for me, will you, Joeff?" He paused and sighed. "I'll join them in a moment."

Draven closed the door behind him. He needed a quiet moment to reorder his thoughts. He walked across the room and opened the windows. Standing there with his eyes closed, he hoped for some clarity on the situation in which he found himself.

What kind of jackass was he that he would burn for this mysterious girl while he was pledged to marry another? In his mind he brought up Cynthia's face. She was a lovely little thing. Big, warm brown eyes, a small turned up nose, creamy rose-tinted cheeks, pouty little bow-shaped lips, and a slender compact body. She was polite and always well-groomed, appropriately attired, and her golden-blonde hair was always arranged perfectly.

"Busy?" Draven spun around. Armond stood half in and half out of the room.

"Yes, but I have a few minutes." Armond nodded once and took a few steps into the room. He wore his usual blank expression but Draven could sense his concern even without looking into his expressive green eyes.

"Mason seems to think you need a woman, Draven." Armond's voice was a smooth deep bass.

"Mason thinks sinking his junior warrior into any hapless woman is the answer to all problems." Draven smirked.

Armond's lips tilted slightly at the corner. "Even so, my friend, we can find someone for you. To help ease your tension."

Draven couldn't help the hard look he pinned Armond with. "Thank you, no."

Armond nodded. That crooked smile of his spread. "I thought not." He paused and shifted uncomfortably. "There's something about the woman, isn't there, Draven?"

Draven turned to the window. Armond walked across the room to stand beside him. Draven knew Armond would say little. He was a confidant, a true friend.

"You want her," Armond said quietly.

Draven took a deep breath. "I've wanted women, Armond, and I've had women. This is something else."

Armond simply watched him. Draven sensed Armond's quiet affection and respect, and took a deep breath. "I believe she shares the gift, or something like it."

"And therefore, you don't trust her."

Draven turned to his friend. "It's all too odd, Armond. She is far from average. Her connection to Gavril unnerves me."

"Draven, you know the elf is not evil. He's a nuisance but he's essentially harmless." Armond tilted his head.

"Yes, I know that. Still, it gives me pause. They are hiding something from me and frankly I don't like it. What the hell are they up to?" Draven frowned and gazed out the window.

"And, you want her."

Draven scowled and shook his head. "Dammit, yes, I want her. God Iybae, how I want her. But I don't trust her. She is somehow familiar. I sense something sinister linked to her and I feel the power she has, the potential to destroy. I cannot let her go till I know her who she is and from where and from whom she came."

"What of Mistress Cynthia?"

Draven reached out and scratched Rolf behind his ear, then stroked Aletha's sleek back. "What of her? We are to be married soon."

"You don't want her."

"I want a queen. My people want a queen." Draven leveled Armond a look with a raised brow. "Cynthia wants me."

"I think Miss Cynthia just wants badly to be wanted by someone." Armond frowned and held Draven's gaze for a moment then slapped him on the back with a sigh. "Very well, my friend. I will do some digging, find out what I can about the girl." He walked across the room and stopped at the large heavy door. "I'll tell Mason you're not interested in the tryst. He'll be sorely disappointed."

Draven scowled. "I hate that for him."

"We'll be in the training yard if you change your mind." Armond flashed a toothy grin, turned and walked out, shutting the door softly behind him.

Draven chuckled and focused his attention back on the immediate issue, Cynthia Randall Madison. She was a widowed woman of thirty-two cycles with a quick smile, many admirers and a reputation for being a bit spoiled. He knew little more about her and this unexpected visit was the perfect opportunity to resolve that. She didn't inspire lust in him, although he knew she wanted him. She was far from repellant and she had his respect. Besides that, Cynthia was born and bred to be a queen. The people needed a queen and he needed an heir.

Draven heard Cynthia's high lilting laugh before he reached the room. Her tight little body sat poised on the edge of the couch, her small, gloved hands folded in her lap. He caught a glimpse of her delicate ankles under her yellow skirts and her beautiful face was tilted up at the young servant girl who poured tea. Her freshly painted bow-shaped lips shimmered like a juicy peach ready to be devoured. He watched her as she leaned forward slightly and spoke softly to her assistant. His gaze traveled her long slender neck, taking in her creamy skin, noticing her small rounded breasts strained against the fine silk bodice of her dress. He sighed inwardly, not so much as a spark.

"Miss Cynthia, I'm sorry to have kept you waiting." He walked toward her as she eagerly stood and offered him her hand. The fragrance of her flowery perfume reached him first. He fought the urge to make a face and took her hand and bent to kiss it. The scent assailed him, tickling his nose. Thankfully, he dropped her hand abruptly and turned away before sneezing. He took the handkerchief from his pocket and wiped his nose.

"Bless you," all three women said in unison.

"I'm terribly sorry, ladies," he murmured as he retreated to the high back armchair behind him and sat. His nose still tingled and he sneezed twice more.

"Bless you," they said again.

He lifted his eyes and gave them a crooked smile. "Well, this is embarrassing."

"No, of course not," Cynthia's assistant said, smiling.

"Are you ill, my lord?" Cynthia asked, her concern apparent.

Draven shook his head and sneezed again.

"Lord Amaranth," the servant girl spoke up. "Is there something I could get for you? Some water maybe, or juice?"

"Thank you, Alma, water would be nice." To Draven's horror his throat felt scratchy, his tongue thick and his eyes began to water. He'd never been sick in his life. Not so much as a cold.

"Lord Amaranth, are you unwell?" Cynthia rose to come to his aid but he held up a hand to stop her.

"No! No, my lady." If he got another whiff of her perfume he was sure he would heave. "Please, don't worry yourself. I'm fine."

He blew his nose and looked up, doing his best to smile at her. She frowned back at him. "This is my assistant, Moria."

He turned and nodded. "Lovely name, Moria." What an enchanting creature, he thought. There were so few faeries in this region. He'd heard about them but he'd never met one. Most dared not leave Ingvar.

"Thank you, Lord Amaranth. And yours is quite handsome as well," she said with a wink.

Draven couldn't help but chuckle, even as his eyes began to burn. She was very small, very short and very pale. Her bright white hair hung like silk down her back. It was tucked behind elegantly curved ears that rose up into delicate points just above the top of her head. Each ear was adorned with a row of gold and crystal piercing rings all along the outer edges. Her violet eyes were bright with laughter. Above her small heart-shaped mouth was a tiny little pug nose that should have been unattractive but was somehow adorable instead. He could see that she had wings. They fluttered close to her back but he couldn't get a good look at them.

"It's a pleasure to meet you, Miss Moria."

Moria's smile was bright. "No, no, Lord Amaranth. Just plain Moria, please," she asked.

He nodded. "I doubt very seriously if there's anything 'just plain' about you." He sniffed and smiled then turned back to Cynthia who was frowning darkly. Lifting a brow he asked, "My lady, how is your father? Why did he not accompany you?"

Cynthia grinned. "We are to marry in two weeks time, Lord Amaranth. I thought it would be wise if we spent some time together before we wed to discuss preparations. Father was preoccupied today so I brought Moria to chaperone." She nodded to her assistant and smiled knowingly at Draven.

"Ah, I see." Draven blew his nose once more, trying not to sneeze. He was thankful that at least he wouldn't have to win her interest. He could feel her yearning now, her desire to touch him, to kiss him. But how in the name of Iybae was he to make love to her if he couldn't get close enough to kiss her without having an attack?

Alma came back with a tall glass of water. "Noon meal is nearly ready, my lord."

"Thank you, Alma." He smiled at her and took the water. He watched Cynthia over the glass as he drank deeply. She glared at Alma, unaware Draven was watching her, and pouted prettily. He wanted to roll his eyes, but they burned and itched and felt sticky. His head began to pound and he could swear he was wheezing.

She frowned at him. "I'd like to have someone do something with my sleeping quarters and I'd like a reading room built on."

He nodded, smiling indulgently. Dear God, this joining was going to be more difficult than he thought. "Give me a week. The room adjacent to mine isn't ready yet," he said, wiping his eyes.

"Oh." She looked disappointed. "Well, all right. When should I send for my things?"

Draven began to cough and sneeze. His stomach became queasy and he thought if he didn't get away from the woman's stench it might revolt. "Ladies, I'm not myself today. I'll send someone for your things at the end of the week. I'll have to excuse myself from our chat now. Go eat. Please, enjoy yourselves."

"I had no idea you were of such a delicate disposition," Cynthia murmured. Her finely sculpted brows knit together with worry.

Draven stared at her incredulously and opened his mouth to dispute her statement when he was beset by another bout of sneezing.

"It's your perfume," Moria snickered.

"My what?" Cynthia's eyes widened.

Moria couldn't stop the laughter that bubbled up. "Your perfume, Miss Cynthia. He's allergic to your perfume."

Cynthia looked from Moria to Draven. Her wide horrified eyes began to fill with tears and her lip began to quiver.

"Lord Amaranth?" Brussoe called from the great hall. Thank Iybae the healer was here, Draven thought as he blew his nose. He stood just as the older man entered the room. Brussoe's expression and tone of voice was less than congenial. He lifted his eyes and shook his head. Why was everyone angry with him?

"Lord Amaranth, with all due respect, my king, what is the meaning of locking that poor girl in her room like that? It's not good for her, considering all she's been through—" Brussoe stopped abruptly and stared at Draven. "What the hell has happened to you? What have you been into?"

Draven turned back to the women. To his horror great tears rolled down Cynthia's face, streaking her rosy cheeks. "Cynthia, darling, I'm sorry to disappoint you. We'll plan an engagement celebration. You may invite anyone you like. I'll have cook prepare a full course meal. We'll dance and laugh and talk as long as you would like." He hesitated and then, with resolve, crossed to her, brushed a tear away with his thumb and quickly kissed her cheek. He turned on his heel and strode from the room in a frenzy of coughing and sneezing.

"But...but I had it mixed, especially for him." Cynthia softly sobbed. "I thought it would entice his male drives. You understand what I mean, don't you?" Her voice lowered to a whisper. "Moria, it's been a long time since...well. And I worked for days with the alchemist in the village to get it just right. And Lord Amaranth doesn't like it. How could he be so insensitive?"

Moria bit her top lip. "No, Miss Cynthia, it's not that he didn't like it, it's just that he's allergic. Come," she said, taking Cynthia's hand. "Let's go home. I'll have a bath drawn for you and we'll discuss preparations for your celebration."

"What do you think the healer was talking about when he said 'poor woman'? What poor woman?"

"I don't know, Miss Cynthia. Perhaps he was referring to a servant girl." Moria glanced up as they passed the staircase. She knew better. She had felt the woman's presence the moment she entered the keep. Moria silently lifted a prayer to Iybae for help in consoling Miss Cynthia when she discovered there would be no wedding.

Chapter Eleven

Draven sat in his war room with his head back, his eyes covered with a cool damp cloth, breathing fresh air from the open windows through his mouth. The healer's anger swirling around inside his mind was not helping.

"Here," Brussoe said gruffly, taking a mug from Joeff. "Drink your tea. It'll help." He set the mug down and continued to pace.

"Ugh," Draven grunted as he lifted a hand to squeeze the bridge of his nose, trying not to sneeze again. He hated tea and to make matters worse, frustration was throbbing inside him in rhythm with his aching head. "Stop your infernal pacing! Can't you see I'm dealing with a rather troublesome issue here, old man?"

Brussoe stopped pacing to look fiercely at Draven, his bushy brows quivering in agitation as he sat reluctantly, his emotions flaring through Draven in staccato waves.

Draven snatched the cloth from his eyes, sat forward and gulped the wretched tea. "How is she healing?" He grimaced.

Brussoe crossed his arms and pursed his lips. "I haven't seen her yet, my lord. I was disallowed."

"Ah." So that was the reason for all this fury. Draven locked gazes with the man. "I'll clear you with the guard."

"Clear me with the... Lord Amaranth, I realize I'm overstepping my bounds here but I cannot stand back and say nothing." He leaned forward. "I have never known you to be an unfairly cruel king. This child was beaten. Beaten like I've never seen before. And for so long, Lord Amaranth. She has scars on top of scars! Please! Tell me why you have locked her up like a devious criminal."

Draven felt the anger crawl up his neck. He'd seen her wounds, knew all too well what had been done to her. It ate at him, haunted his sleep. He would do nothing to mistreat her and yet this man, a man that he respected and loved, insinuated that he was some sort of beast. Before he could control his fury enough to respond, a rapid knock sounded at the door. What now?

"Come!" he growled, his temper teetering precariously on the edge.

"Sorry to interrupt you, my lord." Netta stepped halfway into the room and glared at Draven. "I wanted to inquire as to whether or not you were allowing the girl to eat or was starvation part of your plan for her?"

"For the love of Iybae!" Draven roared. That was it; his patience had reached its limit and the fine thread holding him back snapped. "Have you all forgotten your senses?" He slammed down the mug with a crack. The last of the herbal tea splashed onto the finely polished table. He met Netta's gaze, glare for glare, and struggled to harness his temper. His voice was low and menacing. "Of course the girl can eat. Serve her meals personally and see to her most demanding needs."

With a nod, Netta's lips pursed and her eyes narrowed as she turned to leave.

Draven dropped his head. "Netta." When she paused he lifted it again and met her gaze. "I realize you helped raise me and you have a lot to do with who I am. You are like a mother to me." He watched her expression soften. His voice did not. "However, I am first your king and you will remember that. If you ever defy me with such disrespect again, I will not let it pass."

Netta looked away. "Yes, my lord. I'll send someone to clean up the tea."

"Thank you." He felt the sharp pain start in her heart and spear into her stomach, the tears that threatened to choke her as she quickly left the room. Damn it. He closed his eyes tightly, berating himself for his harshness, and ran his fingers through his hair.

This was getting out of hand. Hurting Netta was the last thing in the world he had intended. He'd have to find her and do whatever it took to fix it. He turned to Brussoe, who had begun to fidget.

"Ahem." Brussoe cleared his throat. "Forgive me, Lord Amaranth. I should never have questioned your actions."

Draven nodded. "You may go see to her, then let me know how she is healing."

Brussoe nodded and moved to go, when Draven stopped him. "Was she violated, Brussoe? Forced to…" His voice was low and husky.

"I don't think so, but I don't know. I suppose it's entirely possible." Brussoe's brows pulled together. "I didn't examine her to that extent." He paused. "I don't think I should now, Lord Amaranth. It may cause her more undue stress. I could ask her if you'd like."

Draven shook his head. "Just tend to the wounds we can see. I'll trust Iybae to deal with those we can't."

"I was wrong to mistrust you," Brussoe murmured and left, closing the door behind him.

Draven laid his head back against the chair and closed his stinging eyes. He was working out his apology to Netta when someone else rapped at his door.

"Come," he muttered without raising his head. He would be glad when this day was finally ended.

"Sire." The urgency in the warrior's gruff voice had Draven opening one eye. "There's a man here from the village who seeks audience with you. It's most pressing."

Alarm shot through Draven as he sat up and nodded. The man slowly entered the war room, holding his cap, his head bowed. The warrior stood at the door, waiting solemnly. Grief washed over Draven, and fear. It seemed he was always being bombarded by fear as of late. "Thomas? What is it?"

Thomas Brighton lifted his face, tears streaming down his weathered cheeks. "My king, Lord Amaranth, they took my daughter. They came into the house while I was in the field."

Draven leaned forward, frowning darkly. "Who?" he asked, even though he suspected — dreaded — that he already knew.

"Kyroks, my lord. Three of them. My wife was beaten when she tried to stop them and...and they took Serina." A cold chill gripped Draven's heart as Thomas stepped between the chairs and grasped Draven's hand. "Please, I need help finding them. I have to save my baby."

"You'll have it, Thomas." He stood, still holding the man's shaking hand, and walked swiftly with him through the door into the great hall. Draven knew the gravity of the situation. Little Serina had only just completed fourteen cycles. She was too young to mate at all, much less endure the mating ritual of a Kyrok. They'd be lucky if they found the girl alive. There was little hope she'd be whole.

Everyone who knew Serina adored her. She was such a precocious and mischievous child. His own stable boy was thoroughly smitten. She left a trail of smiles and laughter wherever she went.

"What of Corrine and Danella?" Draven asked.

"Bless Iybae, they were in the village working for the seamstress. I met Brussoe on my way here. He's headed to my home to tend to my wife," Thomas replied hoarsely.

"Thomas, your wife and girls need you to stay here," Draven said gently, hoping to reason with him. He felt the man's fear and fury, but didn't know what they would encounter when they found Serina. He did know he didn't want this man to ever see his daughter the way Draven feared they'd find her. No father should ever be subjected to that much pain. And yet he already felt Thomas' pain, the kind of suffering he couldn't take away.

Thomas' lips thinned; his jaw tightened as he met Draven's gaze, yet he didn't protest. "Yes, my lord." He grasped Draven's arm in a vise-like grip. "Stop them, Lord Amaranth. Find my Serina and stop them."

Draven laid his hand over Thomas', holding his gaze. "Nathaniel, go get the horses ready. Find Armond and Mason."

"We're here, Draven." Armond strode across the room, sheathing his sword. Mason was right behind him. His intense green eyes took in Thomas' demeanor. "What's happened?"

Draven motioned for them to follow. "Kyroks broke the covenant," he told them as he walked briskly toward the stables. "Serina Brighton has been taken. Mrs. Brighton was attacked."

"Holy God, Draven." Armond looked back to see that Thomas was out of earshot. "Are you aware of Kyrok rituals for mating?"

Draven's frown deepened as he nodded briskly. Of course he knew and it filled him with dread and rage. The little girl would be torn apart by the Kyrok's large spiked cock. If she survived the blood loss, the bites would cause a hellish fever that would be difficult to cure. "Producing half-human offspring is the only way they can enhance their bloodline."

"That's all they'd want her for, isn't it? They just want to breed her," Mason asked, not expecting an answer.

Draven glanced back at Mason and then Armond. "Pray. We must find her. Immediately."

They readied their horses and mounted them in silence. The stable boy looked up at Draven with wide eyes so filled with anguish that Draven's heart clenched. Each of them knew what they were up against, and each was prepared to fight, not only for the precious girl but also for the continued security the people of Lanthor had so cherished. With a shout Draven kicked Mandrake into a gallop and headed toward the thick forest outside the keep walls.

The horses seemed to sense the urgency. Their hooves thundered through the forest. Their riders bent forward, riding close to the animal's neck, dodging low hanging limbs and leaping over thick brush. Draven trusted Mandrake's keen sense of direction as he led the way. He focused with all his energy, mentally searching for Serina.

Soon the lushness of the forest had thinned but not disappeared. The soft moss-covered ground had given way to a coarse rocky terrain that was harder to travel. The waning sunlight had Draven biting back an oath and they were forced to slow their pace; nevertheless, they were getting close. He had begun to feel whispers of emotion from Serina some time ago. Mostly terror, but even terror meant she was alive, so he had been thankful.

Draven pulled back on the reins, slowing his steed further. Mandrake snorted softly in protest. He was receiving Serina's emotions stronger now. Pain—he felt her pain. She was very close. The path they were following would lead them to the Kyrok settlement of Hessum. Draven had discerned that the beasts were taking Serina back to their village.

Evidently they didn't fear censure or punishment from their ambassador and chief warrior, Nezzer Pandrum, or their overseer, Graeme Sierra. Their disregard for the covenant was upsetting and disheartening; their disregard for Sierra's authority was even more disturbing.

The scent of wood smoke had all three men halting suddenly, and the horses tensing. For a moment they listened, moving forward slowly until they heard Serina's cry and the harsh gravelly voices of her captors. Draven eyed Mason and Armond, and then motioned for them to dismount.

They kept low, quietly advancing until they could see the camp in a small clearing. They squatted behind rocks, watching one Kyrok peel the skin from what looked to be a rabbit. Another was poking the fire and preparing the spit. The last sat beside Serina, taunting her, touching her. Draven felt her terror and the pain in her stomach, back and limbs mingle with his own relief and rage.

She was slumped against a large rock. Her arms were tied behind her and her ankles were bound. There were scratches and what appeared to be dirt on her face; Draven knew it was more likely to be bruises. He saw no blood, not like he had expected, and he thanked Iybae. He motioned for Armond to move left and take the Kyrok who was with Serina. Mason went to the right, to take down the one with the rabbit. Draven waited mere seconds before drawing his sword and striding into the camp.

Chapter Twelve

Linea paced the spacious room. Inactivity was grating on her nerves. Surely they could give her some small chore or insignificant task that could keep her hands busy. She was used to smaller quarters and to being alone, but she wasn't used to having nothing to do. There was always clothing to wash or floors to scrub.

She dropped down onto the bed with a sigh of exasperation. Power speared through her like a hot sword from the blacksmith's fire. It filled her and pushed outward. She gasped for breath, trying to cope, to understand what was happening. It consumed her and took her breath away. She couldn't think. Fire that didn't burn engulfed her, making her feel as though she were glowing like a red-hot coal. Her mind couldn't process it.

"My lady, close your eyes. Do not fight. Focus on the energy and breathe in deeply." Gavril stood beside her, his small chubby hand on hers. She wondered briefly when and how he came to be there, as if he just appeared. It didn't matter. She didn't care...she couldn't care. The surging power filled her, leaving no room for anything else. His brows knitted over his sharp purple eyes as they assessed her. "Breathe it in and focus," Gavril commanded.

"I...can't." Linea tried to breathe; she felt the force of whatever had gripped her squeeze and pulse inside her.

"Yes, you can. You will. Focus," he insisted.

Linea had Gavril's hand in a death grip but he met her gaze without flinching. His expression was more serious then she'd ever seen him before. Thoughts were hard to hold onto; her body quaked. Finally she squeezed her eyes shut and tried to concentrate on the explosion of energy inside her.

"That's it...that's it. Gain control of it," Gavril encouraged her.

In her mind she could see it swirling like a tempest. As she focused on it with all her might it grew larger, tighter, denser. "I'm afraid." Her voice sounded foreign as it trembled from her lips.

"You are like a looking glass, Linea. You have it contained now. Reflect the energy and let it flow out." Gavril's voice was a harsh whisper. "It will flow back even stronger. Contain it again and reflect."

"Gavril." She whimpered and clung to him. Just as it had speared into her it speared from her. Seconds later it came back just as Gavril said it would. Draven! She felt him vividly, his rage, his lust for blood. She braced herself, trying to still her trembling as she focused on the power, contained and reflected it again. Tears streamed down her cheeks. She lost sense of time. Her body, mind and soul were consumed with containing and reflecting the power Draven sent to her.

* * * * *

The shocked Kyrok dropped his dinner, grabbed his sword with a curl of his lip and charged. Planting his feet, Draven was prepared for the first blow from the beast's sword. The resounding clang of sword against sword drowned out all other sound.

Draven clenched and bared his teeth, advancing on the Kyrok with all the fury inside him. Power abruptly surged though him, steeling his body and mind. Though it carried a whisper of something suspiciously familiar he had no time to interpret the force or its source. He fought with ease. His heavy sword slashed through flesh and bone as though it were warm butter.

Two others rushed Draven. He didn't have to think about his next step. His body moved, delivering each blow with astonishing speed and precision. He lunged, burying his sword deep into one Kyrok's gut. With a twist of his wrist he pulled it free, ignoring the beast's gurgling roar of pain, and pivoted on his heel. Like lightning he swung his blade, swiping the next Kyrok's head from his shoulders.

* * * * *

Serina's scream echoed through the trees as she stared down into the empty eyes of the hulking Kyrok that lay in her lap. The gaping wound to his throat gushed thick red blood that flowed obscenely down his chest and into her lap.

"Sorry, Serina," Armond whispered as he cut the ropes that bound her. "Shhh, you're safe now. Stop screaming."

She stared up at him glassy-eyed, her face pale, her lips trembling. A mere babe she was, still so vulnerable and innocent. Still innocent, thank Iybae.

"Quickly, take my hand." Armond's voice, though soft and quiet, left no room for discussion. He was afraid she was going into shock and that was unacceptable. She had to be tough beyond her years now, whether she liked it or not.

Taking her forearm in his firm grip, he shoved the wasted Kyrok with his boot while pulling her up and free of him.

She wavered on her feet. Armond could smell the stench of blood, hear the grunts and curses of those still fighting and the clang of crossed swords. His need to assist the other men had him whisking Serina up and swiftly carrying her to where they had tied the horses.

"Serina, stay with the horses," Armond demanded sternly. "You'll be safe here."

"No!" she cried and wrapped her arms around his neck. "No, please don't leave me alone. Please!"

He was a warrior, damn it, not a nurse. He didn't know anything about comforting this girl, nor did he have the leisure to do so. Armond winced as he pulled her little arms away and sat her on his horse. "Serina, I have to go help the king and Lord Mason." He pulled a blanket from his satchel and draped it over her shoulders. "I promise, we'll be back and we'll take you to your mother and father. Now I must go. Stay here. Don't move." Hesitantly, she nodded with a little sob.

Armond drew his bloodstained dagger and sword on his way back to the melee and was more than a bit disappointed to find there was nothing left for him to do. Mason dispatched a repugnant beast to the other world just as Armond entered the clearing. Mason stood over the Kyrok, his chest heaving, his muscles bulging, blood dripping from his sword with that stupid self-satisfied grin on his face. Armond scowled and shook his head. "Where's Draven?"

Mason grinned and pointed with his sword.

Armond followed his directive to the king standing in the clearing, littered now with what seemed to be five dead Kyroks and their body parts. Crouching over one yet in the process of dying, Draven seemed to glow, though he'd barely broken a sweat. The Kyrok was bloody everywhere, his face contorted in pain.

Armond frowned and tilted his head as he approached them. Draven's eyes were as bright as polished silver. His nostrils were flared, his breaths deep and steady. And there was something very different about him, very strong. Energy radiated from him in waves.

"Pandrum..." The Kyrok wheezed. "He knows not..."

"Then why do you not fear the repercussions of breaking the covenant?"

"He knows not...but...he cares not..." The Kyrok sucked in a gurgling breath. "He laughs at you...foul king." The Kyrok sneered, looking Draven in the eye. "Will destroy you...will breed human women...kill human men...Kyrok will rule."

Draven arched a brow. "Merely foul?" His voice was frighteningly deep and abrasive. "I'm the son of the Butcher King, idiotic Kyrok."

He rose with cool indifference and plunged his sword into the throat of the smirking Kyrok.

* * * * *

Armond's apprehensive expression did not go unnoticed, but Draven had no explanation for what had happened to him. It was an exhilarating, enthralling, remarkable power. It was like molten steel coursing through his veins. He felt as though every cell in his body was humming. And he felt the Joan woman. He felt her—not her emotions, not her mind, nor her physical touch—he felt connected to her as though he'd been linked with her spirit.

Draven's gaze slid to Mason. His cousin was too caught up in the glory of his victory to notice, thankfully. Armond, however, was eyeing him, wisps of concern flitting through him, an unmistakable question in his eyes. Draven smiled and spoke quietly. "Later, friend. Let's return the child. She's frightened and cold; she needs her parents and Brussoe."

Chapter Thirteen

Cynthia stomped through the entrance hall and into the small, elegant home she shared with her doting father. It annoyed her that her satin clad feet made no sound on the polished wood floor. She threw her delicately woven shawl at Moria without pausing and ordered her noon meal to be brought out to her in her reading room.

Her precious room, she often found solace here among the lovely soft greens and lilacs. She adored the way the warm midday sun filtered through paper-thin shades, bathing the room in golden light. She would so miss this darling room, she thought as she sat limply on a delicate chaise and arranged the skirt of her dress to cover her feet. How did Draven expect her to move into his keep the way it was? *It was so drab*, she thought, heaving a sigh. So poorly decorated.

And that gardener. The flowerbeds were sparse and there were no pots of greenery in the keep. She had to have fresh flowers and greenery around her. She'd have to talk to Draven about replacing the gardener. No proper lady could reside in that keep and be at peace. The estate had fabulous potential but she had so little time, there was no way around having it done before she'd have to live in it.

She'd wanted a man like Draven for so many years — since she was a young girl and had first set eyes on him. A man like that could give her what she needed. The thought made a shiver skitter up her spine: to belong to someone so strong, potent, a warlord and king. But her father had given her hand to Franklin Madison and destroyed her dreams.

She had liked Franklin well enough; he had been kind and wealthy. He cheerfully gave her anything she wanted, had indulged her every whim. Even when she had tearfully admitted that she didn't love him, he had smiled sadly, taken her in his arms and murmured in her hair that he had enough love for the both of them. But it hadn't been enough and his gentle touch didn't prevent her from fantasizing about big powerful hands squeezing her breasts, a heavy body pounding against hers in the dark.

Her face heated with shame. Those fantasies had defiled her very soul. But Iybae help her, she'd never wanted gentle. She'd wanted to be taken, not with sweet words but with ferocity, rough, fast. Her vagina clenched at the thought of it, her arousal dampening her undergarments. She wanted to touch herself, close her eyes and imagine being impaled swiftly by a big hard cock, slamming into her relentlessly. Her hand went to her breast and she squeezed the tiny bead of her nipple hard and swallowed the cry. She'd be so thankful when darkness fell. When she could lie in bed and bring herself pleasure and scream into the pillow. "Mmm." She shivered.

When Franklin was thrown from that horse, she was truly devastated. She had cared for Franklin; he was such a good man. And when he died, she was crushed and had honestly mourned her husband. But in time she couldn't help but wonder if maybe it was a sign, one she had no choice but to act on.

He'd always tried to please her but she just couldn't get him to understand what she needed. When she had finally found the nerve to ask him he had been so alarmed. He had refused; he loved her too much to treat her like a common street whore, he had said. So she never brought it up again.

Her mourning period was over and she set out to finally get what she wanted. She had to make her father see what her union with Lord Amaranth would mean for the Randall family. Now she had the chance to be with the man she'd always dreamed of, and in doing so, her soul would be absolved of the blackness that marred it. She had to marry a man like Draven; only he could save her from this need and perhaps then she could finally be satisfied and happy.

A servant entered the room with a tray of food, interrupting her thoughts. She scowled at him then noticed Moria following behind him. Cynthia whimpered dramatically, flung herself back onto the plush pillows and began to weep. The servant set the tray down and looked perplexingly at Moria who gently nodded, mouthed "thank you" and motioned for him to leave.

"Oh, Moria, what am I going to do? Nothing is going as I had planned. I'll never be able to get the remodeling done before the marriage." Cynthia rose and looked into Moria's violet eyes. There always seemed to be sympathy there. At least Moria understood her fragile sensitivities. Moria cared; Cynthia was thankful for that. "I'll have to live there before it's ready for me. I can't, I just can't live in that." She took Moria's small hands. "Moria, it's so gray. Everything is so gray."

"Miss Cynthia, you're becoming overwrought and you're underestimating yourself. Lord Amaranth has a lot he's dealing with right now, what with the elves debacle and the Kyrok raids in Callaria. He needs your strength."

Cynthia nodded, her chin quivering. "Yes, Moria. You're right, but I'm not strong. I don't know how to be strong for him."

Moria smiled sweetly. "You are strong, Cynthia. You are a rock; you just don't know it yet. Now eat and you'll feel better."

"You're the faerie. If you say I'm strong, then...whatever." Cynthia wiped the tears from her eyes, made a face and reached for the tray. "Moria," she said without looking up at her. "You mean more to me than you'll ever know."

Moria's pretty white brows dipped over her saddening eyes as she curled into a chair and picked up the book sitting on the table beside her. "I know how much you care, Miss Cynthia."

Cynthia picked at her food, "This is too heavy. It's just not what I want. It's all wrong, everything is wrong," she whined.

Moria sighed. "I'll have them bring you something else."

With a huff Cynthia dropped her napkin and pushed the tray away. "No, I'm not hungry. You can have them clear this away." She waved her hand over the tray. "I'm going to speak with Father." He'd talk to Draven and everything would be fine.

With renewed energy she flounced through the hall to her father's office door and raised her hand to knock, when she heard voices. Her father hated to be interrupted while in a meeting and she loved to eavesdrop, she thought with a sly grin.

"I have heard nothing of it," her father spoke, curiosity in his tone.

"Sir Orbane is distraught. She is, after all, his niece." The male visitor's voice was firm and authoritative.

"Yes, yes, of course. I can only imagine his distress at a time like this. Kidnapped, you say?"

"Yes, but we think she may have escaped her captors."

"Escaped? Well, we shall pray so. If she has escaped, won't she try to make her way home?"

"Not if she's lost or very badly injured." The visitor grew impatient. "Just let us know if you hear or see anything at all of a young woman, possibly injured. She is of twenty-five cycles, taller than average and has long dark hair and blue eyes. Her name is Linea Wyndham."

"I will certainly keep an ear to the wind, sir."

"Good. Sir Orbane and her betrothed, Sir Pandrum, are both willing to pay a hefty ransom for her safe return."

The scraping of chair legs on the floor made Cynthia jump. She scurried back but not fast enough. Two men came from her father's office, pausing briefly to stare down at her. One smiled, the other just grunted and moved on. After the men left the house and the door was closed behind them, she turned to her father.

"I never knew Sir Orbane had a niece," she said.

Her father looked down at her and put his arm around her shoulder. "Yes, he has a niece. His half-sister's daughter, I believe."

He led her back into the small cozy room. She sat in the chair, tucking her feet under her. She watched him walk around his desk and sit across from her. Edward Randall was an elegantly handsome man with closely cropped silver hair and fine-boned features. He wasn't big like Draven but he was a giant to Cynthia. Her hero.

"Oh, I've never met her." Cynthia thought back, trying to remember if she had ever heard anything about her.

"Her mother and father died when she was very young. Sir Orbane has kept her quite sheltered," Edward explained.

"Is she goat-faced?" Cynthia asked, lifting a brow.

"Now, Cyn," he chuckled, shaking his head. "I've never seen her, but I seriously doubt she's…goat-faced."

"Maybe she's lacking in the mind." Cynthia wrinkled her nose. "Did her parents give her to Sir Orbane or did they die? What happened?"

Edward leaned forward on his elbows and steepled his fingers. "They died, I believe, when she was five. Rumor says that Haig Orbane asked the king, who was close friends with her parents, for custody of the child and the king reluctantly granted it."

"Lord Amaranth?" Cynthia asked, her eyes wide.

"No, Cyn," he chuckled again. "Lord Rayne Amaranth was king at that time, Draven's father. Why are you so curious?"

Cynthia shrugged. "It's an intriguing story. I knew I had never seen her at any of the youth gatherings and even though she's seven years my junior, I believe she should have been in attendance at some point."

Edward frowned. "Hmmm…it is peculiar."

"Well, goat-faced and stupid or not, I don't envy her betrothal to Nezzer Pandrum. How ghastly!" She shivered. "She probably wasn't kidnapped at all. If she had any soundness of mind, she probably ran away! Take my word…" She nodded, her eyes wide. "I would have run. Run like the wind, I tell you!"

"Indeed," he murmured. "However, dear, Pandrum is part-human. Perhaps he's not as repulsive as a full-blooded Kyrok."

Cynthia shook her head with a solemn expression. "Regardless, I truly hate it for her. Why would anyone subject their own family to something so hideous?" she said with a sigh and a shake of her head. "Maybe it's not the same with Pandrum as it is with other Kyroks, you know, physically; being that he is part-human and all." She thought for a moment more, then with a shrug she waved her hand. "Anyway, I'd like to discuss my wedding," she said, perking up.

"Hmm…oh yes!" Her father grinned.

Chapter Fourteen

Days had passed since Gavril had helped Linea with the peculiar experience involving the king, and still thoughts of the little elf troubled her. Just as quickly as the looking glass thing began, it ended. Before she could say a word to Gavril, the warrior guarding her door had burst in and dragged him away.

Even though he'd escaped his room several times since in his attempts to reach her, she had yet to talk with him in length. Either a guard, Netta or Joeff had thwarted the little man. Now that the king had returned, Gavril probably wouldn't be able to escape at all. Still, she wondered what exactly had happened to her and what the king had to do with it. Something was changing inside her and though she tried to be logical and overcome it with reason, her heart pounded with fear.

Linea scooted to the edge of the big bed and gently tested her ankle. The blue had turned to a sickly yellow-green, but to her relief, she had more range of motion. The pain in her ankle and throughout her body had waned a great deal. It had become less of a vexation than the restlessness she felt sitting and twiddling her thumbs. Why wouldn't they let her work? Scrubbing floors, emptying bedpans, even. Anything would be better than this infernal idleness.

She stood and walked to the windows. Storm clouds bunched and undulated in the sky, blocking out the afternoon sun. Linea closed her eyes and imagined she could smell the impending rain. Since she had time outside in the fresh air when she ran away from her uncle, she lusted after more every day. But while she had been at the keep, she had been denied even the simple luxury of a breeze through her open window. Her fingers skimmed the window as she studied the nails that held it closed. She had nothing with which to pry them loose. She'd already tried everything short of her own teeth.

Frustration and anger rose in her and she began to pace. *Why was she allowing this to happen to her?* She asked herself. Did she fight against all odds, risk her life to escape from one prison, only to find herself in yet another? No. No, this was wrong. In spite of the fact that Lord Amaranth had fed her well, saw that her wounds were treated, hadn't beat her or had her beaten, she was still in hell; a lesser hell was still hell.

Linea gritted her teeth against the desire to pound the walls with her fists. She would not sit there and pine for freedom; she would take it. Death didn't frighten her; after all, she'd suffered worse. *No,* she screamed inwardly, *she would be no man's captive ever again!* Aletha lifted her head and whimpered.

There had to be a way out, she thought, raising herself up against the windowpane to see as far down the outside wall as she could. Lightning streaked across the darkening sky in staccato flashes of jagged gold. She studied her escape plan for a while until she was confident she could make it out. With determination she snatched up the neatly folded nightgown she'd slept in and wrapped it around her fist.

* * * * *

"I want no more excuses. I'll know how the elf is getting past you." The flustered warrior stood in the great hall before his king and took the dressing-down with as much dignity as he could cling to. "You're a fit warrior of more than six feet tall and you were duped by a pudgy little pest who is straining to reach four feet!" Draven glared. "Have you no pride, man?"

Armond sat on the edge of a chair, his elbows propped on his knees. His solemn mouth curved slightly. Mason pushed himself up from the hearth where he'd been watching the scene with a grin. He sauntered over and laid a hand on the guard's shoulder and whispered, "Don't answer that, I believe it was a rhetorical question." The guard glowered at Mason and shrugged his hand away.

"My apologies, Lord Amaranth. We have yet to find out how Gavril escaped; however, I will see to a thorough re-inspection and we will ensure that the room is secure."

"No more apologies or promises of what you 'will' do. I want it put to an end. I'm adding another man to help you guard the door. I want one of you in the room with the elf."

"Oh! That's not good." Mason stood beside the guard, his arms crossed. He leaned a bit closer and murmured, "Maybe you and the other guy can play a game of patty-cake to decide who has to sleep with the little bastard."

The guard grimaced and shot an irritated glance at Mason as muffled snickers echoed softly throughout the hall. Draven chose to ignore Mason's stinging comment as the girl's fury, strong and vibrant, slammed into him an instant before he knew her mind.

"Damn her," he growled as his own rage erupted like a white-hot flash. He turned and sprinted up the steps, taking them two at a time. The guard registered shock as he moved away quickly. Without taking the time to unlock it, Draven exploded through the door, splintering the frame with a loud crack.

The girl stood at the window, her fist wrapped in cloth, her arm drawn back. Draven grasped her arm before she could thrust her wrapped hand through the pane and whirled her around. Her blue eyes glittered cold and ferocious, her teeth bared. Twisting her body, she tried to pull away. Draven felt her desperation, her fear and anger, melding into a vicious thing. He tried to get his arms around her to hold her still. She swung around with her free hand and slapped him hard across the cheek.

He grabbed her wrist and shoved her hard against the wall and pressed his body against hers. She struggled with all her strength, refusing to give up the fight. Her eyes were blue flames. Sweat beaded across her forehead; her fingers were claws. She tried kicking at him, biting him.

"Stop it!" he roared.

He could feel the pain in her head, her body; pain that he was causing. But she kept twisting against him. He yanked her arms above her and grasped both wrists in one hand. The fear in her peaked; her eyes widened. "*No, not again, never again!*" An image flash of her tied by her wrists accompanying the force of her hoarse inner plea unnerved him.

He grimaced as her foot unexpectedly connected with his shin. Thunder rumbled off in the distance as she writhed and bucked and he pressed himself harder against her. He grasped her jaw and held her head still while his gaze held hers. Slowly, she stilled, struggling boldly against her fear. She panted heavily. Draven felt each breath she took; it was like razors tearing into her ribs, her breasts.

Lightning flashed. She gritted her teeth. Her eyes had gone wide, dark and sharp like the midnight sky and her cheeks were flushed with exertion and stood out in contrast to her stark white face. Her hair had come loose and dark waves clung to her sweaty temple. His eyes moved to her moist parted lips and he grappled with his desire to lower his head and taste them. Her lips clamped together and thinned. Her body finally stilled.

"Don't," she said in a small husky voice.

He held her gaze and tilted his head, moving his knee between her thighs. Evidence of his arousal pressed against her lower stomach. She inhaled sharply, her eyes searching his. He released her chin and brushed her hair away from her face, absorbing her pain. She was a sorceress, he thought. She had come to curse him.

He watched her frown and shake her head slowly.

He felt her moist heat against his thigh and wanted to rip away the fragile fabric of the oversized dress that hung over her body. A helpless expression of worry knit her brows. She tried to think fast, to decide whether she should move her thighs apart or squeeze them together. He arched a brow. Either choice had its advantages, he considered. She looked as horrified as he felt. It was apparent that she knew his mind as he knew hers. Perhaps she was a demon.

She squirmed, trying in vain to pull her wrists free from his grip, and gave him a defiant glare. "I'm no more a demon than you," she snapped.

He lowered his face until his mouth was so close he could taste her. "No, you are something far worse," he murmured, moving his hips against the soft cushion of her lower stomach.

Her awakening desire, the heat of her longing, was intoxicating him. He kissed along the taut line of her jaw to the velvety skin beneath her earlobe and nipped gently. She shuddered as his hand moved down her neck, his thumb caressing her collarbone and lower still, to skim along the rounded side of her breast. She gasped as his thumb moved across the underside and around her budding nipple, absorbing the pain as he went. Everywhere he touched her was hot and she smelled sweet and musky. He groaned as he continued to torture her with his mouth.

"What's happening to me?" It was a silent whisper; a confused whimper of a whisper that was so full of desperate, chaotic emotions Draven couldn't ignore it. He lifted his head suddenly and searched her face. Her eyes were heavy-lidded, dark swirling pools of deep blue fear and lust.

Alarmed, he stepped away. He wanted her badly but not enough to ignore her fear. Gently releasing her wrists, he lowered her arms and rubbed her shoulders. She was confused and anxious and still she hurt. Her chest heaved as she fought for breath. He looked down at her breasts and cursed. Small dots of fresh blood stained the front of her dress.

*   *   *   *   *

Released, Linea swayed on her feet as she watched him prowl to the door, the muscles in his back bunching under his snug gray shirt. His shirtsleeves were rolled up to his elbows. He had her mesmerized. She was sure her desire was evident and that anyone could see her overheated body pulse like that intriguing muscle in Lord Amaranth's jaw.

Her body shook with want of something she couldn't name. It was insanity, she was certain of it. Her fingertips tingled with the urge to trail over the bulging muscles and veins in his forearms and clenched fists. She wondered how it would feel to let her hands explore his bare shoulders and back and...

He spun around, meeting her gaze with a look that should have melted her on the spot. "Stop thinking," he growled tightly.

She trembled and nodded. *Good idea*, she thought, squeezing her eyes closed. He yelled orders to those in the great hall below.

"No, please. I'll change my dressings myself." She couldn't bear being touched by anyone, not even Netta. Not right now, anyway.

Lord Amaranth turned and walked back to her. She looked up at him, noticing for the first time the red imprint of her hand marring his cheek, and bit her lip. Hopelessness enveloped her. She would never be free; she knew that now. She would never be strong enough or smart enough to get away from this man. He would always know her thoughts even before she could act on them.

"Netta is coming to tend to you." Lord Amaranth looked down at her intensely. She let her gaze roam his face. The gray of his eyes were dark smoky rings around black. His mouth was a tight line. He looked hard, angry; it seemed he was always angry like... She stopped herself and lifted her gaze to his. His eyes narrowed. He could rob her of her very thoughts. No, she would never be free.

"Honesty, simple honesty, will buy your freedom. I have no wish to keep you prisoner, woman. But I don't trust you." His voice was deceptively quiet and gentle.

Linea drew in a shaky breath. She knew she appeared weak but she couldn't shake this spell he had her under. "But you have no need to trust me or distrust me. If you'd only give me my medallion back and release the little elf, we'd leave here and you'd be rid of us both."

"Until I know who you are and your intent, I will not let you go," he said. She watched him turn and brush past Netta, speak to the guard who scowled at her in return, and descend the stairs.

Chapter Fifteen

"Here you are, dear." Netta walked in holding a basin of water with a bundle of cloths draped across her arm. She arranged everything on the dressing table. She was always such a soft kind soul. Her sweet voice was like a balm to Linea's ragged emotions.

Linea still burned and now she ached for something she couldn't name, something mysterious and seductive. She felt agitated and unfulfilled in a way she'd never had before. The part of her between her legs felt swollen, slick, overly hot, and sensitive. Rowena, Uncle Haig's house overseer, had promised her that Iybae's curse only came once a moon phase.

Shock slammed into her, tears clogged her throat and she swallowed hard. Panic gripped her heart. This was punishment. Iybae was displeased. He was punishing her by increasing the frequency of the woman's curse and with it adding these odd sensations and aches, to remind her of the evil in her. She'd nearly forgotten.

Uncle Haig had explained that the great Creator, Iybae, regretted creating women for they were inadequate and detestable, sinful in their nature. They were a stumbling block to man. His curse was to remind her of her inherent worthlessness that she might never forget her role. Now, because of her rebellion and her unholy desires, she would be reminded more often. She had always held hope that Uncle had been wrong. It appeared she had hoped in vain.

She clenched her legs together and ripples of sensation cascaded through her. She gulped and tried to hide her surprise from Netta. Something was terribly wrong. "Netta, I would like to tend to my wounds myself." She tried not to appear desperate and avoided Netta's gaze. "If you wouldn't mind. Please."

She could feel Netta watching her. "Well, all right." Netta stepped closer. "Rest, dear heart. You need to sleep. Oh my, you're trembling. Are you cold?"

Linea shook her head.

"Are you afraid of the storm?"

Again she shook her head. "I just want to be alone. I'm sorry."

Netta's forehead creased in concern. "Yes, dear. Send for me if you need anything at all."

Again, Linea nodded and watched as the woman laid out a fresh nightgown and finished her fussing with the bed and the drapes, and then with a wink and a smile shut the damaged door behind her.

Linea took one of the thick cloths and folded it neatly. She pulled the dress over her head and laid it across the back of a chair. Propping a leg up on the end of the bed she reached down with the folded cloth and patted herself. Again sensations flowed through her body. She pulled the cloth away and looked at it, no blood. With a frown she set the cloth aside.

Biting her lip, she gingerly touched herself with her trembling bare fingers. She was slick with something like hot oil and the folds of her flesh were swollen and so tender. She closed her eyes and nearly cried with fear and need. She pulled her hand away and studied the slick fluid that coated her fingers before wiping them on the cloth.

She took her leg down and carefully unbound her breasts. Only a few of the cuts had begun to bleed again. Already they had stopped but they throbbed with something close to but not quite pain. She shook her head and quickly washed her breasts, trying to ignore the feelings they produced in her. She dipped her fingers in the salve Netta had left her and rubbed it gently over her nipples. Her breath caught in her throat as her nipples grew hard against her palm.

She didn't bind them again. She didn't think she could stand to. Besides, even the most badly injured nipple was almost completely healed over. She pulled the gown on over her head and crawled under the covers. She lay there on her back and closed her eyes, but the ache between her legs would not subside.

Curiosity won out as she squeezed her eyes tightly shut, moved her hand down her stomach and pulled her gown up around her waist. Goosebumps danced over her skin with anticipation as she moved her hand lower to the curl-covered mound between her legs. She opened her legs slightly and slid her fingers over the slick swollen flesh there.

Sucking in her breath through her teeth she gathered her courage. Her heart pounded as her finger delved between the hot cleft, slid silkily through the sensitive folds and rasped gently over a tiny hardened knot. She muffled a cry, pulling her hand away, and sat up in her bed panting.

* * * * *

"Draven, you were saying?" Armond spoke, his deep voice full of concern.

Not again, Draven thought as he tried to pace his breathing. Smoldering arousal melted every cell of his body. His pulsating erection thickened and stretched, pushing painfully against the lacings of his leather pants. He still hadn't recovered from being so close to her. Apparently, neither had she.

He looked at Mason and saw the gleam in his eyes. The crooked smile. He glared at him but Mason only winked. "Feeling well, cousin?" he asked.

"Fine," Draven said between clenched teeth. Her desire was much stronger this time; he could feel it surging through her, through him.

Mason shifted in his chair and slouched down, throwing a leg over the arm. "I don't know, Draven, you look pretty, uh, edgy."

Draven glowered at Mason, who chuckled. Turning to the warrior who sat next to Armond, Draven asked, "So they weren't the holy men who were here earlier in the week? Did they mention what they came for before you sent them away?"

"No, my lord, I told them they would not be granted audience with you without the Overseer of Endaria, Sir Orbane."

Draven tensed, trying to concentrate. His lids lowered as a savage wave of sensation hit him and he swallowed a groan. His cock jerked and throbbed painfully.

Mason grinned and murmured quietly, "Think of dead puppies, Draven."

Draven sneered. Appalled, the two other men looked at Mason with astonishment. Mason could hardly contain his laughter and Draven swore if he lived through this, he'd make his dear cousin pay.

Draven leaned forward to speak then closed his eyes and sucked in air through his teeth, his hands gripping the arms of his chair as the exquisite sensations tore through him and showered his body with little pulses of pleasure. *What in hell was she doing? Dear Iybae,* he moaned inwardly, he knew what she was doing. His body was on fire and on the brink of a climax and if he didn't stop her soon, he'd embarrass himself.

"Netta!" he bellowed, trying to breathe. "NETTA! GET IN HERE!"

"Dead puppies, Draven, dead puppies," Mason snorted.

Netta was out of breath when she swung open the door. "What is it, my lord?" Her eyes widened at the sight of him. "Are you well? You look flushed. Are you feverish?"

"Oh aye, my dear Netta, he's definitely hot!" Mason threw back his head and howled with laughter, holding his stomach while the other men looked at him as though he'd gone mad.

Draven gritted his teeth, trying to tamp down the maddening sensations raging through him. "Do something about that girl," he growled. "Do it now!"

"Girl?" Netta frowned and then understanding, said, "Oh, Joan? She's sleeping, my lord."

"No, she's not," Mason sung.

"Shut up, Mason. For God's sake, shut the hell up!" Draven turned to Netta, who looked startled and just a bit frightened. "Go wake her up, check on her, do something."

Netta simply stood staring at him.

"Go, woman. Go now!" His teeth clenched tightly, desperately clinging to composure.

Netta jumped in surprise and went as fast as her pudgy little legs would carry her to do as her lord asked. Silently she prayed to Iybae that He might return sanity to the king.

Chapter Sixteen

Silence had descended on the keep. Everyone had retired to their beds and had long gone to sleep. Draven walked into his room without closing the door behind him. He awkwardly stripped off his clothes and stood swaying, the moonlight caressing his naked body.

He looked down at his erect member. Still achingly hard, it seemed to mock him. The alcohol had softened nothing apart from his brain. At least maybe now, if she decided to diddle with those sweet nether regions of hers, he just might be dull-minded enough not to sense it.

He groaned and fell onto his bed, staring up at the spinning ceiling. Maybe he should reach down and stroke his shaft, give her a taste of her own mischief. No, damn her cold black soul, he wouldn't give her the satisfaction. He rolled over on his stomach, winced, then turned to lie on his side and pulled the blanket over his hips. Quickly he drifted into a restless sleep.

Hours later he woke with a start and sat up. His head felt full of cotton and he fought to clear the web of dark steamy dreams that clouded his mind. He'd heard something, or sensed something, and he had a feeling he knew what it was. He stood and, remembering he was naked, snatched a neatly folded pair of linen pants from the chair. Netta laid them out for him every night. She had made them for him to sleep in, but they had yet to be worn. Thankful he had them now, he pulled them on and absently tied the drawstring that kept them from falling. Still, they hung low on his hips and did nothing to hide his jutting arousal, but he didn't care. He walked rapidly to the girl's room.

The flickering light from the fireplace in the great hall below glowing through the archways along the balcony-like hall illuminated his way. The guard sat beside her door, his chin rested against his chest as he slept. Draven smacked him on the head and the man nearly fell over. "Wha...what's happening?"

"Indeed," Draven said with disgust. Opening the door, he took in the strange sight.

The bed curtains were tied back. The woman lay on her side, her hands fisted in the blankets under her chin. Her dark hair was tossed in wild disarray over her face and across the pillow. The moon lit the gold and copper strands that flowed through the waves and curls. At the foot of the bed lay a sleeping Gavril, curled in a ball and snoring softly like a faithful puppy.

"Hell," Draven muttered. Thinking of puppies, dead or otherwise, would nevermore be the same. In two strides he was standing over the little man. He had been cleaned up and no longer stank, his wooly brown hair was now closely trimmed and his face was clean-shaven, his expression one of peaceful contentment. Draven snarled and reached out, grabbing Gavril by his collar.

Gavril shrieked in shock as he was dangled above the ground, his fat stumpy legs kicking in vain. The woman sat up, panting. "Put him down!"

Draven smiled at Gavril contemptuously. "Not this time, I have had my fill of this little vagabond." He turned his head and looked at her, and the breath caught in his lungs.

She knelt in the middle of the bed. With one arm she swept the great mass of hair back from her face and held it all to one side. Her face was aglow in the moonlight, her cheeks pink. Her lips were parted in outrage. Her full breasts were left unbound and moved provocatively under her thin nightgown with every breath she took. Her dusky rose nipples, brushing against the fabric, tightened under his gaze. His mouth went dry and he nearly dropped the squirming elf.

"And I have had more than enough of you. Lord Amaranth, you're being ridiculous. Put him down, now. I mean it," she warned him. Determination of stone braced her. Her brows furrowed over her sharp gaze. Her eyes were like blue flames licking over his body, pausing at his pelvis.

He watched her widening eyes darken to indigo. She swallowed tightly; the pink in her cheeks turned to scarlet. That little pink tongue darted out to moisten her parted lips. He arched a brow, noting her arousal and her trepidation. He felt her honeyed channel clench in tight little ripples. No, not nearly enough, as far as he was concerned. His cock jerked, straining impatiently, tenting his pants. And it was her fault, all her fault. "You mean it, do you?"

"It's all right, my lady…uh, don't try the king." Gavril scowled up at Draven, his voice strained. "I'll go back to my room."

Oh, she would try the king, Draven thought to himself. He'd suffered at her playful hands enough. She moved to the edge of the bed and stood. He nearly moaned. He wanted to drop the elf, throw her to the bed and sink into her. Taste those round, firm globes and feel her nipples harden in arousal at the rasp of his tongue on her. And she would be aroused; he knew her need. She timidly walked toward him. Her swollen pink-crested breasts swung freely, teasing him, and he gritted his teeth.

"Lord Amaranth, I'm in no mood for clever banter with you tonight."

He tilted his head and narrowed his eyes at her. He knew exactly what mood she was in. What mood she'd been in for days. Her lusty passion mingled with determination and anger, and entwined with his. The mixture of emotions was volatile and it shook him.

"Draven?" Armond stood behind him.

Draven didn't turn from the temptress that stood before him. He handed Gavril to Armond. "Take this runt and make sure he stays in his room this time."

"Draven, you might consider letting the elf stay with her. She seems to have some sort of control over him," Armond reasoned.

"Armond. Leave."

"I'm just…"

"Leave!" he shouted.

"Fine." Armond sighed and left the room with Gavril, who surprisingly didn't fight him.

The door closed softly behind them and Draven took a step closer. "Now, you were saying you're in no mood."

"If you think you're intimidating me, you're mistaken," she said, crossing her arms under her breasts.

He felt her resolve like a red-hot angry wall, and though he knew she fought it, she was intimidated. "You lie. Your mood is quite powerful, sweetness. Even more so than it was earlier, I think."

Confusion flitted over her face. She was strong, courageous, and so beautiful. "I don't understand…"

He took two more steps toward her. The mysterious connection he had with her was more intoxicating than the wine he'd guzzled earlier that evening. "If you are going to tease me with your diddling, you'll learn the correct way to go about it. All you've succeeded at so far has been to frustrate us both." He gently unwrapped her arms from around herself and took her hands in his. Softly he pulled her closer, kissing each palm as he stood over her, quietly watching comprehension spark to life in her eyes.

"You... I didn't know..." she stammered. Embarrassment and shame swirled thickly through her.

He bent his head and kissed her hard. His tongue tracing the line of her closed lips had her opening to him. He groaned as he entered her, even in that small way, possessing her. The heated silken interior of her mouth felt incredible. Her sweet lips timidly moving against his was his undoing. Taking her hand, he pressed her palm against his thick pulsating shaft. "Feel what you're doing to me." His voice was rough and dark.

She was so innocent in her wonder and so filled with shame and fear. He wanted to drive it away. He wanted to fill her with his body, with his pleasure, and drive away all thoughts of anything else. He shook with need as she pulled her hand away, her trembling fingers trailing timidly up the hardness of his shaft.

Her timid touch and ravenous need seared him, driving his ardor higher. "So sweet," he murmured. His hands slid down her back and gripped her bottom as his hips thrust forward.

She held her breath. Her short nails bit into his shoulders as his steel-hard cock pressed against the cleft between her thighs. His lips moved against hers, heating them both, and her shame gave way to craving. He absorbed her shock and fear as the force of his heated arousal surged into her. His tongue probed her mouth, stroking, exploring delicate places, awakening, seducing. Her body shuddered in his arms and he pulled her closer. He knew her uneasiness and her returning heat at the feel of his unyielding cock pressing against her.

She hesitantly touched her tongue to his. The shy caress inflamed him. His tongue plundered the sweet hollow of her mouth as his lips slanted over hers. Wanting her closer, to feel her warm skin against his, he untied the bows at her neck and chest and pushed the fabric slowly past her shoulders until it dropped in folds around her full hips.

Her chest rose and fell as her breaths came faster. He felt the hot molten lust pool deep inside her and he fought to go slow. His hands moved lightly over her shoulders, down her chest, around the sides of her swollen breasts. Her plump, erect nipples grazed his bare chest, sending currents of sensation through them both.

He nibbled at her lips and moved over her jaw to her neck. He closed his eyes and nuzzled her silky hair. She smelled so good, fresh, like morning dew on honeysuckle. He cupped her heavy breasts, lifting them, gently rubbing them, his thumbs softly tracing the outer rim of her areolas. He walked her back until her legs met the side of the bed and slowly laid her down. He met her troubled gaze and she shook her head as he came up over her.

"Shhh, feel me, sweetness," he whispered against her inflamed flesh. He ran his tongue around her tightening areola and took the perfect pink peak gently between his teeth, grazing it lightly as he flicked it with his tongue. Her hands sifted through his hair. Just as he imagined it would, the juicy berry hardened eagerly. She arched her back and pulled him closer.

Her head tilted back as she panted for breath. His mouth moved to her right breast, giving it the same attention. Her body shook with arousal as his hand molded and shaped her left breast, his fingers squeezing and gently rolling the wet aching peak. He softly laved her right breast, careful of her wound.

"Oh, that feels very, very good," she gasped, her breath shuddering from her lips.

"Yes, it does." His hand moved down her abdomen, pushing the gown out of his way, to the soft thatch of curls. "So soft, so silky," he murmured against her breast. His hand moved lower, separating the tender lips to touch the hot swollen folds nestled inside, slippery with the dew of her arousal. His fingers slipped up and down, opening her more and more, saturating his hand. "You're so wet and hot, you're burning for me."

Her pleasure guided him as his mouth caressed her, tasting the tender skin of her thoat, her jaw. She trembled as his thumb found the hard knot nestled at the apex of her cleft and she held her breath. He lightly pressed and rubbed the little jewel then stroked the silken folds lower and lower. She gripped his arm, moving her hips against his hand.

Slowly his tongue glided over her bottom lip and he breathed in her gasps. Sliding his finger deeply into her incredibly tight honeyed channel, he groaned at the intensity of pleasure it gave her, gave him. Inch by inch he stroked her, stretching, sliding deeper still until he felt the thin barrier of her maidenhead. He curled his finger upward, stroking, until he felt the firm sensitive flesh he was searching for. His thumb massaged her clitoris as his finger stroked her sweet spot. Her body tensed; her hands pulled at him, clutching at him, terrified of the urgent need that swelled inside her.

"Don't be afraid, love," he whispered as he carefully slid another finger into her. Blood pumped savagely through her veins. The rapid pulse of it throbbed against his lips. He pressed his thumb lightly against her clit as his fingers moved inside her fiery convulsive sheath. The sensations writhed within her, curled inside of him, driving them both to madness. Her hands left him and fisted in the covers as she moved her hips in rhythm with his hand.

"Let go...feel," he groaned, rising to look down into her widening eyes as her climax gripped her. The hot juice of her arousal gathered and seeped from her tight velvety channel as it clenched hungrily at his fingers, soaking them.

Still, his hand moved against her, inside her. "Beautiful," he growled as the ripples of her pleasure tore through her and washed over him. He lay back against the bed and gathered her against him. Her body shook with her subsiding climax. A fine sheen of sweat covered her body. Her eyes were shut tight and her breath shuddered from her body in little pants as she fought to regain her sanity.

Chapter Seventeen

He frowned as he watched her, brushed the hair from her face and kissed her soft cheek. Her body was still rigid. She never made a sound, not so much as a moan. He kissed her again, focusing on her. He felt no pain, only faint after-ripples and tension…incredible tension.

"You have nothing to fear," he whispered soothingly as his hand smoothed over her bare hip and lifted her leg to rest across his thigh. He clung to his control as his cock thrummed against her saturated vulva. She bit her lip as he moved against her in slow circles, feeling the tension begin to build in her again. He felt her rapid heartbeat against his fingers as he caressed the silken valley between her breasts.

Her lips parted on a silent moan, delicious tingles flooding her system. She arched up, though he knew she fought against it. Her arousal only magnified his own. She was so beautiful in her helplessly eager response it was nearly his undoing. He flooded her with his desire as the breath shuddered from her lungs. His tongue swept her swollen bottom lip then feathered her ripe mouth with soft kisses.

He needed her, to be inside her, to feel her surrounding him. She had to tell him; she must, or he would go mad with lust.

"Tell me your name," he whispered roughly against her lips.

Fear rose inside her and solidified like solid marble, cold and unmoving. Her arousal cooled as quickly as it flared. Draven's hands stilled and he clenched his teeth, knowing her answer before she gave it.

"I'm Joan," she said hoarsely. Draven flinched. She obviously knew her lie was evident, yet she doggedly stuck with that lie.

"Why do you insist on telling me your name is Joan?"

He could see himself in her wide blue eyes as she met his steely gaze. He watched her close off to him, felt her body stiffen in his arms. "Because you insist on asking," she said quietly.

Anger flared to life inside him, mingling with his raging desire. The volatile mixture had his muscles bunching and his teeth clenching. Draven released her and stood, then yanked her up with him. He ignored her gasp, the fear in her widening eyes, her attempts to hide her nakedness.

"Damn you, little liar. Who are you?" He shook her hard. Her ribs ached. Her wounds stung. But his frustration was too great. "I feel it surrounding you, something menacing, something perverse. It's always right there just on the edge."

He narrowed his eyes at her, watching her shake her head in denial. His hands tightened on her arms, biting into her flesh painfully. "Tell me, damn you. Tell me your name!"

Her face remained impassive as though she felt nothing. But he knew what she felt. She was strong and obstinate and he knew she was fighting to keep her mind blank. Her body still. She breathed deeply, raising her stubborn chin a notch.

"Give me a reason not to kill you and be done with it." He felt sudden terror spike out of control, her humiliation and her shame. Not the sort of man who could hurt a woman, much less kill one, he regretted the words as soon as he'd said them but he wouldn't take them back. He had no intention of doing her any harm unless he had no other choice. The thought made him feel ill. He wouldn't entertain the possibility. Not now.

"There is no reason, good or otherwise. So be done with it," she said as she lowered her head and covered her breasts with her arms. Her hair fell across her face, nearly shrouding round, fathomless, cobalt blue pools that began to shimmer with unshed tears.

Dammit, he didn't want to care; she was driving him to madness with this frenzied need. Constructing a block, he closed off his thoughts as quickly as they budded in his mind. Best she didn't know the depth of his concern for her, especially since he didn't understand it himself.

A frustrated growl erupted from deep inside him as his mouth descended on hers in a kiss without constraint or compassion. His lips slanted over hers, taking her mouth in stubborn possession. Breaking away, both of them panting, her swollen lips bruised, he glowered down at her.

"Iybae help me, I will not take you by force." He kissed her deeply, absorbing the last traces of pain from her aching body. Cupping her face in his hands, he captured her gaze. "But believe me, woman, by His holy name you will tell me everything I wish to know or you will never be free again."

He stepped away from her and she dropped weakly to sit on the edge of the bed, pulling the rumpled gown up and over her shoulders. Her fingers trembled as she fumbled with the ties. He turned and walked to the door with the bright blinding swirls of her many emotions swirling around dark strands of hurt. They spun inside him. He ached to chase them away, to replace them with the soft curl of pleasure and contentment, but her stubbornness and fear kept her from letting him.

"Lord Amaranth." Her voice was soft and shaky and sounded like little hiccups.

He spun around. "Yes?" She was sitting there, her hands in her lap, trembling from the residual hum of pleasure he had given her. Tears trickled down her rosy cheeks. He wanted to go to her, make her forgive him, but he couldn't. He wouldn't.

"I have wronged you. Forgive me."

Draven watched her for a moment. "What?" he snapped.

She looked up at him, her face reflecting the misery he felt squeezing her heart. "You are betrothed."

Stunned, Draven stepped back as though she'd punched him. "Yes," he snarled at her. "I was a more than willing participant, so you can save your great remorse. You've committed no sin. And my betrothal is of none of your concern," he sneered and walked out, slamming the door behind him.

* * * * *

Confusion and anger cluttered Linea's mind like obstinate viscid spider webs she couldn't quite clear. It seemed the king would go to any lengths to discover her identity. Her heart felt caught in a vise. He had done those things to her, filled her with such pleasure in order to manipulate her. It shouldn't hurt but it did. The king would not give up and he soon would discover her for what she was. Then he'd either send her back or do as he threatened and be done with her.

Realization of what had happened this night twisted her stomach. She had confirmed Uncle Haig's assessment of her. She had been the whore he'd always said she was. She'd been willing, Iybae help her, and she'd been willing to give the king anything he'd desired.

If he had chosen to take her it wouldn't have been by force. Her body ached with need, and had responded to his every touch and grasped for more. The flesh between her thighs felt engorged and so sensitive, it still throbbed for more attention. She was sodden there with the slick fluid of her arousal. Clenching her legs together sent the hunger coursing through her darkly. Her body still sang from his touch and still she yearned for more of him.

Thinking of the scorching rock-hard shaft prodding her, she remembered wanting him inside her. She shuddered with ripples of pleasure at the thought. His fingers had made her feel so good. She wondered how it would feel to be filled with his hardness, searing her from the inside with pleasure. She nearly moaned out loud at the fantasy. She had to overcome this—this lust, this need for carnal pleasure. If she ever hoped to be accepted, to win the love of Iybae, she had to rid herself of this desire.

She lifted her head and tightened her jaw. She would, no matter. She was not a coward. Lord Amaranth sought to control her and doom her to the hells with her own sin. Her uncle sought to break her and in the process he would eventually destroy her. She would not bow to it. She would not sit and do nothing but wait for Amaranth and her uncle to seal her fate. If they were to kill her, she would not passively endure their torture until they achieved their goal.

Chapter Eighteen

"We really should have at least sent word, Miss Cynthia." Moria sat forward in the carriage, breathing deeply, her eyes closed, her long white hair lifted by the wind. Enjoying the rain-drenched air, Cynthia assumed. The world smelled wonderful after a rain. The sun had yet to peek out from behind the clouds and the day was not as bright as she'd like.

"Yes, Moria, I know, but the king is forever occupied and I feel that he'd prefer that I take care of the celebration details." She smiled, certain he'd appreciate her initiative as well.

A man like him didn't bother with female fancy. A man like him would appreciate her femininity too, her softness against his hardness. She blinked away the erotic visions that seduced her and focused on planning the celebration.

She had sent out invitations, and had, at her father's rather insistent suggestion, kept it to a small crowd. Now she needed to discuss the meal with the cook and see about entertainment. She sighed with delight.

Before she knew it they had arrived at the keep gates. The warrior that stood guard wore a blank expression on his rugged face. He was tall, his shoulders wide, dressed in leather and skins. At his hip hung a vicious looking longsword. He recognized her and granted her entrance with a nod. A shiver ran up her spine and her cheeks heated. Marriage would definitely be a good thing for her. She could scarcely wait.

Joeff offered his hand and a dreary smile as she stepped into the great hall. No one sat chatting around the fireplace. The hall was empty and quiet.

"Good morning, Miss Cynthia, Miss Moria." Joeff nodded politely.

"Joeff, is Netta busy? I have need of her services today. I will also need to speak with the cook," Cynthia said as she scanned the hall making mental notes.

"Yes, my lady, I shall tell her you are asking for her. Follow me."

"Ah, Joeff, I'd rather sit in the great hall since the warriors are not occupying it at the moment. If that would be acceptable?"

He hesitated, and then bowed. "Please make yourself comfortable. I'll send for refreshments."

"Oh, how lovely. Thank you, Joeff." Cynthia cautiously lowered herself onto the massive leather couch.

She watched the man leave then turned to Moria, curling her nose. "After we marry, this room will have to be redone." She gazed around the room. "No more sweaty men draped around, here and there." She met Moria's laughing gaze. "Well, it's simply inappropriate."

"My, my, my, what a glorious sight to behold so early in the morning." The man speaking was only half-dressed. He stood grinning at the top of the stairs, tying the drawstrings of his worn cotton pants. His shoulder-length sandy blonde hair looked more like a nest on top of his head. His eyes were still droopy from sleep, and he rubbed his stubbly face as he sauntered down the steps and swaggered toward them. "Praise Iybae, I must have been a blessing to Him that He should send two beautiful angels to help arouse me," he said, wagging his brows at them.

Cynthia stood transfixed, completely shocked. Her blood quickened in her veins. "What?" she stammered in disbelief.

"You know, help wake me up." He stood over her now, smiling. He wasn't quite as tall as Lord Amaranth but still he stood well above her. He was so close now she could feel the warmth radiating from his smooth naked chest, smell his distinctly masculine scent. With an index finger he lifted her chin and closed her mouth. His light blue eyes sparkled with mischief. "I'm Mason, I'm enchanted and I am definitely..." he held her gaze as he lifted her hand to his lips, "awake."

Cynthia heard Moria cough softly behind her; it sounded suspiciously like a suppressed laugh. The simple kiss sent tingles sparkling through her. To her horror she felt her feminine parts respond with a delicious tightening. She frowned and pulled her hand away. "It's almost midday. You should have been awake hours ago," she said prudishly. "True, but then I would have missed the pleasure of looking upon your beautiful face," he said as his eyes roamed her body, leaving a trail of heat in his wake. He paused at her breasts, taking in the protruding evidence of her arousal at his sultry perusal. He cocked a brow and looked at her with a hooded gaze. He didn't try to hide his interest in her. Horror gripped her throat as she felt her secret place moisten and pout with arousal.

"You are rude," she exclaimed, denying her fierce attraction to this crude male. She tried to ignore her traitorous body. The man looked like a wild, untamed angel. His body was thick with bulging muscle and free of hair. His smooth bare chest muscles flexed, his stomach muscles rippled and Cynthia thought she'd faint. Although his face was hard planes and angles like Lord Amaranth's, he and the king contrasted in other ways. Where Lord Amaranth was dark and foreboding, this rake was fair and flippant.

He took her hand again with an expression of contrition. "Rude? Oh no, I didn't mean to offend you, sweet lady." He kissed her hand again, then her palm. "Quite the opposite."

His lips on her bare skin were sending spirals of sensation through her. She tried to yank her hand away but he held it fast. Her heart was pounding in her chest. This man was too forward, much too forward. If he didn't release her she'd burst into flames. "Let me go!" Her voice was a tremulous squeak and she winced.

He murmured against her wrist, "You haven't told me your name yet, lovely one." He glanced up at her, a plea in his sparkling eyes as he caught her gaze.

"Mason. Unhand Miss Cynthia, and for the love of Iybae put some clothes on." Draven snarled at him with disgust.

The playful glint left Mason's sky blue eyes, his crooked smile melted and Cynthia saw something that looked like disappointment in his expression. "Sorry about that, cousin. I can't imagine why I didn't realize this fine lady was your betrothed."

He released her and Cynthia's sigh sounded more like a whimper. Her body trembled with longing. Mason took a deep breath and winked at her as he backed away. She wondered, but didn't allow herself to look down at his manhood and was thankful when he turned around.

He punched Draven lightly on the shoulder as he passed. "Not fair," she heard him grumble as he left.

Her eyes dropped to his backside, well-defined by the soft clinging material of his pants. She looked back to meet Draven's dark gaze and cleared her throat. His brows were arched and his mouth was turned down. He didn't look happy.

"Well, he was awfully rude." Cynthia swallowed.

Draven leaned down stiffly and kissed her cheek. "Yes, he is. Very. What can I help you with, dear Cynthia?"

Confused, she blinked and looked up at him. Normally any touch from Draven had her tummy fluttering. Now her tummy was still doing crazy things over the attentions of Draven's roguish cousin. She put on her sweetest smile. "I've come to put the last touches on the preparations for the celebration for tomorrow night."

"Ah, I see." He frowned and looked slightly pained. It worried Cynthia. A lot was worrying her at the moment, chiefly the wet heat that inflamed her woman's parts.

"I won't be in your way, my lord," she rushed to explain. "I'll just be discussing arrangements with the cook and Miss Netta."

A warrior stomped in, interrupting her. "My apologies, my lady," he said politely and turned back to Lord Amaranth. He lowered his voice. "We just received word that Sir Orbane will be arriving on the morrow for an audience with you."

"Thank you, Sam," Lord Amaranth said and turned back to the ladies.

"I'm sure it has something to do with his niece," Cynthia said, shaking her head.

"Pardon me?" Lord Amaranth asked, tilting his head, his brows knitting together. "What about his niece?"

"Did you know he had a niece? I had no idea. Father told me the whole sad story."

"Yes, I believe so. Linea, I think is her name. What do you know of her?"

"They say she's been kidnapped." Cynthia frowned. "I don't think that's true, though. I think she ran away."

"What gives you reason to believe that?" Lord Amaranth asked, his hands gripping the back of the chair.

Cynthia wondered if she should go on, considering Lord Amaranth's reaction. "She is betrothed to that horrible beast Nezzer Pandrum. He's half Kyrok, you know. Kyrok women are one thing but for a human female it would be…well, those who have been assaulted in the past do not come away from it whole, if they come away from it at all. The poor girl must have been horror-stricken."

Lord Amaranth went still; his eyes were cold and hard. "Miss Cynthia, you must be mistaken. No man would willingly do that to a woman he was responsible for, especially not his family."

Cynthia watched him cautiously. "Perhaps it's true that Sir Pandrum isn't like the other Kyroks. Perhaps his male appetites aren't as…" She felt the heat infuse her cheeks as she spoke. "I'm told that Pandrum's humanness has caused his…attributes to be more what human women are able to contend with. "

"What possible reason would he have to take such a chance with his niece?" Draven snapped.

Cynthia shuddered, her uneasiness growing, but she continued. "Well, Father said that perhaps Sir Orbane wanted to secure Sir Pandrum's loyalty. Possibly something to do with a trade alliance."

The muscle in Lord Amaranth's jaw jumped and his eyes took on a predatory glimmer. His hands gripped the chair so tightly that his knuckles had gone white. "Do you know what this girl looks like?"

Nervous, Cynthia looked over at Moria, who surprisingly sat calmly, a blank expression on her petite face. Cynthia turned back to Lord Amaranth. "All I know is she's very tall. Rumor was that she has pretty dark hair, blue eyes. I don't know, as I have never had the pleasure of meeting her. She's never been to a ball or social event. I apologize, my lord, I've only heard tales."

Lord Amaranth breathed deeply and closed his eyes. He seemed to vibrate with some emotion; she assumed rage. Lord Amaranth was such a wonderful king that he would be concerned for the lost girl, she thought. She had been praying for her since she heard. Cynthia was glad she told him. Now if he found her, she knew he would see to her safety.

* * * * *

Cynthia had gone to finish her arrangements, leaving Moria sitting cross-legged on a plush stool in the center of the great hall. Moria had watched the king call the men into the war room. He knew now. It was good that he finally knew.

"Psst… Psst." Moria tilted her head at the noise. "Psst…hey you."

114

Little snipe. Moria grinned as she turned and lifted her gaze to scan the arches that ran along the upper level. Then she saw the frisky little elf peeking over the ledge. "Come up here," he whispered harshly.

Intrigued, Moria unfolded her legs, stretched, spread her delicate wings and flew up to him. Landing delicately within the portico, she sat on the ledge and smiled down at him with an arched brow. "Yes?"

"Hrumph. So you can fly, that's no special thing," Gavril grunted.

"No, not really. Not to me it isn't, anyway," Moria said sweetly. "What is it you need from me, elf?"

"Not a thing," he said huffily. "Just forget it."

"As you wish," she said as she went to stand.

"No, wait." He scowled hard at her. "I have an important quest for you."

She chuckled. "Do you?" Oh, this was delightful.

"Yes, I do," he snapped, putting his hands on his hips.

She folded her arms and waited patiently.

"As much as I hate the whole idea, my sweet Miss Linea must wed the foul king, Lord Amaranth."

The corner of her mouth tilted. This was no great revelation. Why else would she risk leaving Ingvar? "Yes, and…?"

"And… And, I need you to take that little prissy thing away." Gavril sneered.

Moria grinned. "Miss Cynthia? Now, Gavril, you know I can not."

"Oh yes, you can. You could make her hate Draven the pig if you so desired," he groused. "You faeries are all alike. You have all these powers and won't use them 'cause you're selfish."

"Oh Gavril, you are a treasure." Moria giggled. She gained control of her laughter and sighed. "Cynthia has her own path. And Lord Amaranth is no pig. You should be ashamed of yourself for saying such awful things." Still she smiled at him, quite enjoying his cantankerous fervor.

Desperation filled his eyes. "Moria, you know Linea and Draven are supposed to be together. If they don't marry, my sweet Linea will never know her true power. Draven will marry that simp of a woman and we will never know the great era that is to come from their union."

Moria frowned. "Things will be as they should be. Be at peace, little one. Linea is already coming into her power."

"The faeries could be free again, Moria," Gavril pleaded.

Moria stood with a sigh and fluttered her wings. "Yes, Gavril, I know. But these things cannot be forced. You will have to trust Iybae to direct their hearts."

"Aah," Gavril grunted, waving his hand. "Iybae is too slow."

Moria laughed. "Iybae's timing is perfect, Gavril. You are impatient." She floated down to the great hall, landing daintily in front of Armond as he strode toward the war room.

* * * * *

"What the…" Armond jumped back in surprise.

Moria grinned up at him. "Oops, sorry about that. I wasn't paying attention."

Armond blinked at the woman but couldn't seem to find his voice. Her eyes glittered and sparkled joyfully at him, enchanting him. She was a faerie. He'd never in his life laid eyes on a faerie and he found himself wondering if they were all as dazzling as she. She was small and fair. The top of her lovely head barely reached the middle of his chest. Her hair was frosty white, cascading like sparkling diamonds down her slender back. Her mouth was small and full, plump, luscious. He was mesmerized; she was the most beautiful thing he'd ever seen.

She held out a small hand in greeting. "I'm Moria, Miss Cynthia's assistant."

Armond took her hand and held it like it was a priceless treasure. So warm, fine and silky, he thought as his thumb stroked the back of her hand between her thumb and forefinger.

"Umm," she began, her voice softer now. "May I ask who you might be?"

He lifted his gaze and lost himself in her fathomless eyes.

"Forgive me," he croaked, then cleared his throat. "I'm Armond. You're a faerie."

Moria smiled and Armond felt the smile warm him from head to toe. "Yes, I am."

"I've never met a faerie before. I'm fortunate to have met you." He was spellbound and couldn't seem to form a reasonable thought.

Her smile spread into a grin and his chest tightened, as did his pants. "Armond, the rumors that we bring good luck are just a lot of fluff. I hope you're not disappointed."

Armond felt his luck had definitely changed for the better. The corner of his mouth twitched. "Never."

There had been something he was in a hurry to do but he couldn't recall what it was at the moment. She had him feeling drunk. He lifted Moria's hand and kissed it, never taking his gaze from hers. Moria's smile faltered and her violet eyes deepened ever so slightly; even so, Armond noticed it. His blood heated in his veins as his mind filled with visions of those eyes darkening with passion and that ivory skin flushed with arousal under his hands. "Mistress Moria, I hope we will meet again."

"I'm very sure we will, sir," she said quietly.

"Please, call me Armond. Till our next meeting." He kissed her hand again before he released it and hurriedly strode to the war room.

Chapter Nineteen

Alone now, Draven sat in his room, his head in his hands and elbows on the desk. Draven remembered little Linea. The one and only time he'd ever seen her was brief. She had been about five cycles old. She'd been reserved, sad and eerily quiet for a child her age. He had barely noticed her, being that he was a young man of sixteen then and just finishing his education. His heart had been filled with excitement and he looked forward to training with his father and the other warriors.

Did Orbane put those marks on her? Did he break her ribs, cut her up? It had to have been him or he had someone else do it. That nagging sense of something sinister surrounding her; he understood it now. Nausea gnawed at his insides. Knowing her uncle was responsible added to the horror of the brutality she'd endured.

He looked up at the fierce image of his father. Rayne was known for his wisdom and evenhandedness in addition to his brutality. Draven had to believe that he would never have turned Linea over to Orbane had he known this would happen to her. Why didn't she just tell him who she was? She was safe here; he would never let Orbane near her again.

Mason knocked twice, swung open the door, walked into the room and dropped into a chair across from him. Draven leaned back. The hard look he gave Mason did nothing to warn him against his usual clever banter.

"Just passed Armond in the great hall chatting with the pretty faerie." Mason motioned behind him with his thumb. "Looked like he'd swallowed a gnat. I think the boy is smitten."

The corner of Draven's mouth lifted and his brows furrowed. "Armond doesn't get smitten. Since I've known him women of every size, shape and beauty have thrown themselves at his feet. He's never given them so much as a second glance. The man is made of stone."

"Perhaps he fancies boys."

"You know better than that. He's had a few affairs. They just never seemed to grab his heart."

"Well, from the look on his face I'd guess that little package out there has grabbed something…looked like maybe his balls."

Draven cut him a glance. "Moria? She's no 'package', Mason. She's a faerie and you will show her respect."

"Yeah, yeah, sorry. She may be fae but she's still female, and a fine one. Now about that female you're going to chain yourself to," Mason muttered. "She is one tender little morsel."

Draven arched a brow. There was an emotion there. Mason was struggling to hide it but Draven felt it, a ribbon of something serious, some truth woven in and out of Mason's playful taunting. "Miss Cynthia?" he asked.

Mason closed his eyes and breathed deeply. "I can still smell her sweet scent."

Draven's brows lowered, as did his voice. "You should have sniffed her 'sweet scent' on her last visit. She could conquer all of Lanthor with that deadly stench."

Mason crossed his arms. "Discord this soon, Draven, is not a good sign."

Laying his head back and feigning exasperation, Draven closed his eyes, sighed heavily and focused on his friend's inner turmoil. "Yes, Mason, I know. I'm hoping that over the years we can develop a fond affection for each other."

It was the truth. He tolerated Cynthia. He didn't hate her, far from it. He had no strong feelings for her whatsoever. It seemed his cousin did not share his opinion of the lovely widow. It gave him a sense of dread.

"Damn, now that is dismal." Mason sat straighter and stared at his cousin.

"Hmm," Draven grunted, feigning indifference.

"I'll tell you what." Mason sat forward, his blue eyes dancing. Draven slanted him a wary look. "I'll bed the little rosebud for you so you won't have to suffer your husbandly duty." Mason inhaled sharply, his voice dropping an octave. "I would take on this tedious task only for you, Draven." He paused for effect. "I would sacrifice my virginity on the altar of this woman's bed."

Draven snorted as he sat up and speared Mason with a steely gaze, then rolled his eyes. "Are you never serious?"

Mason gave Draven an incredulous look. "No. Not if I can help it."

Draven couldn't help but smile. "Poor Miss Cynthia. She'd never live through a night with you. You'd scare her senseless with your insatiable appetites."

Mason seemed to look through him. "I would love to test that theory," he said on a moan. "She has the body of a goddess and there's fire in those doe eyes."

Draven was sure of it now. Armond was not the only one smitten. This was not a good thing, not good at all. His smile melted and his gaze hardened as he watched his cousin. He picked up the strand of desire. It seemed to flare and bank as Mason tried to hide it.

Draven deliberately goaded Mason. "She has the body of a child, Mason, and her eyes are brown. They make you think of things like," his voice took on an edge as he waved his hand in dismissal, "wood, cows, dirt."

Mason looked shocked, honestly offended. He *was* offended; Draven acknowledged the emotion slowly burning through Mason.

"You obviously haven't been looking at her body, friend, and her eyes are intoxicating," Mason objected. "They make you think of hot coffee, dark and rich, or lying by the fire, naked, on warm fur. Melted chocolate, poured all over her small round bottom and…"

"Ah, I get the picture, Mason." Draven's frown deepened as he searched Mason's face. It was a mask and that was unnerving. He paused and lifted a brow. "Cynthia is to be queen—my wife. Although I'm sure you're being your typical roguish self, be careful that you don't step over the line."

Draven watched Mason war with the emotions fighting within him. His strong mouth was a straight line. His ice blue eyes were narrowed and the muscle in his jaw twitched. This new emotion in Mason was cause for concern. He was not only Draven's family but also his closest friend. He trusted Mason. No, Draven could not believe Mason would risk that relationship, nor would he risk his head for cuckolding the king. Not even for Cynthia's chocolate-drenched ass.

"Yes, my lord." His voice dripped in sarcasm. "I'll try to keep my lust to myself."

"It would be best if you didn't lust after her at all." Draven lifted the corner of his mouth. "Did you come in here for anything specific?"

"Yes."

"Well?" Draven was nearing the limit of his patience.

Mason's face finally took on a more solemn expression. "I heard about the girl. I was wondering what you planned to do."

Draven nodded. "I'm thinking about it. I don't want Orbane to know she's here; however, I don't trust her."

Draven heard another knock on the door; this time the one who knocked waited for an invitation.

"Come," Draven said firmly.

Armond stepped in. "I just wanted to inform you that the perimeter patrol has been set up." He gestured to the seat beside Mason and Draven nodded.

Armond nodded a greeting to Mason, who waggled his brows at him. Armond lifted a brow questioningly then met Draven's gaze. "Why is Haig Orbane so intent on your demise?"

"Imagined sins of the father, I suppose," Draven answered, frowning.

"Want me to explain?" Mason spoke quietly.

Draven sighed deeply, pinching the bridge of his nose. "It's a long ugly story, Armond."

"I have time." Armond sat and crossed his ankle over his knee. "And I'm not afraid of ugly."

Mason had something edgy to say on the tip of his tongue. Draven's glare had him swallowing it and slouching back into his seat with a crooked smile.

Draven sat forward. "King Willum Orbane was a foul man and a cursed ruler, as you well know. He chose to marry Allegra Zandorn, much to her family's horror. They knew, however, not to cross the king. They knew one way or another he would have Allegra, so they gave her to him.

"Allegra endured Willum's perverse attentions, his imbalanced temper and his sadistic abuse until finally, she bore him a son. Haig Orbane was a delight to Willum and the only person he ever loved. If a madman can love." Draven paused and looked up again at his father's snarling two-dimensional face.

"My father was known throughout the land as a powerful warlord, intense but honorable. You know of Willum's reign, the laws and taxes he imposed, the atrocities he subjected his people to. Not to mention his alliance with the Council. As you know the origin of the Council is a mystery. Some say they have a pact with Asmodeus. Some say they're harmless. Either way, the Council was founded by Orbane."

"Yes, I've heard the stories," Armond said quietly. "Horrendous."

Mason nodded.

"Many saw my father as the only one who could free them from Willum's legacy of death. Father began holding secret meetings and using trusted messengers, and it wasn't long before he had gathered to him an army of warlords, country men, mages, elves, faeries, gnolls...anyone who was willing to sacrifice himself to free the land from Orbane's rule. Willum didn't fight fair; however, no one expected him to. The battle was long and bloody. Many men died. Women and children were massacred." Draven looked away from the men seated across from him. He hated thinking of this part of history, much less telling anyone. "My mother, Grace, was captured. They wanted to get at my father, you understand."

Mason held his gaze. "You want me to tell him? Or you don't have to tell him at all."

"Yes, Draven, it's all right. I don't mean to push," Armond said.

"No, I'll tell him," Draven interrupted hoarsely. "It's not something I want to remember, Mason, but it's something I never want to forget." He leaned back into his chair stiffly. "I had just been born. I'm told it had been a difficult birth. I was a large baby and though she was a tall, strong woman she was quite slender, small-boned, willowy. She was in bed, recovering. My father had been called away to the fight.

"They came while he was gone in the middle of the night and took her, leaving several of the work staff dead. Netta had hidden in a wardrobe with me; her husband, Javan, had put her in there when he heard them breaking down the door. Javan died defending us." He took a deep breath. "When Rayne finally found Grace, she was dead. Willum had beaten her savagely and shared her with his men. They raped her, repeatedly. She was torn and battered, her body bloody and broken."

Draven thought of Linea the night he found her and clenched his teeth. "My father couldn't be stopped after that. He literally fought day and night, killing all that stood between him and Willum. When he finally found him, he hung Willum from a tree in the middle of town.

From around his chest, not his neck. He cut him up a piece at a time. Willum screamed, cried, begged. Each piece he threw to his wolfdogs; they devoured him while he looked on in agony."

"Willum would pass out from time to time and Rayne would have to work to wake him up again," Mason said with a grimace.

Draven glanced up at Mason then continued. "The people of Lanthor watched in terror and revulsion, and so did Willum's son, Haig. He was seven cycles old at the time. People say that Allegra was there as well and that she never looked away nor shed a tear."

"So now Orbane wants you to pay?" Armond asked.

"Yes. Orbane has a warped sense of righteousness, sins of the father and all that. I think, more importantly, he wants the throne back. Allegra went on to marry a good man, Danner Vallen, and they had Kenna, Orbane's half-sister. Orbane and Kenna never really grew up together. Orbane went to live with Willum's family because as he got older he became unruly."

"I see. Kenna is Linea's mother, correct?" Armond deduced.

"Yes. Kenna married Victor Wyndham, a close friend of my father's."

"And they were killed in a house fire," Mason added.

"Victor got Linea out and went back to get Kenna but they never made it out." Draven thought back. Rayne had insisted Draven accompany him to the entombment of his friends, Victor and Kenna Wyndham. He remembered seeing Linea then, trying to block her. The pain, fear and sadness in her had been unbelievable.

He had thought her pretty standing there in her gray dress, white lace shawl around her shoulders. Her hands were clasped in front of her; a long thick braid hung down her back, wisps of black and copper-colored strands blew across her face. Her unblinking eyes had been devoid of expression. No tears stained her cheeks. She'd been so heartbreakingly quiet, so still.

Haig Orbane had stood beside her, his hand on her shoulder, staring at Rayne. Draven had sensed violent hatred spearing from him like jagged shards of ice. He had felt the cold as if it pierced his flesh and nicked his bones.

How could he have missed that the woman upstairs who claimed to be Joan was actually Linea? It was obvious to him now. She still had that lost, hollow look in her eyes. She still carried the incredible pain, fear and sadness inside her. He'd felt it; even sitting there in his war room he felt it.

"Will you release Linea now?" Armond asked softly. Mason looked at him, wondering how he would respond.

"No. I doubt she's any threat, but I can't be sure, now more than ever. She's Orbane's niece and it is obvious Orbane is formulating an uprising. Either way, she's safer here."

He had gotten too close. Now he wanted her safe, protected, and he wanted to bed her. He wanted her with such passion that he had betrayed his betrothed. No matter what argument he used to try to justify his actions, he had betrayed Cynthia. And all the while Linea could have been plotting with her uncle. Gaining any information she could in order to forward Orbane's cause. No, he didn't believe that, either. If she was spying it was because he forced her, threatened her. But, nothing was ever as it seemed. Only a fool would take anything or anyone at face value.

Chapter Twenty

Linea stood at the window nibbling at her bottom lip. The day was dreary and gray under a thick blanket of ominous clouds. She felt edgy; something stirred inside her she didn't understand. So many strange things had happened since she was brought here.

There was a change in Lord Amaranth. She didn't know how she felt it but there it was. Perhaps she was still a bit weak from what had happened the night before. She'd cried and cried and finally fell asleep, feeling drained and pathetic—and what did it accomplish? She wrapped her arms around herself.

Netta bustled into the room, red-faced and flustered, with a tray of food in her hands and fresh linens tossed over her shoulder.

"Thank you, dear," she mumbled as Linea took the tray from her and she began stripping the bedclothes.

"Netta, I can do that," Linea said, setting the tray on the dressing table.

"No, no," Netta said without looking up from her task. "I'm just a bit harried today with preparations for Sir Orbane's arrival."

Linea felt as though every ounce of blood drained from her body. She held her breath, trying not to heave. Uncle Haig was coming for her. Her mind raced as she tried to push down the fear. She had to keep her thoughts quiet so Lord Amaranth wouldn't know them. *How do you hide your mind?* She thought with frustration.

"Are you all right, dear?" Netta stared at her curiously. "You've gone pale."

"I'm fine, just a bit hungry I guess." Linea resisted the panic seething in her stomach. "Go, Netta, and finish your chores." She sounded a bit frantic as she tugged gently at the clean bed sheet in Netta's hands. "I'm desperate for something to do. Let me take care of this."

"All right," Netta relented. "But eat your noon meal first. I'll be back in a while to check on you."

Linea couldn't speak and merely nodded. Netta patted her cheek, turned and left the room.

There was no other choice, she must move now. Linea waited a moment, listening; her pounding heart seemed deafening. She slowly moved to the door and cracked it open only a sliver. As far as she could tell the balcony was empty except for the guard who appeared to be daydreaming. No voices came from the great hall so she slipped back into the room silently.

Grabbing the crystal glass of juice from the tray, she lifted it and drank as quickly as she could then set it down again. She wrapped her right hand with the sheet and picked up the glass. Gritting her teeth she slammed the glass to the floor and at the same time smashed the windowpane.

"What the hell?" She heard the guard's exclamation and the legs of his chair scrape the floor. She yanked the drapes closed just as he swung open the door and stepped in. His bulk seemed to fill the room and she clenched her teeth against the fear that rose inside her.

Linea stood over the shattered glass, frowning, hands behind her back. "I'm sorry, it slipped from my hand. Lead crystal sounds awful when it breaks, doesn't it?"

He looked at her suspiciously. "I'll send for someone to clean this up."

"No, no, everyone's busy. It's my mess; I'll clean it up. I was just clumsy."

He continued to stare and, for a moment, Linea thought he might not leave. Finally he turned with a grunt and left, closing the door behind him.

Linea whirled around and swept the drapes away from the window. Gently she plucked away the jagged pieces of glass from the edges of the frame and laid them quietly on the tray. She halted when she heard voices below. Looking down, she watched the two women walking along the path until they disappeared around the corner. It wasn't far from the outer wall of the keep. The dreary day would provide her with more hiding places. Her heart leapt with hope. She'd just have to keep focus, no matter what. She reached down, pulled her skirt tail between her legs and tucked it into her waistband. Carefully she stepped through the narrow opening of the broken window onto the ledge.

Suddenly, she wasn't afraid. Her fear had been swallowed by fierce determination and anticipation of the freedom she so longed for. Facing the rough keep wall she clung to the window ledge, looked down to plot her decent, took a deep breath and stepped out onto the first protruding stone.

Even with the cool breeze, sweat beaded on her forehead. She wasn't going fast enough; she could hear the women coming back. Leaning as close to the wall as she could, she gripped the stones with all her might.

"...too spoiled to be queen," one woman was saying.

"Aye, and if ya wanna know what I think, she'll never satisfy a man like Lord Amaranth."

Linea held still. Her fingers began to ache. She gritted her teeth and closed her eyes, praying the women would quit their gossip and speed their pace.

"Ah, but I don't know, Mary. Didja see the way she eyed Lord Mason earlier? She looked as though she'd like to take a chunk out of his arse."

"Aye, and he didn't look like he'd mind at all barin' it!" The woman named Mary chuckled.

The women laughed, their voices fading as they entered the keep.

Linea grappled with the rough protruding stones of the wall the rest of the way down and then jumped to the ground, careful to favor her healing ankle. It was then she realized she didn't have her medallion. When she had left her uncle's house she had meant to go to Ingvar, where the faeries live. Angus told her that if she showed them her medallion, they would offer her sanctuary there. She pressed her lips together. She'd just have to take her chances, plead with the faeries and hope for the best.

She could smell wood smoke and hear male voices only a short distance from where she stood. She raced as fast as she could to hide in the shadows along the wall surrounding the keep. Pressing herself against the wall she looked up. Creator save her, she'd miscalculated. The wall was too tall to scale and the uneven stones didn't jut out as those in the keep.

Closing her eyes she focused on staying calm. Careful to stay in the shadows she moved around the wall until she was facing the front courtyard of the keep. Most of the men stood in the middle talking but two stood at the gate. She thought fast, trying to devise a way to get past them.

The men in the middle began to spread out, each taking a different direction around the keep. Two men were heading her direction, where she'd just come from. Silently she continued to ease toward the stables as the two warriors walked away from where she stood.

The window at the rear of the stables was open. She turned over a bucket sitting there and stood on it to peer in. It seemed deserted of everyone but the horses, who all turned to look at her curiously. "Hello," she whispered.

They all nodded their regal heads but there were no soft whinnies or neighs. Pulling herself up through the window, she dropped silently into a soft pile of hay. Calmness washed over her and she felt strangely welcome. She stood, brushing the hay from her clothes. Slowly she walked by the horses, rubbing their noses as she passed.

The mare in the last stall blinked at her and pawed the ground. She walked to the beautiful chestnut horse and stroked its blonde mane. The horse nuzzled Linea's shoulder. The mare was offering itself in service. How Linea knew that, she didn't know, but she was so tempted to take the mare with her.

Such a strong, beautiful animal would be swift. She had never had a horse or had even been this close to one. She'd never been near an animal of any kind, save for Aletha and Rolf. Uncle Haig had kept her sheltered, separated from everything.

She had never ridden a horse and her inexperience could cause her to get seriously hurt or worse, endanger the horse. She rubbed the mare's cheek and kissed her nose, thanking her. In addition to that, she was more likely to be noticed. No, stealing the horse would not be wise.

Staying close to the wall, she inched quietly to the edge of the stable doors. The horses watched her but remained silent. She felt their good will and it bolstered her confidence. Standing in the shadows, she watched the two men who stood at the great iron gates of the keep wall.

One of the men laughed and struck the other on the shoulder then walked away. For some time, Linea watched the warrior who remained. He rocked back and forth on his heels, rubbing his hands together, his sword in its scabbard.

She moved closer to the opening and her hand ran across a loose board. An idea took shape in her mind. It might work but she hated having to cause someone pain. She bit her bottom lip. *It couldn't be helped*, she thought as she pulled the board free.

Sending a prayer to Iybae that the blow wouldn't hurt the warrior too badly, and at the same time hoping Iybae was still hearing her prayers, she bounded forward, darting in and out of the shadows and around the trees on silent feet. She scurried closer, her body hugging the wall.

She watched the big man, waiting for him to turn his back. When he did she took a deep breath. Holding the board with both hands, she swung back and smacked the warrior on the back of the head as hard as she could. He grunted, reached up to touch the back of his head and fell to his knees. She stood there panting, waiting, set to run. He swayed for a moment before he fell over with a thud.

"I'm so sorry," she whispered on a sob and then darted through the gate and across the field to disappear into the forest.

* * * * *

Draven walked out of the war room and nearly tripped over Gavril. "How in three hells do you keep escaping?" Draven shouted.

"Linea has run away!" Gavril's eyes were urgent as he reached up to stop Draven.

"How do you know?" he asked, his expression darkening.

"I just know," Gavril said. "You're wasting time!"

Draven's eyes narrowed. "I would have felt something."

Gavril gave him a derisive smirk. "You really are impressed with yourself, aren't you? You regal types, you're all alike." He lifted his little arms in supplication. "Dear Iybae, why did it have to be him?"

Draven growled. "I have no time for your asinine games, elf."

"Go! Check then, you insipid oaf!!" Gavril screamed, pointing up the stairs.

Draven snatched the elf by the collar and dragged him up the steps with him. He slammed open Linea's door and stood, taking in the broken glass and the empty window frame in stunned silence.

"She blocked me. The impertinent little wench blocked me. Damn her!" Draven seethed. He should have guessed, he thought, should have never underestimated her power.

"Would you please let me down?" Gavril wheezed.

Draven looked down at the elf he held like a sack of turnips. Swinging him upward, Draven caught Gavril by his shoulders and shook him. "How did you know?"

Gavril's head bobbed on his shoulders and his teeth rattled.

"I said, how did you know?" Draven yelled.

"You're surely not that stupid," Gavril hissed.

Draven pulled him close till they touched noses and Gavril's violet eyes crossed. "Where is she headed? And you'd better tell me true, elf, or I'll have you strapped to a plow for the rest of your miserable little life."

Gavril went still. "She'll be heading to Ingvar."

He shook him hard. "You lie! No one goes to Ingvar without sanction. The faeries will only terminate her."

"She has sanction, you idiot. She has her mother's medallion."

"The medallion." Draven frowned looking away from Gavril. "She doesn't have the medallion."

Gavril shook his head. "No matter, they'll know who she is. They will give her sanctuary even from you."

"You have turned on the one to whom you swore fealty. You are shameful, even for an elf. You dishonor yourself."

Gavril met Draven's gaze and Draven saw something in his eyes he never expected. Wisdom. "I think you're projecting your own sin onto me, Lord Amaranth. I do what I do out of my fealty and love for her and when you see past your own deficient understanding you will show me gratitude. Now put me the hell down and go find her, you ignorant cretin."

Draven snarled and dropped Gavril on his rear. Reining in his temper, Draven faced the shocked guard and ordered that he chain himself to the elf. "If he's not here when I return, I'll have your head."

Draven turned before the big warrior could answer and bolted down the steps to where Mason and Armond waited with stoic expressions. Two men stumbled through the huge heavy doors of the keep, one supporting the other, who moaned and rubbed the back of his head.

Draven felt the sharp headache and the nausea. "What's this?"

"Halvar has been assaulted, my lord!" Arkin, the warrior supporting Halvar said, a hint of anxiety apparent in his voice.

"I'll live," Halvar said. "Iybae willing, long enough to thwart this villain."

Draven slapped a hand on his shoulder and absorbed the man's pain, gritting his teeth as it flowed through him and dissipated. "There will be nothing left to thwart, Halvar, once I am done with her."

"Her?" Halvar met Draven's gaze, dismay filling his eyes. Arkin stifled a chuckle. "Shut it!" Halvar snapped.

Draven turned to Mason, who surprisingly wore a sober expression. "Stay here, and be alert. If I'm not back before tomorrow evening, make up some excuse to Orbane but keep him here. Cynthia's blasted party is tomorrow evening as well," he said, cursing under his breath. "Go ahead with it. Keep her entertained. I'm counting on you, Mason."

Mason nodded. "Be at peace, cousin. All will be well here."

Draven glanced at Armond. "You're with me." Then he looked at Halvar and Arkin. "Are you well enough to ride with me?"

Halvar gave Draven an odd look. "Yes, my lord. Strangely, I feel quite fit now."

"Good." Draven was already heading for the stables. The three warriors hurried to catch up with him.

Chapter Twenty-One

The throbbing ache in Linea's ankle had increased. It felt as though her bone was splintering each time her foot hit the ground, but she couldn't think about that, couldn't stop running. The darkness slowly deepened, making it hard for her to see through the thick foliage. She'd lost track of time, fought the panic and hoped that it was night falling and not increasing bad weather. She watched for flashes of lightning, listened for the rumble of thunder.

Her ears had grown accustomed to the sounds of the birds crying, the various songs of the insects and her own pounding heartbeat. The occasional wail of a wolfdog should have made her cringe. A wolfdog could bring her down in one fell swoop, rip her apart and devour her. Instead of filling her with terror, though, the sound sustained her. She shoved the pain aside as she propelled her body forward and focused her mind on running.

Not sure how far away Ingvar was, Linea knew she would need to rest eventually. She'd never make it over the mountain ridge if she didn't. Vines and branches tore at her clothing, slapping and scraping her skin just as desperation clawed at her heart. Her arms and hands, feet and face, had already gone numb from the cold. Her lungs burned and the screaming pain in her ribs was slowing her down. Her body was beginning to rebel, shut down, as her mind filled with visions of Lord Amaranth.

She imagined his long strong fingers wrapped around her throat, cutting off her breath, her life. She imagined them massaging her swelling breasts, his mouth closing over hers. Linea wanted to scream with the frustration. She was going crazy. She was finally losing her mind, she decided.

She stopped and leaned against an old tree as she fought to catch her breath. She laid her head back against the wide smooth trunk, trying to see the sky through the canopy of leaves. The stately tree was full and lush, its branches thick, protective, beautiful.

She swayed on her feet, a bit lightheaded from fatigue. She was tired, so very tired, bone weary. She slid carefully down to the thick moss ground covering, wincing at the various pains traveling through her. They seemed to meet and merge into one sharp ache as she stretched her legs out in front of her. Her stomach growled and she tried to swallow, but her throat was dry.

A sigh escaped her lips, or was it a whimper? Tears burned the back of her eyes and she clenched her teeth in a battle to keep them unshed. She'd been through worse than this and never shed a tear. She scrubbed her hands over her face and clenched her teeth. Tears did nothing but give her a headache and self-pity was counterproductive, she reminded herself tersely. She had only to wait in the sheltering shadows of the tree. Soon Lord Amaranth would give up on finding her and turn back. The cry of a wolf and the responding call of his mate were strangely soothing to her.

Her eyes drifted closed and she blinked them open wide again. She picked at a short tattered fingernail and reminded herself that she had to stay awake. An hour or two of rest then she'd have to continue on, but she couldn't give in to sleep. She had to keep trying to block him out. He would have her if he could find her consciousness...her soul. His dark image floated through her mind again. A tremble vibrated through her body as she tried to block him out. She wrapped her arms around her stomach. Her breathing had steadied, the pain was a more tolerable throb and she didn't feel quite so cold.

She focused her thoughts on Ingvar and the faerie people. She could find her place there, her purpose. Iybae had to have a plan for her, surely He did not mean for her to be a part of the Kyrok's plan. If He had, wouldn't He have made human women more receptive physically for a Kyrok? Wouldn't He have declared it so through the prophets or the holy men?

Maybe He had and she just wasn't told of it. No. She had to believe He could make a way for her in Ingvar. She would believe. She focused on dreamy thoughts—of warm sun on her face, the sound of laughter. It was all that gave her hope now, it was the only peace she had. It wasn't long till she gave in to the lull of the forest music.

* * * * *

The men rode hard and for as long as they could before the forest became too dense to ride through easily. Draven lifted a hand to stop them, dismounted and smoothed a hand over the great stallion's sleek black neck. The forbidding sternness of his voice had the warriors swallowing their objections to staying behind. Regardless of how they felt, Draven was not willing to risk his horse and theirs traipsing through the gnarled and sometimes thorny vines that tangled along the forest floor.

An awareness of having been through this before only irritated him. He sensed the men waiting behind him as he trudged through the thick undergrowth. This time he knew what he was up against and had his sword drawn. He felt their irritation, their impatience and their unwavering faith in him.

In Halvar he felt embarrassment and anger as well. The damned little fool had hurt the big warrior's pride. Halvar would want a chance to right that, which only made Draven angrier with her. By all rights he owed Halvar retribution but knew he couldn't give him the honor and that would cause problems. He'd have to set rest to it somehow; it would definitely take some deliberating and creative reasoning.

He remembered her stabbing desperation and the sting of fear; however, they did nothing to diminish his fury. His fury did nothing to diminish his lust. The girl was a contradiction of virginal purity and taunting temptress. She'd driven him nearly mad with her timid explorations. He couldn't blot out the memory of how she felt beneath him, the look of ecstasy on her beautiful face, her body hot, her sex dripping with arousal, saturating his hand as he brought her to her peak.

Now that he knew her name and where she came from, he knew her less. He thought of the night he found her, broken and so full of fear. His heart contracted, remembering the pain he'd taken from her. He had believed her either a helpless waif who suffered god-awful atrocities at the hands of her own kinsman, or a devious spy, loyal to the maniacal Haig Orbane. Or was she threatened? Did her uncle threaten her if she didn't do as he said? He shook his head, bared his teeth. He would not let his cursed "gift" or his own carnal desire keep him from performing his rightful duties as king. He would not risk his people, his country.

He was close now, so close to her he could feel her inside him. He pushed aside the wave of relief and smirked to himself. She had tried to block him. He had felt her struggle, but her pitiful attempts had failed.

She didn't seem to realize her failure; she was too tired, her mind too cluttered with pain. He cursed softly. The pain she felt now, even in her shallow sleep, was her own fault, he reminded himself. If she hadn't run from him then she wouldn't be in pain.

He could feel her like he felt his own heartbeat. Halting abruptly, he stood, scanning the surrounding area until his gaze found her slumped against a tree sleeping. He sheathed his sword and quietly crouched in front of her, fighting his desire to pull her into his arms. Though the night was warm, Linea was cold and shivering. The pale blue dress she wore was thin and torn from her escape. Her arms, wrapped tightly around her, were covered with goose bumps and angry scratches.

"Hello, Linea," he growled. Her body jerked, her eyes blinked open and fastened on his. Her terror slammed into him like sharp ragged points.

"No," she breathed. She pressed herself back tightly against the tree, pulled her knees up to her chest and shook her head vigorously.

He set his mind firmly against his protective instinct. It was too late for compassion now. "It's over now. Get up."

He grabbed her arm and jerked her up. He ignored the fiery pain that tore though her body at his rough treatment. She didn't cry out at the pain he'd inflicted and the fact that her firm husky voice held no plea or whimper shocked him. It occurred to him that never had she uttered a cry, neither from pain nor pleasure.

She pressed her lips together and met his infuriated gaze with one of her own. "I'm of no consequence to you, Lord Amaranth. Let go of me." She tried twisting away from him in vain.

He narrowed his eyes and his voice took on an edge. "If you believe that, sweetness, you're not paying attention."

His hands gripped her shoulders and her breath hitched as he pulled her toward him. Looking into her fathomless eyes, feeling the very essence of her spirit blooming inside had him grinding his teeth against the desire to take her, right there in the cooling, damp forest and set her trembling stiff body ablaze with her need for him. He knew he could. Her body had called to his with a wanton eagerness that plagued him. That she had no comprehension of the heat in her own body only made his lust for her worse.

Anything could have happened to her. Orbane could have found her, or worse, a Kyrok. Fury broke free and coursed through him with uncontrollable speed. She stood defiant, her body rigid, her anger, her dogged defiance, radiating into him with a dynamic force mingling with his own spinning into a vortex within him.

Linea's eyes widened as her mind was flooded with his thoughts. She knew his mind and body were in agreement. The force of his need began surging through her, heating her, demanding. He knew what he was doing but didn't want to stop. The feminine flesh between her thighs felt as though it was melting. A groan, low and lustful, escaped his throat as he felt her swell, her vagina flood with a hot slickness, the core of her savagely clenching and pulsing.

Filled with a craving she couldn't control, her lust mingled with a fury that grew and spiraled faster and stronger. It became a heaving thing, growing within him. Her swirling anger, her white-hot hunger, seemed to entwine with his frenzied need and rage. His eyes narrowed as her emotions seemed to mirror his own. She trembled, her hands clinging to him, and he sucked air in through his teeth.

"Focus!" He heard her mental scream as she closed her eyes and her head dropped back. Tears trailed down her cheeks and over her parted lips as she panted for breath and held on. The energy of their combined emotions, the sensations, seemed to take on life, twisting and twirling in a sultry dance until they both felt it being pulled from deep inside of her, snaking out from her to slam into him.

He suddenly shoved her away and she fell back onto the forest floor with a jolt and scooted away from him. She collapsed weakly against an ancient tree, her body throbbing, still somehow connected to his. The surge of power drove him as he withdrew his sword and a roar erupted from deep inside him. He glowed with it as he lifted the heavy sword in both hands.

Linea's mouth dropped open; her eyes were huge, round, turbulent, cobalt pools of wild panic. He spun away from her and swung, burying the blade into a mighty Nako tree. The force of impact sang up his arms as the energy flowed through him and into his weapon. It was a fantastic feeling, as it had been before. He was stunned at the awesome power he suddenly possessed. With a mighty jerk he freed his sword.

The thick tree groaned and crackled. Draven shoved it with his shoulder and watched in amazement as it fell with a loud crash. What in the hell was happening? His body shuddered with unspent energy. Although his muscles were heavy and tense, he felt light and unburdened, ready to fight a war single-handedly. It had come from her—the power; it had come from him and her. He turned and glowered down at her. Her eyes were round and full of raw fear. His mind was swirling with questions as he strode toward her, his body raging with potent energy.

Chapter Twenty-Two

"Don't," she whispered, her attempts to scramble backward thwarted by the wide tree behind her. Still she trembled with the aftereffects of the power surge, just as she had last time. Now he would be convinced that she was a sorceress, a demon, and it made her sick to think that perhaps he would be right. He reached for her and pulled her body against his. She could feel every inch of him hard against her. His chest crushed her breasts. His solid muscular thigh pushed between hers, the steely length of his thick cock pressed greedily at her stomach.

"Stop!" She snarled like a wild cat and pushed against his chest with the palms of her hands, tossing her head from side to side, fighting in spite of the terrible fear that raked her insides. She twisted her body and bucked, kicked and stomped at his feet, pulled and pushed, clawed at his sinewy arms, and still he held her to him as though she were weightless. Her strength was trivial to him. All the strength she had he had taken from her and now he used it against her. He left her feeling drained and so afraid.

"What are you doing to me, Linea?" His question felt like a caress.

Out of breath and hope she collapsed weakly against him, panting. "I could ask you the same thing, Lord Amaranth."

The cool damp air felt like fire ripping through her lungs. Tears simmered right under the surface. She felt them there, beneath her boiling frustration and anger. And she felt him. She clenched her teeth and swallowed, meeting his dark dusky gaze boldly.

"I will know the truth," he promised, his gaze never leaving hers.

He had merely to take her; she wasn't foolish enough to believe she could hold him off and she wasn't sure she wanted to. Her traitorous body screamed for his touch. Her lust was like a rabid dog snapping at her. She wanted to kill him with her bare hands. She wanted to taste him, feel him surrounding her until there was nothing but him in her world.

"Do not hold me against my will, sire," she murmured against his chest. She felt intoxicated and achy. "If you wish to kill me, I beg you to be about it." Her voice sounded foreign to her, hoarse and deep. She pushed away from him shakily. "I will not submit to you willingly, no matter the cost, and I will not go back to him or to anyone with whom he wishes me to breed!" The crescendo of her ragged scream echoed through the forest, briefly silencing the wildlife.

The king's long fingers bit into her waist. She gasped. Bracing herself, she waiting for the mind-numbing blow but it didn't come. She felt dizzy and his face blurred for a moment. She blinked until he came back into focus and wished she'd allowed herself to pass out. His countenance was dark under deeply furrowed brows.

Their dilated pupils made his eyes appear black, ringed with silver. His nostrils flared, lips pressed together, jaw clenched. She felt mesmerized by his frightening beauty, the intensity of his rage and his passion. Taste—she wanted to taste, he wanted to taste. She was losing herself in him.

His teeth bared; he looked like a bloodthirsty wolfdog. "You forget. I know your mind, Linea. I know your hunger." He cupped her chin in his hand. His thumb brushed over her bottom lip as he lowered his head. "If I wish you to surrender to me, you will surrender."

"I...I'll kill you first," she swore roughly. Her heart thumped angrily against her sore ribs. The words were out before she could help herself. The anger was too great, the need too raw. She couldn't think. She wanted to give in to him, let him take her wherever, however, he willed and yet she fought. Her body was raging with heat, her strength returning. She felt aggressive, as though the blood that ran through her veins had been replaced by molten steel, like the hot steel of Lord Amaranth's eyes.

She reached up with her free hand and clutched at the hand that held her face. Locking her gaze with his, she clenched her teeth and drove her knee upward but the king was too quick and turned slightly, catching the blow at his hip. She felt the impact reverberate through her own hip and swallowed a cry. He took advantage of her disorientation and grabbed her wrists and held them in an iron-tight grip.

"You hotheaded little wench!" he growled. She fought to pull her arms free from his grasp. He twisted her around and yanked her back against his chest.

Her breath soughed painfully in and out of her lungs. The hardness of his body pressed against her back; his breathing was labored. Evidence of his lust pressed against her bottom. She closed her eyes and clenched her teeth, fighting the desire to tilt her hips back and rub herself against the long thick ridge of his erection. Her mind filled with the wonder of how it felt to have that bulging rod move against the slick cleft between her legs. The memories of their encounter days ago had her body shaking with the effort to keep still.

"Oh sweet hell! How much more can I endure?" Draven groaned.

"You aren't the one being manhandled." Linea grimaced at the breathless quiver in her voice.

Draven's body stiffened and he spun her around to search her face. His expression was hard, his eyes bright and clear. "You have insulted and disrespected a warrior of high standing. You have defied me, your king, and as absurd as it sounds you have threatened my life. Do you expect to be pardoned so easily for this? After I've been nothing but gracious to you? I should have your head!"

"If you truly mean to have my head, I wish you would quit your dawdling and have it! You, you…jackass!" Shocked at her own words, Linea flinched and prepared again for a blow that did not come. It seemed she was always waiting for a blow that never came, even when she had struck him. She was so tired of being confused. Her head ached from trying to understand.

Draven lifted a brow and tipped her face to meet her gaze. Linea tried to look defiant and strong but she was tired and irritated. She knew that he knew her emotions, felt every exotic one of them. He knew her heat and she knew his. She felt like a wild animal, carnal, frenzied in her urge toward somewhere only he could take her. She watched his eyes and licked her dry lips. His hand held the two of hers between them. His free hand caressed her throat as his gaze caressed her face. She felt heat bloom in her cheeks and pool low in her stomach.

"I don't always do as I should, Linea. But you have put yourself in a shameful situation."

Linea couldn't help but watch his mouth move. She felt his heat, frustration, the throbbing want he had for her. Her hunger for him nearly brought her to tears. His voice was lower now and seductive. He had her under some kind of spell.

"There will be consequences," he said firmly.

Draven's expression was resolute; his heavy-lidded gaze searched hers, reading her thoughts, she knew. As he leaned forward, the soft goatee that framed his sensuous mouth brushed against her. His lips slightly grazed hers, sending sparks through her, teasing her. Her

. mouth opened to him willingly and the tip of his tongue slowly stroked the sensitive skin just inside her lips.

She swayed on her feet, wanting to touch him, pull him to her. She struggled against his iron-fisted grip on her wrists and her hands brushed against the bulge that throbbed against the leather ties of his britches. Her inflamed nipples brushed against his chest. Delicious sensations radiated from the brief contact, irritating them both.

Ravenous for more, Linea pressed harder against him. She couldn't understand her own desperation, couldn't seem to conjure the strength to fight her need for him. It had become so great, so overwhelming. She would give him what he demanded and she would absorb his pleasure and the pleasure she knew he would give her. He had but to take what he would. She despised her weakness.

He released her hands as he wrapped his arms around her. Her hands slid up his back; her fingers bit into his taut muscles. His thigh moved between hers, rubbing against her wet aching flesh. Unexpectedly he pulled back, still holding her, and fought for breath. Fire rushed through her. She couldn't think. She leaned into him. Raising her head she nipped at his throat, then licked the small bite.

"Great Iybae," Draven groaned. Setting her away from him, he took her hand and headed back to the horses and the men who waited for them, his long strides causing her to run to keep up with him.

What had she done? What had possessed her to do something so forward, so wanton? She felt her face flame with embarrassment. The night air did little to cool her hot skin and the stumbling run through the lush greenery only made the sliding friction between her legs worse. Sensations kept slowly building, sliding higher toward that undulating peak. Linea was sure it would drive her mad. Thankfully it wasn't long before they reached an opening in the thick wood.

Chapter Twenty-Three

She wrapped her arms around her stomach as she stood panting behind Draven. Armond caught her attention first. He'd been pacing but now he stood facing them, his hands on his hips. Armond glanced at Lord Amaranth then he turned his hard gaze on her.

She felt his strong disapproval even though he kept his expression blank. Sorry that she had earned Armond's scorn, she lowered her gaze. Gradually she realized that she knew Armond's heart, his concern for his king, his friend. She stood wide-eyed, in awe that she could feel what others were feeling. Until now it had only been Lord Amaranth's emotions that had invaded her consciousness. Now she knew what they all felt.

It was so new, so foreign. Her eyes widened as she embraced it and turned to Arkin and Halvar. Dark hostile emotion swirled into her and she cringed under it. Arkin only frowned, trying to hide his contradicting feelings of admiration and condemnation regarding her. But Halvar hid nothing in his expression.

The mixture of emotions made her feel dazed and sick at her stomach. At the time, she felt that what she had done had been her only choice. It terrified her to think that perhaps she'd never make them understand, and worse, that perhaps she deserved whatever fate they decided for her. Uncle Haig, it seemed, may have been right about her.

She'd believed him wrong, hoped he'd been wrong when she'd been innocent of such emotions, such overwhelming desires. She'd never felt such need. It was wicked. She was wicked. Uncle had tried to keep her safe, he said, to protect her from her own inherent sin. She never knew she had such appetites until she had been exposed to such a potent man as Lord Amaranth.

Now it seemed she had caused him to sin. Her heart conflicted with her mind and it made her want to scream and cry and tear something apart. But she wouldn't scream, she wouldn't cry. She would control her desire to do so—at least that one small desire she could control. She quickly glanced upward and caught Draven's shocked expression. She jerked back from him as she felt his jolt of rage slam through her. She had to try to right her wrongs.

"Um, ah, Sir Halvar, I beg your forgiveness. I would never...had there been another way..."

"Save your wheedling, girl," Halvar snarled.

Linea blinked at the ferocity of his anger. She tried to step forward but Lord Amaranth held her behind him. "Sir, I'm willing to admit my wrong and apologize..."

"Linea, quiet." Did Lord Amaranth speak to her out loud or had she heard it in her head?

"Willing?" Halvar bellowed. Linea trembled involuntarily. "You're *willing*? Why, you useless twit..." He growled the last between his teeth.

Draven caught the man's wrist as he lunged for Linea. She met Halvar's murderous gaze. Immediately she became aware of the big man's embarrassment and what her act had done to a man of such great pride. As far as he was concerned he had failed his king; there was no worse thing he could do.

"Halvar." Draven's face was inches from the warrior's. "You go too far." His voice was deceptively quiet. Linea didn't have to hear it or see it; she could feel the dogmatic warning pulsate from his big body.

"Iybae no, I'm so sorry...if I had any other choice... Please... It wasn't his fault..." Linea thought as the big warrior pulled free of Draven's grip with a grunt and stomped away.

"No, it wasn't his fault, it was yours. But I will not allow him to hurt you." She heard his voice in her mind, clear and angry. She opened her mouth when he pulled her around in front of him. *"Keep silent or I may lose hold of my temper, Linea."*

"Why are you in my head? Why am I in yours? What's happening?" She began to tremble and without thinking leaned back against his chest.

"Hell if I know," Draven answered mentally as he lifted Linea up onto his horse with ease. "Mount up. We'll ride through the night."

Linea's hands were clasped around the saddle horn so tightly her knuckles turned white with the effort. The stallion was huge and, sitting up so high, she felt lightheaded and a bit disoriented. Crossing her ankles tightly she leaned close to Mandrake's neck. Her flimsy dress did nothing to keep her warm, and she ached all over.

She was relieved when Draven swung into the saddle behind her. She caught his spicy scent mingled with leather and earth and her sex tightened. She clenched her thighs together, sending thrilling spirals throughout her aching body. Draven's breath was hot on her neck as he placed both hands on her hips and twisted her to the side.

"Straddle the horse, Linea," he murmured in her ear.

"Lord Amaranth, I'm not properly clothed to ride astraddle a horse."

"Do it," he growled warningly.

Reluctantly she swung one leg over Mandrake's head and winced at the feeling of being spread apart. Her lust had cooled a bit but not so much that her body had stopped pulsing with want for release. She still felt wet and hot; the sensitive flesh nestled within her woman's lips was still swollen and throbbing.

Against the cleft of her backside she felt the pulse of Lord Amaranth's bulging arousal. He steered the stallion toward the keep. Animal and man found a rhythm and Linea bit her lip against the torture of the pounding cadence of the warm leather saddle between her legs. She struggled to keep her breathing even, to think about other things, like how she would get away, how she would get to Ingvar now.

* * * * *

No longer could Draven deny his aspiration to care for her, protect her. Something had happened when he fought the Kyroks and something had happened in the forest that night. Something he couldn't deny. He still felt a hum of untapped power coursing through him.

There had been a fusion of energy between them and it had somehow changed them. Now she could read his thoughts. He could feel her inside him like the air he breathed. Her need for him had increased. Her sweet desire to touch and taste him was making his hunger for her insatiable.

He knew now who had scarred her body, had tortured her, for what looked like most of her life. He was slowly learning why and it sickened him. Orbane would pay for the pain in her eyes, for each and every thin white line that slashed across her voluptuous body. Draven swore silently and pulled her back, tighter against him.

Linea would never hurt like that again; he would make sure of it. Neither Orbane nor Pandrum would ever get near her again. What troubled him most was that his father allowed Orbane to be her guardian. By all rights Rayne himself should have raised Linea. He had been her father's close friend and she had no other family. Rayne knew who had spawned Orbane, so why had he taken the chance?

She was thinking of Ingvar again. Her mind was a flurry of thoughts and ideas as she tried to formulate a plan, anything to distract herself from the fluid sensations that speared into her with every hoof beat. It was a useless endeavor, he thought; he knew so because he'd been trying to ignore them as well. He took the reins in one hand and pressed it low on her stomach as he bent his head to nuzzle her neck. *"No one who enters Ingvar will ever leave Ingvar."*

Her body trembled against his at the words he formed in her mind. *"Yes, I know."*

"No," he murmured in her ear, and ground his pelvis against her bottom. "Little one, you don't know." He closed his eyes and let the sensations wash through him.

She writhed and tried to pull away but he held her tight. His free hand pulled the material of her gown up, exposing her thigh. The muscle of her inner thigh flexed as his fingers grazed the hot moist flesh. Her response was so quick and hot it nearly took his breath. His hand continued to move slowly over her soft skin, his pulse increasing.

"The faeries will protect you but Ingvar is no paradise for humans, Linea. If they choose to accept your sanction and allow you to enter, you will be held there until the New Dawn," Draven explained silently.

He nuzzled her neck with his nose and lightly bit at the tender skin behind her ear as his hand made a circular pattern on her inner thigh. He could feel the heat radiating from the core of her; he was losing himself in the sensations he gave her.

"Ingvar is the land of the faeries. It was never meant for human habitation. Because you don't belong there, the faeries will, with all their compassion, place you in stasis."

"Stasis?" she whimpered as he swept her hair over her shoulder. His mouth left a fiery trail of kisses around the back of her neck.

"Yes." He feasted on her luscious neck with hot licks, sucks and nibbles. *"It's like being frozen, time stops for you but you don't die. You're alive but not living. Do you understand?"*

She arched against him and shook her head. His hand was so close his fingers were damp with the honey of her arousal. *"Mmm, you feel just like a ripe peach off the tree...so soft, warm, sweet, juicy."*

God, he wanted to taste her, wanted to soothe her hot, swollen flesh with his hungry tongue. Linea stiffened as his erotic thoughts filled her mind.

"All around you life will go on, Linea. Everything will change but you will not. No one knows when the New Dawn will come, so only Iybae knows how long you'll be in stasis."

Draven's hand moved from her thigh to cup her breast and gently lift it. He rubbed around her engorged nipple with his thumb. *"Is that what you want?"*

"Yes...no, please stop doing that. I can't think." She bit her lip on a moan.

"What is it you want me to stop, Linea? This?" he asked, gently squeezing the plump berry between his fingers. Linea's head dropped back against his shoulder and she licked her damp parted lips. "Or would you have me stop this?" His moist hand slid to cup her sex. His fingers slid shallowly, teasingly, just slightly moving inside her overly sensitive pouting lips.

Linea panted, clutched at his wrist and rolled her hips against his hand.

Her body bathed his hand in her honey and he shut his eyes against the sensation. Pulling the reins, he directed the horse to a slower gait.

"Hold the reins." His voice was rough with arousal.

She was breathless; her hand shook as he folded her fingers around the leather straps.

"I don't know how to lead a horse, my lord. I..."

"Just hold onto the reins." He moved his hand to massage her other breast and smoothed his drenched fingers up, parting the tender swollen folds opening her against his hand. "The keep isn't far off now and Mandrake knows the way."

"Please, my lord, I don't want..." Her voice was almost a sob.

"You do want. I feel your want," he growled, letting his fingers slide through the wet open folds. "I know your want, Linea."

Linea arched back, biting her lip. He released her breast and, capturing her chin, caught her gaze. Her heavy-lidded blue eyes were glittery with desire. He could feel the excitement firing off inside her like lightning.

"About this, my sweet Linea, you cannot lie."

Transfixed by the power of arousal he saw in her eyes, he bent his head and closed his mouth over hers. His tongue slid between her lips and took possession, stroking, building the wildfire inside her. His thumb slid upward and found the tiny hard bulb nestled at the apex of her saturated silken folds. He teased that tender knot of flesh and allowed a finger to slide slowly into her tight passage. Her body jerked against his hand.

"Cry out for me, sweet Linea."

With a gasp she turned her face away from him and bit her lip as his finger moved inside her. Draven deliberately imagined his cock spearing into her, inch by inch, stretching her open. He felt the currents of pleasure the thoughts gave her and he focused on them, expanded them. Her breath hitched as she thrust her hips, writhing against him.

"I can't, I don't want to…" He heard her thoughts and clenched his teeth against his raging anger and need. His breathing was unsteady, his body strained painfully for release against its leather bounds.

"Your body betrays you, my little liar. Evidence of your want covers my hand." He softly pressed his thumb against the throbbing nub. Her body clutched at his finger as he moved it in and out of her with slow deliberate strokes. *"I want to kiss you here, Linea, lave your swollen aching body, taste your arousal."*

He flicked his tongue over her kiss-swollen lips as he pushed his finger higher to stroke the firm ridged oval inside her. Her channel clenched savagely and her fingers dug into his thigh. He gently inserted another finger, massaging the initial burning sensation into molten desire. He pushed her higher, slowly stretching her, until his fingers met the delicate membrane that blocked her passage. Her hips began to move faster against his hand with the rhythm of the stallion.

Draven's free hand moved down her throat and her stomach, pulling at her gown, wanting to feel her flesh. Her skin was like hot silk where he touched her. He kneaded her breast, loving the soft fullness of it. She bucked against him, pumping her hips against his thrusting fingers.

"Slow, sweetness," he murmured against her neck as Mandrake snorted and nodded his regal head in protest.

All Draven had to do was free his cock, tilt her hips and plunge into her. He closed his eyes and clenched his teeth as he shared with her the fiery mental picture. He could feel her spiraling, tightening, as she knew his thoughts. She was ready to go over, but he was far from ready to let her go. He wanted to make it last and last. Up ahead he saw the keep gates.

"Say it. Say you don't want this and I swear to our great Creator, Iybae, I'll stop now," he groaned at her ear through his clenched teeth.

"I can't stand it," Linea whispered breathlessly.

Draven stilled his hand inside her and he released her jutting nipple. He felt her agonizing frustration. He leaned forward, bracing an arm across her middle, and whispered in her ear. "Say you want it, Linea."

"Yes. Iybae forgive me, please, my lord, don't stop," she panted, clutching the reins and Draven's arm.

Draven plunged his fingers inside her. His thumb slid over and around her little bud. Linea's body tensed as her sheath contracted around them and felt the exquisite pain spike into her.

"Sing for me, Linea, moan for me." She couldn't help the low husky moan that erupted from deep inside her and he pulled her back against him.

"Yes," he whispered, kissing her neck as stroke after stroke of his fingers and thumb pushed her higher, built the erotic tension inside her to the breaking point. She moved against his hand, pressing her body against his back.

"Oh, please," she cried as he cupped her breast again, grazing his thumb across her rock-hard nipple.

"Say my name, Linea."

Linea arched her back, clutching at his arm with her free hand.

"Say it, my sweet Linea. Forget that I am king and cry out for your lover. Call out to me!"

"My lord," she pleaded mentally.

"Draven...say it. Say my name," he whispered roughly.

"Draven... Ah, Draven," she whimpered.

He felt her crest and shatter, her vagina convulse around his fingers, milking them. Ripples ruthlessly tore through her very womb and radiated throughout her body in waves of pleasure. He was captured, riding the tide of her climax as well. Gripped by the intensity of her orgasm, he wanted it to last forever. For her, for him. His cock throbbed painfully. Rocking against her, he held her tightly and kept slowly stroking until she went up and exploded once more.

Depleted and breathless, she lay against him. As each aftershock undulated through her, Draven straightened her dress as much as possible. He grimaced against his need for completion. Taking the reins from her, he led Mandrake through the gate. At the keep door he dismounted and lifted Linea from the saddle. She stood trembling; his arm remained around her, steadying her.

She looked up at him with all the determination she could muster. "I will not honor my betrothal, Lord Amaranth. If you try to force me, I'll only run away again."

He watched the emotion swirling in her eyes, felt it churning inside her. "Where would you go, Linea? I'd only come after you and bring you back again."

"Stasis is better than breed whore for the Kyroks." She shuddered at the thought.

Draven wanted to shudder as well. "The faeries, although kind and generous, are not the answer. I know what he did to you, Linea. I have no intention of sending you back to your uncle. I am your king and I will offer you sanctuary."

"By what authority? Even as king you can't keep me from my family. That's the law—your law. If my uncle wishes me to return to him, by honor you cannot keep me from him."

Draven held her gaze with a sense of dread. She was right; if he were to be honorable, he must release her. If not, he would risk the faith of his people. Right now more than ever he had to have their trust. "Does he know you're here, Linea?"

She frowned up at him, thinking. "I don't know, my lord. I didn't know I'd be here when I ran so there's no reason for him to assume so."

He did not send her, Draven thought with relief as he brushed her hair behind her ear. *"I will think of something."*

She continued to watch him, searching his face, his deep storm-laden eyes, hoping he could save her.

Chapter Twenty-Four

Always stoic, Joeff stood at the doorway, ready to serve. Draven wanted nothing more than to wash up, fill his stomach, take Linea to bed and chase away all her doubt and fear, erase all the horror of her past. The thought of sinking into oblivion surrounded by her heat and her soft sexy purrs of pleasure wreaked havoc with his self-control. His hand tightened on her shoulder and his thumb caressed the nape of her neck in little arousing circles. She shivered. Even to that simple touch, her body responded to him.

Reality slapped him in the face when he saw Cynthia sitting by the fire fidgeting uncomfortably. The tall, plush moss-green chair made her look tiny and frail. Such a lovely lady; her small ankles crossed, her back ramrod straight. Her hands twisted in her lap and she had yet to greet him or even raise her head to grace him with her usual pleasant smile.

Perhaps she sensed his lack of desire for her, or worse, his abundant desire for Linea. She should be preparing to marry a man who was mad with love for her, not a man whose heart was turning toward another. He never thought himself a cad, the type of man who would dishonor his betrothed, and now he saw no way around postponing their wedding, or perhaps canceling it altogether. The urge to punch something or someone had him clenching his fist.

Moria's eyes brightened as she glanced up from her seat on the rock hearth. Draven was taken aback at first, thinking he was the recipient of such a dazzling smile. Realizing it was through him she was gazing, he turned to see Armond returning a crooked smile of his own. Draven's brows lifted and he turned back in time to catch the faerie's wings flutter and her cheeky little wink. It had to be the cutest thing he'd ever seen. He stifled a chuckle and sighed deeply instead.

"Dear child, look at you!" Netta came down the stairs as fast as her stubby legs would carry her. Silver curls had escaped the bun on top of her head and floated around her round red face. Her forehead was wrinkled and her brows knit together over worried green eyes.

"Just look at you." She was huffing and puffing by the time she reached the group standing at the door.

Linea took an instinctive step back, stiffening as she collided with Draven's body. He knew she wanted to disappear as everyone's gaze turned to her. She opened her mouth to reassure Netta that she was fine when the woman took Linea's hands in hers and turned them this way and that. Netta clucked in disgust as she studied the raised scratches that covered Linea's bare arms.

Wrapping her pudgy arm around Linea's waist, Netta strong-armed her toward the baths, all the while fussing and grumbling about fever, infection and death. Draven didn't miss the sharp disapproving glare Netta shot him as she whisked Linea away, nor did he miss the plea for help in Linea's anxious eyes.

"Don't fight her, Linea, the baths will make you feel better," he silently encouraged her. She blinked at him over her shoulder before she disappeared through the big door leading to the underground baths. The corner of his mouth lifted. Their silent communication was beginning to flow easily. He was quite enjoying it, even though it still seemed to take Linea by surprise.

He turned his attention back to the task at hand. Mason had appeared. He was leaning on one of the marble columns that supported the upper balcony. Draven couldn't help but notice the rigidity in his stance and the frustrated restraint and agitation that churned within him. Mason met Draven's piercing gaze with one of his own. Though Mason's expression was stoic, his eyes were a profoundly obstinate arctic blue. Mason wasn't adept at hiding his emotions.

"Where's the elf?" Draven snapped without looking away from Mason.

A large scruffy warrior leaned through an arch of the balcony above and yelled down. "'E's up here, me lord! I've been keepin' a sure eye on the dirty rakehell. You want I should haul 'im down to ya?"

Draven resisted the urge to growl at the man. "No, keep him there. I'll deal with him soon enough."

"Yes, me lord," the warrior replied with a shrug.

Draven cleared his throat. Armond hadn't moved but never took his eyes from the faerie. Armond's struggle with the sensual pull arching between Moria and himself made Draven a bit uncomfortable, much like a voyeur.

Cynthia still watched her lap, dense emotion swarming inside her. He could feel her stomach tighten with it. Mason stood staring straight ahead, anger and frustration swirling around him in vivid colors. Draven always knew what Mason felt; however, he didn't always know why. Normally Draven took it in stride, waited Mason out, but at this moment it irritated the hell out of him, gave him a sense of foreboding. Unfortunately he didn't have the time to focus on it more closely. He had more pressing matters to contend with at present.

"Joeff, please escort Miss Cynthia and Miss Moria to the parlor. Ladies, please excuse my rudeness. I need to confer with my men in private for a moment," Draven said as Halvar and Arkin joined the other warriors present and took a seat on the leather couches.

Cynthia nodded, stood quickly with an artificial smile, turned and with a sigh of relief that had Draven frowning again, followed Joeff gracefully from the room.

Draven watched and waited impatiently until the ladies were behind the parlor door and out of earshot. "Mason, come closer," he said.

Mason cleared his throat and walked across the room, taking a seat on a couch and lazily propping his booted feet up on a wooden table. Mason's brooding manner was odd, very odd, Draven thought, watching his cousin. With a deep breath he shrugged off his apprehension and began to apprise his men of who Linea was, where she'd come from and of his intentions regarding her and Orbane.

"Was Orbane aware of the recent Kyrok attacks then?" Halvar asked.

"I have no way of knowing but I doubt the attacks would concern him either way," Draven answered.

"What of Graeme Sierra, Lord Amaranth?" Arkin looked confused. "Did he not pledge a covenant with the humans?"

"The Kyroks are bound by a covenant, but as you know, with the recent attacks that covenant has been broken. It has come to my attention that Pandrum and Orbane have formed a pact of some sort. I can only speculate what Orbane has in his mind but his arrival here will be a fragile issue. I don't believe he knows his niece is here and I intend to keep him ignorant of it. His belief that I regard him as a devoted subject and that I have faith in him as overseer may not be as strong. Especially in light of all that has happened." Draven was leery of speaking his mind. Still, he suspected a spy was among them.

"He can't honestly believe you don't know of his tyranny." Armond scowled.

Draven shrugged. "I don't have much confidence in the stability of Orbane's thought processes at the moment." Flashes of Linea's wounded body crossed his mind and he ground his teeth. "Linea is lawfully betrothed to Pandrum in return for his loyalty to Orbane."

All eyes cut to him now. Mason's eyes narrowed. "How do you plan to get around that one, Draven? You have no choice but to release the woman to her uncle or her betrothed."

Draven met Mason's gaze, confused by his hostility. "Apart from keeping this pact between Pandrum and Orbane from being sealed, I will not turn the girl over to that maniacal bastard to be abused for his own sick pleasure, nor will I throw her to Pandrum to be brutalized and bred, or killed. I will get around it."

Draven narrowed his eyes in warning as he held Mason's gaze a few seconds more before meeting the concerned gazes of the men around him. He singled out the warrior who guarded the door to Linea's room. "Be sure Linea is in your sight at all times. She's free to roam the keep but she's not to leave or to roam the grounds except the gardens, and at no time is she to be left alone. Netta will attend her personal needs."

The warrior nodded and headed for the baths.

Every man was looking to Draven. It wasn't the first time he was struck with the awesomeness of his responsibility. These were his best warriors, his most trustworthy, most fearless men. They needed to be aware. "There is a change coming. I can't explain it but I know it's coming. Asmodeus is rising."

The air in the great hall seemed to thicken at the sound of the evil god's name. Every man raised somber eyes to Draven's and waited for him to continue.

"I'm no longer concerned about the covenant; it's been broken. I am concerned about the people of Lanthor. This world, though small, will need to become mighty and it's my obligation to prepare you," Draven stated.

Draven crossed the room to stand in front of the blazing fireplace, his hands on his hips. "Don't underestimate the Kyroks. While they lack mental fortitude, Pandrum leads them and Asmodeus is his god. Although he is half Kyrok, he isn't completely brainless. Furthermore, you must remember: Kyroks are incredibly strong and war is their forte. There is no room for ill preparation and oversight. Go, make ready and pray."

The men all wore grave expressions as they left the great hall to do their king's bidding. Some felt respect, some honor, some excitement; all felt an underlying coil of fear. The inundation of so many dark emotions crashing into Draven made him irascible and edgy.

"Have men posted at the gate and set up a watch guard to patrol the wall," Draven snapped as he began to pace. "I cannot allow Cynthia and her assistant to leave here. The whole of Lanthor knows of my betrothal. Orbane may find them useful in his desire to bring me down."

Mason and Armond remained. They continued to look at him with concern on their faces. Both men nodded. Armond's expression turned from solemn to dark and ominous.

"Armond, I'd be blind not to notice your infatuation with Moria. Should I be concerned?" Draven asked sharply.

Armond's brows furrowed. "I'm not sure what you mean, Draven."

"What part do you not understand, Armond?" Draven's sigh was an exasperated one. "The part where I believe you to be falling for a faerie or the part where I'm concerned that your giddy emotions will get in the way of your usually sharp logic?"

He would that he could take the words back as soon as they were out of his mouth. Armond was more than trustworthy; he was Draven's rock. Mason's mouth dropped open. Armond first looked incredulous then anger flashed cold and hard in his green eyes.

Draven opened his mouth to begin his apology when Armond raised his hand to stop him.

"You have nothing to be afraid of, Draven. I have never let you down before, I don't intend to now." Armond spoke through clenched teeth. "If you have no more need of me now I should meet with my men."

Draven felt the sting and wasn't sure if it was his own or Armond's. Damn it to hell.

"No. You'll wait till I've dismissed you." Draven's gaze didn't waver from Armond's glowering gaze. "I was out of line. I trust you implicitly, Armond."

Armond nodded and stood firm, saying nothing.

Draven felt deflated, confused and angry with himself. It wasn't like him to take his irritation out on those he cared about. "You may go now."

He did just that, without a word. Armond would let it fade after a while but Draven could still taste the bitterness of the words in his mouth and it frustrated him all the more.

"I believe you're jealous, cousin." Draven whipped his head around to find Mason slumped on the couch, watching him with a raised brow and a sardonic frown.

"Mason, if you're implying what I think you're implying you're wrong." Draven's laugh was humorless. "I'm enchanted by her, I think she's adorable, but I have no romantic feelings for Moria."

Mason slowly stood and crossed to Draven, laying a hand heavily on his shoulder. "It's not the woman Armond loves that you desire, my beloved cousin. It's his freedom to love her." Mason patted Draven's shoulder twice and then left Draven in the great hall alone.

Standing there, with only his own emotions to deal with, Draven breathed deeply. His betrothed sat waiting for him beyond the ornate doors of the parlor. The wedding would have to be postponed. Only a moron would try to fool himself; he had no intention of wedding Cynthia. Their marriage would be a miserable one for both of them.

His heart would not bend to her; fondness was the strongest emotion he could conjure up for her. And he tried—Iybae knew he tried. The emotions he felt for Linea were another story. They were many and tangled like blackberry vines, painful to delve into but the fruit was oh, so sweet. Blessed Lord Iybae, how would he manage this fine mess? He didn't focus on her; he didn't want to know what she was feeling. Dammit, there was no time for this.

With a grimace he turned and stomped to the parlor door. He paused, his hand on the doorknob, and closed his eyes. He felt the block circle around to encompass him, sheltering him from the chaos of emotions that was sure to come. It was an uncomfortable, unnaturally heavy feeling, but with the task ahead of him, he was sure it was necessary. With another deep breath he walked into the cozy parlor.

Cynthia and Moria halted their hushed conversation and looked up at him. Cynthia sat on the chaise, her body stiff, her big brown eyes wide, her expression childlike. Draven's stomach twisted. Moria sat delicately on a cushioned stool by the fire. She gave him a smile and in her gaze he thought he saw reassurance. Odd, he thought as he cleared his throat and took the seat across from Cynthia.

"It has come to my attention that there is a plot against this keep and the throne. It isn't safe for you to return home. I've sent for your father, Cynthia. You will remain here till the threat has passed."

She simply nodded at him, not really meeting his gaze. "But I didn't bring any of my things. I don't have any clothes, or my combs, or books or anything that's mine."

"I will have Netta get you what you need."

As though she was speaking her thoughts out loud she mumbled as she twisted a handkerchief in her hands, "But they won't be mine."

Draven frowned down at her, praying she didn't start crying or, worse, throw a tantrum. It amazed him that she'd even think of such frivolities when her life was in danger.

"Perhaps I can send for some of your things later if it turns out that you'll be here for a long stay, but not now." His voice was a bit sharper than he'd meant it to be. It was, after all, her association with him that put her in danger in the first place.

Cynthia inhaled sharply, her voice a bit shaky. "It will be fine. I'll make do, and perhaps it won't be for long."

He paused, wondering if he shouldn't put off telling her, then decided it best not to have it hanging over his head. "The wedding will have to be postponed as well."

Her head snapped up and she finally met his gaze. The tears glittering in her eyes did nothing to soften his mood; in fact it annoyed him further. He struggled to curtail his response. "I'm sorry, Cynthia, it can't be helped."

"I understand, my lord. It's completely understandable," Cynthia said as she returned her gaze to her folded hands. Draven narrowed his eyes. Was she smiling?

She took a deep breath and her voice trembled dramatically. "I have a terrible headache. Could someone show me to my room so that I may rest?"

Damn if he'd ever understand the female mind, Draven thought as he rose to leave. "Soon, Cynthia. Your rooms are being readied."

She lifted her brows and pursed her lips. "Lord Amaranth, will you please have your servants air out the room properly? And I will surely need a fresh feather bed and clean linens. Oh, and fresh flowers from the garden would perfume the room nicely. Yes...yes, fresh flowers, and if someone could bring up some nice hot tea. Tea would help calm my nerves and perhaps relieve my aching head."

No one had the time or the inclination to pamper Cynthia and give in to her spoiled requests. Draven clenched his teeth and glanced at Moria, who gave him an apologetic smile and a shrug. He turned and left the room without a word.

Chapter Twenty-Five

Linea held her breath and glided effortlessly through the water, enveloped in warmth and silence. Never in her life had she experienced anything so wonderful. It was like a whole different world where everything wrong seemed to disappear. Her ankle didn't pain her, even slightly, as she pushed off the smooth slate of the pool floor. Surging up she broke the surface and breathed in the sultry spice-scented air.

"Miss Linea, come on now, your skin will wrinkle," Netta scolded from where she stood at the edge, bent slightly, hands on her hips.

Linea blinked water droplets from her eyelashes as she ran a hand over her wet hair. "I'm absolutely fine, Netta," she panted. "This is an amazing place."

The oblong pool was fed by an underground hot spring that kept it the perfect degree of warmth. Netta had told her that it was the abundant minerals in the water that made it feel so soft against her skin. Linea stood on her tiptoes to keep her head above the water and took it all in.

The pool room was walled completely, floor to ceiling, in light gray slate. Candles were lit all around, giving the room a soft glow. The large pots that sat here and there with profuse lush plants intrigued Linea the most. How could they thrive so in such a dim environment? There were so many things happening to her that she didn't understand.

"You've been in there long enough, my dear. You can't spend the entire day in the baths. You've been up all night traipsing through the woods like a mischievous badger. You need to rest. Come now and dry off so you can get dressed."

"But I don't feel a bit tired. I feel wonderful." Linea tried not to pout.

"The baths can trick you. You will feel like a cooked dumpling once you've gotten out and dried off."

"Just a little longer please, Netta," she begged as she lay back, letting the water lift her and hold her aloft.

"Really, Miss Linea, you act as if you've never had a swim before." Netta scowled down at her.

"I never have!" Linea stood up in the wide pool and looked up at Netta wide-eyed and smiling. Hoping she'd give in.

Netta gave her a look of utter disbelief. "You expect me to believe you've never bathed?"

"No, no, I've bathed." Linea bobbed up and down. "In a metal tub. But the water was cold and it didn't smell so delicious or feel so nice." She plunged underwater again and tilting her head back, then surfaced again. "It's simply wonderful," she said breathlessly.

Netta rolled her eyes. "All right, child, I'm so pleased that the baths have made you happy, but enough is enough. The pool isn't going anywhere. You can enjoy the water another time. Now, out with you."

"Yes, Netta, soon...but not yet," Linea said as she dove underwater and swam to the end of the pool.

"Linea, you're acting like an ill-behaved child." Netta scowled at her and stamped her tiny foot. "Now I have had enough of this!"

Linea dove down again and used her arms to pull her through the water. She swam back and forth several times. She lost count, surfacing only when her lungs burned from the lack of air. She felt a twinge of regret that she'd made Netta angry. She just couldn't leave the sanctuary of this watery cocoon. Sanctuary was something she'd never experienced. This feeling of safety, freedom, she'd never known before and she wasn't ready to give it up. Not yet, not until she had her fill.

* * * * *

"Netta, what are you looking for?" Draven stood outside the storeroom door patting Aletha's broad head as he watched the woman nearly standing on her head digging through a trunk.

"Looking for a length of rope," she grumbled.

Draven raised his brow. "Is there someone you're looking to hang?"

Netta straightened, her face red and dotted with beads of sweat. She met his gaze, her eyes bright green, flashing with irritation. "My lord, it would be wise not to give me any ideas!"

Draven worked to stifle a smile and rubbed his goatee. "May I ask who the unfortunate soul might be that has incurred your wrath?"

Netta nodded vigorously, her topknot bouncing up and down. "That stubborn lass refuses to leave the pool so I'm going to rope her and pull her out!"

"Linea?"

She lifted her arms in frustration. "Who else?" Then turned to search the shelves.

Draven arched a brow as a thought occurred to him. "Where is the man I sent to guard her?"

"He'd better be sitting right where I told him to sit and stay. The girl's nude, you know," she snapped, blowing the hair out of her face without turning.

"Netta dear, go see to Linea's room and I'll deal with her." He patted her on the shoulder. "Oh, and could you have someone find some things for Miss Cynthia and Miss Moria, and see that they have nice rooms?" He walked away, calling over his shoulder, "They'll inform you of their needs."

"Yes, I have no doubt of that. Spoiled little sparrow," Netta grumbled.

Draven didn't bother to hide his grin as he left Netta grumbling to herself and headed quickly down into the baths. The warrior guarding Linea sat where he'd been told, though he looked fidgety and bored. Straightening, he looked up as Draven entered and nodded his acknowledgement.

"You can go now, thank you," Draven said to him, briefly patting his shoulder.

"Thank you, my lord," the man answered with relief. Draven nodded to him and walked through the opening leading to the bath.

She looked like a seductive water nymph, Draven thought as he watched her glide through the crystal water, his body responding readily. Her hair rippled behind her as her body undulated. Her perfect heart-shaped bottom flexed as her long well-formed legs spread and came together, propelling her forward. Draven forgot to breathe and his mouth had gone dry.

The sharp staccato sound of Aletha's barking had Linea breaking the surface of the water with a gasp. She fought in vain with her long tangle of wet hair before finally ducking under again and re-emerging with her head back, her hair a shiny black fall of water smoothed away from her face and down her back. Her breasts thrust forward and rivulets of water slid over her face, her parted lips, her pert pink nipples. Draven wanted to draw those pretty berries into his mouth. His cock pressed painfully against its bindings.

* * * * *

She ran a hand over her face. Finally, her eyes focused on the wolfdog at the end of the pool. Aletha barked again and danced as though she wanted to join Linea. A laugh bubbled up from deep inside her and surprised her so that she gasped. The sound was so foreign to her. She couldn't remember the last time she laughed.

"Musical," Draven murmured as he crouched at the edge of the pool watching her.

The candlelight dancing in his intense gray gaze made her think of a hungry wolf stalking his prey. His eyes moved to her breasts bobbing in the water as she panted for breath. She froze. Her smile melted as she crossed her arms over her chest and watched him with wide eyes. He arched a brow and the corner of his lips tilted, drawing her attention to his mouth. She felt her blood quicken and heat infuse her. She was becoming familiar with this arousal he caused in her.

The humidity had his hair curling around his rugged face. Even crouched down he was a hulk of a man. His elbows rested on his powerful thighs, his hands dangling between them. She remembered what those hands could do, the pleasure they had brought her, and she trembled.

"Your eyes are red, Linea, and you're more tired than you think." His voice was dark, warm and as smooth as warm butter. He stood and bent toward her, extending his hand. "Come, time to get out."

Swallowing hard, she shook her head.

Aletha barked. Slowly Draven's lips parted into a toothy grin and he pulled his shirt over his head. His hands went to the ties of his pants and Linea shuddered again. Her eyes grew wider. He was coming in for her. Curiosity had her gaze fixed on his groin. She'd felt the hot, pulsing length of him but she still didn't know what he looked like.

Her body responded as if his hands were already on her. Without trying to deny her need anymore she clenched her legs together, her body throbbing for him. She could feel her nipples hardening against her arms. She wanted to rub them so badly; she wanted him to rub them, cup her breasts as he'd done before and take her into his mouth. But she was still afraid of what was happening, afraid to give in to her need.

"I...I'll get out. Wait, I just need a towel. I'll get out!"

"Too late, no more second chances, love." He pushed his pants down over his hips, freeing his manhood. The shaft was long and thick; the veins wrapping around it seemed to pulse. The dark and dusky tip was round and wide, resembling a ripe plum. She couldn't help but wonder if it was as soft as it looked, what it would feel like to kiss it, what it would taste like.

She remembered too late that he knew her mind but she couldn't seem to tame her lusty train of thought. Without lifting her head her eyes met his darkening gaze. Anticipation and apprehension grew in her heart as he turned and lowered himself into the pool. The muscles of his shoulders and back bunched and bulged. His hind parts were round, smooth, firm and as arousing as his front parts. She appreciated the beauty of his form, recalled the feel of his warm skin against hers, and wanted to moan just looking at him.

He stalked toward her, the movement of the water causing her body to sway. Even though she was tall in stature she stood on her tiptoes to keep her head above the surface. The water came to just below Draven's broad shoulders. Overwhelmed and feeling perplexed she shook her head and stepped back. She had to gain control of herself, of her lust. She gasped as his hands found her bare waist and dragged her to him. Her eyes fluttered closed as her body collided with his.

He lifted her against him and just that simple contact she needed so badly, that light silky friction, had luscious sensations spiraling through her. He moved one hand up her body to cup her breast and fondle her nipple gently. The pleasure was so sharp, so consuming. As pathetically weak as she felt, she couldn't pull away, and with a sigh she surrendered to her passion. She wrapped her arms around his neck and pressed her body closer. His hands smoothed down her back and gripped her backside.

Lost in the softness of the water, the heat of his body and the slow liquid arousal pouring over her, she lifted her head and kissed him. Timidly she let her tongue stroke his bottom lip, tasting him. He growled, deepening the kiss, and pulled her legs up around his hips, his fingers playing along the crease of her bottom. Desire, raw and heady, came from him and whipped through her. She sighed with need, hers and his, as his cock slipped between the folds of her sex, rubbing against the inflamed flesh.

"Linea, wait…" he groaned.

"Draven," she murmured, her voice husky and weak, her mind spinning beyond reason. "Please, help me."

She felt something both pulling and pushing her toward those wonderful explosions he'd given her before. She wanted it; she needed more. Her hips moved urgently against him and she gasped as the wide round head of his cock pressed inside her, stretching her. Deeper…she wanted to feel him slide deeper inside her.

"Slow down, love," he groaned as hot desire undulated through her, flooding her system, blocking out all reason. He'd gone stone still. His muscles felt like warm steel beneath her hands. She shuddered as his hands pushed her legs from around his hips and lifted her into his arms. Laying her head on his shoulder she nipped at his neck then ran her tongue over the bite. How could he feel so hot? Was that his moan or hers? He tasted so good, felt so wonderful.

"Wonderful…I feel wonderful," she murmured against his neck. "You feel wonderful." She began kissing his jaw, his ear, licking him.

"Dear God, Linea," he said through bared, clenched teeth. "If you don't stop, I'll have you against the damn wall." His voice was hoarse and tight.

She shivered, but not so much from the cool air that hit her body as it was from the image of him pressing her against the wall with his body, stroking her inside with that hard thick shaft. Her inner walls contracted, releasing the slick juice of her arousal, begging to be filled.

He groaned, his arms tightened around her and his mouth took her as her fantasy flitted through his mind. She smiled and wiggled against him without opening her eyes. He struggled for control, draping a blanket around her body. She breathed in the scent of him. She felt his warm skin against her smile and let herself sink into the safety and strength of his arms.

Chapter Twenty-Six

Draven was thankful he didn't meet anyone as he made his way through the great hall and the staircase. He'd had no time to pull on his pants. He took two steps at a time and darted into Linea's bedchamber.

"Draven," she whispered against his lips as he laid her on the bed and claimed her mouth. Her hands moved lightly, eagerly, over his body. Lost in her desire for him, her body seemed to throb languidly. The heat radiating from her, her eager innocence, consumed him, making him feel like an untried boy.

"Wait, sweetness." He kissed her jaw, nibbled her neck as he cupped her breasts. She arched up. Her brows furrowed over her heavy-lidded eyes."I'll be right back, love." She groaned in protest as he unwrapped her arms and quickly moved away from her to shut the door.

Just as he turned the key in the lock he heard it, the whisper of a soft snore. He spun around and went to sit beside her on the bed. She moaned and turned to her side, tugging the blanket around her. He thought for a moment to wake her, but she was so tired and he wanted her completely alert when he came inside her. He wanted her to feel every reality of the pleasure he would give her, of the pleasure she gave him.

He stared down at his throbbing member with a frustrated sigh and ran his hands through his hair. It was wrong and he knew it. He shouldn't want her, definitely shouldn't touch her. Not with his betrothed wandering the keep all the while. *Dear God, what had he been thinking?* He'd dashed naked from the baths, carrying Linea, naked, while she did incredibly seductive things to his neck with her sweet mouth. This issue had to be resolved. He had to find some way, a loophole of some sort that would allow him to back out of this wedding. His stomach twisted at the thought. *What kind of man had he become? What had this little broken bird done to him?* He rose from the bed and with a bit of a struggle took the damp blanket from her and covered her with the heavy bed coverlet. Wrapping the blanket around his hips he leaned down and kissed her temple. "Sleep well, sweet Linea."

In his own room he drew the curtains and sprawled across the huge bed. He worked at distracting himself from his hunger by thinking of all the other things needing his attention. His men were busy preparing for Orbane and Pandrum's next move. He was anxious to settle the matter. Thinking of what the cowardly sod had done to Linea caused his palms to itch for his sword. He suspected that someone close to him was betraying him. If so, Orbane would soon know that he sheltered Linea.

Linea. He was drawn to her spirit, her courage. He was humbled by her strength and determination. His lust for her was greater than he'd ever known. But she presented a well of complications. He needed to understand this connection she seemed to have with him and his gift. Gavril had the answers. Gavril, and he suspected Moria had some insight into what was occurring.

Draven closed his eyes, willing himself to sleep. He could afford a few hours of rest at the most; he could not afford to waste that time tossing and turning. Yet, his urgently throbbing cock was becoming painful. His hand moved down his stomach. His fingers curled around the thick shaft, lightly trailing up and down the hard length of his member.

* * * * *

Linea woke softly as strong sensations ribboned through her body. It softly spread from between her thighs like wisps of warm smoke, floating, caressing stroking. Long, softly sliding strokes. Her body seemed to move closer to it, wanting more, needing more. Confused, she tried to ignore it as she turned to lie on her back. But the sensations kept teasing her. Her breath quickened and her hands clutched the sheets. This couldn't be a dream, no dream felt this real.

* * * * *

Draven breathed in deeply as his thumb passed over the tip of his cock, spreading the pearl of cream over the hot pulsing plum. His hand moved steadily up and down, caressing the thick ridge that throbbed along the underside. Thoughts of Linea, her softness, the tight entrance of her honeyed sheath, urged him forward. He milked the rigid shaft, sharpening the pleasure. The sensation built and spread through him as his thumb rasped the ring at the base of the head and tightened his grip.

* * * * *

Linea's mind was still foggy with sleep, but her body was on fire. She pressed herself against the bed and clenched her thighs together. A soft cry escaped her throat. *What was happening?*

"Draven?" Her lips formed the soundless words as she tried to thrust against the unseen hand driving her upward.

Reaching down, her fingers found her sex slick with her arousal, her curls coated with her cream. Her forehead beaded with sweat and she kicked at the covers. Sharp pleasure seared through her and she arched her back, pressing her lips together against the need to cry out as wave after wave of pleasure pulsed through her.

* * * * *

Moisture welled up, coating the engorged head of Draven's shaft as his hand pumped up and down. His glistening cock pulsated, sending waves of pleasure radiating from his loins. With his other hand he reached down, cupping his balls, and gently massaged them.

Soon they tightened against his body. His hips drove upward on a groan as his hand clenched on his steely rod, pistoning harder, urging him higher. He clenched his teeth as his ejaculation gripped him. His hot seed pumped from him, coating his shaft, his hand, as it slid up and down.

* * * * *

Linea's eyes flew open wide as her body flamed with a mysterious desire so strong she didn't have time to be afraid. She whimpered and gasped for air as the pleasure mounted. Yanking the pillow from under her head, she pushed it between her legs and held it tight against her mound as erotic waves pulsed through her. She was on the verge of another explosion and she had no control, none at all.

It hit her with startling power and she threw the pillow aside. Her vagina clenched powerfully and she clamped her hand over her sex, rubbing hard as the climax tore through her. Her juices flooded from her core and soaked her hand. For a long moment she lay there wide-eyed, clutching herself, panting as the ripples gripping her slowly faded.

* * * * *

Draven lay there for a moment waiting for his breathing to regulate. His climax had been a bit more intense than usual, he thought with a frown as he rose from the bed, cleaned up and dressed in a white button-up shirt and thickly woven black cotton pants.

He laid back down across the bed and felt the faint familiar pulses of his climax, as though they ricocheted from some other place. He focused, trying to understand, and as sleep enveloped him it dawned on him. He grinned with satisfaction. *"So glad you shared in my pleasure, love. After all, you were the inspiration…"*

Chapter Twenty-Seven

Linea descended the wide staircase slowly. She gripped the banister with one hand and fingered the skirts of her dress with the other. It was the prettiest she'd been given to wear so far. It was so soft and it very nearly fit, just a few inches short. The deep wine-colored velvet hung in full folds from the empire waist. Wine and gold cording trimmed the dress and draped delicately over the cap sleeves.

Netta had brushed her hair till it seemed to glow, braided it with the same wine and gold cording and arranged it in a lovely configuration on top of her head. Linea felt like royalty, but she knew better — she was nothing of the sort. She was an orphan without a home, without a purpose, and suddenly the fine clothing felt uncomfortable. She frowned down at the plump tops of her breasts. She could see the tips of a few of the scars. She tugged at the low rounded neckline.

Her body still vibrated from her...dream...or whatever it was. "*...you were the inspiration...*" Had it been Draven's voice, or was she just dreaming? She took a deep breath and tried to push it from her mind.

"Are you sure this is appropriate?" Linea asked nervously.

"The dress? Of course, child," Netta said, smiling up at her. "It's lovely on you. Quit pulling at it." She met Linea's worried gaze, leaned in and whispered, "No one will see the scars, dear, they're so very faint."

Linea swallowed and nodded. "Is...should I be taking evening meal at the king's table? Is that appropriate?"

"Certainly." Netta gave her a serious look. "Miss Linea, you have but to explain things to Lord Amaranth. He's a compassionate king."

"I was made to believe he hated my family and wanted to see us dead, all of us, brutally dead."

Netta skewed up her face. "Oh posh. Lord Amaranth is a fierce man but he has a gift for compassion." A secretive smile lit up her round face. "Now, I'll have no more of that way of thinking from you. You need to eat. You're a rack of bones, you are."

The dining chamber faced the keep's entrance hall doors. The etched glass doors to the room were held open with two large silver urns potted with tall plants, their lace-like leaves deep glossy green. The delectable scent of something savory, spicy, made Linea's stomach growl. She stood at the bottom of the stairs, her heart in her throat. The doors must have been closed when she entered the keep before, otherwise she would have never missed this room.

Draven sat at the end of a long, light oak table that ran down the middle of the room, perfectly centered to be the focal point. Two silver candelabras were evenly spaced in the center of the table. Each held three blue candles, their flames dancing cheerfully. Matching sconces holding matching candles hung intermittently along the blue silk brocade covered walls. Wide oak chairs with thick blue cushions were arranged around the table. Draven's chair was the same light polished oak. Much larger than the other chairs, it was majestic, hand-carved, and beautiful.

The woman Linea had seen briefly in the great hall that morning was perched to Draven's right. She was small, fair and beautiful. Her hair shimmered like gold, held back from her perfect face with jeweled clasps and cascaded past her bare shoulders.

Linea couldn't help but admire the way the deep emerald dress shimmered against her creamy, flawless skin. She had never seen material like it before. It glowed, the flickering candles sending shadows and light dancing over the incandescent cloth. A swath of the same material wrapped around her back and over her upper arms.

Her hands were sheathed in soft emerald gloves from the tips of the tiny fingers of her hands to her dainty elbows. Linea looked at her own hands with her long fingers and short nails. Unlike the lovely lady, Linea was neither petite nor delicate. This was Draven's betrothed, Linea surmised as guilt twisted her insides. She suddenly felt over-tall and cumbersome. Her heart felt as though it were in a vise.

She swallowed and let her gaze travel the room. Beside Draven's betrothed sat an enchanting, odd little woman. Linea couldn't recall meeting or ever seeing anyone so fascinating before, but she felt a spark of recognition, a connection of some sort.

The woman was leaning forward; wisps of her pure white hair fluttered around her pretty face. It was straight, parted in the middle of her head and pulled to the side to flow over one shoulder and down past the table. Linea wondered if it covered her knees.

The little woman's eyes were unusually wide, a brilliant violet, and they watched Linea intently. Her muted silver gown wasn't ornate but somehow seemed to sparkle. It fit her diminutive body loosely; its cap sleeves were much like those of the gown Linea herself wore.

To Draven's left sat Armond, beside him two chairs were empty. All the other chairs were filled with Draven's men, the Lanthor Warriors. The chair nearest her, a smaller version of Draven's, also sat empty. Halvar and Arkin were there, as well as a few Linea had not met. Draven stood; his silvery gaze was fixed on her as Netta nudged her forward. The other men set their glasses of wine down and stood, clearing their throats and mumbling to themselves.

"Come, Miss Linea, you may sit beside me." Armond spoke softly and though he did not smile his green eyes were bright and friendly.

"Thank you," she whispered as he pulled out her chair.

She felt as though she had miles to walk as she made her way to her seat. The fire of Draven's lust instantly infused her. She was aware of his erotic thought processes as he watched her. The vision of his throbbing manhood glistening, pistoning in his strong hands, filled her mind. Recalling every sensation his long fingers coaxed from her as they slid up and over his shaft had her shuddering with returning arousal.

She could feel his eyes on her. Everyone was watching her, assessing her. Could they feel it, the incredible heat? Did they see her lust? It irritated her, frightened her. She wanted to turn and run. But she wouldn't. *No, running no longer seemed a viable option*, she thought, pressing her lips together. Instead she sat, keeping her trembling hands clasped tightly in her lap.

"Linea." Draven waited until she met his gaze. "You already know Armond. This is Mistress Cynthia Madison."

Linea cleared her throat. "Nice to meet you," she said quietly, meeting Cynthia's curious gaze.

Draven motioned to the small woman sitting beside Cynthia. "And her assistant, Moria."

Linea turned her attention in time to see fine diaphanous wings flutter behind Moria as she lifted a brow and winked at her. Linea nearly gasped. A faerie. There was so much she wanted to say, so much she wanted to ask. "Oh...I..."

Moria narrowed her eyes quickly and formed a silent 'shush' with her lips, then smiled brightly. "So nice to meet you, Miss Linea."

Linea couldn't contain the smile that spread across her face. "Likewise, Miss Moria."

From the corner of her eye, Linea saw Draven tilt his head and narrow his eyes as he continued to watch her. *"You're beautiful, Linea."*

His words were dark and silky in her mind, like an intimate caress, and her body responded voluntarily. Her womb clenched and she pressed her clasped hands against her stomach. *"Stop it."*

"Stop what?" The vision of his hot wet mouth drawing on her nipple wavered in her mind. Her nipples became erect and hard. Linea nearly whimpered. She looked down at her lap and squeezed her eyes shut.

"Are you all right, Miss Linea?" Cynthia's sweet bell-like voice was muffled by the sound of Linea's blood as it pounded through her veins.

"Yes…yes, Miss Cynthia. I'm fine." She cleared her throat and tried not to scowl at Draven, who was smirking at her now.

Cynthia's fine brows knit together. "Where is the meal? The girl looks peaked. She probably needs to eat."

Linea smiled at Cynthia quickly then looked away, trying to swallow the lump in her throat. "Yes, I'm feeling a bit hungry."

"As am I, sweet Linea. I'm nearly starved." Draven shifted in his chair and Linea sincerely hoped he was feeling as uncomfortable as he was making her. "It has been a while since you've had the slightest…nibble. I would think you'd be famished."

Linea could have sworn she felt his hands on the aching flesh between her legs. She felt herself grow damp. She jerked her head around and gave him a dumbfounded look. He lifted a brow and held her gaze; his eyes were darker, the corner of his full lips tilted slightly. Damn him, he had no right, no right at all to toy with her in this way. Her body vibrated with arousal. She narrowed her eyes at him. "I imagine you must be right, Lord Amaranth."

Cook came in with the meal then. He set wide bowls of thick, rich soup in front of each of them. Baskets of warm crusty bread were set down along the center of the table and a young man followed behind Cook, pouring wine in every sparkling crystal goblet. Linea thanked them, turning her attention to the food and worked on shutting out the erotic play Draven tortured her with.

"Well, well, well. Looks like I showed up at just the right moment." Mason ambled into the room. His rugged face was stubbly and his light eyes were glassy and heavy-lidded. His shirt was wrinkled and hung over his leather pants. The legs scraped noisily across the fine wood floor as he pulled out the empty chair next to Linea. He sat or, rather, fell into the chair facing her without hiding his admiration for her bosom. Was he looking at her scars? She wanted to cover her chest. She didn't know whether to be embarrassed or angry. He leaned close to her, his breath reeking of ale. "Hey there, Miss Linea. Wow, you're pretty."

Linea blinked. "Uh, thank you."

"Mmmm, smell pretty too." Mason leaned closer until she could feel his breath on her neck and chest.

"Mason." Armond's voice held a note of warning.

Linea didn't look up as she felt the heat of Draven's emotions shift, his arousal mingle with fury. It was a heady combination. Instead she leaned away from Mason until she bumped into Armond. "Excuse me," she said quietly.

Mason raised a hand and licked his lips. To her horror, he seemed as though he was going to touch her breast.

"Do it and lose your hand," Draven said through clenched teeth.

Running his hand through his disheveled blonde hair instead, he raised his gaze to Draven. "Do what, cousin?" Even in his ragged state his wide toothy smile made him endearingly handsome, like a mischievous boy.

"Show some respect, Mason." Draven's voice was deceptively quiet.

Draven's countenance would have made anyone else run shrieking in fear. Mason continued to grin and turned to face the table, lowering his head in remorse. "Whatever you say, King Draven. I am but your humble servant."

Draven continued to glare at him. The men began to mumble to their neighbors, averting their eyes from the hostile exchange. Cynthia was frowning deeply. Armond shifted uncomfortably. Linea saw that Moria seemed to completely remove herself from the faction.

With the most serene expression on her delicate features, she ate her soup and nibbled her bread with poise and grace. Linea watched her for a while until Moria looked up and winked at her ever so slightly. Linea blinked as she picked up her spoon and began eating as well. The soup was thick, smooth and flavorful. Linea ate slowly, savoring every delicious spoonful.

Mason laid his hand firmly on Linea's knee and gently squeezed. She nearly choked. Raising her head, her eyes flew to Mason but he seemed absorbed in consuming his soup. Then she met Draven's gaze. Not a good idea. The instant her eyes met his, she knew he was aware of what had rattled her. She could swear lightning flashed in his eyes. Mason's hand moved higher and panic rose up inside her. With widening eyes that never left Draven's narrowing ones, she grabbed Mason's wrist.

"Mason." Draven's voice rumbled low and menacing.

Mason looked up smiling innocently. "Yes, my lord?"

"Remove your hand." Draven's words thundered through Linea to the very pit of her stomach. Fury infused her and her grip tightened.

"Hey, ease up there, dove." Mason smirked as he tugged his hand away.

Linea let go of him, eyeing him. He rubbed at his abused wrist and she gasped at the redness she'd caused, the angry half moon indentions her nails had left. But she wasn't sorry; she wouldn't say she was sorry. He'd had no right to touch her. Suddenly she felt energized, powerful and nearly told him just what she thought of his obnoxious behavior.

"Boy!" Mason swayed in his chair. "Where is that damn boy with the wine?"

Everyone tried desperately to disregard the tension that hung thickly in the room. Cook came in smiling, his beautiful roast and fresh spring vegetables plated up in glorious fashion.

"You've had enough to drink, Mason. Either shut up and eat or excuse yourself." Draven glared, his body rigid.

Cook's smile faltered and his hand shook ever so slightly as he placed the artful plates before each guest.

"Well, I've lost my appetite." Cynthia sniffed angrily, but everyone ignored her.

"Of course. You're right, you're right." Mason nodded as he picked up his knife and fork. "The King of Lanthor!" he sang around a bite of meat. "In what universe could he ever be wrong?"

"For the love of Iybae, Mason, shut the hell up," Armond grumbled.

"And Mason," Draven said without looking up from his plate. "If you dare once more to lay a hand on her, I'll separate you from your favorite part and feed it to Rolf."

A shiver ran up Linea's spine as Draven's perfect white teeth scraped the meat from his pewter fork. Enveloped in his rage, her blood pounded hotly through her veins. The flesh between her legs felt on fire, swollen, slick with arousal. Her nipples ached against the fabric of her dress. She wanted to scream for him to restrain his emotion. It seemed no matter the path his passion took it was volatile to her senses.

Mason stared, heavy-lidded, at Draven, taking his grave threat in stride. "What a fair, compassionate king you are," he said. "My beloved cousin." He speared Draven with a look that was anything but jovial. "No one could blame you for wanting to sink your royal teeth into such a tasty morsel as our Miss Linea here," he said as he gestured with his head in Linea's direction. "And still set to marry the beautiful Miss Cynthia. How nice for you to be given the privilege of having your pussy and eating it, too."

Cynthia's hands trembled and she dropped her spoon, disregarding the loud clank of metal against porcelain. Her eyes widened and glittered with unshed tears. Moria patted her back, whispering to her softly. Linea clenched her teeth against the violent outrage that pervaded her every cell.

A roar tore from Draven as he stood suddenly, his heavy chair nearly tipping over. Like a flash he had Mason by his shirt and was dragging him forcefully from the room, both men growling curses as they went. Silence descended on the room. Linea's stomach churned as she regarded the others. The warriors went back to their meal without a word or a mumble.

"He loses what little reason he possesses when he drinks," Armond said blandly.

Mortified, Linea stared at the far wall, struggling to keep her breath even. She could feel heat crawling up her neck. Such words she'd only heard from her uncle, and hearing them again brought back the shame and humiliation they embodied. Hope that maybe she was something other than what her uncle had said she was had teased her into a sense of security. Now…now she was left confused, angry and aroused. The mixture was driving her mad.

Cynthia looked up at Linea, her dark brown eyes shimmering with tears, her body shaking.

"I'm...uh... If you'll excuse me I've had my fill for tonight." Linea stood on shaky legs, bowed her head and slowly walked from the room.

Her pace increased as she went until she was running up the stairs. Once in her room she sat on the bed, her breath soughing in and out of her lungs, and tried to sort out the whirling thoughts and emotions that had her stomach in knots.

Because of her wicked lust for Draven, Linea had caused Cynthia to hurt. She had felt the sharp anger as jealousy knifed into the woman. Then there had been pain, only pain. And it had been her fault, Linea berated herself. After all those years of hoping he was wrong she had finally proven Uncle Haig right. Shame sank its vile fangs into her heart as tears rolled down her cheeks. She was a whore. Now everyone knew it to be true.

Chapter Twenty-Eight

"You go too far, Mason!" Draven slammed the door behind him as he shoved Mason into the war room. Mason stumbled then righted himself.

"I go too far? I go..." Mason swayed on his feet.

Anger and resentment flared hotly in Mason, their sharp tendrils reaching Draven, wrapping around him. His own anger was enough, he didn't need Mason's too. "You disgrace yourself, drinking like a sod till you're revolting to look upon. What is your problem?"

"You! You're my fuckin' problem, you greedy fop." He launched himself at Draven, his fist ready. Draven stopped him easily enough as his fist connected with Mason's stubborn jaw. Mason fell back into the chair, shook his head then vaulted back for another attack. Once again Draven outmaneuvered him with another blow to the jaw.

"Dammit, Mason, you're being a jackass!" Draven roared as he threw Mason up against the wall.

Mason wiped the blood from his lip and snarled, "Yeah? Then we're two of a kind, cuz."

Draven held his angry gaze for a tense moment, wishing he could read his cousin's mind as easily as he read Linea's. He suspected he knew the reason for Mason's fury, which only heightened his own. He bared his teeth and shoved Mason hard before turning away to pace the room. The guilt was gnawing at Draven's insides.

The truth was Mason was right about one thing. Linea was a tasty morsel and he did want her. He craved her and it pissed him off that Mason wanted her too, and to further complicate things he'd embarrassed and humiliated Cynthia. He'd never been the sort to treat a woman so savagely as to scorn her in public and leave her tearful and in the throes of such raging jealousy. Draven ran a hand through his hair and sighed.

"What the hell is it that you want from me, Mason?" he asked gruffly.

"It doesn't matter what I want, does it, Draven?" Mason mumbled in reply, licking at his cut lip.

"Fuck you, Mason!" Draven hurled back.

"Yeah, fuck me." Mason slouched down in the big chair and threw one long leg over the arm.

"It matters, you ignorant ass. You matter. And it's damn insulting for you to say otherwise, even if you are acting like a whining titty baby. You're all the fucking family I have left. By Iybae, Mason! I'd damn you to hell if you weren't," Draven growled, his voice hoarse with emotion.

Mason worked his aching jaw and said nothing.

"I didn't know you had fallen in love with Linea…"

Mason's eyes cut to Draven then he laughed out loud, a laugh that held more contempt than humor. "For the love of Iybae, you really are a dolt." He shook his head.

Draven grabbed Mason by the collar of his shirt and yanked him up until they were face to face. "Mason, cut the games and speak your mind like the man you should be or I'll cut your fucking tongue out with a dull butter knife. I've had enough!" he shouted, throwing him back into the chair.

Mason sat forward, his elbows on his knees, and scrubbed his hands over his stubbly face.

Draven roared, "What?"

"Cynthia! I want Cynthia! She's everything, she's all I want. God help me, Draven, I love her!"

Draven froze, staring down at Mason in shock. It seemed every emotion inside him froze as well and for the first time, he didn't know what to feel, he didn't know what to say.

"Aw hell, Draven, I think I'm gonna puke." Mason grabbed his stomach.

Draven sat in the chair across from him. "You damn well better not, you sniveling milksop."

Mason tried to scowl but it looked more like a sulk. He rubbed his temples and breathed deeply. "Draven, it happened so fast. I told you I found her attractive… no…more than that. Hell, you knew what I felt."

Draven looked at him with disgust. "You're trying to make this my fault."

Mason shook his head gently. "No…well, not really."

"Not really?"

"It's not like we planned it…" Mason looked up pleadingly. Draven narrowed his eyes as revelation came to him. "We had been talking all day. Those big warm eyes of hers were so alive, so bright. It was late, you still hadn't returned with Linea. I suggested Cynthia and Moria stay. They agreed and went to bed. Cynthia and I were up in the middle of the night and I passed her in the corridor. She was adorable when she was flustered so I thought I'd…at first I was just teasing, Draven, I swear."

"Oh, I wanted to touch her, don't misunderstand, but…I just wasn't thinking. I got close to her and she smelled so good and I got closer…" Draven watched Mason closely as he seemed to lose himself in the shadows of his memory. "I leaned in and her lips were so close. I thought, one taste, one little taste. But I was like a starved man, Draven. Her sweet little hands were moving over me, touching me and before I knew it I had her against the wall and I was deep inside her, she was…"

"Stop, Mason, I get the picture." Draven felt torn between the joy he felt and the disgrace for what he was supposed to feel that he didn't.

Mason looked up and met his gaze. "I'm sorry."

"Was this mutual? Please tell me you didn't take advantage of her, Mason."

Mason's expression was incredulous. "Fuck no! She was always a step ahead of me; hell, she had my stiff and ready cock in her hand before I could even formulate a plan. And Draven, her tongue did things I didn't know could be done."

Draven squeezed his eyes shut and lifted a hand to stop him. It was hard to believe they were talking about the same woman. He'd always considered Cynthia to be an ice queen. He stood and turned his back to Mason. It did nothing for Draven's ego that Mason brought out the temptress in her. But he'd never wanted to, not like he wanted to with Linea.

"But she was hurt and angry, she was…ah, I see. She was upset over your flirting with Linea," Draven said softly.

Mason winced.

"As was I." Draven's voice took on an edge as he pinned Mason with a sharp look, glowering at him.

"What?" Mason frowned.

Draven continued to glare at him. "I'll have to mull over this. Out."

"Draven, I…"

"Get out, Mason. Now!"

A look of utter despair crossed Mason's face. "You want me to leave the keep?"

Draven rolled his eyes and snarled at him. "No, you half-wit. Just get the hell out of my sight."

Mason breathed a sigh of relief and rose. His wide shoulders were slumped as he walked out of the room, quietly shutting the door behind him. Draven's hand itched to smack him on the head. Mason was no idiot, though he could act like one on occasion. That his cock led him was no surprise. Although, Draven suspected there was more to this attraction than sex. He'd never seen his cousin this shaken. And Mason would never have risked such a scandal had he not been smitten. Now Mason and Cynthia's tryst had altered everything. Draven couldn't help but smile with relief.

* * * * *

Linea finally found Gavril lounging on a chaise near the fire with a book in his hand, a tiny glass of port in the other.

"I've been looking everywhere for you, little man." She stood in the doorway, her hands on her hips.

He closed his book carefully and sat up grinning. "Miss Linea! I'm glad you found me!" He patted the space beside him on the velvet seat. "Come sit with me."

Linea stood where she was and frowned down at him. "I'm confused. Why have you not come to fight with the king or even to see about me? You don't even have a guard anymore. Has Lord Amaranth come to his senses?"

Gavril's grin faded. "That ass, he has no sense. Come, sit with me. There is much we should talk about."

Reluctantly Linea crossed the room to sit beside the elf. He took her hand in his and looked up at her adoringly. She could see that his violet eyes held secrets, secrets that irritated her curious nature. "Tell me what you know, Gavril. I need to understand."

"Ha! As though I should know so much." Gavril patted her hand. "I'll tell you what I knew. I knew your mother and father, during the dark time. I pledged the allegiance of the elf folk to them and their cause. I am forever their servant."

Linea's chest tightened and she swallowed hard. "Then you are free. They're dead. Didn't you know that?"

"Nay, dear Linea, they live in you. I see your mother in your eyes and your father in your stubborn chin. You are their legacy. "

Linea's brows knit together and she struggled not to shed the tears that burned behind her eyes. No one had ever spoken of her mother and father. She could barely remember them now. They had left her a legacy of pain.

Gavril frowned deeply. "I couldn't find you, Linea. I tried. I was unable to go anywhere near Orbane's keep. I was hunted and for the safety of my people we had to stay away. I'm so sorry, my sweet Linea. I knew he would bully you, keep you down. He knew your power. I had no idea he was beating you."

Linea met his gaze. "I have no power."

Gavril winked at her. "Aye, ya do. But, it's been dormant. Heh, you're strong enough, though, without it. You're bull-stubborn, tall as a reed and built. Damn if ya ain't built, girl."

"Don't be crass, Gavril." She scowled at him but softened it with a crooked smile. "I have to go. I don't want to be found here. Tomorrow…we'll talk more tomorrow."

Gavril blinked at her. "Aye, my lady. You do what your gut tells you, you hear?"

Linea just shook her head. Odd little fellow said so little and told her so much. She felt like she had one of those itches that wouldn't go away no matter how hard she scratched. She wanted to hear more about her parents, more about this power she supposedly had, and Gavril never did explain why Draven had given him freedom. Frustration had her grumbling as she left the room, closing the door behind her.

It had grown quite late. Everyone had retired to his or her room and the keep was silent. Her way was lit only by the fire from the great hall below. She moved slowly down the dimly lit corridor, careful to keep her footfalls quiet.

A warm sensation seemed to tickle her brain and bathe her in heat. Her nipples pushed against the soft material of her gown and her sex tightened, sending tingles dancing through her body. She trembled, knowing Draven was near. She tiptoed to the edge of the balcony, staying in the shadows, and looked down into the vast space of the hall. He was busy stirring the fire. His back was to her, bent slightly.

Her breath quickened as she watched from her shadowed alcove by the archway in the balcony. She couldn't help but think he had such a fine round backside. His back was strong, wide, his thick muscles rippling as he moved. Her hands fisted at her side as she imagined them gliding over that back to grip his smooth, hard butt, pulling him closer, deeper into her.

It was always the same when he was near. Lust flamed through her veins, reminding her of her wantonness. She wasn't sure she could control her passions if she wanted to, but she didn't want to. She trembled at the mental image of him straining over her, the thick hardness of him filling her, moving inside her like his fingers had, invading her softness. He stood then, replacing the poker in its holder.

"You're playing with fire, Linea."

Deciding to let her true nature reign, her eyelids lowered seductively as she eyed Draven. Her heart pounded against her ribs; goose bumps rose over her arms. She could hide nothing from him anyway. *"I'm not a child, Draven, that I should need to play."*

He tilted his head, his eyes widening. Ha. She could do some taunting of her own. She stepped out of the shadows and crossed her arms under her swelling breasts. She knew he could see her erect nipples straining against the thin fabric of her gown and she didn't care. The smirk tilting her lips slowly evaporated as a wicked grin slid across his face. Oh those lips of his, so full, so firm and soft at the same time. Her confidence faltered a bit and she moved toward her bedchamber door, which unfortunately faced the staircase.

"No, you're right." He began to walk toward her, stopping at the bottom of the steps. Her breath caught in her chest. *"You're no child, but you are young, too young…"* She felt his lust flow into her, heating her, raising her blood pressure. He took two steps at a time, melting her with his mental torture. *"So…innocent, Linea, and you are playing."*

Dear Iybae, she was in over her head. He kept advancing on her. She gasped, and then grimaced as she bumped into her door, wedged between the cold wood and his hot rock-hard body. She squeezed her eyes closed against the torrential tide of emotion that seductively enveloped and penetrated her. In her mind she could see the rosy-gold waves of heat coming from him, washing over her. She felt dizzy, her body swaying toward him.

She slowly opened her eyes, letting her gaze travel his body until she looked up into his eyes. The grin was gone but his eyes still held that wicked glint. They were hard and serious, piercing. A shiver crawled up her spine and her breath was coming in pants. Her lips parted on a silent moan.

He leaned down till his lips were a fraction away from hers. She could taste his wine-flavored breath as it feathered over her lips. Without thinking she licked them and felt him stiffen. Why was he holding back? Her imagination filled with thoughts of wrapping herself around him just to feel him envelope her, permeate her very being.

"I don't play, Linea." His whisper seemed loud, like thunder. It shook her. She had no time to respond before he reached around her, opened the door and gently pushed her into her room, closing the door in her face. She wanted to stamp her foot with frustration. Her skin felt ultra sensitive, and the need was becoming painful. He did this; he made her burn for him.

She stood there vibrating with raw lust, with intensifying anger. She wasn't sure how long she'd stood there when she took a step back, turned and crossed to the dressing table beside her bed. Her chest was heaving with fury, her teeth clenched so hard her jaw began to ache. The flesh between her thighs was swollen, throbbing, sodden with her juices. Each step sent ribbons of sensation curling through her womb, making her breasts grow heavy, her nipples painfully erect, wanting, ready for attention.

He couldn't hide that he'd wanted her. She'd felt him straining against the hunger gnawing at him, the warm heaviness low in his stomach and the spiraling arousal that wound through him. Yet he held back. He seemed to find more pleasure in denying her. Even if she had not felt the incredible desire in him, she had noticed that the front of his pants were tented.

She was naïve but she had learned what that meant, he had taught her. He did this to her, gave her this horrible craving that never left her. She grabbed a tall slender vase that held two blood-red feathery flowers and hurled it with a roar that came from deep within. The delicate vase smashed against the door; its shards tinkled across the floor.

She spun around and stood staring at her image in the mirror. Her cheeks were deeply flushed; her eyes were bright with emotion, and she shoved the burning feelings of shame roughly aside. She knew she couldn't compete with Cynthia's fair beauty but she was not ugly, and though she wasn't guiltless she did not deserve this. This was cruel, hurtful, infuriating.

She pressed her lips together as she reached up and undid the clasp holding her hair back. He doesn't play? Ha! She pulled the pins loose, freeing her thick hair, letting it tumble down her back. She dragged the brush vigorously through her hair, ignoring the painful twinges the few tangles caused. Damn him and his games! In spite of what style and application the man chose to use, torture was torture. "I'll be damned if I let a man torture me again!" she declared defiantly, not caring who may hear her.

Before she could change her mind she was heading down the corridor to his room. She opened his door, shut it quietly behind her and lit the thick candle sitting on the desk near the door. Evidently he had just settled into bed and had pulled the cover over his hips. She felt his surprise, his concern, as he sat up raising a brow. Yes, he had need to be concerned. She would have him, rape him if need be. "Linea...what the hell..."

She marched over to the side of the bed, her hands on her hips. "I am very sorry for Mistress Cynthia. I never wanted to hurt her. She's very sweet and hopefully one day she'll forgive you and me. But I can't help that now..."

Confusion had him frowning and he shook his head. "What, wh..."

"Just shut up! You started this and you're going to finish it. Right now. This night."

Chapter Twenty-Nine

Draven turned in the bed and put his feet on the floor, careful to keep his hips covered. Feeling brazen, Linea unabashedly let her gaze travel his body, from his long narrow feet to his wide silvery eyes. He was a masterpiece of manhood. His strong features and potent body were sculpted to exhibit Iybae's exquisite creative nature.

Heavy muscles contoured his hairy calves and powerful thighs. Dark curls dusted his wide chest and tapered down his finely corded stomach. His expansive shoulders and biceps bulged. Sinewy muscle snaked tightly over his forearms. His broad hands were perfect, their long fingers curled in the material that kept her eyes from drinking in all of him.

The man exuded power and for a moment she felt overmatched. Hesitating, she focused on him but couldn't feel him or hear his thoughts. She briefly closed her eyes and gathered her courage. The vision of those long fingers curled around his cock filled her with need and anticipation. The ache between her legs mounted; the intoxicating sensations pervaded her system and she swallowed hard.

Frowning, he reached out to her and touched her forehead. "Linea, what's happened? Are you ill?"

How could he be so blind, this man who could see into a person's very soul? She slapped at his hand. "No! Damn you!"

Stiffening with resolve, she took a step back and crossed her arms over her middle, grasping the sides of her gown. She met his gaze then lifted it over her head and threw it aside. Praying he wouldn't reject her again, she stood before him naked, trembling, her hands on her hips, resisting the urge to cover the ugly scars that marred her body.

If he rejected her now…well, he just couldn't. If he did, her heart would shatter. She lifted her chin and thrust out her chest in defiance, trying to conjure up her bravado. "I am sick to death of your games and your insipid torture. I'm done with it. I'm not leaving until you have satisfied me properly and well."

He was staring at her as though in shock. She could swear in the painful silence that she could hear her heart crack. She cleared her throat and tried to still her raging emotions. Her voice was a bit softer. "You won't notice the scars so much in the dim light. Just ignore them."

He sat there, his mouth open, his eyes darkening as his pupils dilated. She felt heat flash through him, through her, and fought the urge to run crying from the room.

"Linea." His voice was dark and husky.

Her body trembled from his heated scrutiny. If he didn't touch her soon she thought she would burst into flames. A breath shuddered from her shaking body and she gritted her teeth.

"Spare me this torment now, Draven," she demanded in a deep sultry growl. Nerves fueled her frustration and she moved like lightning, jerking the covers away from him. A relieved smile tugged at her lips as her gaze took in his erect member. It was a magnificent sight, standing up so proudly, it seemed to stretch out, reaching for her.

Hungry for him, she took his face between her hands and kissed him lightly. She took her time, testing, teasing him with slow little kisses. She loved the feel of his soft goatee against her hands. His smoky, spicy scent assailed her senses as he opened his mouth and met each soft kiss.

His mouth felt wonderful against hers. Warm and firm, his full bottom lip tempted her and she took it between her lips, letting her tongue skim over it. His hands were so warm as they grasped her waist just above her hips. Encouraged, she hesitantly slipped her tongue into his mouth to stroke the sensitive skin on the inside of his lips. He groaned into her mouth and pulled her closer until she stood between his thighs.

Opening to her, he flooded her mind and body with his passion, his hunger. They only served to stimulate her frenzied senses even more. He kissed her neck, her throat. His hands moved up her body, leaving a trail of fire as they went. His mouth did hot, moist exquisite things to the area where her neck met her shoulder as his hands cupped the sides of her breasts.

Heated arousal curled through her and she felt herself quickly losing the advantage. Afraid that he would tease her and leave her to burn alone again she fought through the fog of desire, planted her palms on his shoulders and shoved him hard. He fell back on the bed;

his gaze locked on hers as she lowered her head and planted wet kisses over his stomach.

She nuzzled the taut, tanned skin then licked his navel. His stomach quivered beneath her tongue, fueling her passion. Her hands roamed over his stomach, his hips, loving the feel of smooth skin and crisp hair against her palms. She bit into his tough but supple skin and licked him again, smiling triumphantly at his lusty growl and the pleasure she felt surge though him.

She moved lower. Her long hair brushed over his stomach, hips and thighs. Gently she touched his shaft with her fingertips; a tingling sensation danced over her as she let them softly wander up and down the velvety length of it. Her thumb found the thick ridge that ran underneath.

"So hard and so soft, it's like velvet over steel," she whispered, not trying to mask the wonder in her voice. Her lips were so near she could feel the heat from him. She lowered her head and ran her tongue over it. "Mmmm," she groaned huskily.

Draven inhaled sharply, arching toward her. She could feel his arousal mounting and his struggle to rein it in. She wanted to make his control snap. She wanted him to lose all logic and reason and take her, devour her. Her own hunger pounded through her, demanded more sensation, more touch.

She raised her head and met his gaze, watching him as she took the plum-like head of his cock into her mouth, tasting, laving it with her tongue. He breathed through his teeth and his hands sifted through her hair. Her lips moved over his shaft, taking him deeper into her mouth.

"Stop. God, Linea, stop," he rasped. Her tongue rubbed against his rigid flesh and curled around the base of the head. "Dammit! Linea. Come here. I said stop!"

His cock left her mouth with a pop. She knew she had been doing it right. She felt the vibrations that pulsed in him, in her, and she had let them guide her. She squeezed her thighs together as the waves undulated through her. She needed this, desperately.

"It feels too good. I don't want to stop." Her voice was deep, sultry. It sounded as though it came from someone else.

"Yes," he said roughly. "Just not now, not yet." He wore the expression of a man in great pain, though she knew for a fact the pain he was in was glorious. She felt the same kind of pain and she never wanted it to end. It was so good, every inch of her ached with need for more of him. And she loved the feel of her lips gliding over him and the feel of his passion rising with each stroke of her tongue.

"It will only get better, sweetness, I promise. Come here."

She stood slowly, tossing her hair back from her face. He was taking control again. Making her wait. She couldn't, not anymore. He began to sit up and with a leap that shocked even her she jumped up on the bed and straddled him. "No," she panted.

Linea needed to be in control. She was captivated by the sensations she received from him, his emotions flowing though her. She wanted them, all of them, she wanted him unguarded and he was always so strong, so controlled, and so cautious. She didn't care that she was young or that she was clumsy in her exploration.

She'd known too many years filled with pain, without so much as a kind pat on the shoulder from anyone. This was like paradise and she was probably turned over to a reprobate mind, but she couldn't help it. She couldn't think about her sin, she needed this. Greedy…she was so greedy, she thought biting her lip, but she was past caring. Tonight she would take from him what she had needed and give him her all.

Desperately she fell forward across his body, kissing him. Pressing her mouth hard against his she rocked back and forth, brushing her breasts against the crisp hair of his chest. She couldn't help moving against his cock as it nestled against the crease of her butt. Oh, it felt so good she wanted to cry or scream or growl but she had control. For the first time in her miserable life she had joy and she had control.

In one smooth motion Draven took that control away, flipping her to her back, pinning her arms over her head. His thigh pressed against the swollen lips of her sex, opening her. She lay there looking up at him with frustrated defiance. The hot blood surging through her veins pounded loudly in her ears.

His dark eyes were like a wild thunderstorm as he watched her, saw her mind. She bit her lip to keep from begging him. She writhed under him, undulating against his thigh. The roughness pressing and rubbing against her sensitive flesh felt so amazing. Her head tilted back as she cried out softly. He moved his thigh away and she whimpered in protest and fought to get closer to him.

"Stop, Linea. My love, slow down," he growled.

She wanted to scream. "Draven, please, don't make me stop. I hurt…I need…" she pleaded with him, nearly crying.

Draven kissed her. "Shhh Linea, sweet Linea," he murmured. His hot mouth moved down her neck and between her breasts, kissing, nipping and licking as he went. One hand cupped her breast, stroked and massaged her, avoiding her nipple. "It's all right, I'll fix it."

But he was taking too long, moving too slowly. The folds between her legs felt full and engorged, sodden with her hunger. The tips of her aching breasts throbbed and tightened painfully. Finally, he took her nipple in his mouth and drew on it gently, laving it with his tongue as she had the head of his cock. She arched up, crying out. "Harder, Draven, please…"

His lips gripped the hardening bead as his tongue rasped over it. He then kissed his way slowly to the other.

"It feels so good. Please, don't make me suffer," Linea silently pleaded.

The ache spread through her and set her aflame. "Please don't stop," she cried out in frustration.

He raised his head and met her gaze. His somber eyes reflected the heat in hers. "No, love, I won't stop this time."

Releasing her hands, he took each breast in a hand and kneaded them, rolling her hard nipples gently between his fingers. His mouth moved lower, faster, leaving a hot moist trail down her body to the thatch of mahogany curls that covered her mound. He kissed her there.

Grasping her thighs he pulled her legs up and opened her. He was killing her; she was going to die, and she knew it. His tongue speared inside her at the apex of the folds to lightly stroke the hard little knot of flesh nestled there. Sensations—every kind of sensation—took her over, searing into her, radiating through her, winding her tighter and tighter. Linea gasped, arching and twisting in his grasp. Her fingers tangled in his hair.

"So sweet, just like honey. Linea, so wet and hot." He dipped lower, laving her juice as if it were the nectar from Iybae Himself. Nibbling at the pouting lips of her sex, she felt him smile against her.

"So it is, sweetness, a precious gift from Iybae." His words, soft and warm inside her mind drove her wild. "Mmm, so good," he murmured against sensitive flesh.

Her body tensed as the pleasure built, intensified, coiled tightly inside her.

"Let go, Linea," he mentally whispered to her, gently squeezing the lips of her sex together as he drew his tongue through the narrow cleft.

Her head tossed from side to side. Whimpering cries came from somewhere. Was that her?

"Oh, it's too much, I can't." Her breath was shallow.

His thumbs stroked her, opening her again. "Mmm. Yes you can." He moaned. "No one will hear. I want to hear you scream."

Her vagina contracted as his tongue thrust into her, and then firmly stroked from her tight opening upward through the swollen folds of her sex and circled her clit. "*Cry out for me.*"

She arched up, groaning through clenched teeth as her fingers threaded through his hair, pulling him closer.

"*Let go, love.*" He took her clit between his lips and sucked gently on it. She writhed against him as the pressure grew. His hands moved over her, touching her, inflaming her. She felt like she was going to shatter, like that vase she'd thrown against the door. Linea sucked her breath, crying out as waves of sensation pulsed outward and coursed through her. It was like a living thing, a force Linea had never known.

Again, Draven moaned against her heated flesh, vibrating the swollen bud as he felt the effects of what he did to her. Linea seemed to hover for sheer seconds on the precipice of ecstasy before she broke apart in an explosion of pleasure.

He wouldn't stop and neither would the orgasm. She couldn't contain the cry that erupted from her. She cried out hoarsely, fisting her hands in Draven's thick silky hair as she flew into pieces. He stroked and sucked and licked and groaned as each wave crested and crashed over her, leaving her weak and trembling. Draven moved to lie beside her and took her into his arms. She turned to him, nestling her head against his shoulder, shuddering in the aftershocks.

"So beautiful," he murmured.

Chapter Thirty

Linea lay there, slowly regaining her senses. It had been incredible to lose control and cry out like that, to feel him feel her. It was like a mirror image of their emotions, a ricochet of sensation that built one on another, adding more and more until...*pow*!

Draven chuckled and she felt the rumble against her cheek. "Better?"

"Um hmm," she mumbled against his chest. She felt him closing her off, just a little, but still, he was blocking her.

"Good," he said softly, pulling her closer.

Her brow furrowed as she focused on him. Though it was fading, she could still feel his need, the desire left unsatisfied throbbing inside him. Not to mention the rock-hard shaft that pressed against her belly. Although her orgasm had been amazing, she wanted more. She wanted to know the feel of him inside her physically. To be completely filled with him.

"Don't stop now, Draven," she said huskily as she kissed his chest, flicking her tongue over his nipple. "I'm not finished." Her hand slid down his body; her fingers wrapped around his pulsing cock. Rising, she watched as her thumb smoothed the pearl of arousal beading at the tip over the fully engorged head. He sucked air through his teeth and let go of the block.

"Dear Iybae." He pulled her down to him and his mouth closed over hers. His tongue plundered her mouth, rubbing and stroking. He tasted exotic, like seduction, spicy and a bit musky. His hand moved over her breasts, down her stomach to her still throbbing wet flesh. His passion surged into her, taking her breath, filling her with urgent need for him.

His hand was firm but gentle as he slid his fingers through the slick, overly sensitive folds. She tried to lay still, relax, but his touch incited her senses to riot. It was as though her body had never been satisfied and began aching for more. The familiar tightening sent spirals careening up through her womb to her breasts, from her breasts down to her womb. It flowed out from her and reflected back, slamming into her with force.

Linea gripped his cock lightly, sliding her hand up and down the shaft. She was amazed at the intensity of pleasure he felt. It spiraled around her own, spiking her passion. The feeling was astonishing; it overwhelmed her. Her fingers caressed the crease below the flared head. She moaned into his mouth and he clasped her wrist and moved her hand away.

"Too fast," he panted huskily. "You're driving me crazy."

"Good. It feels so good." Her body began to tremble with urgency. She wanted him crazy. His desperate want for her made her feel strong and invincible. Anxious to feel his body surging into her as his emotions were, she clung to him, her lips moving over his, greedy for all he would give her.

His finger slowly entered her convulsing channel as his tongue stroked the sensitive interior of her mouth. Her mind clouded and she pressed closer to him. Her sheath clenched around his finger as he slid it slowly in and out. With each stroke she felt the pressure tightening within her, the pleasure intensify. A moan came from deep inside her as her hands smoothed over his tanned skin. She trailed a hand down his arm and covered his hand, urging him closer, further inside her.

"Easy, love," he murmured against her lips as he inserted another finger, stretching her.

His mouth covered her breast and nibbled at the taut nipple. She arched against him, pulling at his hips, and cried out, "Oh God, I can't stand it. Please, Draven, now."

He rose over her and settled between her thighs. She grasped his hips and pulled him closer.

"Wait, Linea." He rested his forehead on hers. "Woman, you're going to kill me."

"I want you inside me. Deep, deep inside me." She gulped. "I can't help it. I need you." He met her gaze and she could see her wild-eyed expression reflected in his eyes.

His breathing was ragged as he kissed her deeply, struggling to go slowly. He moved his upper body against hers. "I want that too, love, but it's your first time. We have to go slow."

"I don't want to go slow." Her voice was low and raspy as she reached for his cock.

"Linea!" He stopped her hand before it found him. "Next time, I promise but this time it will hurt a little. I must go slowly so I can help you with it. If I take you like I want to take you, I could hurt you a lot before I can take the pain from you and I don't want to hurt you."

It would hurt? How could it hurt? Everything he'd done to her had felt wonderful, glorious, amazing. It didn't hurt. She frowned up at him. "I don't understand. You're confusing me. I know you feel…"

Draven groaned. "Linea, just relax and let me take you."

Linea nodded reluctantly, but she still didn't understand. He nuzzled her neck. Kissing and nibbling, doing those incredible things to her. He reached between them and took his cock in his hand, guiding it up and down through the creamy folds of her tormented sex. The hot round head circled her engorged clit.

She couldn't think. Everything grew fuzzy in the sharp rush of passion. Her hands moved up his chest and over his shoulders. Her nails bit into his flesh as the round swollen head of his cock pressed into the entrance of her vagina. "Ah…Linea, you're so tight, so hot," he rasped.

Oh, dear Creator, this was what she had hungered for. Linea's breath was shallow with the intense pleasure.

"More," she cried, arching upward, taking him deeper inside her. Why? Why did he do this to her? She wanted all of him and he kept torturing her. Her body convulsed around him, urging him in further.

"Dammit, Linea!" He sounded angry but his eyes didn't reflect anger and she didn't feel anger from him. What she did feel was his voracious need to plunge into her, which only contradicted his actions and his words.

He took a deep shuddering breath. "Wrap your legs around me…tightly."

She obeyed as she looked up at him and smiled. He made her feel so good, so incredibly good after she'd lived so many years filled with pain and hurt. Her body shook with desire as he touched her cheek, softly rubbing his thumb along her lower lip. She took it into her mouth and sucked it, licked it then moved her hips, taking him a bit deeper. The muscled walls of her channel stretched to accommodate his thick shaft. The ache it caused was not unpleasant. She closed her eyes, drinking in the feel of the broad bulbous head pulsing inside her as the sensations washed over her. Her vagina closed around him, molding to him.

Draven gripped her hips and moved into her slowly, a fraction at a time. His teeth clenched. A sheen of sweat had coated their bodies with the exertion. The pleasure and the promise of more were driving her insane. This wasn't making sense; none of it made sense. Her body screamed for the driving force of him. It took over her mind. All of him, now! She wanted it now.

Linea moaned and bit her lip, then with all her strength she thrust her hips upward. His cock tore her maidenhead and drove up into her, stretching her, forcing her open, filling her completely.

She wasn't prepared for the harsh bite of pain. He had tried to save her from it, but she hadn't understood. Her eyes flew open wide and she held her breath as pain seared her. The sharpness slowly faded to a burn and she blinked up at Draven and gasped for air. His face flushed with restraint, his glittering eyes were shuttered. Was he snarling?

Her eyes widened. "I'm sorry," she whispered, afraid he would pull away.

"No, love, I won't leave you." She frowned at the strange pulling she felt as Draven drew the pain from her. It left her body and filled his like a dull fog. Then as quickly as it spread through him, the pain dispersed and faded away.

Draven bent then, kissing her so gently, so sweetly. His goatee rubbed softly against her cheek; his warm lips moved over hers deliberately, tenderly, making her forget the pain ever existed. His thumb wiped the tears she didn't notice from her cheeks.

Linea's fingertips grazed over his back, down to the dip in his spine. His tongue delved into her mouth, possessing her, teasing her tongue with his as he began to move inside her. The pain was completely gone, replaced with a different kind of pain—a pain she was quickly becoming addicted to. Her hips began moving in rhythm with his.

He pulled almost completely free of her convulsing channel then slid in to the hilt. The sensations were euphoric. Her body seemed to be made for his. He sucked her nipples, his tongue rasping over each hardened berry, giving equal attention to both as his hands moved over her body, stroking and fondling. "You belong to me, Linea, now and forever."

Draven drove into her with slow and steady strokes. Soon he picked up momentum. Linea groaned. Following her instincts she gripped his ass in her hands, lifting her hips to meet each thrust. He reached between them. His palm pressed against her, right below her stomach, as his thumb slid around and over her clit, circling, pressing.

She arched up. A lusty cry escaped her as she surrendered every tiny control to him. She threw her head back, thrusting her hips up as she bore down on the heightening pleasure, moaning and whimpering with each stroke. She flexed the muscles of her sheath, clenching around his cock as he speared up into her.

"Mmm...yes," he hissed, fighting against his own release as he forced her higher and higher.

She finally let go, wavered, then she splintered, hurled into the all-consuming throes of her violent climax. It seemed to have a mind of its own. She was helpless against it as it gripped her and tossed her body into an intense world of pleasure. She had never felt freer.

Draven growled as he rammed hard into her soft hot flesh, completely filling her. Her channel spasmed tightly around him.

"My Linea." His shaft thickened, filling her beyond what she thought possible. He growled as he drew in and out in long, hard, steady strokes. Linea held on to him and cried out as her second release overtook her. She felt the juice of her release gather and flood from her, coating his burgeoning cock and the tender swollen folds caressing it.

The slick slide of his shaft against her felt so good. She moaned as he thrust inside her, his body rubbing against hers. He lifted his face and roared as his climax seized him and surged into her. It ricocheted as each orgasm fed off the other until they both were caught up in a spasmodic torrent of sensation. Linea screamed his name as another orgasm seized her. She gritted her teeth, her body shuddering with the overwhelming sensations. She felt the hot fluid filling her, soothing her inflamed, convulsing flesh. Her sheath tugged and milked him for every precious drop.

She lay there for a long time, his weight holding her down. It was a strange but comforting feeling to have the weight of this man on her. Her breathing was shallow, as was his. They were both slick with sweat and arousal. Her bones felt like liquid and for the first time in a long time she felt full, warm, peaceful.

Chapter Thirty-One

It was done; there was no turning back. She belonged to him. Stubborn woman, she had given him her all, surrendered completely. He kissed the top of her head and cuddled her closer. She slept so peacefully now. Her dark copper-tipped lashes lay against her pale skin. Her full lips were still swollen and rosy from his kisses. Her leg lay possessively over his; her hand rested over his heart. His body still felt the aftereffects of their climax. His shaft lay, semi-erect, against his leg but it wouldn't take much to make him ready to love Linea again.

He breathed deeply, frowning up at the folds in the canopy over his bed. Of all the women he'd had sex with before, he had never experienced their climaxes. He could feel their emotions, but not their bodies, not the sensations he produced in them. Linea and Draven seemed to reflect each other when emotions were high. When battling the Kyroks, and also in the woods, he had felt the odd power surge when his anger and frustration had soared.

So Linea was gifted as well. Isn't that what the elf had told him? It was time he accepted the fact that he needed to spend some time with the little bastard. Gavril knew and understood what was happening, and Draven needed to know everything. But first he needed to deal with Mason and Cynthia.

He looked down at Linea again. Reluctantly he shifted and began carefully untangling himself from her. She frowned, her bottom lip protruding as she groaned in protest. He grinned at her, fighting the urge to take that voluptuous lip in his mouth and nibble at it until she kissed him back and… "Damn," he whispered, shaking his head.

She groaned again and turned over, pulling her knees up to her chest. Her hair fanned out over her face, across his pillow. Draven's brow shot up as his gaze devoured the shape of her long straight back that tapered down to her waist and then flared out in the finest backside he'd ever seen. Her hips were wide and her ass was full and round and inviting. His shaft throbbed to life. He grimaced. Now it was his turn to groan.

With a sigh he pulled on his pants and quietly left the room. The light from the fire below had dimmed, leaving the balcony dark. He passed Linea's room and turned right, carefully making his way to Mason's room. He stood before Mason's door and raised his fist to knock when he heard a guttural sound coming from inside. Frowning, he quietly turned the knob and silently opened the door.

The first thing he saw was Mason's ass cheeks flexing frantically as he pumped into the small woman he had bent over in front of him. Draven leaned against the doorjamb. That tiny little ass could only belong to the lovely Cynthia and apparently, Mason now. His lips tilted in a sarcastic smile as he took in the humorous but arousing scene: his sweet demure betrothed, her tiny hands grasping the headboard railing of Mason's bed for all she was worth, her head bobbing up and down as she cried out like a yapping puppy.

"Yes, yes, oh Mason, harder oh yes, deeper, right there, oh, oh." She punctuated each thrust.

Mason gripped her minute waist, his thighs on either side of her legs, grunting as he pumped. "Yes! Take it all," he groaned.

The whole scene was definitely giving Draven ideas and he would have waited till they were sated but from the looks of them going at it, who knew when that would be? Then Mason smacked Cynthia's tiny butt and she screamed. "Yes! Spank me again. Do it harder, Mason!"

Draven rolled his lips inward to keep from laughing and cleared his throat. Both of them jumped apart. Cynthia grabbed the cover from the floor and dragged it up to her neck. He watched her with arched brows as her chin began to quiver. Mason was cussing like a madman looking for his pants. Finally giving up he put his hands on his hips and glowered at him. Draven let his gaze drop pointedly to Mason's very erect, very wet cock straining up from his hips. Mason could have pulled off the angry affronted look if he hadn't looked so much like what he was. A boy caught with his pants down.

"Mason, grab a towel or something. You're dribbling Cynthia's 'love juice' all over that very expensive rug." Cynthia paled at that, her hands covering her face.

Mason grabbed his shirt and covered his pelvis. "Iybae damn you, Draven. Damn you to fucking hell."

Draven pushed away from the door and tilted his head. "Why, shouldn't I be the angry one here, Mason? I mean, you were fucking my betrothed."

Mason had the good sense to look down.

Cynthia looked up, her gaze meeting Draven's. "Oh, Iybae, forgive me," she whispered then she began to sob.

Draven watched her, his face stern, his brow arched. "Fucking her quite thoroughly, I must add." He turned and left the room. "Follow, Mason," he said without looking back.

He left no room for argument and Mason knew it. With a sigh he sauntered from the room, leaving Cynthia to sob into her pillow. He closed the door softly behind him. Holding the shirt against himself with one hand and scrubbing a hand over his face with the other, Mason leaned against the wall.

"I wonder if she's more upset about being caught or being interrupted?" Draven asked, staring at the closed door.

Mason chuckled, shaking his head. "So, what now? What are you going to do?"

"I'm not doing anything. However, I'll tell you what *you* will do."

"Me?" Mason's brows furrowed with worry.

"Yes. You tasted the honey, my dear cousin, you'll buy the pot," Draven said, crossing his arms over his chest.

"Huh?" Mason looked befuddled.

"Huh? Don't pretend you're brainless now. Even though brainless is exactly how you behaved — witless, simple." Mason shifted from foot to foot, contemplating exactly what Draven meant.

"Exactly what do you mean, 'buying the...'" Mason croaked.

"I mean, my dear cousin, you and your hot little honey pot will be betrothed. You, not I, will be wed to the lovely Cynthia. I will announce that Cynthia requested to be released from her covenant with me and I granted her request. You two can explain your..." he waved his hand frowning, "...love affair, however you wish."

Mason nodded without saying a word.

Draven's brows pulled together over curious eyes. "Does she really like it when you smack her ass like that?"

Mason looked up and rolled his eyes. "Oh yeah, she's like a wild animal. She wants it fast and hard. She loves it when I pinch her tits and smack her ass."

"Hmm," Draven said, shaking his head. He turned, leaving Mason standing there, and headed back to Linea.

She lay in the bed the way he had left her, curled up with her back to him. He tilted his head and studied her ass. Thin white lines crisscrossed her round, luscious, perfectly heart-shaped bottom. They reminded him that never would he want to hit Linea, for any reason. Perhaps if circumstances had been different they could have indulged in such love play but he never wanted her to experience anything that even remotely resembled what she'd gone through.

He dropped his pants and climbed into bed behind her. His hand smoothed over the warm downy skin of her arm. Brushing her hair away he kissed the back of her neck. She tasted warm and sweet as he licked and kissed down the length of her spine. He nipped and licked at the hollow of her back.

Linea began to squirm. "Draven?" she moaned softly.

"Mine. You're mine," he murmured low and husky against her, licking the goose bumps that rose on her skin.

He moved back up her body. His thick cock wedged between her thighs. She moved her hips, pressing against him, trying to get closer. He groaned into her hair. "Iybae made you perfect, and He made you for me."

His hand slid around her body, moving up to cup the full round globe of her aching breast. He nuzzled her neck, teasing her impossibly hard nipples with his thumb. His hand moved down, splaying over her softly rounded stomach. He lingered there, massaging her moments before smoothing his hand lower to tangle in the patch of curls at the apex of her thighs. She started to turn toward him but he stopped her. "No, trust me."

"But I want to touch you," she whispered shyly. So sweet and hot, her innocent need was intoxicating.

"Soon enough. Let me love you my way this time." His fingers delved into her heat, sliding through her slick arousal, rasping the tender skin made swollen and sensitive with her desire for him.

She shuddered hesitantly. "What do you want me to do? How should I lay?" It was so tempting to just turn her over and sink into her, and let himself be carried away by the current of sensation that enveloped them.

"I want you to take pleasure in me. I'll put you where I want you." Her clit hardened as his long calloused finger circled it.

"Mmm." She pressed her sweet butt against him. His cock slid through the slick folds of her sex. She squeezed her thighs together and moved against him. He could feel his cock growing thicker, longer. If he didn't move quickly she'd have him coming.

He rose up on his knees and looked down at his throbbing shaft glistening with her juices then turned her onto her stomach, straddling her thighs. Such an erotic view was so enticing. He couldn't resist leaning down to gently bite her beautiful ass. She yelped then exhaled shakily as he licked where he nipped her.

"Rest your head on the pillows, Linea."

She nodded, lowering her head, and tilted her hips upward until she was on her knees.

Draven gripped her hips and straddled her legs. Heat seared into him as he guided his engorged cock through the drenched silky folds of her sex. He drew the soreness from her and heard her sharp intake of breath, felt her frustration, her savage need as he slowly sank into her hot, tight softness.

"Draven." Her voice was low and sultry as she rocked back against him, taking him deeper still.

Draven snarled, showing strong white teeth. He drank in the feel of her sheath stretching, accommodating him, clenching tightly around him. He breathed deeply and ran his hands over her back and around her sides, soothing her. She tilted her hips upward and he impaled her deeper. Soft mewling sounds escaped her lips as he pushed farther into her, the pain giving way to pleasure. Her rippling channel tugged at him, squeezing him. His hands found her breasts and he molded them, massaged them, and pushed still deeper.

"Draven!" Linea cried out and rocked against him, wanting more.

He fought for his breath, fought to focus, but didn't register any pain from her. There was only an incredible stretching and full feeling woven within the delicious ripples of her greedy vagina constricting, enveloping him. Both sensations convulsed through him, through her, back through him with each small thrust, infusing them with a need for more. It filled him with wonder, filled them both with a savage desire. The walls of her hot slick sheath convulsed around him, urging him further.

"Feel me, Linea, feel what you're doing to me." His deep voice rumbled through her.

"...so good. Oh, Draven, I can't stand it. I need..." she begged, her voice low and guttural, struggling for breath.

With a final eager thrust he filled her completely. He felt the round firmness of her womb against the smooth head of his cock, the hot blood pounding through his cock making it thicken, throb for release. The slight pinch of pain heightened the pleasure. The musky sweet scent of her desire, mixed with her throaty moans and soft panting cries, was enough to send him careening out of control. The pulsing, driving waves of pleasure combined with his swelling arousal were a heady mix.

His hand smoothed over her ass and slid between their trembling bodies to spread her open wide. He loved the feel of her body, the slick silken lips of her sex, the hard knot of ultra sensitive flesh nestled within their folds. He loved the way she trembled when he stroked her. Not an inch was left to give her and not an inch more could she take, he so completely filled her. She cried out, rocking harder, panting as his balls slapped against her exposed clit. Her frustration and need assailed him and Draven clenched his teeth as he struggled to hold onto his restraint.

Focusing on her and the pleasure she felt, he withdrew until only the broad head of his cock remained inside her. Ripples danced over her, over him. He held her open and slammed into her, grinding and rotating his hips against her. She screamed as the sensations wrapped around them. The intense pleasure overrode all thought. Faster and faster, he pulled out and slammed into her over and over again. Grinding and pivoting, twisting, rolling his hips with each forceful thrust. Erotic sensations throbbed through her, through him.

He groaned as salacious need sizzled along every nerve ending. His calloused thumbs rasped her petal-soft inner lips and the delicate flesh behind her entrance. His balls slapped against her clit until she was moaning, begging, crying out with wild eager passion. Fire rushed over him, blazed through him with frantic emotion.

She was his and he wanted her. He wanted her safe, warm and well-pleasured. Draven moved, focused and reflected the torrent of emotion and sensation back to her.

"*Linea, my love,*" he whispered silently as he felt their souls flow together and blend into one.

Linea whimpered and buried her face in the pillow, her knuckles white as she gripped the cloth. She rocked with him, meeting him thrust for thrust and screamed as she shattered. Her violent orgasm pulled at him, threatening to take him with her as he rammed into her repeatedly. His fingers dug into the soft flesh of her hips.

Draven felt his scrotum tighten, the pressure build to nearly unbearable measure. The tight contracting muscles of her sheath pushed him over and he lost control, erupted. Driving deep, he seated himself inside her body and threw his head back with a rough groan as his seed burst into her hard, fast and hot. He flooded her womb, her vagina, his cream drenching her delicate folds, coating her clit.

He pulled her down with him, holding her close to him as he tried to regain his sanity. She wiggled within his arms, turning to face him, and snuggled against him. He smoothed her hair back from her face and kissed her. Clear, deep blue eyes looked up into his. They were so expressive. He heard her silent questions, her doubt and dread. But it was the cold ugly thread of shame snaking through her that disturbed him. In time, he swore he'd drive it away. He'd find the root and cut it away. Until then, he would protect her.

He covered her mouth with his, pleased with her willing, giving response. His tongue swept her sweet, honeyed mouth; nibbled and sucked at her full, voluptuous lips. She gently, shyly, sipped at his tongue and his voracious cock began thickening again, still throbbing and wet, glistening with spent arousal. His desire for her was insatiable. He'd never get enough of her. He'd never let her go. The emotions rioted inside him and he pulled her tightly against his chest. Holding her head to his violently pounding heart, he vowed to kill Orbane for what he'd done, and Pandrum for what he wanted to do.

Chapter Thirty-Two

Haig Orbane licked the honey from his stubby thumb and then wiped it on his napkin. Again, the damn cook fried the bacon too long. She knew he liked it soft and chewy. "Rowena!" he bellowed. "Damn bitch. Rowena!"

Rowena came bursting from the kitchen, out of breath. Rivulets of sweat trickled down along her temples and rounded red cheeks. "Yes, my lord?" Her voice softly shook with nerves.

"This bacon is unacceptable! You should know better by now!" He scowled at her.

"Yes, my lord. I'm sorry, my lord. I'll bring more." She turned and rushed from the room, taking his grunt as a sign to go about it in short order.

He tugged at the crisp white ruffles under his silk lavender jacket, then sipped at his tea and nibbled at his morning cake. With all the trouble he'd been having it would seem he'd be able to enjoy his breakfast. Stupid, incompetent twit. By the time the wench got back with his bacon the rest of his meal would be cold.

"Rowena!" Could no one do anything correctly in this damn keep? He thought.

"Yes, my lord," she said, emerging and wiping her hands on her apron.

Orbane said nothing as he picked up his plate and hurled it at her. Rowena tried to duck but wasn't fast enough. The edge of the fragile china plate caught her in the forehead, opening a long gash above her right eye. He watched her coldly as she stooped to clean up the mess and curled his lip in disgust.

"Mayhap, next time you'll get it right." He crossed his arms over his fat stomach and sat back without looking at her. "You had damn well better, otherwise, you'll be taught the importance of respect and honor." He folded his arms over his chest and looked down his sharp nose at her.

Rowena stood, the ruined plate and food in her arms.

"Bring more tea. And warm the honey next time. And my napkin is soiled!" he complained, his voice escalating with each sentence.

Rowena didn't look up but bowed. "Yes, my lord," she said as she turned and left the room.

"Damn bitch. Stupid ugly bitch!"

* * * * *

"Great Iybae, Rowena, what happened?"

Rowena clenched her teeth as the blood flowed into her eye, blurring her vision. She brushed the girls away gently. "Sonya dear, hand me a towel. Brody," she called to the young man preparing the bread for noon meal. "Brody, let that rise for now. Here, take this fresh pot of tea out to Sir Orbane. Careful, it's hot."

Brody took the pot, frowning at her, his lips thinning in anger. "Brody, the last thing we need right now is your death. Just take the tea in there to him."

"I'm a man, I can stand up to a coward that would do this." He gestured to her wound.

"You are seventeen and if it were only him you'd need to fight, I'd say have at him." She patted his cheek. "Now, let's hurry. He's in an ugly mood." She went to the sink and rinsed the blood from the small towel Sonya had given her, wrung it and held it back to the wound.

"Laws, Row, you need to sit," Carol whispered. "Sonya, go fetch the healer."

Rowena snorted as she took up the skillet and the raw bacon. "Do you want him to take off our heads? Just get busy, it's just a little cut. I'll deal with it later."

"A gash more like," Carol grumbled.

Rowena shook her head. "It's my fault. I should have told you he likes his bacon underdone."

"Aw hell, I'm sorry, Row. 'Twas I who prepared the bacon," Annie mumbled.

"Annie. I just said I failed to let you know. How could you be to blame? And I'll not have that language in my kitchen." Rowena blinked the sweat and blood from her eyes and gave Annie a piercing look that had the headstrong girl lowering her gaze. Turning her attention back to the bacon she shook her head. "I apologize for snapping. I'm feeling a bit of a grouch myself. My mind has been filled with worry over Linea."

"Is she the girl everyone's been whispering about?" Annie asked, propping her hip on the counter as she began peeling more potatoes.

"Who's been whispering?" Rowena asked.

"Everyone," Annie said wide-eyed. "They say she escaped and no one knew exactly how, but everyone suspected the gnoll helped for he'd gone missing as well."

"I heard that too," Carol said as she shaped and placed the morning cakes on the baking tray.

"I'm glad she got away. The things he did to her..." Sonya said softly.

Rowena gave Sonya a sharp glance.

"What'd he do?" Annie asked.

"Well, there were nights when I heard things. Terrible noises. His voice, high-pitched and unnatural." Carol spoke sadly. The other girls listened intently. "I would stand outside my room listening, waiting...I never heard her scream."

"Nevertheless," Rowena and Sonya exchanged looks, "he'll have her back in his clutches soon enough," Rowena continued.

"No. Oh Row, no!" Sonya cried.

Rowena nodded without looking up. "The king has her held in his keep. The way I see it, he's honor-bound to return her to her family."

Sonya thought fast. "Not if he married her! The king may marry whomever he wishes and the family must give consent."

"Foolish girl, the king is betrothed to the daughter of Sir Simmons, the widow Mistress Randall."

"Oh." Sonya looked nearly ready to cry. She knew exactly what would happen when Linea was returned. She'd tended to the hideous wounds he'd afflicted on her body. No salve in the world could heal those he left on her heart, mind and soul. He'd lock her away again and he'd continue his torture, possibly more severely now that his anger had time to grow and fester. "She can't be brought back, Row." Tears streamed down her cheeks. "She can't. I can't stand by and..."

"Sonya!" Rowena's hazel eyes grew cold. She was aware of the other women staring curiously, wanting to know more. "Hush. Now, you will stand by. If you don't, no one else will. She'll need you again. Do you understand me?"

"Yes ma'am." Sonya bowed her head and sniffed. "I'm sorry."

Carol swallowed hard. Annie looked at each of them. "From what I heard, she won't be coming back here."

"What?" Rowena turned her sharp countenance on Annie as she held out her skillet. Rowena poured in most of the bacon grease, saving only enough to prepare the gravy.

"I heard it but, mind you, it may not be truth."

"Just tell us," Carol snapped.

Annie dropped the potatoes into the hot grease and frowned at Carol. "I heard that Linea was promised to Lord Nezzer Pandrum."

"Dear Iybae, no!" Sonya exclaimed. The other women stared, dumbfounded.

Rowena took a deep breath, struggling to hold back her emotions. Her stomach churned at the thought.

"What?" Annie asked, looking from woman to woman. "What's wrong with Sir Pandrum?"

"Are you ignorant or just plain stupid?" Carol asked.

"Ignorant," Annie said with an arched brow.

"Pandrum is half Kyrok. Do you know anything about Kyroks?"

"Only that they're ugly and stupid." Annie shrugged.

"He's still ugly but only half as stupid. He's the liaison between humans and Kyroks. The Kyroks wish to breed with humans but Lord Amaranth has prohibited it."

"Why?"

"Why, she asks?" Carol rolled her eyes. "Have you just arrived on the planet, Annie? Kyroks have enormous, you know, male members."

Rowena clenched her teeth against her desire to scream at them all.

"And this is a bad thing how?" Annie asked, wagging her brows.

"It's a bad thing, you little tramp, because these quite large…ah…members are covered with needle-like barbs. They can tear a human woman to shreds."

Annie wrinkled her nose and hissed.

"Exactly. If she lives through it the first few times without bleeding to death, eventually she'll become calloused inside and he can soon have her breeding."

Rowena's hands shook as she plated up the newly prepared food.

"So if the king has prohibited it, how can Sir Orbane promise Linea to Pandrum?" Annie questioned.

"Pandrum is half-human and is believed to have a human-like man thing." Carol sighed with exasperation.

"So what's the problem?"

"There are other issues involved in a Kyrok mating ritual, Annie, and no one has actually seen Pandrum's endowment to know whether it's spiked or not."

"Stop it. No more of this talk." Rowena's voice wavered. Sonya was softly sobbing so she handed the plate to Carol. "Take it to him, Carol. I don't think I can, I'm going to be sick," she said as she clung with one hand to the counter.

"Of course, Row. Sonya, dry it up and tend to Rowena, won't you?" Carol said as she headed to the dining room and the loathsome lord waiting for his meal.

Chapter Thirty-Three

Orbane finished his meal with a belch, thinking he'd have to punish Rowena and her staff for their carelessness in the first preparation. He should have them beaten. He would withhold their pay for the month. The kitchen and pantry should be scrubbed as well.

He was downing his last cup of tea when Pandrum stomped into the room with none other than the traitorous gnoll, Angus, dangling from the scruff of his collar. Pandrum's hairy frame filled the doorway. His grin revealed teeth gone black and green with rot. Evidently, Orbane thought, his morning meal was destined to cause him indigestion.

"Look what I dug up." Pandrum chuckled as Angus squirmed and snarled, trying to get free. His face was nearly purple from being held in that manner.

"Wonderful. Kill him," Orbane said, wiping his hands and mouth on a linen napkin and tossing it on his empty plate.

Pandrum's hideous smile faded. "Even I know this gnoll could serve a purpose, Orbane."

Orbane narrowed his eyes, considering.

"We'll use him to retrieve my wife, then we'll kill him," Pandrum said, lifting his ugly head haughtily.

Orbane nodded, rising from the table. "She's not your wife yet. And fine, we'll use the traitor, as long as we eventually kill him. Now remove your filthy self from where I dine. Your stench will permeate everything and I'll not be able to eat again without retching."

"How very inhospitable of you, Orbane. No offer of sustenance? Why that's inexcusably rude." Laughing, Pandrum dragged Angus from the room. Orbane followed, watching the retreating back of the bulky warrior. How he hated Pandrum and his foul ways, but he must be tolerated. He and his army were a necessary evil, for now. When he became king, he would destroy the entire race, starting with Pandrum and that fool, Graeme Sierra.

They crossed the small front hall where Pandrum handed Angus off to one of his Kyrok men. "Let him loose and die," Pandrum uttered blandly.

They entered Orbane's office and Pandrum dropped into the first chair he came to, Orbane's red silk chair with a high back. The dirty Kyrok was soiling his chair now. It was too much, just too much.

"How about some coffee, Orbane? Could you part with some coffee for a guest? After all, we both know you couldn't reach your goal without my help—our help."

Orbane clenched his teeth and fisted his hands at his sides. "I have no coffee, Pandrum. I don't keep the foul stuff in my stores."

"Ah…shame. I first tasted some at the king's keep. Decadent stuff that is, hard to get, very valuable."

"Soon I will be king and ensconced in the king's keep as I should be." Orbane scowled. And he would rid himself and the country of every filthy Kyrok who had the misfortune of being born. Then, Linea would be his again. "When that happens you are welcome to any and all the coffee stored there."

"Excellent, excellent." Pandrum rubbed his hands together greedily.

Glutton. Orbane narrowed his eyes, frowning as Pandrum went on talking. Orbane's mind wandered. His informant had let him know that Linea was ensconced in the Amaranth keep and the thought of Linea being with Amaranth was driving him to madness. He wondered if she'd let Amaranth touch her. Was she the whore he always feared she'd be? Oh yes, he was sure of it. He was nearly certain she had spread her long silky legs for the king, wrapped them around him as he rutted her like the bitch she was.

Just like her mother, his sister. Just like their mother before them. Orbane sat in the uncomfortable chair across from Pandrum and pretended to listen as the beast droned on about how he'd captured the gnoll. Pride. Orbane just shook his head. He was surrounded by sin.

He had struggled to keep Linea pure and sanctified before Iybae. As soon as he'd noticed her strength of will along with the curving and developing of her enticing body he knew he must act. Though she was a young girl, only five cycles old, he had undertaken the demanding task of instructing her, teaching her of the wickedness of her sex.

And yet she'd brought iniquity to him, filling him with lust, causing him to sin. She led him to stumble in the eyes of the Almighty

God, Iybae. He'd punished her and began working to keep her clean, beating the sin from her body. She was a temptress, created to cause sin.

He had hoped that wedding her to Pandrum would consecrate her once again to Iybae. He knew she was strong enough to live through the first few times the beast took his marital rights. Not once had she screamed at his punishment. No matter the severity, he could never wrench a cry from her. The plan had been from Iybae Himself.

After Pandrum had prepared the polluted part of her body, she would no longer wish for a man. Then when Pandrum was dead and she once again belonged to him she would be wholesome, virtuous, in the sight of Iybae. But now, after all he'd done to keep her unsullied, she'd fucked the king and probably his whole army. After Pandrum was killed, if she lived, he would once again purify her. He would ready her for the King of all kings, the great Lord Iybae, and he would send her to Him.

"Orbane, did you hear me?" the Kyrok spat.

"Yes...no, what did you say?"

Pandrum tilted his big head to the side. "See, now that's just impolite."

"I have much on my mind, Pandrum, forgive me." Blasted Kyrok, wouldn't know polite if it bit his ass.

"I was saying that we have a problem, another reason I have need to pluck my wife...to be..." His voice slurred with sarcasm. "From the safety of the king's lair."

"I cannot guarantee her purity at this point, Pandrum."

Pandrum waved his meaty hand. "Makes no difference. I'll still marry her and stick her till she's round with my sons." His thick lips pulled back over his scraggly green teeth in a parody of a grin.

Dear Iybae, Orbane hoped the beast did not get Linea with child before he could have him dispatched into the Netherworld. He took a breath. Well, there would be no guessing. It would displease God greatly to send her to him with an evil being embedded inside her. He'd simply have to clean her womb, make sure she carried no Kyrok parasite before he sent her to be with Iybae.

"Besides my personal reasons we need her because the Orb is useless without her, Orbane. She's needed to focus the power."

Orbane stared, dumbfounded. "What do you mean?"

Pandrum scowled. "I mean, the Council has discovered that in order to wield the power of the Orb of Ingvar they must have one who can focus and channel the energy."

Orbane's head began to ache and he rubbed at his forehead. "And what does this have to do with Linea? She can't..."

"She can." Pandrum smirked, nodding once.

Orbane narrowed his eyes. "How do you know this?"

Pandrum shrugged. "The Council knew."

This was very disconcerting, Orbane thought. The Council should have discussed this with him. They should know nothing apart from what he knew. It was very disturbing. If indeed she was needed then it was all the more urgent that they reclaim her. Thinking back he tried to remember one instance, one occurrence that would have given him a clue that she was a channel. This changed everything. "Send a message to our man. Have him get it to Linea."

Pandrum grinned. "That will be easily accomplished."

Chapter Thirty-Four

The warmth of the morning light warmed Linea as she lay on her back gazing up into the wide blue sky. She smiled and her cheeks heated with the thought of how it might feel to have the light's rays on her bare skin. She imagined Draven nude as well rising over her, his body moving against hers, and she stifled a moan. The mere memory of him stirred up a craving in her that she had not been able to cool and she hadn't been left alone long enough to touch herself and dream that the touch came from him.

Absently, she scratched Aletha's ear and offered prayers of thanksgiving to Iybae. The last few days had been surreal to her. Uncle Haig had not come. Draven had left to meet with the overseers of the villages and to minister to the needs of the people. He'd been gone for three days now and she sincerely hoped he'd be back soon.

"Soon, love. I'll return soon, and when I do we'll make your daydreams reality."

Linea's eyes widened, her lips curved as she heard Draven's voice faintly invade her thoughts. So far away and yet he could touch her. Her body instantly responded, and she sighed.

"My lady, are you well?" Gavril cried out to her as he came running down the steps of the keep as fast as his stubby legs would carry him.

Linea pulled herself from the fog of arousal, turned her head to the side and grinned. "Yes, Gavril. I'm very well." Aletha opened one eye and silently bared her long fangs.

"Hrumph," Gavril grunted as he bared his short blocky teeth to Aletha.

Linea laughed and sat up, crossing her legs, picking the grass out of her hair. Aletha shifted to rest her head in Linea's lap.

"Were you lying there on purpose?" he asked her wide-eyed.

"Mm hm." She ran her hands over the lush blue-green grass.

"What a queer thing to do." Gavril eyed her closely. "Are you tired?"

"No, Gavril. Will you stop your incessant mothering?"

Gavril shrugged his shoulders. "Can't help it. I've searched for you for so long. You were my charge and I didn't save you from the horrors you suffered..."

Linea held up a hand stained with dirt and grass. "I don't want to think about that, Gavril. Not until I have to." She looked up and around the courtyard, her gaze resting on the men practicing with their swords in the training field. "Soon enough, Gavril. I can feel it coming." She rested her fist below her breasts. "It's like a stone, right here. I know a struggle is coming."

Gavril nodded and patted her arm. Aletha opened her eyes and softly growled a warning. "Ack, filthy animal."

"Be nice, Gavril," Linea said as she gently stroked the wolfdog's big head. "Aletha is with child."

"Oh really? And how would you know that?" he asked rolling his eyes.

Linea shrugged. "She told me."

"Oh, she... She what?"

Linea grinned at him. Gavril was so funny when he was surprised. His lavender eyes were huge and his mouth made a circle. He was adorable and she loved him. She winked at him and his pursed lips slid into a smile.

"Well, isn't that something. Have you told the brute?"

"If you mean Draven, no. She only told me yesterday. And Gavril, don't call him names." Gavril gave her a sheepish look. "I did tell Rolf, though, and he's quite pleased. He'd like to know how many and if there'd be sons. I told him that was something he'd have to wait to discover."

"So you've been spending your time conversing with wolfdogs." Gavril grunted as he plopped down beside her.

"Yes, and Duncan. Oh, and a bird or two but those were very brief. Birds are very cordial but very busy."

Gavril sighed. "I'll be ashamed I asked, but who is Duncan?"

Linea frowned at him. "Duncan, my darling elf, is a horse. A very frustrated horse who wants to be allowed to run more."

"Ah, of course, what was I thinking?"

"Are you scoffing at me, Gavril?" Linea cut him a disgruntled look.

"Nay, nay, never, my lady. It's just that you never cease to amaze me." He took her hand in his. "Miss Linea, there are things we must discuss."

"Yes, there are." She watched him, waiting. She'd known he had the answers to all the questions rioting in her mind, but somehow she knew he would come tell her when it was time.

Gavril took a deep steadying breath and met Linea's gaze. "You were born with many gifts. The Fae people knew when you were born that you were the chosen Channel." He lifted a hand to stop her as she opened her mouth to speak. "Let me finish then you can ask all the questions you want."

Linea nodded. "Go on."

"We elves knew it as well. Although he is not as great as Iybae, Asmodeus has much power. Those who follow him are manipulated by his evil. The Orb of Ingvar is a great and mighty source protected by the Fae people. Our God, Iybae, gave it to provide for, heal, and protect all who choose Him. However, in the wrong hands the Orb can be used as a mighty weapon of evil. The Orb was stolen from Ingvar a few years after you were born. This is why the Fae have sequestered themselves in Ingvar and have allowed no one to enter or leave."

"Gavril, that can't be so. Moria is a faerie. She isn't sequestered." Linea frowned. She had suddenly gone cold from her very core outward.

"Yes, but Linea, she is here for you. For Miss Cynthia, yes, but her main mission is to guide you. As is mine."

Linea blinked. "I don't understand."

"Yes, you do." Gavril's countenance was more somber than she'd ever seen him. "You've felt the gift within you. The focusing, reflecting of the king's power. Remember?"

Linea swallowed hard and nodded.

"You can also hear his thoughts, feel what he feels…as well as others."

Linea's stomach tightened and her body trembled. "Only when there's passion…in one form or another."

"Yes." Gavril nodded. "But it will grow inside you and develop as you train. Miss Linea, the council abducted several faeries. Some they tortured, some they forced to aid the Council's cause. Only you can channel the Orb; that's why you must be protected."

Linea struggled to process the information. "Nezzer Pandrum, my uncle…"

"Yes." Gavril squeezed her hand. "You and Lord Amaranth…" He paused, making a face. "Your gifts are compatible and they work as one. Though I had no knowledge of this 'talking to animals' thing." Gavril smiled and winked at her. "You are more gifted than I thought."

"I see. What steps are being made to retrieve the Orb?" Things became clearer to Linea now. She felt an urgency to understand and do what needed to be done.

"In time, dear, in time." He struggled to his feet and kissed her hand. "I'm thinking the cook may have a treat for me!" He headed back inside, whistling.

Linea watched him leave and stood brushing at her skirts. She needed some time to think, to sort out the information Gavril had given her.

"Aletha, I'm going for a walk in the gardens. You should go see if you can charm the cook as well," Linea said, smiling down at the wolfdog.

Aletha looked up at her with golden eyes filled with wisdom, then ambled in behind Gavril.

"Be nice to Gavril," she yelled to the wolfdog.

"*I won't bite him*," came Aletha's gruff reply.

"Good enough." Linea chuckled and strolled around to the garden gate.

She lifted the latch and pushed the iron bars open with a screech. "Ooh, needs some oil," she mumbled.

The garden was in desperate need of attention. The various bushes needed trimming and shaping, and weeds were choking out the flowers. Did Draven not have a gardener? She spotted a swing across the garden among the overgrowth and made her way through the brush, lifting her skirts as she went.

Not knowing much about plants or gardening didn't stop her from taking on the task of ridding the lovely garden of weeds. It would be fun to have a project to occupy her hands as her mind worked around this Orb issue. She sat down at a bed at the farthest corner and began carefully tugging the weeds from around the tender flowers.

"Miss Linea?" Joeff called to her.

"Over here," she called out, raising a hand. She got up and looked at her filthy hands. She brushed them together, not wanting to stain her dress anymore than necessary. Netta would have a fit as it was.

"Stay there. I'll come to you, miss." The manservant made his way through the garden and held a small square envelope out to her.

A chill sent prickles up her spine as she looked at it. "Wh...who is it from?"

"I don't know, miss. He said it was from a friend. I thought perhaps the king sent it. A note of affection?" Joeff tilted his head and smiled awkwardly.

"But, I don't..." The mysterious cold seemed to seep into her bones. Linea met Joeff's gaze.

"I'm sorry, miss, I didn't mean to startle you. I can go try and find the messenger if you like."

She held out a trembling hand, took the envelope and held it to her chest. "No, no that's quite all right. Thank you."

He nodded to her, took two steps back then turned and walked away. Linea waited until she heard the gate close then looked down at the little square. There was no seal in the wax, no writing on the outside. She took a deep breath, broke the wax and read the message.

Angus has been captured

If you wish to save him

come to the Hunting Cave

on the south end of

King's Forest.

Tell no one or Angus dies.

Linea's heart pounded in her ears, her hand trembled and the letters blurred as her eyes filled with tears. Surprised by the strength of the violence that flared inside her she gritted her teeth. Her uncle had underestimated her and her trust in her king. She folded the note and tucked it between her breasts, praying Draven would return swiftly.

Chapter Thirty-Five

The temple was filled with countrymen and women from three villages. All the seats were taken and some stood around the walls.

"Here we have enough food and we are safe. Others are not so fortunate; many of my family members are still there. Lord Amaranth, something must be done about him."

Draven wore a stern expression as he listened to the man tell of his liberation from Sir Orbane's oppression. He felt the concern and fear of his people. He knew their trust as well. It made him all the more committed to resolve the situation with Orbane once and for all.

"You have my word. He shall be dealt with…" Furious anger, violently strong, hit Draven like a fist to the stomach. He frowned, focusing on the source. "Swiftly."

"Yes, my lord." The man took Draven's hand in both of his and shook it. Fear, a familiar fear, and desperation swirled in his gut…from where? The man looked up at him. "Are you well, my king?"

Draven shook his head then met the man's gaze. "Yes, yes, I'm fine." Linea…it came from Linea. It hadn't been long ago that he had shared in her stimulating vision of love play. He wasn't expecting this. He spun on his heel, found Armond and motioned to him.

"What is it? You've gone pale," Armond said as he walked up.

"We must head back. Now." Draven's voice left no room for question.

Armond nodded with a frown and turned to the other men. "Ready your steeds. We return home tonight," he said quietly but sternly.

Draven turned back to the crowd standing before him with curious stares. "I regret I must leave now." Groans of disappointment filled the stifling air. "As soon as possible I will return and I will see you in the temples of your own villages. You will not have to travel. Until then your overseer will see to your needs." He gave the men standing close by a pointed look. "You have but to confer with him."

With that he made his way down the aisle through the people. He grasped their hands and patted shoulders as he walked past them. Once outside he mounted Mandrake and kicked him into a gallop. Armond, Mason and two other warriors followed in his dust.

* * * * *

Aware of the eyes watching her, Linea stood in the great hall over a lounging Halvar. "Have you no notion of when Lord Amaranth will return? Does anyone?" she asked glancing around the room. Some men lifted brows at her and she knew what they were thinking. But she didn't care. She didn't know how much time Angus had. Knowing that if she ventured out on her own they'd both be killed eventually, she had no choice but to go to the king. She needed Draven, and she needed him now.

"Miss Linea, Lord Amaranth could be away for days or weeks. It will all depend on what's needed of him," a rugged warrior spoke up.

"No," she whimpered. "That's too long." She chose to ignore the snorts of laughter and tried to think.

Halvar sat up, concern clear on his rugged face. "Is there some way I can help, miss?"

"Yeah, me too. I can help too," another warrior offered with a snicker.

Halvar moved so fast Linea jumped, a tiny yelp escaping her lips. He stood over the boorish warrior, his sword at his throat. "You embarrass yourself." Halvar's lip curled as he spoke, his gravelly voice leaving no question. "You will show the lady respect and keep your filthy thoughts to yourself."

"Aw, come on, Halv…" The tip of Halvar's sword nicked the warrior's Adam's apple. The man shuddered and swallowed.

"Do you have something else to say, dumbass?" Halvar asked with an arched brow.

"Ah…I…I apologize, Miss Linea," he stuttered, his eyes wide.

Halvar sheathed his sword. "Go home. Pray Iybae forgives your impertinence and blesses you with some common sense."

He turned on his heel, watching each warrior. "Does anyone else have something to say to this fine lady?" They each cleared their throats, remaining silent, and avoided his gaze.

"Forgive them, Miss Linea. Is there anything I can help you with?"

Linea chewed on her bottom lip and shook her head. "I don't think so. I don't know." She headed for the steps. "I'll let you know if..." She started up the steps, stopped halfway up and turned. "Thank you, Havlar...for...for..." Her eyes widened; her mind was a whirl.

He smiled and it lit up his harsh features. "You're welcome, miss."

She nodded and turned to continue up the steps when the heavy wooden doors flew open.

"Where is she?" Draven roared.

Halvar just pointed. Linea breathed heavily, trying not to sob with relief. She didn't have time to move or say anything. Draven bounded up the steps two at a time and pulled her into his arms. His hands moved over her arms, her back. "What is it, Linea? What's the matter? What's happened?"

She clung to him, breathing in the scent that was his alone: spice, leather and the outdoors. He was safety, her refuge. She noticed the grave expressions Armond and Mason wore as they came in behind him.

He took her by the arms, his chest heaving with his labored breathing. "Dammit, Linea, what is it!" he bellowed.

"Can we... I need to talk to you. Somewhere private." He turned, dragging her to his war room. She didn't even remember descending the stairs. She'd never been in his war room and she wasn't sure she wanted to be here now, surely not ever again.

He slammed the door behind them then turned to her. His expression, made savage by the flickering shadows and light of the fire, was frightening. The muscle in his jaw jumped. His dark steel-gray eyes searched her face. His hand combed through her hair and cupped her scalp, angling her head as he lowered his. He took her mouth with a possessive force. His tongue plundered, stroked and teased, dueling with hers as she whimpered and surrendered. Her arms wrapped around his waist, pressing him closer to her.

One hand released her scalp and slid down to cup her bottom. Lifting her, he ground the incredible bulge of his hard cock against her. Heated arousal spiraled through her womb. Hot liquid seeped from her contracting vagina to soak her swelling flesh, preparing for him. He let go of her head and grasped her waist, lifting her. She kissed him back with the force of a wanton woman out of control.

She sucked the tip of his tongue and bit his lip as he lifted and set her on a hard surface. She didn't care what he did anymore, as long as it was hard and fast. Her body was on fire, her juice flowing from her. She felt the powerful throbbing of his body, his sharp need pulse through her. Her nipples strained, begging for attention.

He shoved her dress up past her thighs. His mouth traveled over her jaw to her ear, nibbling and sucking on her earlobe. Her hands moved down his chest to frantically struggle with the ties of his pants. The storm of emotion and sensation swirling inside him engulfed her and she couldn't distinguish his desire from her own. His hands grasped her breasts and squeezed, pinching her hard nipples. Her head fell back and she cried out as his mouth closed over one eager nipple through her dress. He sucked hard as his free hand moved between her thighs, opening her folds to his rough stroking. He took the other nipple and sucked it, biting gently.

His tongue stroked her bottom lip and he took it between his, devouring her mouth again, swallowing her cries as he thrust his three middle fingers inside her contracting channel. She rocked, leaning back until he touched that hypersensitive spot inside her sheath. The slide of his thumb through her drenched cleft had her writhing, rotating her hips against his hand, as frenzied need took over.

Finally she freed his cock from his pants. With both hands she massaged the thick shaft. The feel of the small beads of cream that seeped from him felt glorious as she smeared the fluid over his smooth bulging tip. Draven groaned, laid her back on the desk and pushed her dress up farther.

He grasped her hips, pulling her to the edge as he drove his steel-hard cock into her. Draping her legs over his shoulders helped him pump harder, deeper. Voracious hunger gripped her and had her arching up trying to get more of him. At that moment nothing mattered, nothing but the feel of his energy surging through her, his body ramming into her. She opened her eyes and watched with wonder the beauty of his rugged face glowing with sweat in the firelight. Dark sultry cries came from deep within her as she undulated on the desk, pushing harder against him.

She tossed her head back, frantically meeting Draven's powerful thrusts as her world came apart and her body disintegrated in a starburst of intense, all-consuming pleasure. He reached down and took her swollen clit gently, rolling it between his finger and thumb. A low ecstatic scream tore from her as he drove up into her over again and again building the sensations, layering them one on top of another.

He gave and took and gave again until her body shuddered with the power of her second release. With one last surge into her gripping channel the building pleasure fractured and burst into her. Waves of sensation poured over her, reflecting back and forth. Gasping for breath Linea thought it might never end, she didn't want it to end.

Shaking with the aftershocks of his climax, Draven gently lowered her legs and lifted her. He carried her, still impaled on his shaft, and sat in the nearest chair. Pulling her close against his chest, he rubbed her back.

"Linea," he panted, his voice husky with passion. "Tell me now what happened."

She shook her head, not willing to spoil the moment. Instead she moved her hip, clenched the walls of her sheath and moaned as she felt his cock thicken, lengthen and begin to fill her again. To feel this man, this warlord, respond to her on so many levels was more than incredible; it felt like a miracle, her miracle.

He nuzzled her neck, sucked and licked at the sensitive skin there. "Linea," he whispered roughly. "Tell me."

She raised her head and searched his face. *Not yet,* she thought as she laid a hand against his cheek and watched her thumb stroke his full bottom lip, savoring the feel of his groan reverberate through her. She lowered her mouth to his and sucked gently on his lower lip.

Linea pushed away, spreading her legs as much as the wide chair would let her, and slowly began to ride him. Gripping the arms of the chair she let her head fall back. Drawing the pleasure out as much as she could, she moved painfully slow, rising and falling, his cock sliding slickly inside her, stroking her inner walls.

Intently he watched her as his hands cupped her butt, his fingers delving into the crease of her bottom, caressing lower until he touched the place where his shaft entered her. She met his gaze, though her vision blurred. Gauging the sensations she received from him, she began to move faster. A whimper of protest escaped her lips as he grasped her hips and held her still. His silver eyes glinted with arousal and intent, his expression deadly serious. "Now, Linea. Tell me now."

Without looking away she reached down the front of her dress, took out the note and handed it to him. She sat still, closing her eyes, bathing in the fluid sensation of him throbbing inside her. She didn't want reality. She wanted this cherished feeling, and only this pleasure he gave her.

Chapter Thirty-Six

His body tensed as he read the note again and again, then tossed it on the desk. With ease Draven pulled her dress up over her head and unabashedly surveyed her naked body. It was her first response to feeling utterly exposed that had her crossing her arms over her chest. The tiny white scars stood out against her flushed skin and, though her nipple had healed nicely, it would forever be a bit misshapen. A reminder of what she came from, who she was.

"You trusted me." Draven's voice was low, foreboding.

Gently he took her hands and laid them on his shoulders as he looked into her eyes. Linea watched him nervously, gripping his shoulders. Trying to understand the mixed sensations she received from him, she focused on them and let them wash over her.

His hands moved over her breasts, cupping them, teasing her nipples to contract into round berries and she could think only of him, only the freedom he allowed her to believe in. A soft moan escaped her lips and she closed her eyes. The warm lazy waves of lingering arousal blossomed into yearning pulses as she flexed her hips.

His hand caressed one breast, gently massaging, while his mouth devoured the other. His hands were always so warm; his mouth was so hot. The soft brush of his goatee against her sensitive skin felt like licks of flame. Wild, dark waves of his sweat-dampened hair clung to his forehead and cheekbones and brushed against her chest. The struggle to move slowly on his lap was killing her. She bit her lip and wove her fingers through his thick mane of hair, holding his head against her. His mouth covered her nipple, laving it with his tongue as he sucked.

It felt so good, like incredibly hot waves flowing over her, pulling her toward a peak. She didn't want to rush, but what he was doing to her breasts with his mouth was inflaming her. He shifted, needing to be deeper inside her. She shuddered, concentrating on sheathing him deeper, withdrawing and then slowly driving him deeper still.

"You're beautiful," she whispered, her hands combing through his long thick hair. She smoothed his hair back and kissed his forehead, such a proud masculine forehead. Her lips moved over his brows, his closed eyelids.

"Linea," he breathed, thrusting up to meet her slow gyrations.

She felt his urgency; his body shook with it as he grasped her hips and tilted her. Every thrust rubbed against her clit. And her body strained toward release. Fire infused her from her very core; her body was consumed in the pleasure and pain that they shared. She tried moving faster but he held her pelvis firmly in his grip slowly torturing her, pushing her further and further. Her cries shuddered from her body as waves of ecstasy pounded against her, only building the sensations one on top of the other.

She thought she would die as his thumb found her clit, pressed and rotated gently. She stopped breathing as she felt his orgasm rip through him, through her. Helpless, unable to think in the vortex of sensation, she lost control of rational thought. He pulled her tight against him, his mouth savagely claiming hers, swallowing her screams. In that one brilliant moment there was nothing, nothing but the feel of his arms surrounding her, his body pressed so tight against hers, his seed filling her, coating the hot folds of her sex as his thumb pressed firmly, circling, smearing his cream over the hard knot of flesh.

Never given the chance to come down, her climax surged up and crested once more before she slumped against his sweat-drenched body, bone weary, her mind numb. She wanted to lie there forever, his breath fanning her hair. At that moment, she felt accepted. She felt safe.

"Linea." His husky voice vibrated through her. She cuddled closer and moaned into his neck. *No,* she thought, *don't let this end.* His warm fingertips trailing over her back felt so good. Her legs cramped but she didn't care, she wanted to stay like this forever. Though his shaft had softened it was still well lodged inside her. Still warm, slick with their arousal. He kissed her shoulder.

"Linea." He kissed her again. "I'm going to carry you to bed now."

Linea whimpered in protest. Pressing closer, she rotated her hips once, twice, and bit his neck. Smiling against his warm skin she felt him growing hard, filling her again.

"Linea." He groaned. "I've made love to you twice now and I still have my pants on. Please."

She giggled; she couldn't help it. Her sheath's walls contracted around him and she sighed.

"Oh, don't laugh," he groaned again. "Love, don't move."

Linea murmured, "I don't want to move. Let's stay like this all night."

Draven chuckled and pulled her away. He kissed her, his tongue swiping her pouting bottom lip. "We can't stay like this all night. I need to talk to Armond and Mason about this damned note and decide what to do. Besides, our muscles will stiffen and we'll fuse together."

Joy…she felt joy. The emotion was so new and bright. Linea smiled at him and nipped at his nose. "Would that be so bad?"

His silvery eyes widened. "Yes! I'm an old man. I need flexible muscles to keep up with your insatiable appetite."

Linea was lost in his eyes for moments before she finally sighed and reluctantly pulled away with a grimace. She hadn't expected to be so sore. Draven stood and took off his shirt. She pulled her dress over her head, adjusting it as best she could. Linea watched as he used his shirt to wipe their come from his leather pants, his cock jutting out proudly. She pressed a hand to her mouth but couldn't contain her giggles.

He shot her a look without raising his head. "Do you find me amusing?" he asked gruffly.

She grinned. "Maybe, just a little." She inched toward the door.

Wincing, he worked his erect member back inside his tight pants. "Remember, sweetness." He grunted as he tied the laces as best he could. "Turnabout is fair play."

She exaggerated a yawn and patted her mouth "Well, I'm off to bed," she said, darting from the room.

* * * * *

Draven watched her go, thankful she wasn't fearful anymore, and decidedly pleased with himself that he'd made her laugh. He picked up the note and re-read it, his smile melting into an expression far from pleasant. She had trusted him to protect her. He wouldn't give her reason to regret it. There were no lengths to which he would not go to keep her safe. Orbane would pay for every tiny white line marring Linea's beautiful body, every unshed tear, every second she felt even the slightest twinge of shame, and more...much more. And he would pay with his blood.

Mason was in the great hall with Halvar, Nathaniel and a few other warriors. He was sitting in front of the fire, chomping enthusiastically on a roll filled with meat left from the evening meal.

"Where's Armond?" The men turned to Draven, giving him their undivided attention. Fear...he felt a faint zing of fear...from someone. Draven gritted his teeth. That was not a good sign. Mason shrugged and then looked up, catching Draven's expression. He stopped chewing and swallowed hard.

"Uh, he went upstairs as soon as you went to the war room to...uh..." He had the decency to forgo his usual teasing manner. "...confer with Miss Linea."

Draven's eyes narrowed. The faint tension radiating subtly from the men didn't go unnoticed, nor did the stern expression on Halvar's face. Draven's gaze surveyed the faces there. One man kept his eyes averted. There...there was the source of the fear.

"Joel." Draven's voice was deep and held a hint of warning. Reluctantly the man looked up. Dried blood crusted in a line that ran from a small cut at the man's throat and disappeared below his collar.

"My lord," Joel answered.

Draven tilted his head. "What happened to your neck?"

Joel's gaze darted to Halvar, back to Draven then to his lap. "My lord, I foolishly made disrespectful remarks regarding Miss Linea and yourself. I'm truly sorry, my lord, and humbly ask for your forgiveness."

The muscle in Draven's jaw pulsed. He cleared his throat. "What happened to your neck?"

"Halvar, my lord, he...rightfully reprimanded me and demanded my apology." Joel looked up, meeting Draven's gaze. "Which I gave, my lord, as I ask for your forgiveness now."

"Lord Amaranth," Halvar said quietly. Draven continued to watch Joel. "Miss Linea was asking after you and Joel commented..."

"Halvar, I don't think telling me would be wise. Joel seems quite repentant. Let it rest." Draven stared hard at Joel. He was young and hot-blooded and a bit of a smart ass. Unfortunately Draven was in no mood to tolerate his foolishness, especially when it affected his Linea.

"As you wish, my lord." Halvar nodded.

"Joel." Draven's voice rumbled with barely restrained anger.

"Yes, my lord." The young warrior shuddered.

"You're forgiven. Unfortunately, I'm still pissed off. Therefore, you should take care not to give me the slightest reason to beat you senseless."

"Yes, of course. Thank you, my lord." Joel nodded tremulously.

Draven spoke sternly, his eyes narrowing. "If I so much as suspect any of you of even thinking disparaging thoughts about Miss Linea, you will, at the very least, no longer be welcome in this kingdom." He paused, surveying the room. "For what I'm about to do I need men I can trust, unequivocally. Go home, Joel. You'll need to earn my trust again."

"Yes, my lord," Joel murmured as he got to his feet and walked away.

Draven waited until he heard the echo of the doors closing behind the dejected Joel. Damn fool, he thought. "Mason, will you inhale that thing and go find Armond?"

Mason stuffed the last bite in his mouth and chewed vigorously as he stood. "Sure thing, cuz," he mumbled around his food. Draven's lip curled and he rolled his eyes.

* * * * *

The small space was filled with warm moist steam that smelled of him. Linea breathed deeply and closed her eyes. She lay submerged to her chin in the wide oval-shaped basin in a dreamlike state. It was made of smooth slate like the rest of the chamber. Such an intriguing place was this bath, with its walls and floors of slate glittering in the abundant candlelight, its incredible warmth and comfort, and that spicy musky scent that was distinctly Draven.

There was a small cluster of three rooms each designated for one purpose or another, and there was the mineral bath. She had grown to love this cleansing tub, as Netta had called it. It was very large and smooth. Sweet Netta. She had told her of the lightly scented powders that made the water soft and rich with thick foam.

Oh, this must be Paradise, she thought. But no, it couldn't be. She would have no place there. It was written there would be no whores in Paradise. And there was no mistake that she had made herself a whore. Wasn't it written? She frowned and opened her eyes. Uncle Haig had told her it was so. It sounded reasonable but something deep inside her contradicted that belief.

Draven had made her so happy; he made her feel like there was good in her. Linea sighed; she was so full of conflicting emotions. On the other hand, her heart ached with the guilt she felt for what she'd done to Miss Cynthia. It would be best if she stayed away from Draven but, Iybae help her, she could not.

She needed him like the air she breathed. He made her smile and laugh when she'd never known either. Not since she was old enough to remember. He never seemed to see her sin, never treated her like the whore she was. He had saved her, harbored her, healed her and sheltered her. When he had turned that extraordinary silver gaze on her, he had looked beyond the scars and made her feel beautiful. He touched her so deeply; he'd touched her soul as surely as he'd touched her womb.

She so desperately needed him that she could never turn away, not of her own will, not of her own power. "My holy God Iybae, I long to please you but it seems as though I have not the goodness in me to do so," she whispered. "I cannot let him go, if it is your pleasure for him to be free of me you will have to rip him from my very arms."

The foam had, for the most part, melted away. Linea sighed and rose from the water. Her muscles felt fluid and the aching pull between her legs had eased almost completely. Feeling rejuvenated, yet troubled, she stepped out of the tub, wrapped herself in the thick billowing towel and made her way from the underground haven.

* * * * *

"Two things disturb me. One... Orbane knows Linea is here. He got that information from someone close to me and wisely didn't show up for the meeting. I have not heard from his escorts and I have the sick feeling I won't. Two... Orbane took the chance that I wouldn't discover the note. He handled this thing very carelessly." Draven sat on the hearth, his elbows on his knees, holding the note in his hands.

"You're expecting an ambush?" Armond asked.

"It would be stupid not to, I think. The bastard is demented and he's hungry for your blood, Draven." Mason spoke gruffly.

Draven's head jerked up at the soft gasp. "No," Linea whispered as she stood trembling at the bottom of the staircase wrapped head to toe in a large towel. Her wet hair clung to her head and her feet were bare.

Alarmed at the strength of emotion, dark and desperate, twisting inside her, he stood and quickly crossed to her. "I thought you were in bed. How long have you been standing there?" He took her gently by her shoulders, his voice steady yet stern. "You're shaking. Linea, look at me."

Linea looked up at him and his heart clenched at the bleakness in her eyes. She shook her head. "You can't go, Draven. Please don't go."

He pulled her to him, holding her trembling body close to him. Dear Iybae, he'd never seen her so frightened. "Linea, I'm not going alone."

Her hands fisted in his shirt. "What have I done? Oh my God, blessed Iybae, I didn't mean this, not this way."

"Linea, you're not making any sense." He brushed the wet strands of hair away from her face and lifted her chin. "You said you trusted me." Draven said and to his horror, her ocean blue eyes filled with tears.

"Don't cry, love." He kissed her cheek, the corner of her mouth, and tasted her tears.

"He wants to kill you, Draven. He hates you. You have no idea how much he hates you. Let me go. He wants me. I'll go. I'll convince him to free Angus." Her fear was building, driving away common sense, and choking all logic.

"Stop it. Stop it now!" Draven held Linea's head against his shoulder, absorbing her shuddering sobs, feeling her tears dampen his shirt.

He turned his head to the men who looked on with shock. His expression was grim, his voice harsh. "Be ready to leave in the morning. No later than an hour past dawn."

He lifted Linea into his arms, carried her up the stairs to his bedchamber and laid her on the bed. She sat up, holding the towel around her. She watched him as he unbuttoned his shirt. Guilt and shame moved through her, filling her like dark bitter sap. His own stomach churned with it.

"Gavril told me, Draven. It's about the Orb of Ingvar and the Council. They think I'm a channel and I can make it work." Linea looked at him, her head tilted, her eyes red-rimmed from crying. "Angus is already being abused because of me. Draven, if you go to help Angus and you get hurt..." she swallowed hard, "or worse, it would be because of me. I don't want you hurt, Draven, if something worse happened. I can't lose you."

He had suspected that she was a channel. It was the only way to explain the power surges he'd had. It only solidified his resolve that she belonged to him. *And she was right*, he thought with rising fury. Those gorgeous eyes of hers pleaded with him. She was so young, so selfless, yet so full of the ugliness Orbane had force-fed her day in and day out since...Iybae only knew.

Linea's memory swam before Draven like a vision. Orbane's furious red face, his fat lips peeled back from his teeth, his dull blue eyes glittering with sinister pleasure took shape in his mind. The whip in Orbane's hand flicked and snapped as he hurled indictments and accusations along with scripture, prayer and his spittle in Linea's sweaty face.

Draven's body tensed, feeling the snap and sting of the whip that left burning slashes of pain across his stomach and chest as she had felt it. Orbane moved around, punching and hitting her as she dangled from her hands by a rope. Her shoulders burned and the ache was nearly unbearable as she struggled to keep her body from swinging around. The vision evaporated as quickly as it appeared, only a second or two, though it seemed to Draven that he had been caught in it for much longer.

Fury exploded inside Draven. His body shook with it. His shoulders lifted and fell with each deep breath that seared his lungs. His blood pressure rose, his teeth clenched, as did his hands at his sides. Years...for years he had been careful to keep his emotions under control. Not only because of the cursed gift but also because of the stigma of the legacy his father had left him. He'd worked hard at keeping an even manner, his emotions in check. Now, for the first time in his life, he understood his father and the passion that drove him to butcher a man.

He looked down at Linea and caught her weary, watery gaze. She stilled as their gazes locked and she shuddered, the rage blazing within him licking at her. He spun around and, with a roar that shook the keep, drove his fist through the wall. Without looking back, he stalked from the room. He felt Linea as she sat on the bed, her chest heaving, her body trembling so hard her teeth clattered together. He hated that he frightened her but he couldn't soothe her now, he couldn't find it in him. She would have to believe in him.

Chapter Thirty-Seven

Draven's body sliced through the warm healing water smoothly. It did nothing to cool his wrath. Fantasies of killing the sick freak of nature in all the many ways one can kill a man with his bare hands filled Draven's thoughts. Reaching the end of the pool he flipped underwater, swiftly bolted from the side, and swam for the other end.

His arms and legs pumped furiously, muscles bulging, tightening, propelling him forward. He'd constructed a block, not wanting to contaminate Linea with his rancid hatred. Yet he could feel her trying to reach through it. She wanted to feel him, to share what he felt. This he couldn't allow. On the final lap he submerged himself, gliding effortlessly to the slate steps.

He rose from the water, went to the rain chamber and stepped inside. Still dripping wet he took the bar of soap and washed. His cock was heavy with arousal and his soapy hand sliding over it felt good, turning his thoughts to Linea and her tight slick sheath. Dammit, would he ever get enough of the woman?

No matter what emotion gripped him he was always in need of her, on fire for her soft, responsive body. He pulled the chain and the same hot spring water that was pumped into the pool showered over him, rinsing the soap from him. He snatched a towel from the shelf and dried himself haphazardly as he walked, tossing the towel aside before he left the baths.

Draven walked back through the great hall naked, ignoring Armond's scowl and Moria's appreciative once-over. He bounded up the stairs and stalked down the balcony to his room. Linea stood in the middle of the room buttoning his shirt over her ample breasts, her dusky nipples visible through the thin white material. She looked so damn good standing there in his shirt, its hem ending mid-thigh. Her long legs were incredibly sexy. Her feet had healed and were shaped beautifully. He growled with lust and slammed the door as her head snapped up.

"Draven," she breathed. "I'm...I was..."

She had no time to say anything else. He advanced on her like a wolf after his prey and yanked her body against his. Linea gasped. Her nails bit into the hard muscle of his upper arms as his mouth descended on her neck, biting, sucking, licking. There was no tenderness in him now. He was wild, driven by animal instinct.

He backed her against the wall. "I need you now," he rasped.

Linea could only yield. Her breath hitched in her throat as he shoved his thigh between hers and ground it up against her tender flesh already damp with arousal. He ripped the shirt away, exposing her breasts, groaning as he watched them sway from his rough treatment. His hungry mouth closed over one peaking nipple, squeezing and massaging the other.

To his delight, Linea growled and bit into his shoulder. She rode his hard thigh; sharp ripples of pleasure pulsed through him with each jerk of her hips. His thigh became drenched in her hot slick honey. She was so close and his cock was unbelievably hard pressing against her stomach.

He took her mouth, his tongue plundering the soft moist territory. Her tongue mated wantonly with his as his hands smoothed down her sides to cup her ass. She writhed against him as his fingers spread her, trailing along the tender crease separating her luscious round cheeks. He growled into her mouth and she whimpered.

The maddening sensations swirled through them both until he couldn't separate them. He lifted her and spread her open further, exploring the saturated silken folds of her sex. Thick creamy arousal coated his finger as it circled her tight opening. It dipped inside, stroking her slick rippling inner walls as his tongue grazed over her parted lips.

"Now, Draven, shove it in. Please!" she moaned.

Gripping her bottom he lifted her off the floor and lodged the thick pulsing head of his cock at the entrance of her sheath. He lifted his head, wrapped her legs around his hips and met her drugged gaze.

"Hold onto me," he snarled, baring his teeth, and with one powerful thrust filled her to the hilt.

Linea cried out, arching against him, her arms clasped around him. Draven couldn't think. His mind was filled with need, his body flooded with pleasure. He braced her against the wall and pounded into her with hard long thrusts. A lusty groan rumbled through him as her tight channel convulsed around his swelling shaft, hugging him, surrounding him in liquid fire. The wet sucking sound of flesh pounding against flesh, his balls slapping against her butt, drove him higher. Their passion merged, melted together into a living vortex spinning wildly out of control.

"Sweet Linea," he croaked.

"Harder, Draven, harder," she whimpered, writhing against him. Her legs tightened around him.

She sunk her teeth into his neck; her nails dug into his back, her hips pistoning with him. He felt their climaxes crest at the same time. Linea clung to him, his neck muffling her screams. They shattered together, their bodies racked hard with the force of their orgasms. With two more powerful thrusts he buried himself deep inside her as they both hurled into oblivion.

Linea held him tightly. Her body jerked against him as the aftershocks rocked her. Gently, Draven unwrapped her legs and pulled her into his arms. He laid her on the bed and settled down beside her. He moved her hair from her face and lifted her chin to look into her eyes. His breath caught in his lungs at the sight of her tears. He didn't feel any pain and yet she was crying. He hurt her. How had he missed it?

She shook her head. "You didn't hurt me, Draven." She closed her eyes as another aftershock vibrated through her. "You make me feel so good," she whispered.

"Mmm, very good," he said, breathing deeply as the feeling washed over him.

"I should go to my own bedchamber, Draven. This is wrong, all wrong. I've caused you to sin against Miss Cynthia and Iybae."

Draven would have laughed had she not been so serious. He kissed her forehead. "Linea, we haven't sinned. You certainly haven't." He caressed her cheek. "Miss Cynthia has chosen another," he said, pushing her hair aside.

"What? I don't understand," she mumbled. Her stopped-up nose gave her voice a nasal quality and made Draven smile.

She looked up at him with that look of hunger and curiosity that had him instantly hard and throbbing again. His hands held her face, his thumb brushing over her incredibly sexy full bottom lip.

"Cynthia is happily betrothed to another now. We were never suited. Everything has worked out fine. All you need to understand is that I love you, Linea, and I would happily lay down my life to keep you safe. However, I'm very capable of doing what needs to be done concerning Haig Orbane. As a matter of fact, my love, I'm quite good at it. I will come back to you and when I do, I will announce to the entire kingdom that I have made you my queen." Draven paused as her eyes widened and filled with tears. "You are my queen, Linea." Taking her bottom lip between his, he flicked his tongue over it. "You belong to me," he whispered.

He tilted his head. His lips softly moved over hers, deepening the kiss, breathing her in. His hands moved down to her neck until his thumb rested over her pulse. He felt it quicken as he slowly pushed the fear from her, replacing it with hot desire. One day, he vowed, there would be no fear.

Her passion was like a drug rushing through his veins, intoxicating him, tantalizing him. Reluctantly Draven pulled away from her. Rising from the bed he went to his dresser. Linea watched Draven pour fresh water from a pitcher into the shallow shaving basin. He dipped a clean cloth in the cool water, and brought the basin and cloth back to the bed.

He spanned a hand over her hip and gently urged her onto her back. "Open your legs for me, love."

Linea looked up at him, frowning, but spread her legs. Draven wrung out the cloth and began washing her thighs, rinsing and wringing as he went.

Chapter Thirty-Eight

One touch, the smallest caress of his skin against hers, inflamed her, reduced her to a wanton woman in dire need of all he could give her. Draven loved her. She hadn't known love since her parents died and it was so long ago. So long. Her heart clenched. The cool damp cloth against her sex felt wonderful. Draven was so gentle, so caring.

"Uncle said you hated me and my family. He said you wanted me dead." Her voice was soft and desire-laden.

Draven's hand paused and he looked up into her eyes. What she saw in them sent a shiver down her spine. "Your uncle lies."

She rubbed her hands across her stomach and hugged herself. "He didn't lie about me."

Draven watched her, his brows knitting together as he pulled her legs together and covered her naked body with the bedcover. "What about you?"

She looked away from him. "That I am shameful, led by wickedness."

He washed himself quickly before dropping the cloth in the bowl and setting it back on his dressing table. "Your uncle lies. What makes you believe those things, Linea?"

She sat up, holding the cover to her chest. "I'm filled with lust for you, Draven. Even now. Even though I know you belong to someone else."

"I do not belong to anyone else."

"But you did," Linea argued.

"No, I never did," he said sternly.

Linea sighed, giving up the argument. "The things I feel, Uncle said they're evil. A woman isn't supposed to lust, he said, and if she's pleasing to Iybae she will not cause lust."

She looked up at him then, wanting desperately to understand. Hoping he wouldn't turn away once he knew the truth. "He said my mother and her mother were whores. He said that even so, he'd had hopes for me, but..." She paused and took a deep breath. Draven silently watched her and listened. "None of my grandfather's superior blood was evident in me. I was a whore, nothing more than a stumbling block to good, righteous men."

Even as she spoke resentment and fury built in her. "He tried to whip it from me." She swallowed hard and closed her eyes, remembering. "He...he beat me. For hours I hung from my wrists, my shoulders ached so badly. There were times, if Uncle were especially fervent, when he would beat me till I twirled and swung. The blows would sometimes jerk me hard and my arm would jerk free from my shoulder. Rowena and Angus had to shove my arm back in place."

"Linea." Draven reached for her, folding her shaking body into his arms.

"He said I was wicked but I never believed him. I worked hard and tried to do everything he commanded. I never even knew what he meant by lust. Now, Draven, I do. Have I made him right? Was he right all along? Is this all I'm good for?"

"Your uncle is the evil one, Linea." He lifted her face; she felt anger and sadness solidifying in him. "You are incomparable, my greatest gift. For the rest of my life I'll fight to make you see that."

He bent and kissed her, flooding her with his love. His hand caressed her jaw. His tongue gently teased hers before he pulled away and kissed her throat. "I love you, Linea. Dear God, how I love you," he groaned, moving up to capture her mouth.

Hungrily she kissed him back, taking from him and demanding more. He was offering her everything, all she'd ever dreamed of and never believed in. Her body was wild with need. Trembling, she reached for him, her hands grasping his arms. At that moment he seemed too much. He was larger than life. She couldn't seem to get enough of him and she wanted all.

She whimpered with frustration. When he pulled away from her and looked into her eyes, she couldn't look away. She watched with fascination the storm brewing there. She knew he felt her desperation as he nudged her over, taking her hand and stretching out beside her.

He placed her hand over his heart and looked up at her. "I'm yours, Linea. Take what you need."

She blinked at him, then let her gaze drink in the sight of his naked body. "Mine," she murmured, a shiver of arousal quivering through her.

He put his hands behind his head and gave her a sexy smile. His body was tanned, hard, sprinkled with dark crisp curls. Nestled in a thatch of those same dark curls, at the apex of two incredibly long and powerful thighs, his shaft stood thick and unyielding at an angle toward his chest. Her hand explored the smooth contours and muscular ridges of his hot flesh.

She felt the tingles that sparkled from her fingertips and fanned through his body. Would she ever get used to feeling what he felt? Her other hand released the blanket that covered her body and began moving over his chest as it rose and fell faster now. She moaned, loving the way her moan made his body heat.

Curiously, her fingers grazed one flat nipple. Immediately it peaked, radiating pleasure throughout his body. She glanced up at him; his gaze was still focused on her face. Without looking away, she leaned down and flicked her tongue over the tiny bead. She felt him flinch at the sharp sensation. His eyes narrowed as she did it again. Then, copying what he'd done to her, she took it between her lips and drew on it gently.

His lids drifted closed, arousal spiraled and coiled and he inhaled sharply. She moved to the other, laving it with the same attention. Her hand trailed down his stomach to comb through the thick hair at the base of his cock. His biceps bunched as his hands clenched behind his head.

Driven by the arousal that grew within both of them, Linea rose and grazed his lips with her tongue. His mouth opened to her, wanting more. She held back. Her tongue slipped just barely between his lips, licking the silken skin inside. He tasted so good. She sipped at his mouth then kissed him. She could feel his restraint, his need urging her on. Eagerly she stroked his invading tongue with hers while her fingers curled around his pulsing shaft, not quite meeting.

His groan vibrated through her as spasms gripped her vagina. She pulled away from him and moved to kneel between his thighs. She couldn't help smiling as she began inspecting him for the first time. Her fingertips trailed from the base to the tip, feeling every pulsing vein. His thickening shaft jerked in her hands, his hot response coiled through her. Underneath the length of his shaft she discovered a rounded column. She stroked it, fascinated by the way it throbbed against her touch, the way it made him feel.

"Draven?"

"Mmm?" he moaned, trying his best to keep still.

"What is this?" she asked quietly.

"Huh?" he croaked as her hand continued to touch, explore.

"This rounded part. I like the way it feels." She tilted her head, studying him.

"Yes. It's…uh…Linea, sweetheart, … I can't think right now."

"All right," she mumbled. She pressed her thumb against it at the base of his shaft and stroked upward to the plump head. Tight gripping pleasure surged through him, spearing into her. Her breath hitched, a strangled groan escaped him; his cock thickened, pulsed and he arched his hips. She grimaced. She didn't think she felt pain in him but she wanted to be sure.

"Oh Draven, did that hurt?"

"No, not really," he muttered tightly.

Linea frowned. "I didn't mean to hurt you." She leaned down and followed the path her thumb had taken with her tongue. "Does that feel better?"

"Sweet Iybae," Draven breathed. "Both…have their merits."

Captivating, she thought, so hot and long and hard. She felt her swollen flesh throb with every sensation she gave him; every titillating response seemed to stoke her own arousal. With one finger she circled the velvety-soft rim of the head of his cock. It felt so good. His low groan confirmed it. He arched his hips, clenching his teeth.

She leaned down again, her hair brushing over his cock and thighs, and let her passion guide her. She carefully stroked the soft sac that hung below his shaft, gently lifted it, fondling it in her palm. The way it seemed to contract and release of its own accord intrigued her.

He gasped. "Oh, dear God, please be careful with that."

She frowned at him. "But this feels good, I can feel the sensation it gives you." Carefully she massaged them, feeling the hard balls inside.

He was breathless and she felt his trepidation. "Yes, wonderful, it feels amazing, just… please, love, don't squeeze too hard."

She smiled, scooted down and leaned forward. That she was bringing him such pleasure made her feel strong, powerful. Nuzzling the corded muscles of his inner thigh, she nipped playfully, then licked the bite. Her hands splayed on his hips and slid up and over his sides. The warm arousal washing over them guided her. Her hands swept higher as her mouth moved upward. Moaning softly she let her tongue timidly glide over his ridged scrotum. Draven growled and arched his back. Thrilled with his response she continued her torture, bathing him with long slow strokes, her lips gently caressing the tight sac until his hands came from behind his head and fisted in the sheets.

Desire claimed her and pushed her on as she rose over his cock and licked the salty pearl of dew that gathered at the tip. The dusky round head seemed to pulse and throb. It was soft, like velvet against her lips as she kissed the tip, then held the shaft with both hands. Slowly, cautiously, she took the swollen head into her mouth, her tongue rasping firmly over the tiny slit along the head as she sucked gently.

Encouraged by his lusty groan, her lips drew more of him inside her mouth until her tongue could sweep around the base of the head. All she could hear was the sound of her blood pounding through her veins. Draven's pleasure swirled through her as she opened her mouth wider and took him deeper. Her lips moved over him as her tongue stroked, circled and teased. She sucked harder as she felt the intense sensations envelope her. She moaned, sending vibrations through him. His hands speared into her hair.

"Ah yes. Linea, my Linea," he cried as he thrust into her mouth. She took him in as far as she could, swallowing him, sucking harder, her rasping tongue rubbing the sensitive tissue that flared beneath the head. The pleasure expanded, she could feel his climax building.

Sure her own body was visibly pulsing, she wanted to draw it out. He had pleasured her, loved her. Now it was her chance to give to him. She pulled away, licking the head of his cock, nipping with her lips. It glistened with her saliva and his cream. He was teetering on the brink and she endeavored to keep him there, for just a while longer. Slowly she caressed his balls as she took him into her mouth again. Her head moved back and forth as fast as she could, sucking him, licking him as his impending orgasm mounted higher.

"Linea," he croaked as his hands framed her face. He was writhing, fighting for control, trying to push her away.

"No, Draven, don't make me stop. I want this, I want to taste you."

"Damn," Draven snarled, his teeth bared, his brows furrowed. He arched up, thrusting into her warm eager mouth. His hands fisted in her hair as she felt the orgasm seize him, sending hot waves of pleasure pounding through her. With a roar his head fell back. His hips arched up as his seed burst into her mouth, hitting the back of her throat. Swallowing as fast as she could, taking as much as she could, she held him in her mouth, drawing the very last portion from him.

He shuddered, stroking her face, and reached for her. Sensations fired from her nipples as he dragged her up his body, their hard peaks grazing over his hard planes. Using his rumpled shirt he wiped the remains of his climax from her lips then tossed it aside.

Chapter Thirty-Nine

Draven pulled her head down and kissed her hard, possessively. His hands moved over her back, eager for the feel of her. He kissed her jaw, her neck. "I want more, Linea, I need more." His body still quivered with the power of his release. Pinned between their bodies, his cock, rigid and throbbing, never diminished. Her skin felt so hot, supple and satiny.

Linea braced herself above him and lifted her head, exposing her neck to his ravenous mouth. "Mmm, Draven, you make me feel so good," she murmured.

His hands moved lower and smoothed over the rounded contours of her bottom, his fingers caressing along the crease, damp with her arousal. Her body, infused with heat, demanded more of his touch. Moving his fingers lower he opened her drenched folds, thickly coated with her honey. He lifted her hips, setting each luscious thigh on either side of him. Released, his cock sprung free. The plump head pressed against her slick flesh. He guided it through her swollen folds.

His groan was loud and harsh as he was enveloped in her hunger. So ready, so wet, her heat permeated him, radiated back through her. Silky and on fire, the feel of his cock rubbing slowly up and down the cleft of her sex was incredible. Never would he get enough of her, never would he be satisfied, he thought desperately as he grasped her hips and pulled her down, impaling her. Dark and thick, her cascade of curls fell forward, sweeping over his chest as her guttural cry vibrated through him.

She threw her head back and rocked her hips against him. Mesmerized by the way her expression revealed her every pleasure, he couldn't take his eyes from her. The deep blue of her eyes had darkened; her pink kiss-swollen lips were parted. Small white teeth bit her bottom lip as a moan bubbled up from deep inside her.

Control wasn't so hard to give up watching her, feeling her take her pleasure. Mirroring each other became more and more natural. Being inside her was like finding home, peace. Leaning back a bit she found the angle that had his turgid cock rubbing against that wonderful spot within her clenching sheath. Quickly he was losing himself in the storm of sensations, hers and his, they intertwined, intensified and doubled. Lifting her breasts, he kneaded them; he squeezed her taut nipples, gently rolling them between his thumb and finger.

Draven gritted his teeth, trying to retain some control of the frenzied emotions tearing through them. Panting, Linea lifted up and leaned forward, bracing her hands on his chest. The throbbing head of his cock pulsed just inside her channel entrance before she plunged down over him again and white-hot pleasure sang through him. With his cock seated inside her, utterly filling her, stretching her to the limit, she could feel the head resting against her cervix. Soft mewling sounds escaped her throat as she clenched the walls of her sheath, hugging him tightly. No longer could he remain passive. A growl tore from him as he grasped her hips and withdrew as much as he could stand before driving upward.

Each relentless thrust of his hips and each soft moan vibrated through him, making him wild, savage with desire. Linea panted, cries erupting from her as she held on and rode him harder. The honey of her arousal drenched him and somewhere he got lost in the friction of each thrust, each gripping contraction of her vagina around his cock, stroking him, in her all-consuming pleasure. The sensations hurled them upward. His blood pounded through his body in rhythm with hers and he strained to hold off, drawing it out. Watching her as she surged over him, her expression caught between extreme pleasure and pain, she was beyond beautiful; she was awe inspiriting. His.

They were one, in body, in spirit. She screamed as her orgasm slammed into her, viciously exploding through her. She clutched at him as she rammed her hips against his.

His hand moved over her damp chest, slid down her quivering stomach to separate her cream-soaked lips. With clenched teeth, his thumb lightly grazed her hard, throbbing clit. Slowly his thumb continued its unrelenting massage, unwilling to let her descend, and she was catapulted up and up, her cries growing weak and hoarse.

Struggling against the force of her climax as the power of it slammed into him again and again, Draven arched up, gripping her hips, his fingers biting into her soft flesh. He threw his head back in a savage roar that shook the walls as he arched off the bed. They both shuddered as hot bursts of his semen gushed into her. She collapsed against him with a sob as he brushed the damp hair from her face and feathered her with kisses and words of love. Almost immediately she was asleep as he pulled the covers over them both and kissed the top of her head. He cradled her to his chest, turned to his side taking her with him, and possessively moved his leg between hers. Orbane would die at his hands, that was his silent promise.

✳ ✳ ✳ ✳ ✳

No, he couldn't be gone! Linea sat in the middle of the large bed and clung to the covers. She didn't get to say goodbye. She didn't get to kiss him, touch him before he left. There was so much she needed to say. She scrambled across the bed, her heart seized in her chest. So much could happen. A sob escaped her throat as she clawed at the sheer material.

Finally finding an opening, she leapt from the bed and stumbled to the window. "Oh please, oh please," she pleaded. Holding her breath she scanned the courtyard. There was no sight of him or Mason or Armond. Her forehead hit the cold window; her shoulders sagged under the weight of despair. "Draven," she cried.

"Linea?" She spun around and there he stood, holding a towel around his hips. Water dripped from his hair, sending little rivulets over his shoulders; beads of water glistened in the fine curls of his chest hair. She sighed with relief and ran to him. The towel was forgotten in a heap on the floor as he caught her in his arms. She kissed his chest, his neck, his jaw and captured his mouth. She kissed him hard, her hands circling his neck.

Draven pulled her arms from around his neck and held her away. His eyes were full of concern. "What is it?" he asked, trying to make her meet his gaze.

She touched his cheek then buried her face in his chest, nuzzling him, inhaling his scent. Her arms went around his waist. "I thought you had left already." She couldn't shake her apprehension.

"I wouldn't have left without kissing you goodbye." He held her tight and rubbed her back.

He wasn't overwhelmed with heated anger or hatred. She only felt strength in him, confidence, resolve. She should have been comforted but there was a shadow of warning inside that wouldn't go away. She looked up at him. "Take me with you. Please, Draven."

His brows furrowed. "No. I want you safe. You'll be safer here at the keep."

Tears blurred her vision. "You don't understand. I love you. I have love again. I can't lose you, Draven. I can't."

His expression hardened and he moved her away from him, roughly taking her face between his hands. "You are dead wrong. I do understand. I understand that this jackal get threatened my woman. I will not cower like a spineless twit and ignore that. Nor will I deliberately put my woman in danger by dragging her into the battle with me."

She felt anger in him now; he trembled with it. She watched him through a blur of tears. "I'm not a weak kitten, Draven."

"Ha, no, you're a stubborn wild cat." His eyes turned smoky, sultry as his hands moved down her neck and shoulders, sending warmth cascading over her. Large powerful hands that were always so warm, almost hot. He gripped her upper arms and yanked her against him, capturing her mouth. She surrendered to him immediately, taking from him, giving back. Easily she would give her life for this man. She wondered if she would ever tire of touching him, tasting him. Her hands roamed the hollow of his lower back; her fingertips grazed lightly over the tiny dimples above the crease of his butt.

"A very enticing wild cat," he growled, grinding his thickening erection against her.

"Love me, Draven," she breathed, licking his chest.

"Great Creator, I do," he murmured, kissing her again then setting her away. "Linea, I will come back to you." He lifted her face to his. "And when I do, you will be free. You will have no cause to fear again."

She nodded and backed away from him. "But I will be sick with worry." She hopped up on the bed, wiggled back until she sat in the middle and crossed her legs. She pulled the covers up over her shoulders and watched Draven.

"Focus on me, love. You'll feel me. I'm always inside you." Draven paused. "If it were only physically possible," he said with a wink and a wicked grin.

"If only." Linea laughed softly. Her body hummed with arousal as she watched him bend to retrieve his towel and dry his long muscular legs. He dried his balls and his burgeoning erection as he turned his head slightly and gave her a knowing look. She lowered her lids and breathed deeply. With one glance he could set her aflame. With one kiss she was open and slick with need of him.

"Will you be gone very long?" she asked quietly.

"No, I don't foresee it taking overly long." He pulled on a thick pair of black leathers. Grimacing, he tucked his throbbing cock inside, laced and tied them up. Reaching between his thighs he pulled up a placket of leather, triangular in shape, and fastened it over his groin. "It's a codpiece, Linea. It protects my privates," he explained when he noticed her staring intently, her brows lifted.

"Oh." She tilted her head. "I like that idea."

He turned from her and she couldn't help but appreciate the way the pants fit him. The glowing black leather hugged him lovingly, emphasizing his hard round butt and his tight bulge. They molded snuggly to his slender hips and thick thighs. She sighed with rising desire. He could feel it too, her sex filling with blood, just as his was. He had his shirt on now. It was crisp, very white, with long billowing sleeves that buttoned at the wrist. He had tucked it in his pants and buttoned up the front, all except the top four buttons. Could he feel her growing wet, preparing for him?

"Yes, I feel it and it's becoming damned uncomfortable." He gave her a wicked, toothy grin as he reached for his vest.

The thought of those teeth nipping at her breast caused Linea to shudder. "Draven." Her voice was low and husky.

He seemed focused on hooking the metal clasps of his leather vest tightly over his flat stomach and broad chest. He buttoned the last of the shirt buttons then finished fastening his vest. "Mmm?"

"Uh…" she licked her lips and he speared her with a look without lifting his head, "I…you could easily untie that cod thing and untie your pants and love me quickly…before you go." She spoke softly, slowly.

He didn't say a word as he sat and pulled on his boots. She wondered if she'd made him mad. He stood swiftly, running his hands through his long damp hair as he strode quickly to the end of the bed. He held her gaze; his eyes were hot molten steel. His full mouth didn't smile. She watched him nervously; he was intimidating when he looked like that.

Like lightning his hands reached out and grabbed her feet. She yelped as he yanked her to the end of the bed. He leaned over her, drawing her turgid peaked nipple into his mouth, then moved to the other. He sucked on her savagely. She almost climaxed from the mixture of pain and pleasure his hungry mouth gave her as his hands worked to free his aching member.

Her hands went to his hair and neck. She felt that wonderful round head of his cock rub against her sex and she whimpered. He grasped her wrists and put them over her head. She writhed against his jutting erection. His dark gaze locked with hers.

"Don't move your hands," he growled.

She swallowed and nodded. He grabbed a pillow from behind her and propped up her hips with it. He grasped her hips and slammed into her, filling her with one fluid stroke. She cried out, clasping her hands in the sheets over her head. With no time to recover or think or breathe, he pounded into her hard, tilting her hips so that every powerful stroke rasped against her clit. The orgasm was sharp, fast. It gripped her quickly as she wrapped her legs around him.

The feel of the warm smooth leather and his thick, rock-hard cock pistoning into her was incredible. She felt herself building again, faster. The feverish pace thrilled her, setting her body on fire. Her inner walls clenched around him furiously. She felt so hot inside she thought she might burst into flames. The second orgasm was stronger than the first. She screamed, her eyes flew open and she bucked urgently against him.

Draven arched his head back and snarled as he erupted inside her. It felt so good, so free, she screamed again. He slammed into her once more, filling her to overflowing with his hot seed. She moaned as aftershocks of both their orgasms shook her body. He leaned over her, fighting for breath, and kissed her gently on the mouth, chin and neck. He shuddered as he withdrew from her.

"I will never get enough of you," he panted.

Feeling the same way she shook her head, unable to form the words. She moaned again, her body still undulating with delightful sensations. Draven kissed her again then walked to the basin and washed, adjusted himself and retied his pants. She sat up, her legs dangling off the edge of the bed.

"Wow," she muttered.

"Indeed," he said as he buckled his belt and scabbard around him. Then picking up his long sword he sheathed it and crossed back to stand before her. He wrapped his arms around her and covered her mouth with his. He tilted his head, deepening the kiss even more, his tongue caressing hers, his lips nipping at hers.

"What a wonderful idea that was. A perfect goodbye gift," he whispered against her mouth.

She smiled. "I love you, Draven."

He rubbed her nose with his. "I love you, Linea." He kissed her one last time. "I'll be right back."

* * * * *

Armond and Mason stood waiting at the bottom of the stairs. Armond looked embarrassed and Mason wore his usual sardonic grin. "Is the girl still alive, cousin?"

Draven scowled. "What?" Then he lifted a hand. "Ah, forget it. I don't care."

Armond squeezed his eyes shut. A look of disgust crossed his angular features. "I'm going to make sure the men and horses are ready to ride," he mumbled.

Mason raised his brows. "You sounded like you were murdering the woman."

"Shut up, Mason," Draven snapped and walked on toward the door. Joeff met him in the great hall with his cloak. Draven took it from the man and draped it around his shoulders.

"Thank you. Joeff, there is a book with a note on top of it on my desk in the war room. If you would take the time to wrap it in pretty paper and give it to Linea after I leave, I would greatly appreciate it," Draven said without looking at him.

"Certainly, my lord," Joeff said with a smile and headed for the war room.

"Sounded pretty damn hot," Mason said after Joeff was out of earshot.

Draven spun on his heel, crossed his arms and glared at Mason.

"What?" Mason asked, shrugging uncomfortably.

"Go ahead, Mason, get all the snide remarks out of your system."

"Well damn, cuz. Can't help but wonder what would bring a woman to cry out so...so rapturously."

Draven rolled his eyes and turned to walk out the door.

Mason followed behind, whispering loudly as they left the house and headed out across the courtyard. "Aw come on, Draven, you can tell me. What did ya do to her? Was it a special maneuver? Some kind of kinky trick? I have to know."

"I'll tell you this, my dear cousin. It wasn't a few slaps to the bottom." Draven winked at him and mounted Mandrake.

The men sitting atop their horses turned their eyes to Mason. A few chuckled. Mason grinned sheepishly, his neck turning red. He mounted his horse and pulled in line with the others. Draven led the men on horseback through the gates and collectively they kicked their horses into a gallop. It wasn't long until they entered the thick forest surrounding the keep. They followed the wide path for some time when over the rise came two riders. Draven signaled the men behind him to halt and they waited for the riders to approach.

"Lord Amaranth," one rider spoke. "Haig Orbane has three men with him and he is accompanied by Nezzer Pandrum."

"How many Kyroks?"

"Besides Pandrum we only saw two. We spread out, scoured the area. That's all we saw."

Draven sat silent for a moment, planning.

"They're hard to miss, my lord. I'm sure we are accurate," the other rider spoke up.

"The gnoll, Angus?"

"He's with Orbane. Uh, he's in pretty bad shape."

Draven welcomed the rush of fury. Breathing deeply he turned to the men following him. "Fan out and come around Hunting Cave silently. I will dismount a few yards from the cave's opening and come in on foot. You're prepared, you know what to do."

Chapter Forty

Draven watched for the slightest glimpse of movement through the lush foliage. He stood stone-silent, mere feet from the mouth of the cave, waiting. He didn't have to wait for long. An annoyed, overdressed Orbane came out of the cave and paced the clearing, scanning the wood for Linea. Draven felt rage surging through his veins as he stepped from the blind. He drew his sword and walked purposefully toward Orbane.

Orbane stiffened. "The stupid bitch showed you the letter. I was sure her concern for Angus would overshadow her fear."

"She didn't show me the note out of fear, Orbane. She gave it to me because she trusted me and she knew what I would do." He heard the rapid footfalls on the cave floor as he smashed Orbane's smirking face with his elbow.

Orbane squealed and fell to the ground as he tried to stem the fountain of blood pouring from his nose. Draven's men came out from the wood behind him and flanked him. The three men froze in their tracks as they took in the scene. The hulking warriors stood on either side of Draven, who stood over Orbane, his hands gripping the hilt of the sword resting on Orbane's chest.

Orbane's men glared at Draven, their bodies braced, their minds racing. Draven lifted a brow as the finely honed tip of his sword sliced easily through Orbane's overcoat and ornate vest. The two warriors drew their swords, preparing for battle.

Draven shook his head and looked down at Orbane. "Should have worn leather, Orbane. It would have made it a little more difficult to slide my blade into your black heart." He speared Orbane's men a glance. "Bring the gnoll."

Orbane coughed and gurgled, "Do as he said!" His eyes were wide with panic. "You can't kill me, Amaranth. You owe me."

Draven blocked the thick cloying fear that radiated from Orbane as he scowled down at him. "Quite the opposite. You owe me and you will pay," he snarled; each word bore his vast abhorrence for the worm.

"Your father butchered my father!" Orbane screamed. "He did it to steal the throne from my family! YOU OWE ME!"

Draven felt the pain from the cave, felt it grow. He clenched his teeth as the Endarian warrior dragged Angus to the clearing. The gnoll's legs were broken, his clothing splattered with blood. There was so much pain. Angus struggled for breath and blinked his swollen eyes, trying to adjust to the bright sunlight. Draven focused, absorbing as much of the pain from Angus as he could tolerate.

"Your father was evil, a waste of carbon. Just as you are." Draven put his boot on Orbane's stomach, pressing till his eyes bulged and air whooshed from his lungs. Pain...he wanted Orbane to feel excruciating pain.

Without hesitation, Draven's men moved to the mouth of the cave where the nervous Endarian warriors held Angus. Warrior faced warrior; the scrape of drawing swords filled the air. Two other men, faithful to their king, came from the darkness. Angus was quickly carried back to the horses. Halvar came running from the woods with a war cry, his sword raised, and joined the fight.

"Pandrum! Where are you, you bastard?" Orbane wailed and broke into high-pitched sobs.

Arkin joined the fight then, swords slashing, men crying out in pain as Draven's warriors cut down Orbane's deficient army. Awareness flitted through Draven and he went cold. He didn't feel Linea. She wasn't reflecting his fury, and Pandrum was missing. He'd have to rush. There wasn't much time.

He so wanted to draw out Orbane's agony but he had to get to Linea, now! He leaned down until their gazes met. "For what you did to Linea, every lie you made her believe, every scar you left on her heart, her body. I only regret that I can't make this pain last." He pushed down, sinking the heavy sword into Orbane's fat body, ignoring his screams; he shoved hard through bone to pierce his black heart. He twisted his sword and with a sick gurgle of blood and crunch of bone, pulled it free.

Draven spun around to see his men standing over three ruined bodies. "Pandrum. Where's Pandrum?"

Halvar's face was contorted into a savage expression. "We killed the two Kyroks but Pandrum escaped. Mason and Armond went after him."

"We lost him, Draven!" Mason panted as he pulled his horse to a halt on the edge of the clearing. Draven felt the searing pain just as he saw the blood oozing around Mason's fingers that were pressing against his side.

"Take Angus and Mason to the keep. Get Brussoe there. I'll be there soon." Draven roared his orders.

Mason shook his head and opened his mouth to speak.

"Shut up, Mason, and for once do as I say," Draven snapped.

Mason clenched his teeth and nodded as his reins were taken from him and he was led quickly away.

Draven sheathed his bloody sword and ran, mounted his horse in one fluid leap and kicked Mandrake into a gallop.

* * * * *

Sitting cross-legged on a mound of moss-covered earth, Linea smoothed her hand over the pretty wrapped package. She had focused all through her bath, while she dressed and through her late breakfast, trying to feel him. She kept hitting a wall. Netta said that was a good thing. She said if there was no wall and no sense of him there would be no Draven. The thought sent a ripple of fear through her. She breathed in the scent of the flowers surrounding her. They were blooming now, bursting with color. The garden was starting to take shape. It was so much lovelier now that the weeds had been pulled and the bushes and hedges trimmed or cut back.

She sighed and gingerly opened the gift Draven left her, careful not to tear the paper. It was a book. A beautiful book, richly bound in mahogany colored leather. She opened the note and read.

My precious Linea,
Within these pages you will find
the truth that will set you free.
All my love,
Draven

Linea opened to the first page: *The Words of Iybae* was printed there in strong bold letters. Linea forgot to breathe, afraid of what she might learn. She began turning the pages and found that Draven had marked certain passages.

Time seemed to stop as she pored over the words written there. She swiped at the tears that streamed down her cheeks as she learned that all had sinned and all could be forgiven. Iybae loved women and men equally, as a matter of fact. He didn't distinguish at all between the two. One particular sentence Draven drew a heart beside: "Iybae created woman for man so that he may know love." Linea was overcome with happiness. They were all lies—Uncle Haig's declarations. She was torn between elation and anger. She laughed out loud and brushed her hands over her cheeks.

"Linea!" Moria darted through the garden gate. "Come in, you need to come in." A look of panic marred her angelic face.

"I'm here, Moria." Linea gathered her book and the neatly folded wrapping paper and stood brushing at her skirt. Her smile faded when her gaze met Moria's.

"NO! Run, Linea," Moria shouted.

Linea frowned and started forward when a huge arm grabbed her around the waist and yanked her against an unyielding body.

"Little whore! Your presence is required elsewhere." The voice was raspy. *Pandrum!* Linea lost her breath. The foul stench of rotted meat and blood made Linea retch as she clawed and kicked at her attacker.

Moria ran at them, her face glowing, her fingers outstretched. Pandrum raised one great arm and knocked Moria aside, then moved to where the faerie lay and kicked her hard in the stomach.

"No! Stop. Stop it! I'll go with you! Stop it!" Linea sobbed as she watched blood trickle from the corner of Moria's mouth. "*Iybae, please don't let her die,*" she pleaded silently.

Pandrum howled and sprinted to the garden wall. He tossed Linea over the side. She hit the ground with a thud that rattled her bones, knocking the breath from her lungs. Linea scrambled to her feet, struggling to breathe. She managed two steps when he had her again. She opened her mouth to scream and he hit her hard on the head. Blackness threatened to overtake her but Linea fought against it.

* * * * *

"Send for the healer!" Gavril bellowed. He didn't want to believe what he'd seen. He'd sensed something wrong all day. He should have known; he should have stayed by her side. He hurried across the garden toward Moria as fast as he could. "Someone go find the king!"

Cynthia stood at the door screaming. "Moria, oh Iybae! Moria!"

"Quit squalling and go for help, Cynthia!" Gavril yelled at her. He touched his fingers to Moria's throat. There was a pulse, thank Iybae. "Where the hell is the warrior charged with guarding Linea?"

Netta and Joeff appeared at the garden gate at the same time, taking in the horrid scene.

"He took Linea! Nezzer Pandrum took Linea!" Fear clawed at Gavril's throat. *Where was Draven?* Dear Iybae, he had to save her. Pandrum would kill her. "Send the warriors after Pandrum! Someone has to find Draven." His voice was shrill with panic. Joeff hesitated then turned back into the great hall to go for help.

Netta picked up her skirts and ran to Moria. Cynthia was on her knees crying. Shock held her frozen and no one could get through to her.

Netta jerked her hands away from her face and slapped her smartly. "Get it together, girl."

Stunned, Cynthia rubbed her cheek and frowned at Netta. "Do something productive. Go get some warm water and clean cloths. Ask one of the girls to help you find them," Netta snapped.

Cynthia nodded. Tears streaming down her face, she stood and ran to do as she was told.

Chapter Forty-One

The urge to heave was so great Linea had to keep her eyes shut. She couldn't think, couldn't focus. The pounding of the massive horse's hooves and the powerful arm that bound her to her captor made it hard for her to breathe. She'd been unconscious and lost track of time.

"Almost there, little bird." Pandrum bent his head, his hot foul breath fanning her hair. "When the Council is through with you, I'll take you as my own. My dick is aching to pierce your every hole." He ground against her and grunted. "Until your entire little body is slick with my seed and your blood."

Linea shuddered and clenched her teeth. "If Draven doesn't get to you first." Her voice trembled with rage and fear.

"Your true love, is he? I'll kill him easily if he finds us. Now, precious, we have arrived. Let the festivities begin." Pandrum's head fell back with his lusty laughter as he dismounted, jerking her off the horse with him.

He tugged her along behind him as he burst noisily into the large stone building. Several men, Kyroks, gnolls and other beings she'd never seen before turned surprised faces to her, their eyes glittering with greed. They sat on benches surrounding a marble pillar. Atop the pillar hovered a gleaming silver sphere.

A pale man dressed in black velvet stood and smiled at her. He was tall and thin; his silver hair was slicked back and tied with a black cord. His eyes were dark gray, nearly black, tiny lines fanned from their corners. His lips were thin, bracketed by deep-set grooves. Though he wore a kind expression on his clean-shaven, oval-shaped face, Linea sensed the malevolence within him.

"Welcome, Linea. We require your assistance, dear." His voice was rich and deceptively gentle.

"That's unfortunate for you. I have no intention of being helpful," Linea sneered, too angry to worry about the consequences of her snipe. All the lies, all the beatings she'd passively endured in silence for years...well, no more. Never again. Now she knew the truth and she would not lie down and accept brutality anymore. Someone loved her and that's all the reason she needed to fight.

The man's eyes hardened and his smile faded. He leisurely crossed the room and stood before her. She lifted her face and met his dark gaze, bracing herself. The blow had her head snapping back painfully against Pandrum's shoulder. His meaty fists tightened their hold on her upper arms; his claws bit into her flesh. Pain flashed through her head and she tasted blood. Inhaling deeply she turned her head. Lifting her chin she met his gaze again.

Triumph glowed there and his thin lips curled into a parody of a smile. "Your impudence will be to your detriment, dear. I suggest you be a good little girl and do as you're told."

✷ ✷ ✷ ✷ ✷

Armond came through the great front doors. Mason leaned heavily against him, his legs collapsing under him. "Someone help me get him to the baths. I need the healer, Brussoe. I need him now!" Armond shouted.

"Mason! Oh Iybae!" Cynthia burst from the kitchen, her arms loaded with cloths. *This would not be helpful,* Armond thought. Cynthia handed the cloths to the girls following her and swiftly crossed the room to them. The last thing Mason needed was an overwrought lover. To Armond's surprise, she put her arm around Mason and braced his weight.

"Help me, dammit!" Cynthia screamed at the men who came rushing from the stables and the fields.

Armond watched her as she took control of the situation without complaint. Two warriors came around them, picked up Mason and carried him down into the baths.

Cynthia turned before she went after them. "Armond," she whispered.

What now? Armond thought, looking at her. Her eyes filled with tears and her chin began to quiver. He didn't want to be harsh with her but he needed to find Draven in case he needed aiding. She continued to stare at him as the tears spilled down her face. He glared at her and narrowed his eyes. "What, woman, what?" he asked, holding out his hands in frustration.

Cynthia swallowed and shook her head, trying to gain control. "Pandrum scaled the wall. He took Linea and..."

Armond's mind was spinning. He had to get word to Draven. They would have to find her. Not wanting to encourage her in her melodrama he turned to walk away. "I have to go, Cynthia."

"Moria. Armond, it's Moria."

Armond stopped. He felt as if someone had punched him in the gut. Slowly he turned and walked toward her. "Tell me," he growled.

Cynthia backed away, as well she should. He was feeling like strangling the little priss. "She's hurt, Armond. She's in the garden."

Anything else Cynthia had to say Armond didn't hear. He rushed from the room out to the garden. Netta knelt over Moria, wiping the blood from her face. Everything in him went cold and he dropped to his knees beside her. He took her tiny limp hand in his and smoothed her brow with the other. She was warm, so warm.

He looked up at Netta. Her eyes widened as she met his gaze. "She's alive. The blood is from a cut in her mouth. I don't know if there's any damage otherwise. 'Twas Nezzer Pandrum. He took Linea. He...he kicked little Moria."

Armond looked back at the delicate woman and swallowed the panic and the fear. He kissed her lips gently, scooped her into his arms and carried her into the great hall. Several men gathered there, preparing to leave with the king when he arrived.

"Has the healer arrived?" Armond snapped.

"Not yet, Armond. Soon," someone said. He didn't know whom; it didn't matter. He rushed down the steps to the baths and laid her on the bench, glancing over at Mason. Visibly shaking, Cynthia was sniffling and didn't look up as she went about treating the wound in Mason's side. Mason whispered to her softly as she worked. On another bench lay the gnoll, Angus. The warrior cleaning his face must have brought him in. He hadn't noticed.

* * * * *

Heading back to the keep seemed to be Draven's only option at the moment. He found no sign of Pandrum. It would have been so much easier if the Kyrok would have just gone back to Hessum but Draven knew that was not the case. He felt as though his chest was in a vise. He felt a summons to arms of sorts; alarm nagged at him.

His human blood had done nothing to temper the Kyrok in Pandrum. If anything, it had made him more volatile than a purebred Kyrok. Pandrum had to know Orbane was dead. Now that their scheme was ineffective, could he still want Linea? There was more to it. The Council was behind this.

Someone shouted in the distance and Draven heard horses galloping toward him. He pulled back on Mandrake's reins. He listened, focused, as the pounding hooves came closer. Halvar and Nathaniel came into view and Draven waited for them to reach him. Odd how time progressed like normal all around him when Draven knew his world was balanced on the tip of a trembling sword.

"My lord! Nezzer Pandrum somehow gained entrance to the keep." Nathaniel gasped for breath and swallowed hard. "He attacked Miss Moria and took Miss Linea and escaped over the wall!"

"*Razor Rock Peak.*" The soft voice wafted through his mind.

Draven took no time to analyze the words he heard or wonder from whom they came. With a yank on the reins, he turned Mandrake and headed up the mountain at full gallop. His head was down, rage boiling his blood as he mentally reached out for Linea and drove Mandrake harder than ever before.

Chapter Forty-Two

The man hit Linea hard once more in the ribs and once to the stomach. She gasped in pain, wondering if she would survive. Her face stung from the blows, and though her stomach ached she'd managed to keep from throwing up. She twisted and clawed at Pandrum's arm and kicked at his shins as he yanked her across the room to stand before the sphere. But she was nothing to him, certainly not a threat.

"Be still." Pandrum chuckled. "Eager little bitch," he grunted. His dark tongue flicked over her cheek and she recoiled at the revolting stench.

The tall man rolled his eyes. "Later, Kyrok." He sighed, turning to Linea. "Now, darling, already your pretty face is swelling, your elegant high cheekbones marred an unattractive blue." His fingers were cold and unnaturally soft as they caressed her cheek. "Now be a good girl and place your lovely little hands on either side of the Orb and we'll get started. The mighty king of Lanthor has a mindset we long to change."

Linea's fury burned past the pain. Her eyes narrowed. "No." She would not help them destroy Draven or Lanthor.

"Tsk, tsk, tsk." He shook his head; his hand lashed out like a snake striking and slapped her again. Then grasping her throat he took a step closer. His nose wrinkled and his lip curled at Pandrum's offensive odor. "Such an intelligent girl to behave so foolishly." He leaned close; his thin cold lips pressed a kiss right beside her ear. "Linea, we can do this the hard way or the easy way, it's your choice. But know that you will do this for me, for the Council."

Icy tremors snaked up Linea's spine. She met his gaze and tried to feel him but she couldn't. The corner of his mouth lifted as he took her hands and held them against the Orb under his own. The Orb heated under her hands and the thought occurred to her that perhaps she could use the Orb to destroy the Council.

Focusing on the Orb she let her gaze scan the faces. Her eyes drifted closed as the heat from the Orb traveled up her arms and filled her body. Nothing was happening. It trembled in her hands and seemed to be waiting…waiting for something more.

Linea's knees went weak as she felt the man in her mind. Frigid black and bitter, he crept through her brain. Scraping like claws over stone he invaded her mind. She cried out in pain and rage as she fought to expel him. Suddenly he left her and she collapsed. Pain, so much pain. Too much.

"Aaahhh!" the man roared. "It's not working! Why is it not working? She has the gift; I can feel the gift in her!" He spun around, glaring at the members watching.

He swiftly bent and grabbed Linea by the throat. She choked and struggled for breath, clawing at his hands as he lifted her off her feet.

"You are useless," she heard him growl as blackness closed in on her. Finally he tossed her to the ground. She clutched at her throat, gasping for air, unable to move.

Pandrum reached down and hefted her up over his shoulder. "If you're through with her then, Lord Vanseri?"

Vanseri spared Pandrum a glance then waved his hand in disgust. "Yes, go, take her. Fuck her, kill her, do whatever you wish."

Pandrum's thick lips parted in a macabre grin and he carried Linea out the door. Once outside he tilted his head back and laughed. "Stupid fool. Even I could have told him the king is needed to complete the triad. Without the power of his life force, the Orb has nothing to enhance, nothing for you to channel."

Every step the Kyrok made was like knives piercing Linea's ribs. The pain in her head was subsiding but her thoughts wouldn't flow.

"Why?" Her voice cracked.

"Why what?" Pandrum chuckled as she heard a door squeak open. He carried her into a dark musty room and threw her down on a small lumpy bed. Dust rose around her and she coughed. Blinking, she tried to make out her surroundings.

"Why didn't I tell 'em? Heh, 'cause then, my little bitch, they would want to keep you. And I had other plans."

Grinning at her, he grasped the neckline of her dress and tore it away from her. Four shallow scratches wept blood from between her exposed breasts. She yelped involuntarily. *Think, think*, she told herself. There had to be a way to get free. What did that man do to her mind?

She felt so befuddled, but she had to overcome it. She couldn't come this far to die like this.

Garnering all the strength she could, Linea jumped up, intent on running. Pandrum grabbed her arm and twisted. She bit back a scream. Drawing back a fist she drove it as hard as she could up under his chin. His head snapped back and he growled but he never loosened his grip on her arm. He jerked it brutally. The blinding pain nearly overwhelmed her. He slapped her with his palm, then backhanded her on her other cheek.

He gripped her breast, one in each meaty hand. "You wanna fight, huh?" He squeezed painfully.

Linea gritted her teeth against the pain as she clawed at his arms. Kicking at him had proven fruitless. She stomped at his feet. He only grinned, showing those green craggy teeth. She swallowed the bile that rushed into her throat. He leaned down and bit into her shoulder, growling as he sucked the blood from her wound. She couldn't contain the scream that erupted from her. He rose, laughing, her blood dripping from his lips and hit her again.

Momentarily stunned by the blow, she fell to the cot. Knowing she couldn't give in to the pain, the nausea, she struggled against him but he was too strong. He laughed at her, licking her blood from his lips as he held her down and tied her hands and feet. Moving down her body, he tore away the material, biting her breast, her ribs, her stomach, her hip. She tried crying out for Draven in her mind. Fear was strangling her, stealing her breath, her sanity. She had to fight it, she had to clear her mind, and she had to fight. She tried to block out his cruel, groping hands as he knelt between her legs.

"You will pay!" She couldn't help the tears now, the fury at the helplessness she felt. "I belong to Lord Draven Amaranth."

Pandrum leaned in close to her face. She could smell his foul breath and her blood. She didn't look away from his empty black eyes. "You stupid breed bitch, you belong to me!" He hit her again and this time she couldn't push through the darkness that claimed her.

* * * * *

Draven rode hard, thundering through the rough terrain, his mind trained on what he was picking up from Linea. In pain and horror, she trembled as she reached out for him. Draven kicked Mandrake. He had to ride harder. He'd found her; he just prayed he'd get to her in time.

He tried to take the pain but he was too far — too far away, but almost there. The scream ripped through him like an arrow tearing through his flesh. He lowered his head and drove the horse harder still. The pain enveloped him and he faltered at its intensity. Fear had teeth and they sank into him now. He rode upward over the rise. He saw the shack; he was there, but he'd lost her. He felt nothing, nothing from Linea at all.

He jumped from the horse without slowing and unsheathed his dagger. The door splintered from the force as he smashed through it. Pandrum was kneeling between Linea's legs as he turned to face Draven. With a roar, Draven grabbed the Kyrok as he jumped up and grappled to gain control.

Draven pushed the beast away then charged him. Pandrum had no time to retrieve his weapon as Draven slung him against the wall of the lair, his dagger at the beast's throat. Draven glanced back at Linea. Her ankles and wrists were tied to stakes, her dress was torn away, her naked breasts bathed in blood.

Pandrum took the advantage and rammed Draven in the stomach in a failed attempt to take Draven to the floor. Draven struggled with Pandrum, returning blow for blow. Finally Draven grabbed Pandrum by the throat with a roar and shoved him back against the wall. Sweat dripped from Draven's face as he pounded the beast's head against the wall twice. He locked gazes with soulless black eyes that glittered in glee. Fury washed over him at the sight of Linea's blood dripping from Pandrum's grinning mouth.

"Sweet," Pandrum groaned as his dark tongue darted out and licked his lip.

In a lightning flash Draven drove his dagger into the Kyrok's gut and savored the wide-eyed surprise that registered on his face. With a grunt Draven forced the dagger up, ripping through tough flesh until it lodged in bone, relishing the feel of the Kyrok's blood as it flowed thick and lukewarm over his fist. He watched Pandrum convulse and cough, the blood gurgle oddly from his mouth, mingling with Linea's. Draven leaned in with a scowl, twisting the dagger as he wrenched it from Pandrum's ruined flesh.

"Sweet," Draven growled, wiping blood and torn meat onto Pandrum's dirty sleeve as the giant slid limply down the wall.

Draven knelt beside Linea and cut the ropes that bound her. "I'm here, love." He lifted her to him and, pressing his lips to her neck, felt her pulse, slow but strong.

With his clean hand, he probed at the bite wounds on her body. They were deep and ugly and needed to be cleaned, soon. He unhooked his vest and pulled it off, then did the same with his shirt. He folded it into a square and held it against the deepest wound at Linea's neck. The shirt was damp with sweat but it would do. He stood and picked her up, hugging her against his bare chest. Nathaniel and Halvar stood at the door, their expressions guarded. They moved aside to let him carry her through. Halvar picked up Draven's vest.

"She gonna be all right, my lord?" Nathaniel asked.

"She will be fine," Draven snapped, anger and fear still churning inside him. He drew the pain from her, amazed at its ferocity. The wound in her shoulder burned. Infection was spreading. Her ribs were broken again; his body trembled with fury at the thought.

Draven handed Linea to Halvar and mounted Mandrake. Halvar laid her in Draven's arms. Nathaniel brought the blanket from his pack and gave it to Draven to wrap around her naked body. The warlord and his warriors rode away from Razor Rock Peak.

Draven looked down at Linea's pale face. Her cheeks were swollen and bruised and her lip was bleeding. He kissed her forehead. Linea opened her eyes and gasped. Draven held her closer and looked down into her cobalt blue eyes. "My love, my queen."

* * * * *

The great hall was filled with warriors, the keep staff, and neighbors. Draven walked in with Linea in his arms. A hush fell over the crowd and they all turned questioning eyes on him.

"My lord, is she alive?" The gnoll spoke timidly from somewhere in the middle of the gathering. The people parted and Draven saw him sitting on the chaise, his face battered and bruised. Each leg had been bound, wrapped tightly to keep them from moving. His eyes were round and pleading.

Draven nodded. "She's hurt badly," he said, his voice husky with emotion. He turned and carried her to the baths.

"Angus. I heard Angus." Linea opened her eyes. Her whisper was hoarse.

"Yes, love, he's fine," Draven reassured her. "Linea?"

She raised her gaze to his without speaking.

"This is the second time I've done this. I don't want to carry your broken body to the baths again. My heart can't take it."

She smiled, lifted her hand and touched his stubbly cheek. Her eyes widened. "Draven Amaranth, don't you dare cry. Don't you dare." She moaned as tears rolled down her cheeks.

Draven stared down at her and swallowed the lump in his throat. He walked into the cavernous room.

Netta met them, breathing deeply. "Is Miss Linea...will she...?"

"Lady Linea, and yes, she'll be fine."

"Lady Linea." Netta grinned, her green eyes sparkling like a garden pond. "Lay her here, my lord," she said, indicating a bench she hurriedly cleaned.

Draven felt Brussoe enter the room as he gently laid Linea on the cushioned bench. He drew more pain from her and motioned the healer to come as he knelt down beside her.

Draven kissed her tenderly. "I'm sorry I didn't protect you. I'm so sorry."

"You did, Draven," she murmured, her voice husky. "You saved my life. You set me free."

Draven strained against the tears. He kissed her cheek, her lips, her brow. This love was overwhelming. He'd almost lost her. He knew his father's heart, the pain he must have felt, and he thanked Iybae for sparing Linea and him that agony.

"Was she raped, Draven?" Brussoe asked, his eyes full of strain.

He shook his head. He'd just barely saved her from that horror.

"Good, good." Brussoe nodded. "Oh yes, this is nasty. Infection has already set in." He grumbled as he looked under Draven's makeshift bandage. Then he looked up at Draven and smiled that comforting smile of his. "But, not so bad that we can't fix it. You should go clean up, you're covered in blood and dirt and other things I'd rather not contemplate."

Draven agreed, gently kissing Linea's bruised lips. "Stay with me, love," he whispered in her ear. "I will return soon."

Chapter Forty-Three

Most of the people from the neighboring villages just wanted reassurance. Now that they had all left, Draven sat in the great hall. Staring at the fire he began to realize how tired he was, emotionally and physically. Armond sat across from him, just as exhausted.

"Brussoe says Moria will be fine," Armond said stoically.

Draven gave him a crooked smile. "That's good to hear. I'm sure you're relieved."

Armond nodded and stood. "I'm going on to bed. Good night, Draven."

"Good night, Armond." Draven leaned back in the chair and rubbed his eyes with the heels of his hands.

"Why don't you carry your carcass to bed before you annoy us all with your incessant snoring?"

"I don't snore, elf." Draven eyed Gavril.

"Hrumph." Gavril plopped down on the couch beside him.

"What is the Orb, Gavril?"

Gavril sighed. "It's difficult to explain. And you being of such low intelligence, I'm confident you wouldn't understand if I told you."

"Try me." Draven speared him a look.

Gavril shrugged. "It's a volatile power source, but it requires a supply of sorts. Your empathic gift is only part of your true gift, Draven. You are the power supply. You always have been. However, you are ineffective without a channel. Linea is a channel, likewise ineffective without a supplier. That's why the Orb didn't work...actually even if you had been present, it wouldn't have worked."

"Explain." Draven sat up.

"Linea's heart would have to be tuned in; it would need to be her choice to channel. Also, her desire to use the Orb would have to be pure, not forced."

"Ah, I see. What is this Orb for?" Draven pressed him.

"It's for Linea." Gavril smirked.

Draven scowled at him. "Explain."

Gavril rolled his eyes. "With it, the two of you will bring healing to the land of Lanthor and all who abide here. It's in the wrong hands. It's very doubtful that there will be another channel and source so compatible and so strongly gifted as to be able to use the Orb."

"And if there were?" Draven asked holding his breath.

Gavril shook his head. "It'd be near impossible to—"

"If there were?" Draven interrupted.

Gavril met Draven's gaze, serious for the first time in his ornery little life. "I'm not sure, Lord Amaranth. But I know it would be devastating."

Draven leaned back in the chair, again contemplating the situation. The Orb would have to be returned to Ingvar. It was the only way he would be assured of Linea's safety and the safety of Lanthor.

"Moria, when she has recovered, will work with Lady Linea. She will train her. Then she will return to Ingvar. She has already taken a grave chance being outside their protection. The Council would pay well for a faerie, then they would use whatever means necessary to extract from the fragile faerie whatever they may need."

Draven nodded. "Armond and I will protect Moria. Thank you, elf, for your help."

"Does this mean I don't have to shovel animal shit anymore?"

Draven snorted. "Yes, Gavril, you don't have to work anymore."

Gavril lifted his small arms in silent thanksgiving. Then looked at Draven and winced. "I'll, uh…not do any more thievery or cause destructive mischief."

"I'll hold you to that, elf." Draven speared him a hard look.

Gavril frowned. "Yes, I know," he murmured, looking very uncomfortable.

"What is it, elf?"

"You plan to wed Linea," he stated looking at his little hands.

"Yes." Draven waited.

"But the ceremony is for the people of Lanthor only. You've already made covenant with her. You were gifted from birth, Draven, as was Linea. Her gift remained dormant until you bonded with her. Now you're fused together and the gift has become a greater power in its own right. Not just for the Orb."

Draven held the elf's gaze, trying to absorb what he had said.

"Now you're just silly with love. In time you will know the gravity of your union." Gavril shook his head; his violet eyes seemed to glow as he spoke. "Just know this, Lord Amaranth. In the service of Iybae you will be blessed, as will your children and your children's children. And through those precious blessings, Lanthor and her people will know prosperity, joy and freedom."

Draven narrowed his eyes. He didn't take what the elf said lightly. He'd always hated the gift. His father told him he'd gotten it from his mother. It wasn't a comfortable thing and Gavril was right, it had grown stronger since he found Linea, his true gift.

"There is...one more blessing," Gavril said quietly.

Draven looked up at him without lifting his head and said nothing.

"For the rest of your days, you'll have me!" He grinned.

"By what stretch of the imagination could that be a blessing?"

"You will grow to love me, foul king!" Gavril laughed at Draven's snarl.

* * * * *

The bedchamber was dark save for the fire in the fireplace. Linea sat in the wide chair, draped in a white gown, her legs tucked under her. She stared into the flames, her fingers idly twirling strands of her damp hair. Draven felt in her all the emotions that went with the hideous scenes marching through her memory. He felt in her body the twinges of pain and leftover aches. Rage and heartbreak bloomed inside him all at once as he crossed the floor to her. He needed to be near her now, to touch her.

She turned her head and looked up at him. Her eyes were dark blue pools of emotion. Slowly she unfolded from the chair and came to stand in front of him. So beautiful was this woman...his woman, his gift. He couldn't stand the pain he felt in her. He lifted a hand and touched her bruised cheek. There was no fever, thank Iybae. His thumb lightly caressed her smooth skin as the pain filled him and evaporated.

"Are you all right?" she asked softly.

He nodded and searched her face, her brows furrowed over intense blue eyes. He was nearly undone by the question. All she'd been through and her concern was for him.

"Come to bed. You're exhausted," he said more gruffly than he intended.

She climbed up on the bed and crawled under the covers. He sat beside her and pulled off his boots then stood and began unbuttoning his shirt. She watched him as he finished undressing; her eyes left a trail of heat as they traveled over his naked body.

His cock stiffened uncomfortably at her perusal. He needed her but he refused to push or even suggest anything from her. She'd need space, time to let the memories of today fade. He climbed into bed and took her into his arms. She snuggled close, wedged her leg between his and laid her hand over his heart. He felt her body heating. Perhaps he'd been wrong and she was growing sicker.

"Do you have a fever?" He pulled back, feeling her forehead, her cheeks. She simply shook her head. He looked at her for a moment then pulled her close again.

Her hand moved over his chest and she kissed the hollow between his collarbones then nuzzled it with her nose. His cock thickened, throbbed.

"Draven?" Her voice was like velvet against his skin.

"Yes, love?"

"I don't need space from you. Please don't make me go to sleep with these memories," she said quietly, her body cuddling closer.

He wanted her, always wanted her. But she was so fragile now. She'd endured so much.

"Linea."

"Draven, I need new memories." She arched against him and kissed his neck. "Give me new memories." She kissed his jaw. "Please, my king, my love." She moaned. "I need you," she whispered as her mouth found his.

He couldn't resist as her arousal seeped into him, mixing with his own. His hand cupped her neck then slid up into her hair, holding her head still as he deepened the kiss. He gently turned her onto her back and nipped at her throat.

Draven smoothed a hand over the rounded side of her breast, cupped and lifted as he massaged gently. He kissed the scrapes along her breastbone then nibbled and licked her other breast. Linea moved against him, rubbing her hip against his straining erection. He groaned and circled one tightening areola with his thumb as his tongue circled the other.

Linea bit her lip and moaned, running her fingers through his hair, pulling him closer. Finally his mouth covered her aching nipple, drawing on it as his finger and thumb gently rolled the hard peak of the other. Draven felt the gripping coil of arousal slide through her body. He moved lower, licking and nibbling his way down. He kissed her perfect tiny belly button, licked it, sucked it. He traced a line down her tummy with his tongue then he blew on it. She gasped, arching against him. He pulled her knees up as he settled between her thighs, kissing up and down each thigh; he nibbled the taut muscles at her groin.

Her mahogany curls glistened with the dew of her arousal, her musky scent fueled his hunger. "Mmm, you smell so good," he whispered as he kissed the silken skin all around her woman's lips.

He grasped her hips and held her as his tongue slid slowly up and down between her sodden folds. His tongue unfurled her as he moved it side to side and all around inside, opening her further, spreading her slick honey, sliding up to the tight bud nestled at the top of her folds. Draven put his hand on top of her mound and gently pushed back, exposing her little pink clit. He moaned as his tongue licked around it slowly then faster. He laved it, tasting, feeling it pulse against his tongue with every beat of her heart. He took it between his lips and moaned.

She gasped, a soft cry escaping her lips. "Ah, that feels good."

He laved her again and again; up and down. He loved it; the taste of her, the sound of her soft cries as he moved his tongue through the sweet beautiful folds of her flesh, long, smooth, firm strokes. She was breathing heavy, fisting her hands in the sheets then his hair as he slid two fingers inside her and curled them slightly. He moved them back and forth until he found that elusive spot.

She arched her hips against his mouth. Her groan, low and husky, sent sensations radiating through him. His lips closed around her clit and he sucked, flicking his tongue over it as his fingers stroked her. She panted, writhing against him. He felt the pleasure building until finally it crashed over her. She cried out, undulating with wave after wave of sensation.

Chapter Forty-Four

Draven rose over Linea and his intense expression sent shivers through her. He looked fierce and wild and beautiful. His hair brushed against her ultra sensitive skin as his mouth devoured her breasts. She hissed at the incredible pleasure he gave her. His need wrapped around her and she moaned, whimpered at the heightened passion that spiraled inside her. His hands touched her everywhere. His mouth claimed every inch of her, possessing her. It was so good, so incredibly good; it was almost too much.

She couldn't contain her cry as his cock slid through her slick flesh, then sunk into her tight sheath. She loved the feel of his thickness stretching her, filling her. The weight of his body felt amazing. She arched up, taking him deeper. He moved slowly out until he almost left her then filled her again in fluid strokes. He took her aching nipple into his mouth and groaned as he picked up the pace, gliding in and out of her. She clenched the walls of her vagina around him.

"Linea," he groaned as he moved within her, gradually stroking her, filling her with swells of pleasure.

She threw her head back and writhed against him. Her hands smoothed over the sweat-slicked muscles of his back feeling them ripple sensually as he pumped into her. Roaming lower she gripped his butt and pulled him deeper, lifting her hips to meet each urgent thrust. The pressure was building, pushing her closer to her climax. She didn't want it to stop, not ever, this hot liquid pleasure that washed over her, launching her upward.

She felt the passion in him, his mounting desire. She also felt the savage hunger and possessiveness. The musky, spicy scent of him, the sound of slick flesh pounding against slick flesh. He was so hard, so thick; the delicious friction set her on fire. She couldn't get enough of him. She pistoned upward driving him deeper, accelerating the pace.

"Draven," she pleaded as she felt herself being hurled closer, out of control. She struggled for breath as her orgasm tore through her. Her nails bit into the muscles of his shoulders. Her head fell back and she screamed her release.

Draven drove into her faster. She felt the pleasure expand inside her, sending sensations pulsing through her then build again, taking her back up toward another orgasm. She didn't think she could take another.

"Look at me," he demanded.

Her eyes opened wide as her body was racked with powerful sensations. He opened his eyes and looked down at her.

"Linea," he growled as he ground against her, claiming her. "My Linea."

Captivated by his dark desire-filled gaze, she couldn't look away as her second orgasm gripped her. She lost her breath. Her body shook. She gripped his arms as his muscles trembled under her hands. He lowered his head, still holding her gaze, and snarled. His body jerked against her, lodged deep inside her, filling her with hot streams of his thick cream.

Ripples still shook her as he rolled over onto his back and pulled her up on top of him. She lay on his chest and listened to his pounding heartbeat as she tried to catch her breath. His hands moved up and down her back. After a while he pulled the covers up and over them. His cock, still inside her, hadn't softened much. She loved the way it pulsed and jumped inside her occasionally. She moaned and smiled against him when it did.

She found his mouth and kissed him. "I love your beard," she whispered.

"Mmm, do you?"

"I do. I like the way it feels against my skin." Her voice was husky. She felt his cock thicken.

"I like the way your skin feels against my mouth..." He groaned. Pulling her down, he kissed her neck. Gently he bit, grazing his teeth over her. "...my tongue." He rasped his tongue over her heated skin.

"Draven, you're turning me into a raving sex fiend," she panted, moving her hips against him.

"And this would be a bad thing?" he said huskily. His hands gripped her waist, his mouth moved over her chest, between her breasts.

"Uh...oh...it...ah...seemed so a minute ago."

He sucked firmly on her nipple, his tongue flicking over the tip. She rocked her hips against his thickening erection. Her walls rippled, gripping him, gathering moisture, coating him in the honey of her growing arousal.

His low chuckle rumbled through her. His hands roamed over her thighs to cup her ass as he drove up into her. She braced her knees wider. Her hands smoothed over his stomach, tracing circles around his navel. His stomach quivered at her touch and she smiled down at him.

"I love you so," she whispered and closed her eyes. She focused on the feeling of him stretching her, filling her; the glide of his rock-hard cock stroking her to ecstasy; his hands lovingly cupping her breasts, massaging them, teasing her throbbing nipples. The sensations he felt speared through her suddenly. Her head fell back, a deep groan escaping her throat.

In an instant he had her flipped over on her back, then he lifted her against him. He nuzzled her, devouring her breasts, her taut nipples, as he moved in short strokes inside her. Her arms went around his head as she held him against her breast; the pleasure spiked straight into her womb.

She felt her moisture flowing over him, coating them both in the thick rich cream. He pulled her hips closer, grinding upward, rotating his hips against hers. She felt herself being pressed open. The sliding of his cock rasped against her clit. Her breath was coming in short shallow pants as he groaned and growled, his mouth sucking, biting and licking her to madness.

"Oh God, Linea," he groaned as he held her at an angle, his arms braced behind her. Her head fell back as he slammed into her. He took her hard and fast, driving steel-hard shaft into soft velvet. It felt so good she thought she might die. She cried out over and over again, screaming as the orgasm pounded through them both. His, hers...they couldn't distinguish. Draven roared, his fingers digging into her soft flesh as he rammed into her, his seed pumping like a geyser, flooding her.

Linea collapsed in his arms, sighing as the aftershocks shuddered through her. Draven eased her down onto the cool sheets and lay down beside her. Gathering her to him, he kissed her cheeks, her eyelids, her forehead.

"I love you, Linea." His mouth covered hers and his sipped tenderly at her tongue, stroking the sensitive skin inside her lips. "I need you." His lips moved over hers, nipping at her bottom lip. "Mine, my queen, my woman. Forever." Linea could only sigh and hold him closer.

* * * * *

The sun streaming through the windows made Linea smile. She struggled with her chemise; wiggling, she tugged it over her body. She couldn't dress fast enough. Fresh from the bath she was rapidly becoming addicted to, Linea's body felt fluid and flexible. Freedom intoxicated her and she wanted to work in the garden and the green smell of the outdoors. But her stomach rumbled and she'd have to have breakfast first.

The great hall below was filled with chatter. She hurried down the balcony corridor and skipped down the steps with a grin and a "good morning" on her lips. There stood Angus, grinning his stubby-toothed grin. His face was swollen and cut-up but his golden eyes glowed with joy. Those animated bushy brows of his rose as she ran and grabbed him full force and hugged him tight. "Angus!" She couldn't stop the tears from rolling down her cheeks.

"Hey there, Mi...Lady Linea!" He hesitantly put his arms around her and hugged her back.

Something inside her broke and she couldn't stop it. She held onto Angus tightly as she sobbed. She couldn't stop, couldn't control the torrent of emotion wrenched from deep inside. The joy and fear, all the emotion she'd hidden deep inside her whole life suddenly came pouring out. Angus just held her and patted her back.

"Go find Lord Amaranth," she heard someone whisper.

"No!" she cried. "I'm all right. I am," she sobbed. She didn't want him to see her this way but it was too late, he'd already sensed her. He rushed into the room and strode to her. Taking her into his arms he held her.

"It's all right, love, I'm here," he whispered into her hair.

She shook her head against his chest. He picked her up and, holding her in his arms, sat down in a chair. Settling her in his lap more comfortably he held her head against his shoulder and stroked her hair.

He listened to her cry, endured every heartbreaking image that floated through her mind and shared with her the emotions they tore from her.

She didn't know how long she had lain against him. Her sobs had digressed into little hiccups. She felt drained and lighter, as if all the bad things in her past had been lifted from her. She sat up. Draven handed her a handkerchief and she wiped her eyes and nose.

"Oh, I got your shirt wet," she mumbled hoarsely.

Draven brushed her hair away from her face and smiled. His hand grasped the back of her neck gently and pulled her close, kissing her. "It will dry," he whispered. "How do you feel?"

She snorted. "As if you would need to ask." She twisted the delicate material in her hands. "I feel silly."

Draven kissed her nose. "You're not silly. I was expecting this. I just didn't know when or how. You can't really deny your emotions, sweetness. You pushed them down till you just couldn't hide them anymore. Eventually they burst from you with a vengeance. You had years of emotion that you refused to allow yourself to feel." He ran his finger over her lower lip then kissed her. "If you need to cry some more, I'll be here. I'll always be here, Linea."

Linea looked around at the compassionate faces that watched her and felt the heat crawl up her neck. She cleared her throat.

"I'm hungry," she said and stood, giving Draven a sheepish smile.

He gave her behind a little squeeze. Chuckling at her scowl he took her hand and led her into the dining room. *"Couldn't be helped, you have such a fine round juicy ass. Mmm, I can't wait till I can get my hands on it again, sink my teeth into it."*

"Stop it."

"I can feel you heating up. You love it."

"Draven!"

"I love it. It's so firm and full, fits in my hands perfectly."

"Draven, please."

"Sweetness, you don't have to beg." He stopped mid-stride. *"I don't need breakfast. I have a greater hunger."*

"Well, I do need breakfast."

He squeezed her hand and gave her an exaggerated pout.

"First…then you can bite my ass."

Draven blinked down at her then threw back his head and laughed a deep lusty laugh that rumbled through the room.

Epilogue

"It won't be an easy transition, Mason, but I'm confident in your abilities," Draven said without taking his eyes from Linea. She looked like a child sitting on the blanket with Cynthia and Moria, rubbing Aletha's swelling belly. It still amazed him that she connected with the animals. She was an amazing woman.

Mason shifted from foot to foot. "I have some ideas."

Draven nodded.

Mason crossed his arms and tapped his foot.

Draven cocked a brow at him. "Do you have a problem?"

"Yeah, yeah I do," Mason grumbled.

"Well?"

"Cynthia talked me into shaving my balls," he grumbled.

"What?" Draven tried not to laugh.

"The hair is growing back and it itches like hell." He shifted again.

"You fool, of course it itches." Draven raised his brows.

"Draven, you don't know what she did for me when I shaved my balls," Mason said in a low secretive voice. "She sucked 'em, Draven. Took the whole sac in her loving mouth and sucked them till I thought I'd lose my mind. Damn, that woman and her magic mouth!"

Draven bit his lip and nodded. "So, why don't you just shave them again?"

Mason gave him a stern look. "Let's just drop it."

"Fine with me." Draven snickered.

Armond came into the garden, his green eyes focused on Moria, and ambled over to where Draven and Mason stood.

"Is it true that Graeme Sierra knew nothing of the Kyrok attacks and Pandrum's plans?" Armond asked.

Mason nodded. "That's the rumor."

Draven remained silent. His expression was shadowed.

"The ground should have just opened up and swallowed them all." Armond squinted against the sunlight.

"That's an idea," Mason said, tugging at his pants again. "What do you think, Draven?"

"I think that it's possible that some Kyroks are honorable. At any rate, we'll soon find out. Some men and I are going to travel to Hessum. I quite honestly don't know what to expect. I've done my best to stay out of Kyrok business for so long."

"What about Sir Graeme Sierra?" Mason asked.

"I've heard word that he's been killed. I'll have to find out for sure," Draven replied.

"And if he has?" Mason gritted his teeth.

Draven looked at Armond. "I'll need to appoint another overseer."

"No, Draven, I don't want that kind of responsibility," Armond said.

Draven watched Armond for a moment. "We'll discuss it if it comes to making a new appointment."

Mason turned around and scratched his balls. "Ah...damn her fine ass."

Armond's brows knit together. "What's with him?"

Draven closed his eyes and shook his head. "Don't ask."

Armond watched Mason for a few more minutes, then leaned closer to him. "Use mineral oil next time and just shave them every morning when you shave your face." Armond shrugged. "No big deal. But the secret is mineral oil, lots of mineral oil. Feels good, too."

Mason and Draven stared at Armond, dumbfounded, then exploded with laughter. Armond frowned at them. The girls stopped chatting and looked up at them. A smile curved Armond's lips and it wasn't long until he was laughing as well. Draven wiped his eyes and put his arms around his friend's shoulders. He caught Linea's gaze as she smiled up at him. The crabby little elf was right; he was blessed and with Linea the future was brilliant with promise.

MOVING VIOLATIONS

By: Lora Leigh and Veronica Chadwick

Excerpt

Deceit and treachery mix with treason in a small Tennessee town. When Becca returns to Jericho as the new deputy, she wasn't expecting that the man she's loved for ten years would welcome her with a night of passion and lust. Nor did she expect that he was actually her new boss, the newly appointed sheriff.

Now Becca and Jackson must find their way amid a growing desire and a love deeper than they imagined, as well as a danger that could destroy more than just their lives. It could destroy a nation.

About the author:

As a young impassioned girl with a vivid imagination, Veronica Chadwick learned to express her thoughts, ideas and emotions through writing. As an adult she dabbled restlessly here and there with both poetry and prose. Finally, Veronica was introduced to Ellora's Cave and Erotica/Romantica. Her hot, rugged heroes and headstrong, vibrant heroines took control, helping her focus her energies and she knew without a doubt she had found her perfect niche.

In addition to writing, Veronica divides her time between home schooling her two gorgeous children, spending time with her wonderful husband who thankfully loves to cook and caring for their five cats and one very sweet beagle. Veronica has very eclectic tastes in just about every aspect of her life. Though she needs and cherishes all the quiet alone time she can manage to steal, she loves spending time with friends and chatting over a great cup of coffee.

Veronica welcomes mail from readers. You can write to her c/o Ellora's Cave Publishing at 1337 Commerce Drive, Suite 13, Stow OH 44224.

Also by Veronica Chadwick:

Why an electronic book?

We live in the Information Age—an exciting time in the history of human civilization in which technology rules supreme and continues to progress in leaps and bounds every minute of every hour of every day. For a multitude of reasons, more and more avid literary fans are opting to purchase e-books instead of paperbacks. The question to those not yet initiated to the world of electronic reading is simply: *why?*

1. *Price.* An electronic title at Ellora's Cave Publishing runs anywhere from 40-75% less than the cover price of the <u>exact same title</u> in paperback format. Why? Cold mathematics. It is less expensive to publish an e-book than it is to publish a paperback, so the savings are passed along to the consumer.

2. *Space.* Running out of room to house your paperback books? That is one worry you will never have with electronic novels. For a low one-time cost, you can purchase a handheld computer designed specifically for e-reading purposes. Many e-readers are larger than the average handheld, giving you plenty of screen room. Better yet, hundreds of titles can be stored within your new library—a single microchip. (Please note that Ellora's Cave does not endorse any specific brands. You can check our website at www.ellorascave.com for customer

recommendations we make available to new consumers.)

3. *Mobility.* Because your new library now consists of only a microchip, your entire cache of books can be taken with you wherever you go.

4. *Personal preferences are accounted for.* Are the words you are currently reading too small? Too large? Too...**ANNOYING**? Paperback books cannot be modified according to personal preferences, but e-books can.

5. *Innovation.* The way you read a book is not the only advancement the Information Age has gifted the literary community with. There is also the factor of what you can read. Ellora's Cave Publishing will be introducing a new line of interactive titles that are available in e-book format only.

6. *Instant gratification.* Is it the middle of the night and all the bookstores are closed? Are you tired of waiting days—sometimes weeks—for online and offline bookstores to ship the novels you bought? Ellora's Cave Publishing sells instantaneous downloads 24 hours a day, 7 days a week, 365 days a year. Our e-book delivery system is 100% automated, meaning your order is filled as soon as you pay for it.

Those are a few of the top reasons why electronic novels are displacing paperbacks for many an avid reader. As always, Ellora's Cave Publishing welcomes your questions and comments. We invite you to email us at service@ellorascave.com or write to us directly at: 1337 Commerce Drive, Suite 13, Stow OH 44224.

Printed in the United States
38124LVS00001B/271-315